THE KINSELLA SISTERS

Kate Thompson is an award-winning former actress. She is happily married with one daughter, and divides her time between Dublin and the West of Ireland, where she swims off some of the most beautiful beaches in the world.

For more information about Kate, please go to
www.kate-thompson.com

KATE THOMPSON

The Kinsella Sisters

AVON

This novel is entirely a work of fiction.
The names, characters and incidents portrayed in it are
the work of the author's imagination. Any resemblance to
actual persons, living or dead, events or localities is
entirely coincidental.

AVON

A division of HarperCollins*Publishers*
77–85 Fulham Palace Road,
London W6 8JB

www.harpercollins.co.uk

A Paperback Original 2009

3

Copyright © Kate Thompson 2009

Kate Thompson asserts the moral right to
be identified as the author of this work

A catalogue record for this book is
available from the British Library

ISBN-13: 978-1-84756-099-5

Set in Minion by Palimpsest Book Production Limited,
Grangemouth, Stirlingshire

Printed and bound in Great Britain by
Clays Ltd, St Ives plc

Mixed Sources
Product group from well-managed
forests and other controlled sources
www.fsc.org Cert no. SW-COC-1806
© 1996 Forest Stewardship Council

FSC is a non-profit international organisation established to promote the
responsible management of the world's forests. Products carrying the FSC
label are independently certified to assure consumers that they come
from forests that are managed to meet the social, economic and
ecological needs of present and future generations.

Find out more about HarperCollins and the environment at
www.harpercollins.co.uk/green

These are the people to whom I owe a thousand thanks: each of you knows why.

Tony Baines; Barbara Bradshaw; Maxine Hitchcock; Yvonne Holland; Cathy Kelly; Marian Keyes; Padraig Murray; Keshini Naidoo; Fiona O'Brien; Tory Lyne-Pirkis; Sammia Rafique; Hilary Reynolds; Moira Reilly.

My husband, Malcolm; my daughter, Clara.

For Padraig

The light of evening, Lissadell,
Great windows open to the south,
Two girls in silk kimonos, both
Beautiful, one a gazelle.

W. B. Yeats

Prologue
Summer 2001

'Hey, you! What do you think you're doing?'

It was a girl's voice, brittle as cut crystal. Río, daydreaming amongst sea pinks, wondered if the words were directed at her. Lazily, she turned over onto her tummy, pushed a strand of hair back from her face, and leaned her chin on her forearms. From her vantage point atop the low cliff she had a clear view of the shore, picture-postcard pretty today, with lacy wavelets fringing the sand. Below, on the old slipway that fronted Coral Cottage, a girl of around twelve years old stood, arms ramrod stiff, hands clenched into fists.

'You!' said the girl again. 'Didn't you hear me? I asked what you were doing.'

The boy squatting on the sandstone glanced up, took in the blonde curls, the belly top, the day-glo-pink pedal-pushers, the strappy sandals, then resumed his scrutiny of the rock pool that had been formed by the receding tide. 'I'm looking for crabs,' he told her.

'Smartarse. I didn't mean that. I meant – what are you doing on my land?'

'Your land, is it?' murmured the boy. 'I don't think so, Barbie-girl.'

'You may not think so, but I *know* so. That's my daddy's

slipway, and you're trespassing. And don't call me Barbie-girl, farm-boy.'

Río smiled, and reached for her sunglasses. Bogtrotter versus city slicker made for the best spectator sport.

'Shut up your yapping, will you? There's a donkey up in the field beyond trying to feed her newborn. You'll put the frighteners on the pair of them.'

Río saw the girl's mouth open, then shut again. 'A donkey? You mean there's a donkey with a baby?'

'Yip.' The boy rose to his feet. 'I'll show you, if you like.'

The girl looked uncertain. 'I'm not supposed to go beyond the slipway.'

'Why's that?'

'I've got new sandals on. I might get them dirty.'

The boy shrugged. 'Take 'em off.'

'Take my shoes *off*?'

'They're not nailed to your feet, are they?'

From the field beyond came a melancholy bray.

'What's that?' asked the girl.

'That's Dorcas.'

'Dorcas is the mother donkey?'

'Yip.'

'What's her baby called?'

'She doesn't have a name yet.'

'What age is she?'

'A week.'

'A week! Cute!'

'She's cute, all right,' said the boy, moving away from the slipway.

The girl gave a covert glance over her shoulder, then reached down, unfastened her sandals and stepped down from the slipway onto the sand.

'My name's Isabella,' she said, as she caught up with him. 'What's yours?'

'Finn. Do you want some liquorice?'

'Hel*lo*? Don't you know the rule about not taking sweets from strangers?'

'Liquorice isn't really a sweet. It's a kind of plant. Have you clapped eyes on a donkey before?'

'Yes, of course. On the telly. What's that stuff?'

'That's spraint.'

'What's spraint?'

'Otter poo.'

'Ew!'

Finn laughed. 'Wait till you see donkey poo.'

The children's voices receded as they moved further down the beach. Río was just about to call out to Finn, to warn him to mind Isabella's feet on the cattle grid, when new voices made her turn and look to her left.

Two men were strolling along the embankment that flanked the shoreline. One sported a shooting stick, the other had a leather folder tucked under his arm. Both were muttering into mobile phones, and both wore unweathered Barbours and pristine green wellies. City boys playing at being country squires, Río decided.

The men clambered down the embankment, then meandered along the sand until they came to a standstill directly below Río's eyrie.

'Get your people to call mine,' barked one man into his Nokia, and: 'I'll get my people to call yours,' barked the other into his, and then both men snapped their phones shut and slid them into their pockets.

As Isabella and Finn disappeared round the headland, Río heard Dorcas greet them with an enthusiastic bray. One of the men looked up, then raised a hand to shade his eyes from the sun. Leaning as he was on his shooting stick, he looked like a male model from one of the naffer Sunday supplements.

'What's that bloody racket, James?' he asked.

3

'A donkey. You'd better get used to it,' said the man with the folder. 'Noise pollution in the country is as rampant as it is in the city, only different. You'll be waking up to the sound of sheep baaing all over the place.'

'And birdsong. Felicity's having a statue of some Indian goddess shipped in from Nepal, so she can greet the dawn every morning from her yoga pavilion.'

Yay! Río realised she was in for some top-quality eavesdropping. Yoga pavilions! Indian goddesses! What kind of half-wits were these?

'Did Felicity mention that she wants me to relocate the pavilion further up the garden,' asked the man called James, 'in order to maximise the view?'

Sunday Supplement Man swivelled round to survey the bay, then nodded. 'She's right. Imagine starting the day with that vista spread out in front of you.'

'She'll be like stout Cortez.'

'I beg your pardon?'

'Stout Cortez. Upon his peak in Darien. It's Keats, you know.'

'Oh, yes.'

Río smiled. Something about the man's demeanour told her he was bluffing, and that he didn't have a clue about stout Cortez or Keats.

'You'll be able to moor your pleasure craft there,' observed James, indicating a buoy that bobbed some fifty yards out to sea. 'That's where the previous owners used to moor their row boat, according to the agent.'

'I'll need a rigid inflatable to take me out. I assume there'll be space in the garage for an RIB as well as the Cherokee?'

'Of course. And space for the garden tractor too. I was mindful of all that when I drew up the dimensions. But while you're in residence you'll be able to leave your RIB on the foreshore below the gate.' James indicated the five-bar gate that opened onto the foreshore. It was the gate into the old orchard that adjoined

4

the property, the orchard where Río had often picnicked as a child because it was a designated right of way onto the beach.

'That's commonage, yeah?'

'Strictly speaking, yes.' James opened his folder, and drew out an A6 sheet. 'But if you plant a lawn – see here, where it's marked on the plan – that stretch of foreshore could easily be incorporated into the garden.'

'Could be dodgy. People can be very territorial.'

James shrugged. 'Only someone with local knowledge will know it's an established right of way, Adair. And I don't imagine many locals go strolling here, away from the beaten track.'

I do! thought Río indignantly. *I* go strolling here! And not only that, but I go skinny-dipping here too. And picnicking. And once upon a time I even managed some alfresco lovemaking here. Try planting a lawn on that foreshore, *Adair*, and I'll tether Dorcas there and have her crap all over it!

'I don't want to make any enemies, James,' said Adair. 'It's going to look bad enough, pulling down the cottage and putting up a structure ten times its size.'

'I shouldn't worry too much about that. The cottage would be sure to have a demolition order slapped on it within the next year or so in any case – if you hadn't had the nous to snap it up first. Derelict buildings are anathema to the boys in Health and Safety.'

'And anathema to every developer worth the name.' Spreading an expansive arm that took in the foreshore, the embankment and the cottage that Río knew lay nestled in the tangle of ancient trees beyond, Adair – looking more like Sunday Supplement Man then ever – sighed with contentment and said: 'This will be our bucolic retreat, far from the maddening crowd. Our very own Withering Heights. There's a literary reference for you!'

If Río hadn't felt so pissed off, she might have sniggered.

'Have you dreamed up a new name?' James asked, with alacrity. '"Coral Cottage" will be a serious misnomer once you've increased the square footage.'

'How about "Coral Castle"?' suggested Adair, with a laugh.

'That may be more accurate,' agreed James. 'But it's hardly the most diplomatic of choices, if you want to keep the locals on your side.'

'You're right. As I said, I don't want to make any enemies.'

Río bit down hard on her lip in an effort to stop herself shouting out the retort that sprang instantly to mind. But she was hungry for more insider knowledge and had no wish to alert these city gents to her presence – not just yet, anyway.

'I've done a fair amount of tweaking since we last spoke.'

'Good man, James!'

'Allow me to show you the redrafts.' James spread a sheaf of plans over a flat rock, and both men hunkered down to study the drawings. 'As I said, I've changed the aspect of the yoga pavilion. It'll mean less privacy, but by angling it a fraction more to the east it will catch the morning sun full on, and . . .'

And on. And on. And *on* the architect went. Several more minutes of prime eavesdropping went by, during which time Río learned the following: the house was to have underfloor heating. It was also to have a vast feature fireplace in the sitting room, floor-to-ceiling triple-glazed windows throughout, and state-of-the art white goods in the catering kitchen. It was to have two family bathrooms, three en suite bathrooms, a downstairs shower room, and a hot tub on the deck. It was to have an entertainment suite, a games room and a bar, as well as a home gym and a home spa and a home office so that Adair could keep in touch with his business associates in Dublin and London and New York. It was to have a guest suite with *more* en suite bathrooms, where Felicity's friends could take up residence when they came down from Dublin for house parties. It was to have a swimming pool – a swimming pool, fifty yards from the sea! – and, of course, it was to have a walk-in wardrobe-cum-dressing room in Felicity's suite, where, Río presumed, the lady of the house could stash her Ralph Lauren casuals. It was – in James's words – 'a home with a kick'.

A home with a *kick*? Whatever happened to a home with a heart? Or was home in Celtic Tiger Ireland no longer where the heart was? Was it more imperative to construct a great big kick-arse des res that announced to the world your great big kick-arse status?

'Felicity can start compiling her invitation list,' was Adair's final observation, as the two men got up to go. 'She's planning some serious parties. She's asked Louis if Boyzone might be available for the house-warming.'

Boyzone! What planet were these people living on? Río rose stiffly to her feet and followed their progress from behind the dark lenses of her sunglasses. Their voices came back to her intermittently on the breeze as they trudged along the sand. They were talking money now. They were talking millions.

'Adair?' A woman wearing a butterscotch suede shirtwaister and matching loafers was making her way with difficulty along the overgrown path that flanked Coral Cottage. Her hair was swishy and stripy with highlights, her tan looked airbrushed, and her accent was a grown-up version of Isabella's. '*Adair!*' she called again. 'Where's Izzy got to?'

'I thought she was with you?' said Adair.

'No, no! I thought she was with *you*. Where on earth *is* she?'

'Maybe she's exploring.'

'Well, I hope she's not. I told her if she set foot on the beach that she was *not* to go beyond the slipway. Izzy? *Isabella!*' The woman's eyes scanned the shoreline, and then her hands flew to her neck and clasped at the pearls that encircled it. 'Ohmigod. There are her sandals.'

'Where?'

'There, on the slipway. See? But *where is Isabella*?'

The tableau the three of them struck looked so much like something out of a Greek tragedy that Río felt like a *deus ex machina* as she stepped forward to the edge of the cliff.

'It's OK,' she told them. 'I know where she is.' Raising a hand to her mouth and forming an 'O' with the tips of her thumb and middle finger, she blew robustly. Her second whistle drew a corresponding one from beyond the western headland, and within moments Finn was silhouetted against the skyline.

'Finn!' shouted Río. 'Bring the girl back here. Her mammy wants her.'

'Coming!'

Twisting her hair into a knot, Río bent down to scoop up her espadrilles and her backpack, then proceeded down the cliff path towards where the gobsmacked trio of adults was standing. When she drew abreast with them, she slid off her sunglasses and gave them the benefit of her steely, green-grey gaze.

'Hi,' she said. 'Your girl went off to have a look at the donkeys.'

'Well, goodness!' said a clearly discomfited Felicity. 'She really shouldn't have done that without asking me first! I emphatically told her not to go beyond the slipway.'

'Hey, Ma!'

Turning, Río smiled at Finn as he approached the slipway. The sure-footed stride, the intelligent face, the lean-limbed grace – all these traits evoked the Celtic chieftain after whom he was named. And the liquorice smeared around his mouth only served to emphasise the lopsided beauty of his grin.

Isabella was loping along beside him, gloriously dishevelled. Her blonde curls were tousled, her face was flushed, and her hot-pink pedal-pushers were covered in grass stains. Her mouth, like Finn's, bore telltale traces of liquorice, and her smile was radiant.

'Mummy!' she cried, dancing over to where Felicity stood, still clasping her pearls as if they were rosary beads. 'You should have seen the baby donkey! She was *sooooooooo* cute! And guess what we've called her? Pinkie!'

'Hello? *You* called her that,' said Finn.

Felicity stepped onto the slipway, and looked pointedly at Isabella's abandoned sandals. 'Put your shoes back on, Isabella,' she said. Then she turned to Río. The smile that she stapled onto her face made her look as if she were sucking on a lemon. 'How do you do?' she said. 'I'm Felicity Bolger. This is my husband, Adair, and this is our architect, James McDermot.'

'I'm Río,' said Río. 'And this is my son, Finn.'

Felicity Bolger looked at Finn with ill-concealed distaste, then turned back to Isabella.

'Can we get a donkey, Mummy?' breezed Isabella, fastening her sandals. 'We could keep it down here and Finn could look after it for me when we're in town. Finn says donkey races are great craic. He says he could organise them and we could charge people money to come and watch and take bets on which donkey's going to win. I had a go on Dorcas, and even though I fell off, Finn says I have quite a good seat and—'

'Oh, do stop your chattering, Isabella, and concentrate on what you're doing,' snapped Felicity. 'We're going to be late for this reception.'

Isabella gave her mother a mutinous look. 'I don't want to go to a stupid reception,' she said. 'I'd rather stay here and ride Dorcas.'

There was an ominous silence. Then James cleared his throat, Adair whistled a bar of some random tune, and Felicity drew in a small, shuddery sigh.

'All right, then!' she said in a tremulous voice. 'Stay here and ride Dorcas, if that's what you want. I can't bring you to the reception, anyway, looking the way you do. You can travel back with Daddy in James's Jeep. I'm going on by myself. Give me the keys to the Merc, please, Adair.'

'Felicity—'

'Give me the *keys*.'

Reaching into the pocket of his Barbour, Adair drew out a set of car keys and handed them over.

Then, with a barely audible: 'Thank you. Have fun . . .' Felicity flicked back her frosted hair and fled without another word.

Another silence fell, and then Adair Bolger said, 'Go after her, darling.'

'But, Daddy—'

'Go on. I'll join you in an hour.'

'But—'

'*Please*, sweet-cheeks. This reception means a lot to Mummy. It'll be her first big social event in Coolnamara.'

Isabella gazed after her mother, who was stumbling along the shore, looking wretched and unloved. Then she looked back at Finn, who had resumed his scrutiny of the rock pool.

'Oh, all right,' she said. She quickly finished fastening her sandals, then jumped off the slipway. 'Mummy, Mummy!' she called. 'Hang on! I'm coming!'

Felicity paused, drooped, then made a helpless gesture with her hands. 'But your clothes . . .'

'She can change in the hotel,' replied Adair, quickly. 'Run, Isabella.'

Isabella ran. Halfway up the beach, she turned, and waved at Finn. 'Next time I see her, she could be ready for racing!' she called, before continuing on after her mother. 'Mummy – wait up! Finn's going to allow me to ride Pinkie when she's old enough. Maybe I could get jodhpurs and proper riding boots? And a hard hat.'

'Don't be stupid, Isabella. You're talking about riding a donkey, not a thoroughbred pony.'

'But it could be fun! Remember that film where . . .'

Isabella's voice grew reedier and reedier, and then mother and daughter disappeared along the path that led to Coral Cottage.

'I think you said your name was Río?' enquired James, turning to Río with a polite smile. 'Río . . . um . . . ?'

Río knew the architect was fishing for her surname, but she was damned if she'd volunteer it. 'It's short for Ríonach,' she told him.

'That's an unusual name.'

10

'It's Irish; it means "queenly".'

'How fascinating. Well, nice to meet you, Río,' said James.

'Likewise,' said Adair. Now that Río saw him up close, he didn't look like a male model at all, she realised. There was something about him that was a bit rough around the edges, despite the country gent casuals. 'Do you live locally?' he asked her politely.

'Yes,' said Río. 'I've lived in Lissamore all my life.'

'In the village? Or – um . . . ?'

'In the village. But here is my favourite place. It's so unspoiled. Did you know that it's a designated area of outstanding natural beauty?'

Adair and James exchanged neutral looks. 'Is that so?' said Adair.

'You mean you weren't aware of that when you made the decision to bulldoze Coral Cottage and build your Legoland mansion?' Río gave him a disingenuous smile. 'That's a shame. You might want to take things a bit more slowly, Mr Bolger. People in the country don't like it when things happen too fast.'

'I'd hardly describe the planning procedure as "fast",' said James, with a supercilious smirk. 'Each application is subject to rigorous examination by the relevant department and—'

'Don't patronise me, and don't push your luck,' returned Río. 'You might just about squeeze permission to stable a donkey here. But I've never heard of planning permission being granted for a yoga pavilion in Lissamore. And as for mooring a pleasure craft . . .' Raising her chin, she gave them a challenging look. 'Let's just say you could find yourselves with a fight on your hands. *Slán*, lads.'

With a toss of her head, Río strode away from them, back in the direction she'd come. The climb up the cliff path was a stiff one, and by the time she got to the top she was breathless with exertion and anger. Looking down, she saw that the beach was deserted now but for Finn, poised above his rock pool. Fishing in her backpack for her phone, she dragged a couple of deep breaths into her lungs before jabbing the keypad. What she was about to do was going to take some nerve. She was going to phone her sister.

Río had read some aphorism somewhere, about sisters being bonded by childhood memories and grown-up dreams. She and her sister, Dervla, shared plenty of childhood memories, but she hadn't a clue what Dervla's grown-up dreams might be. The Kinsella sisters hadn't spoken in any meaningful way for over a decade, and the reason for this was quite simple. They had learned to loathe one other.

'Dervla?' said Río, when the number picked up. 'Why didn't you tell me that Coral Cottage was on the market?'

'Because it never was on the market,' came the cool response. 'It was sold privately.'

'Did you handle the sale?'

'I may have had something to do with it, yes.'

'How could you, Dervla? You *know* it's always had my name on it.'

'Oh, Río – give me a break! It never had your name on it. It never *will* have your name on it. I thought you'd given up on *that* dream years ago. Oh, excuse me one moment, will you? I have a call coming in.'

'On-hold' music jangled down the line, and Río repressed an urge to fling the bogging phone off the cliff. Then she took another deep breath, bit down hard on her bottom lip, and decided instead to use this 'Greensleeves' interlude to count to ten, the way she'd learned to do any time she had dealings with Dervla.

As she counted, she compared herself to stout Cortez in the poem, except she was viewing the Atlantic, not the Pacific, and this view was her birthright. To the west, the bay gleamed lapis lazuli, its islets blazing emerald in the low-slung sun. Below her, a low, fluting call and the glissando of wings announced the arrival of curlews on the foreshore. An early season Cabbage

White fluttered past – insubstantial as tissue paper – and a honeybee buzzed over the bright cotton of her skirt, thinking, perhaps, that Río might be a flower. And then, beyond the headland, came the riotous, discordant guffaw of the donkey.

'Is that a friend of yours I hear?'

Dervla was back on the line, and because Río had only got as far as seven, her voice shook with rage when she spoke again.

'You, Dervla Cecilia Kinsella, are a conniving bitch. I will *never* forgive you for this.'

'I'm quaking in my Manolos, darling. Incidentally, what sartorial statement is *your* footwear making today? Are you sporting espadrilles? Or Birkenstocks? Or are you wandering lonely as a cloud, barefoot along the beach in Lissamore with sea pinks in your hair and—'

This time, Río did obey the inner voice that had urged her to hurl her phone off the cliff. She followed its trajectory as it sailed through the air, bounced off a boulder and fell with a splash into the sea.

Shit, shit, *shit*! she thought. That impulse, that fit of pique, that little act of what my sister would describe as *lunacy*, just cost me the best part of sixty bogging punts . . .

Chapter One

Several Years Later

'You're like Baa, baa, Black Sheep, Ma.'

'Baa, baa, Black Sheep?'

'You've got three bags full by the kitchen door.' Finn was leaning against the doorjamb of Río's bedroom, watching her curiously. 'What are you *doing*?'

'I'm decluttering.' Río looked up at her son from where she was sitting on the floor, surrounded by junk. 'It's my New Year's resolution. I heard someone on the radio this morning say that every time you buy something new, you should discard at least two items of your old stuff, and I haven't thrown anything out since the cat died.'

'The cat dying hardly counts as throwing something out.'

'No, but throwing out her bed and her kitty toys did. So now I'm making up for the fact that I haven't trashed anything for ages by dumping *loads* of things. Like this.' Río tossed a theatre programme over her shoulder. 'And this.' A desk diary went flying. 'And these. Go, go, go!' A bunch of Christmas cards fluttered after the desk diary. 'Decluttering's proving to be surprisingly therapeutic. How's your hangover?'

'Not too bad.'

'Last night was fun, wasn't it?'

Río and Finn had rung in the New Year in O'Toole's pub,

15

where Río worked part time as a barmaid. But for once she hadn't been pulling pints – she'd been singing and laughing and dancing into the small hours. She and Finn had swung home around three a.m., and then Skyped Finn's dad and left a recording of 'Auld Lang Syne' on his answering machine in LA.

'Last night was a blast.' Finn moved across to the pile of debris that Río had fecked into the middle of the floor, and pushed it about a bit with his bare foot. 'Anything here I might want to keep?'

'Nope.'

'What about the bags in the kitchen?'

'They're full of crap too.'

In the kitchen Río had bagged – amongst numerous other useless objects – a torn peg bag, half a dozen broken corkscrews, a copy of a GI diet book (never read), a cracked wine cooler and a yoghurt maker still in its box.

Upstairs, she had decided to attack her bureau before attempting to cull her wardrobe. She suspected that if she opened the closet door, her clothes would start pleading with her not to discard them – especially those heart-stoppingly beautiful garments she'd earmarked for herself when she'd dealt in vintage clothing. The chiffon tea dresses, the cobwebby scarves, the silk peignoirs – all had their own stories to tell, and all had the power to bring her hurtling back to the past.

As did the photographs. They were mostly of Finn. Finn aged seven, in a rowing boat with his father, both squinting with identical green eyes against the sun; Finn at thirteen, climbing a mast, black hair a-tangle with wind and sea salt; Finn at fifteen, kitted up in scuba gear, poised to perform a backward roll from a dive boat; Finn on his twentieth birthday, smiling to camera with a pint of Guinness in his hand . . .

'Ha! Get a load of Dad's ponytail!'

'What? Show me!'

'I could blackmail him with this if he had any money. Look.' From out of the bureau Finn handed Río a yellowed newspaper cutting. Underneath a headline that read 'Flawed *Hamlet* Fails to Engage' was a picture of Shane gazing moodily at a skull. 'What year was this taken?'

Río frowned, thinking back. 'It must have been 'eighty-seven, because I was pregnant with you during the run of that show. I remember climbing ladders to paint the backdrop, and trying desperately to hide my bump – I was scared they'd fire me for health and safety reasons if they found out. No wonder you've a head for heights.'

'And depths. I was down at forty metres this morning.'

'Finn! Don't scare me!'

'Pah! It's a piece of piss, Ma. I could dive in my sleep now. I got gills.' Finn started rummaging in the drawer again, and produced a carrier bag stuffed with mementoes. 'Baby shoes!' he said, pulling out a pair of teensy bootees. 'Jeepers! Were my feet ever that small?'

'Give me those!' Río grabbed the bootees from him, and set them reverently aside in a box she'd labelled 'Things to Keep'.

'And here's more newspaper stuff about Dad. Hey! Listen to this. "Shane Byrne glowers sexily as Macheath, but he should not also be required to sing." Was Dad a really crap actor, Ma?'

Río laughed. 'No, he wasn't. He just never got the breaks he deserved. Good-looking actors can be at a real disadvantage. Casting directors tend to want to bed them rather than hire them.'

Finn gave her a cautious look. 'Ahem. Casting directors are mostly women, yeah?'

'Yip.'

'Thank Jaysus for that. You want to keep this?'

Río shook her head, and Finn screwed the newspaper cutting into a ball and batted it across the room. Next out of the carrier bag was a photograph mounted on pretty, marbled card.

'Well, hel*lo*!' said Finn. 'Who are these foxy ladeez? Don't tell me it's you and Dervla, Ma? Take a look!'

17

Río looked – and looking took her straight back to the spring of 1987, the year her mother had died. The picture showed a seventeen-year-old Río walking hand in hand with her sister through the garden of their childhood home. Both girls were wearing silk kimonos – one patterned with birds of paradise, the other with cherry blossom – and both were barefoot. Yellow-faced monkey flowers and blushing meadowsweet stippled the banks of the pond in which a lamenting willow trailed her arms, and a pair of lazy koi drifted. You could practically smell the damp earth.

Río remembered that Shane had taken the photograph – from the sitting-room window, to gauge from the angle. And sure enough, when she turned the print over, there on the back were some lines he had adapted from a Yeats poem, written in his scrawly black script:

> The light of morning, Lissamore,
> Sash windows, open to the south,
> Two girls in silk kimonos, both
> Beautiful, one I adore.

'You were beautiful, all right,' observed Finn. 'Both of you. Jaysus, if I'd been Dad, I'd have been hard-pressed to choose between the pair of you.'

Río looked up from the photograph. 'What do you mean?' she asked uncertainly.

'Well, he'd obviously already made his choice, hadn't he? You were the adored one. Otherwise *I* would never have happened.'

'Oh. Yes.' Río's eyes dropped back to the image on the photograph, of the two girls wandering through an Impressionist garden, waiting in anguish for their mother to die. She remembered how her older sister's hand had felt in hers, the reassuring coolness of her palm, the comforting pressure of her fingers. They'd held hands again at the funeral the following week, and slept together in their mother's bed afterwards, with their arms wrapped around one another. But just months later, Dervla had turned on her heel and stalked out of Río's life.

Río looked at the photograph for a long time, and then she reached for an envelope and slid it inside.

'What went wrong between you and Dervla, Ma?' asked Finn.

Río affected a careless attitude. 'Sisters fall out. It happens all the time.'

'But you must have been close once. You can tell by that photograph.'

'Dervla and I were all each other had for a couple of years. On the day that picture was taken, my father was most likely slumped over the desk in his study with a whiskey bottle beside him, while Mama lay dying in the bedroom above.'

'What about friends? Had you no one to help you?'

'Young people are no good at handling death, Finn. It embarrasses them. Most of our friends tended to steer clear. Apart from Shane.'

'Good for Dad.'

'He was a rock, all right.' Río set the envelope aside in the 'Things to Keep' box, then looked back up at Finn, who was unfolding another press cutting.

'Hey – here's a pic of you in the paper,' he remarked. 'I remember that dress from when I was about ten.'

'You were nearer thirteen,' Río remarked, peering over his shoulder. 'That was taken in my activist days, when I kicked up a stink about Bully Boy Bolger pulling down Coral Cottage.'

'I thought Coral Cottage had fallen down years before?'

'It was derelict, but not a ruin. And it was slap-bang in an area of outstanding natural beauty. It should have been resurrected, not built over. It still makes me mad when I think about that barnacle of Bolger's getting planning permission.'

'How did he wangle it?'

'Brown envelopes stuffed with cash, presumably. That kind of carry-on was rampant in those days.' Río took the cutting from Finn, scanned it, then sat back on her heels and tossed it onto the pile, where it joined the jetsam of her past. 'I suppose I wouldn't mind so much if anybody actually *lived* there. But apart from this Christmas, the Bolgers haven't been near the joint for yonks. Imagine spending all that money on building a holiday home with all mod cons, and mooring for a boat, and a fecking yoga pavilion, that you never even bother to visit!'

'Maybe they bugger off to Martinique and the Seychelles and places like that instead. I wouldn't blame them, given this climate.'

'I wonder what it's like to have that kind of dosh. Lucky Mrs Bolger will get a tasty settlement when her divorce comes through.'

'They're getting divorced?'

'That's what the dogs on the street are saying.'

Shaking back her hair, Río stretched, got to her feet, and wandered to the window. On the street below, there were indeed dogs – quite a few of them. Her neighbour's Yorkshire terrier was sitting on the harbour wall chatting to the postmistress's Airedale, and Seamus Moynihan's lurcher was looking out to sea, waiting for his master's trawler to arrive back with the lobster pots. The bichon frise that belonged to Fleur of Fleurissima was posing prettily in the doorway of the shop, waiting for one of the local curs to pluck up the courage to ask her for a date.

Fleurissima was the village's sole boutique. Río's friend Fleur specialised in non-mainstream designers sourced from all over Europe: her beautiful shop was a mecca for those with some wealth and a lot of taste, who were seeking unusual and elegant one-offs. It opened for just nine months of the year, because it didn't make financial sense to stay open after October. In winter-time there were no well-heeled visitors around to snap up her exquisite garments, so Fleur opened the shop only in the run-up to Christmas, but she always took New Year off to fly to some exotic location with her latest lover. This year, she planned to celebrate New Year's Day by swimming in the Blue Lagoon in Jamaica.

Río had helped run the shop once upon a time; now she just dressed the window. In the old days, she and Fleur had acquired their stock from the house auctions that were held every few weeks in estates and big houses all over Ireland. They'd pull up in Río's ancient, battered Renault, and drive away with cardboard boxes crammed with silk and satin and velvet and chenille, some bearing labels with legendary names: Ossie Clark, Yves Saint Laurent, Mary Quant. It broke their hearts to sell their spoils – in fact, sometimes they 'borrowed' the frocks themselves before they sold them – but that had been how they made their living in the days before Lissamore had become a playground for plutocrats.

Lissamore was one of the prettiest, most picture-postcard-perfect villages in the whole of the west of Ireland: there was even a sign to say so, a quarter of a mile down the road from Río's house. It read: 'You are now entering Lissamore – possibly the most picturesque village in Ireland.'

Since the sign had gone up a couple of years earlier, Río had been tempted to deface it by crossing out the word 'possibly'. Opposite her front door, fishing boats bobbed cheerfully in a photogenic harbour against a backdrop of purple mountains. Islands shimmered in the bay beyond, rimmed with golden beaches – the kind of beaches that would be bound to win awards if only Condé Nast copped on to them. On the outskirts of the village, leafy boreens wound their way here and there, mostly leading to random beauty spots. Boats and boreens, mountains and islands – all could have been designed by a deity in a benevolent mood, or by the Irish Tourist Board.

Río's house was on the main street, one of a nineteenth-century terrace of two-storey cottages. It was the kind of house that epitomised the estate agent cliché 'oozing with character', the kind of house that tourists chose to pose in front of for photos.

There were, however, two major drawbacks to the property as far as Río was concerned. She didn't actually own it, and it didn't have a garden.

All her life Río had dreamed of tending a garden by the sea. When her mother had lain dying, she had sat by her bedside and told her stories about how one day she, Río, would own Coral Cottage, where she and Mama had used to go to fetch freshly laid eggs. She promised to plant there all the flowers her mother had grown in the garden of their family home, and build a bower for Mama to rest in on warm summer days, and a tree house for her future grandchildren to play in, and a picnic table, for when they felt like entertaining. And she'd promised her mother that when she died – and oh! she could have years ahead of her still! Mama could outlive Río! – her ashes would be scattered on the promontory by Coral Cottage, which overlooked the Atlantic. This last promise Río had kept; but of course the bower and the tree house and the picnic table had never been built. Instead there was an ostentatious yoga pavilion in the garden of what had once been Coral Cottage, and which was now known locally as Coral Mansion.

'Ma? What are you daydreaming about?' Finn's voice brought Río back to the here and now, and she turned to him and smiled.

'I was thinking about Coral Cottage, and the way it used to be. It was the loveliest place, Finn. My mother used to take me and Dervla to buy eggs from the old woman who lived there when we were small. There was always a smell of baking in the kitchen, and there were geraniums in pots on all the windowsills, and there would be a turf fire lighting and a cat on the hearth and hens in the henhouse, and I always used to dream that one day I might own a place like that and live the good life.'

Finn gave his mother a 'get real' look. 'Come on, Ma! Who lives like that any more? Even you'd be lost without broadband and Skype.'

22

'I was always a romantic, I guess. And the fact that you were conceived there made me—'

'What! I was conceived in a derelict cottage?'

'No. You were conceived under an apple tree in the orchard. I remember there was a full moon that night and—'

'*Ew*, Ma! Too much information!'

'Sorry. I'll shut up.' Río returned to her bureau, absently leafed through an old notebook, then lobbed it onto the rubbish heap. Kneeling down and reaching randomly for something else to trash she said: 'You should do this, Finn, in your room. Declutter your life. Isn't it about time you got rid of a load of your old computer games?'

'Funny you should say that. I was just thinking it was about time for me to do a blitz. I've been doing some thinking, Ma, and—'

'Oh, look! One of your old school reports. Listen to this: "Finn is a popular and outgoing boy. However, he tends to concentrate overly on the physical aspect of his education. This is, unfortunately, to the detriment of his academic work, at which he could be very successful if he applied himself more rigorously." I used to get that sort of thing in my school reports too. "Could do better. Must try harder."'

'Ma?' Getting to his feet, Finn swept his hair back from his face, and the gesture reminded Río – as it always did – of his father.

'Mm-hm?'

'Carl's decided he's going to do the round-the-world thing this year.'

'Good for Carl. When's he going?'

'In about three weeks.'

'And he's going for a whole year?'

'Yeah.'

'You'll miss him. What do you fancy for dinner this evening, by the way? Or maybe we should forget about cooking and head down to O'Toole's for chowder? My treat.'

23

'I hadn't really thought about it. You see, Ma, the thing is that Carl's asked me to go with him.'

Río paused in her perusal of a mail-order catalogue. 'Oh?'

'Yeah. And I've really been thinking about it. It would be a really amazing experience, wouldn't it?'

'Yes. It would.'

'He's – um – planning on hitting Australia, New Zealand, Thailand, South America . . .'

'That's going to cost a lot of money.' Río turned a page automatically. A garden gnome that was great value at only €22.99 winked up at her with unseemly cheerfulness. How could it wink at her when her world was about to cave in?

'Well, yeah. But there are ways of doing it on the cheap. You can get a ticket with a certain amount of stops on it, and it works out pretty good, depending on how many stops you take. It actually costs less than you might think. And I've been saving.'

Río wrenched her attention away from the gnome and forced herself to meet her son's eyes. 'You were saving up to go to college, Finn. I thought that's what we agreed.'

'I'm sorry, Ma. But I don't want to study Marine Biology. I want to dive.'

'But a degree in Marine Biology can help you as a diver. It can—'

'Ma – I'm not an academic. I'm a hands-on kind of guy. I don't want to pootle about underwater collecting specimens for analysis. I want to dive deep, I want to dive hard, I want to experience—'

'You sound like some stupid slogan on one of your dive T-shirts.'

There was a silence, and then Finn said, 'Shit, Ma. Are we going to fall out over this?'

'I'm sorry. I shouldn't have said that.' Río chewed her lip, hating herself. 'I don't mean to rain on your parade, Finn – really I don't – it's just that you've taken me a bit by surprise, that's all.'

Finn shuffled his feet. 'You probably think that I haven't put very much thought into this, Ma, but I have. It's not like it's going to be a holiday. We'll pick up work as we go, me and Carl. There's always work for Irish in bars, and we can help out in the scuba resorts we visit. And if I pick up enough work, I might be able to afford further training. Maybe even get my instructorship certification at last.'

'Your big dream.'

'My big dream.'

Río closed the mail-order catalogue and added it to the heap of junk. 'Then go for it, Finn.'

'You mean it?'

'Yes, I do.' She gave a rueful smile. 'If we were in a movie now I'd say something meaningful like: "Follow your dream, son. That's the only thing that matters in life." Blah, blah, blah . . .'

'But we're not in a movie, Ma. I want to know what you really think.'

'It doesn't matter what I really think.'

'Yes, it does.'

'OK. Here goes,' she said, taking a deep breath. 'This is what I think. I love you more than my own life, Finn. You are the best thing that ever happened to me. And because I was responsible for bringing you into the world, I am responsible for your happiness. At the very least I owe you that—'

'But, Ma, I owe you too. I owe—'

'No, no. Listen to me. *I* owe it to you to be happy because there is no point – no point at all – in bringing into this world a human being who is going to end up a miserable son-of-a-bitch who resents his mother for standing in the way of what he really wants to do and turns into a – a big seething ball of bitter and twistedness. Oh God, how crap am I at this sort of thing! Let me try again.' Folding her hands on her lap, Río looked down, waiting for the right words to come. 'I didn't make you so that you could care for me in my old age, Finn,' she resumed,

25

'or because I wanted to mould someone in my image. I couldn't have done that even if I'd wanted to, because you were always your own man, even as a toddler. And now that you're grown, it's time for me to start letting go. Oh!' Río stood up briskly. 'I'm sounding like a character in one of your dad's schmaltzier pilots. This is where I should get out your baby pictures and gaze at them tearfully.'

'Here.' Finn held out his baby bootees. 'Gaze at these, instead.'

Río laughed, even though she actually did feel very choked up. 'You've always been able to make me laugh, you brat.'

'Maybe I've missed my vocation. Maybe I should do stand-up.'

'No. Being a stand-up is more dangerous than being a scuba-diver.'

Mother and son shared a smile; then Finn gave Río one of those self-conscious hugs that twenty-year-olds give their parents, patting her shoulder and depositing a clumsy kiss on her cheek before disengaging.

'Thanks, Ma,' he said.

And then the phone went.

'Get that, will you, Finn?' said Río, reaching for a packet of tissues. She wasn't going to cry. She just needed to blow her nose. She had nothing to cry about. She had reared a beautiful, confident, gregarious son, and she had done it all by herself. She had *nothing* to cry about.

Finn picked up. 'Hi, Dervla,' he said. 'Yeah. I'll put you on to her.'

'Dervla?' mouthed Río, giving Finn a sceptical look. '*Dervla?*'

He nodded, and Río wondered, as she took the handset from him, if this was one of Finn's jokes. What had started as a fissure, just after their mother's death, had developed into a rift between the sisters as wide and unbridgeable as the Grand Canyon. Dervla rarely phoned, and if they happened to meet on the street they would cross to the other side to avoid each other – to the private amusement of the rest of the village. For two decades Río's sister's preferred method of communication had been via terse reminders sent in the post or dropped through the letterbox. These billets-doux bore such legends as: 'When was the last time you cleaned Dad's kitchen?' (A major chore.) Or: 'Your turn to organise a chimney sweep for that fire hazard of a house.' Or: 'Please defrost Dad's fridge. I did it last time.' Since the advent of text messaging, the reminders had become terser still. 'Lite bulbs need replacing.' Or: 'Washing machine broken.'

'Hi, Dervla,' Río said into the receiver, assuming a bright, faux-friendly expression to cover her confusion. 'What's up?'

'There's no easy way to say this, Río,' came Dervla's voice over the receiver. 'But then there never is a good way to break bad news.'

'What's wrong?' Río asked, antsy now.

'Daddy's dead,' said Dervla.

Chapter Two

The sisters arranged to have their father buried in the graveyard near the beach, where all the headstones faced the sea, on Friday the fourth of January. The notice Dervla had composed for the paper read: 'Kinsella, Frank. Husband of the late Rosaleen, beloved father to Dervla and Ríonach, and grandfather to Finn. At home, peacefully.' Both observations were lies. Their father had not been beloved by either of his daughters, and, although he had died in the comfort of his own bed, there was no way it could have been a peaceful leave-taking.

'I'm hardly going to put the real cause of death in the paper,' Dervla had said waspishly, when Río questioned the wording. 'Everybody in the village knows he was a complete lush—'

'And everybody in the village will know exactly how he died, Dervla.'

'I realise that. Of course word will get out about what really happened, but there's no reason to announce to all and sundry via the obituaries page that our father choked to death on a lamb chop.'

'I wonder why he was eating a lamb chop in bed,' mused Río.

Dervla shuddered. 'Let's not go there.'

Dervla and Río were sitting on the sea wall opposite their father's house, trying to pluck up the courage to go in. Since

Dervla had phoned Río with the grim news of their father's undignified demise, the sisters had forged the kind of uneasy *entente cordiale* that is always necessary when families get hit by flak. Río had spoken to the local GP and the priest, while Dervla had spoken to Frank's solicitor and the funeral parlour in Galway. Together they had started to compile a list of other people who should be contacted personally, but had given up when they realised that there was actually no one outside of the village who would be in any way affected by their father's death.

Dervla had noticed that Río was wearing red shoes today, which seemed a little inappropriate given the circumstances, but she'd resisted the temptation to be critical of her sister during this difficult time. She'd even managed a morose smile at Río's latest alcoholic joke which went: 'A drunk was walking through the woods when he found a skull. The first thing he did was call the police. But then he got curious and picked it up, and started wondering who this person was, and why this person had antlers.'

During their childhood, Dervla and Río had found that the best way to cope with their father's alcoholism was by developing a sense of humour around it. The incident that had made them crease up most had been the evening they'd spotted Frank careering home along the coast road in his Volkswagen, clearly well over the limit. The car had lost one of its back wheels, which meant that sparks were ricocheting up from where the undercarriage was scraping the asphalt. Frank was hunched over the steering wheel – a manic expression on his face – and a garda patrol car was in hot pursuit. Dervla and Río had adapted 'Three Wheels on My Wagon' to fit the occasion, and for days afterwards simply humming the opening bars of the song had made them cry with laughter.

They'd even managed to make their mother laugh sometimes, and when the three of them started, they couldn't stop. A musician friend had once remarked that the sound of the Kinsella women's laughter had inspired him to write a ballad.

That had been Before Shane. When Shane Byrne entered their lives, everything changed.

Dervla had spotted him first, when he'd played Macheath in a student production of *The Threepenny Opera* in Galway, where she was studying Auctioneering and he was studying Photography. She had been blown away by Shane: she attended every production he was in, she volunteered her services backstage as an assistant stage manager, and she spent hours boring all her friends – including Río – about what a god he was. She'd even snogged him one memorable evening, when a friend of a friend had thrown an opening-night party. That had been the defining moment of their relationship: for Dervla it had been such a celestial experience that she couldn't admit to herself that it might not have been quite so earth-shattering for Shane. But she was determined to make him realise how good they could be together, too infatuated to care that she was in danger of making a laughing stock of herself. When it came to Shane Byrne, Dervla had no pride left. And one night she decided she was going to bite the bullet and seduce him backstage, after the show.

But Río had got there first. Beautiful Río, gregarious Río, Río who had been their mother's favourite and was beloved by everyone who met her. Río, who danced on the sand like the girl in the song, and who turned heads when she walked down the street, and who could fall out of bed looking like a young Brigitte Bardot. Río, who had landed an apprenticeship with a scenic artist because she painted so beautifully; Río, who looked adorable standing on a step ladder with a smudge of Crimson Lake on her nose; Río, who had invited Shane back to the house in Lissamore to take photographs, so that she could parade in front of him in her bird-of-paradise kimono just days before their mother died . . .

Dervla had never forgotten how she'd walked into the prop room that evening to find her sister and 'her' man in a hot clinch. Río had jumped like the guilty creature she was, then become abject. Dervla remembered the halting sentences, the pleas, the lamenting: 'Please understand . . .' 'It's been agony . . .' 'We couldn't help ourselves . . .' 'I beg you, Dervla . . .' Dervla had listened stony-faced, without comment, watching her sister stew while Shane sat on the sofa looking bemused. Then she had turned on her heel and made a dignified exit. The sisters had barely spoken since, and the cold war had continued to the present day.

What had upset Dervla most had been that the betrayal had taken place a bare two months after their mother had died. Until then, she and Río had been a force united against a home life blighted by cancer and soured by alcoholism. When Río betrayed her, Dervla had never felt more alone in her life.

She'd moved out of the family home and landed a job in an estate agency in Galway city, forty kilometres away from Lissamore, determined to become the most successful, most highly regarded estate agent in the entire region of Coolnamara. Because, after all, bricks and mortar were the only things that could be depended upon. Property was the most solid, most tangible, most proven form of investment there was, and Dervla craved constancy in her life. Other women sought constancy in the shape of a husband and children, but Dervla knew that there was no such thing as constancy in families. Her daddy had disregarded her, her mother had abandoned her, and her sister had betrayed her. Her ultimate aim was to own a house so classy that it would announce to the world that, in terms of self-sufficiency, she – Dervla Kinsella – was at the top of her game.

And Dervla had achieved that ultimate aim. She had set up on her own, worked her ass off, and assembled a team of razor-sharp agents. Her name was writ large on 'For Sale' boards all over the Galway/Coolnamara region, many of which boasted 'Sale Agreed' or 'Sold' banners. She hadn't found her dream house yet, but she had found its urban equivalent in a gleaming penthouse apartment in a newly fashionable area of Galway city.

'You do realise that we'll have to clear the place before the funeral?' she said, resuming scrutiny of her father's scuffed front door. Behind that door, she knew, lurked unspeakable chaos.

'Oh God.' Río started swinging a scarlet-shod foot. 'Can't we leave it until afterwards?'

'Of course not. We'll be having the wake there. When was the last time you visited Dad, incidentally?'

'A couple of days ago. I brought him some chicken casserole.'

'So you know what kind of state it's in?'

'Yes. Worse than Francis Bacon's studio. I volunteered to clean up for him, but he told me to eff off, as usual.'

'That's what he told me when I last visited, bearing Tesco's Finest lasagne.'

'Did you bring him the lamb chops?'

'No, thank God. Did you?'

'No.'

'Well, at least neither of us is guilty of patricide.' Dervla gave her sister a grim smile, then swung herself off the sea wall. 'C'mon, Río. Let's get cracking.'

Leading the way across the road, she produced a key from her bag, and inserted it in the lock. Next door, she saw a net curtain twitch, revealing the sparkle of Christmas tree lights. She hoped that her neighbour had invited her father in for mince pies and mulled wine at some point over the Christmas period.

'Mrs Murphy's on our case,' she observed. 'We'd better say hello.'

'Maybe she brought him the chops,' Río said in an undertone.

Mrs Murphy emerged onto her front step, wiping her hands on her apron, and wearing a lugubrious expression. Dervla found herself wondering why her father's neighbour had phoned her in her Galway office with the news that Frank had popped his clogs, rather than phoning Río, who lived just down the road. But when she saw Mrs Murphy glance reprovingly at Río's red shoes, she concluded that it must be because Río had always been seen as the less responsible of the two sisters. She, Dervla, was the sensible one, while Río was the flibbertigibbet. Dervla was the level-headed career girl, Río the boho vagabond. It made sense to contact Dervla rather than the giddy one on an occasion that required a degree of gravitas.

'I'm sorry for your trouble, girls,' said Mrs Murphy. 'Will you come in for a cup of tea?'

Dervla returned her doleful smile. 'That's very kind of you, Mrs Murphy, but we'd best be getting stuck in to cleaning.'

'I managed to tidy the upstairs a little, after your father . . . you know.'

The sisters nodded solemnly. 'Thank you so much. And thank you for taking care of the removal and—'

'I would have done the downstairs too,' resumed Mrs Murphy hastily, clearly reluctant to dwell on any morbid particulars, 'but my back started giving me gyp. I'm sorry I couldn't have been of more help.'

'No worries, Mrs Murphy. You've been a real trouper. Daddy couldn't have wished for a better neighbour.'

It was true. Frank could never have survived without the help of Mrs Murphy and the other denizens of the village who 'kept an eye' on him. The care in the community myth actually existed in Lissamore, where twitching curtains were less a sign of nosiness than of a genuine concern. The villagers looked out for each other, and nobody had been 'looked out for' more than Frank Kinsella. People dropped food in to him, they saw him safely home at closing time, and every so often somebody would slip into his house while he slept, to wash dishes or clothes or floors.

Río and Dervla did their bit too, of course, but both drew the line at moving in with Frank. There was no way Dervla would consider leaving her penthouse and her business in Galway, and it would be unfair to expect Río – who'd already reared one child single-handedly – to become full-time carer to a father who was more demanding and irresponsible than any adolescent.

33

'I'll bake a fruit cake for the wake,' said Mrs Murphy. 'And if there's anything else I can do, just ask.'

'Thank you.'

'It'll be hard, living without your da next door.' To Dervla's astonishment, the elderly lady's eyes filled with tears. 'I'll miss him, so I will. He had the gift of the gab, did Frank. Better than the radio, he was, with those stories of his.'

For the first time, Dervla entertained the possibility that people had actually *liked* her father. She had dreaded it when he'd launch into one of his stories when she had brought friends home as a child. Frank would go on and on about some mythical Irish hero of the Celtic twilight, or sing rebel songs, or spout Yeats's poetry endlessly while her mates tried hard not to yawn or snigger.

From inside the house came the musical intro to the lunchtime radio chat show.

'Oh!' said Mrs Murphy. 'I'd better get back in. They're talking about rip-off funeral parlours. Oh! Saving your presence.'

Bowing her head, she made a tragic little *moue* before disappearing back behind her front door.

'Poor Mrs Murphy,' said Dervla, turning to Río. 'She's genuinely gutted about Dad.'

'Do you think she fancied him?' Río asked.

Dervla considered the possibility of Mrs Murphy fancying her father. 'I dunno. I suppose he was a handsome dude once upon a time, in a Rabelaisian kind of way.'

'He certainly knew how to charm the ladies. Didn't he sweep our poor mama off her feet? How long did they know each other before they got married? Two months, or something stupid?'

'Two months and two days, Mam told me. Kinda proves the point about marrying in haste and repenting at leisure.'

'She certainly did that. I wonder why she never divorced him?'

'Divorce wasn't allowed, in those days.'

'I guess they were just young and foolish. I guess we all were once.'

There was a pause as the sisters regarded each other. Then Dervla turned the key, pushed open the door to their father's house, and stepped over the threshold. To the right of the hallway, the sitting room was in darkness. She flicked a switch, then strode into the room and yanked open the curtains.

Sunlight made a reluctant entrance through grimy window-panes, and dust motes could be seen spiralling sluggishly around the room. The curtains had evidently not been opened for some time.

'Jesus,' said Río. 'What's that smell?'

'There's a dead mouse somewhere. We may have to lift a floor-board.'

'Ugh. You're sure it's not just rotting food?'

'Sure. I've smelled enough mice corpses in my time. You wouldn't believe some of the house-of-horror recces I've done. Let's just hope it's not a rat, and that it isn't survived by its dearly beloved wife and children.'

The women stood in the middle of the floor and surveyed the room where, on rainy Sunday evenings, they had once played board games in front of the fire. In those days their mother would make sandwiches – chicken or lamb or beef left over from the roast they'd had at lunchtime – and sometimes as a treat they'd have marshmallows to toast, and then they'd watch the Sunday evening soap opera with Rosaleen, while Frank dozed under the newspaper. And then they'd pack their school books into their satchels in readiness for the next day, and kiss their parents good night, and go upstairs to the big attic bedroom, which ran the length of the house, and tell each other stories about what their futures would be.

Dervla was going to live in a Great House, while Río was going to live in a cottage by the sea. Dervla's garden was going to have manicured lawns and a topiary, while Río's was going to have apple trees and hollyhocks. Dervla was going to have a Dalmatian, while Río was going to have a marmalade cat. They were both going to marry tall, dark and handsome men who looked like Pierce Brosnan in *Remington Steele*, and they were both going to have two children each, and it didn't matter whether they were boys or girls as long as the babies were healthy and had all ten fingers and all ten toes.

'What are you thinking about, Dervla?' Río asked.

'Those Sunday evenings. The ones that seemed happy until we realised that Dad wasn't snoozing contentedly under his paper, but was comatose with the drink.'

'Remember how he'd head off to the pub after lunch, and when he came back he'd be in flying form, and give us piggy-backs, and roll down the slope in the garden with us, and we thought he was great craic? And all the time, Mama would be in the study doing the weekly accounts and we always wondered why her eyes were so red, and she told us she'd got allergic to the cat.'

'God. We were like something in a novel by John McGahern.'

Río laughed. 'At least it wasn't out of a novel by that bloke who wrote *Angela's Ashes*.'

'Frank McCourt.' Dervla looked at the black cast-iron fire-place that was grey now with ash and dust, and that boasted not the art nouveau figurines that their mother had collected, but a battalion of empty bottles and sticky-looking glasses and dirty ashtrays. 'Maybe we should write a misery memoir,' she said. 'We could go on *Oprah* or *Richard and Judy* and make a fortune.'

Dervla and Río turned to each other, but this time they didn't laugh. 'Poor Dad,' they said simultaneously, each reaching for the other's hand.

And then they had their arms wrapped around each other, and they were crying, and Río was saying, 'I'm so, so sorry about the thing with Shane.'

And Dervla was saying, 'Don't be sorry – sure, wasn't it ages ago and wasn't he an awful eejit anyway. And weren't we the

36

awful eejits to let something as petty as a teenage crush mess us up.'

'And for so long!' exclaimed Río. 'Twenty stupid, stupid years we've wasted, acting like characters in a Dostoevsky novel.'

'Except in a Dostoevsky novel the characters would never kiss and make up.'

'Is that what we're doing?'

'I think so. Don't you? Don't you think it's possible to wipe a slate clean after twenty pointless bloody years of resentment and strop?'

'Yes,' said Río. 'I do. I'm so sorry.' And leaning forward, she gave Dervla a kiss on the cheek.

Dervla kissed her back. 'I'm the one who should be sorry, for overreacting the way I did.'

'No, no – I'm the one who should be sorry for stealing him.'

'No, no – you didn't steal him. He was never mine anyway.' And then they were laughing again, but it was a kind of snuffly laughter.

'Do you have a tissue?' Río asked finally, wiping her cheeks.

Dervla undid the clasp of her shoulder bag, and passed over a packet of Kleenex.

A plaintive mew from the doorway made them turn. There, arching his back and rubbing his muzzle against the door jamb was W.B., their father's cat. His marmalade fur was bedraggled, and the leather collar dangling loosely round his neck told them he'd lost weight.

'Oh, W.B.!' cried Río, bending to scoop him up. 'Poor you! I'd forgotten all about you – you must be starving. Let's see if there's anything to eat in the kitchen, puss cat.'

'Apart from mouse pie, you mean?' remarked Dervla.

'Ew. I'd forgotten about them. You'd better go first, since you're so used to them.'

Dervla moved down the hall. A lozenge of light on the tiles indicated that the kitchen light was still on. Inside, the big table in the centre of the floor was covered in detritus. More bottles and glasses, half-empty mugs of tea with mould floating on the surface, cereal packets, milk cartons, a box of Complan, empty tins, books, newspapers and magazines.

W.B. pitter-pattered into the room and immediately leaped onto a work surface upon which boxes of dried cat food were stacked alongside a wine rack.

'Wow,' said Dervla. 'There's an entire bottle of wine in there. He actually left us some drink. Fancy a glass of Dutch courage?'

'Definitely.' Río moved to a drawer, rooted among its haphazard contents for a corkscrew, and reached for the bottle. 'Merlot,' she said, deftly inserting the corkscrew. 'Château-bottled, interesting vintage.' There came a *plop!* as the cork slid out. Río sniffed it. 'Mm. Plum pudding fruit, spicy vanilla oak, peppery nose, a touch of stewed mulberries.'

Dervla gave Río a curious look, as she poured cat food into W.B.'s bowl. 'I didn't know you were a wine buff.'

'I'm not, I'm just spoofing. It's plonk. Here's a challenge for you. Find a couple of clean glasses.'

'There aren't any.' Dervla moved to the sink, which was piled high with dirty dishes. There were half a dozen or so dead blue-bottles on the inside windowsill, and half a dozen or so dead snails on the outside one. She selected two of the least disgusting wineglasses, and rinsed them under the tap. 'Well,' she said, clearing a space on the table and setting the glasses down. 'That's interesting. Dad was still able to do the cryptic crossword.' She picked up a backdated copy of the *Irish Times* and scrutinised the Crosaire. 'There's only one he missed,' she said. '"Sounds like fifty ended like this." Eight letters, second letter "e".'

'Deceased,' said Río. 'Here's to him.' She sloshed red into the wineglasses, then passed one to Dervla.

'Here's to our daddy,' said Dervla, raising her glass.

'And to our mama.' Río raised hers likewise. 'We're officially orphans now, Dervla.'

'I've felt like an orphan for years,' Dervla observed, matter-of-factly. She took a sip of her wine and made a face. 'Ew. Nasty.'

'Very nasty,' agreed Río. 'But don't let that stop us from finishing the bottle.'

Dervla sat down at the table and looked around the room. The framed photograph of her parents on their wedding day hung, as it had always done, next to the dresser full of their wedding china. Dervla noticed abstractedly how intact the dinner service was; but then, she supposed, throwing plates had never been their mother's style. 'Here's hoping Ma and Pa don't run into each other in the big blue hereafter,' she remarked.

'Oh, I dunno,' said Río, taking the seat opposite her sister. 'I reckon Dad yearned always to be reunited with her, like Heathcliff and Cathy. I don't think he ever stopped loving her. I wonder what made her put up with him?'

'She stayed put because of us, of course,' said Dervla.

'I suppose this is where we give each other thoughtful looks and start reminiscing about the past.'

'Somebody once said that the past's another country. Let's not go there.'

'Unless we can travel first class. And this ain't no luxury state-room.' Río looked round the kitchen with distaste. 'How could he have *lived* like this?'

'You'd be surprised at how many men who live on their own, live in squalor. I could tell you stories that would make you puke.'

'Houses you've seen?'

'Yes. Sometimes I'm scared that I might actually puke, then and there, all over the kitchen floor. One woman used to cook pigs' feet for her husband every evening—'

'Gross!'

'And because he was incontinent, he smelled perpetually of wee. I used to have to spray the house with Jo Malone before every viewing.'

'Business must be good if you can afford Jo Malone.'

'It is. Very good. I'm going to have to recruit another girl.'

'Is someone leaving?'

'No. I'm expanding. I'm going to offer my clients a home-staging service.'

'A home-staging service? What's that?'

'For an extra charge, I turn the house into a really desirable property – the kind of place where a prospective buyer will walk in the door and say, "Wow! I simply must have it!"'

'How could you possibly do that in a house that smelled of pigs' trotters and wee?'

'That one was a challenge, all right. But some places can be really dramatically transformed. Statistics prove that a house that has been home-staged is far more likely to sell than a house that hasn't.'

'Isn't it a waste of money for the owners, since they're going to be moving out anyway?'

'Not if it guarantees a sale. And makeovers don't need to cost a fortune.'

Río gave Dervla an interested look, then leaned her elbows on the tabletop. 'Really? What would you do with this place?'

'Clean it. Paint it. Highlight the original features – the fireplaces, cornices, coving. Perhaps hire a few good pieces of furniture, plants, some paintings. Tidy up the garden.'

Both women looked towards the window that framed the view of overgrown ferns and rampantly rambling roses and leggy geraniums.

'It's like a Rousseauesque jungle, except not as pretty,' observed Río. 'I looked after it as best I could, but gave up on it a couple of years ago. He just wasn't interested. The garden was Mama's domain.'

Dervla took a thoughtful sip of wine, not noticing this time how disgusting it was. 'Shane took a picture of us on the lawn, once, by the pond. Do you remember? We were trailing around in our dressing gowns. It was shortly before Mama died.'

'I still have that photograph. I found it just this morning.' Río turned remorseful eyes on Dervla. 'I meant what I said earlier, Dervla. I am beyond sorry about what happened with Shane.'

'I know you are. And I'm sorry too that I didn't accept your apology. I should have been bigger than that. We were going through such a horrible time then. I guess neither of us was thinking straight.'

'Were you in love with him?'

Dervla considered. 'No. I barely even knew him. I was just insanely infatuated – like a woman possessed, or a demented fan of some rock god. Were you?'

'In love with him? No. I just thought I was. He was so good to me when Mama died.'

'He was in love with you?'

'I guess so. He was so supportive. I couldn't have got through that time without him.'

'I did pick up the phone to you a couple of times, you know, to say let's make amends,' said Dervla. 'But you didn't answer.'

'I tried phoning you too. And then I got pregnant, and I couldn't bear to tell you that Finn was Shane's baby.'

'I knew he was. He takes after his dad, does Finn. He's a good-looking boy – and charming, to boot. Any time I meet him on the street he's full of chat. I'm glad you never put an embargo on him fraternising with his auntie. I'd have hated him to cold-shoulder me.'

'He's my best friend,' said Río. 'I adore him. I've been very lucky, to have produced something so fine when there are thousands of delinquents roaming the country.'

'Does Shane have much input?'

Río shook her head. 'No. Finn's practically all my own work. Shane sends money from time to time, though he's always broke. We keep in touch by Skype and e-mail.'

'When was the last time you saw him?'

'About five years ago. He had a small part in a movie being made in Killary.'

'Was he as winsome as ever?'

'Yes.'

'And you weren't tempted?'

'No. I had a man in my life at that stage. But he was a waster too. That's why I had my tubes tied. I couldn't bear the idea of having another child with an irresponsible father.'

'We've got a lot of catching up to do,' said Dervla. As she reached for the wine bottle, she wondered who Río might have talked to when she made the decision to undergo surgery; who might have picked her up from the day ward; who might have made her a cup of tea afterwards. She guessed that it would have been Fleur, and wished now that it might have been her. 'I know hardly anything about you, little sister. Tell me more.'

'There's not much to tell,' said Río. 'I work hard, but at nothing in particular. I guess I'm a jack of all trades.'

'What do you mean, jack of all trades?'

Río shrugged. 'Sometimes I work in O'Toole's—'

'In the restaurant?'

'No, downstairs in the bar. Sometimes I drive a taxi, sometimes I work in other people's gardens. I do Fleur's window display for her. Sometimes – if I'm lucky – one of my paintings might sell—'

'You're still painting?'

Río nodded. 'Mostly landscapes. Some portraits. I'd prefer to do more portraits, but tourists tend to go for the landscapes.'

'Where do you sell them?'

'Fleur's opened a little wine bar at the back of the shop. Some of my stuff's on display there.'

'Does she take commission?'

'No. She does it for me as a friend.'

'I knew you were driving,' said Dervla. 'And Fleur told me you were doing her window. But I never knew about the gardening. Where did the green fingers come from?'

'I guess I inherited them from Mama.'

Dervla gave Río a speculative look. 'You were wrong, you know, when you said there wasn't much to know about you. There's lots to know.'

'Not as much as there is to know about you. I've been keeping tabs on you.'

'You have?'

'Yep. I know, for instance, that you have no man in your life right now because you're "married to your career".'

'What? How do you know that?'

'I hired a private investigator. Joke. I read a profile in *The Gloss* magazine when you were up for Female Entrepreneur of the Year, and I saw you on breakfast television, and I heard you being interviewed on Galway Bay FM last week. And your picture's always cropping up in the society pages.'

'You don't strike me as the type of gal who bothers with the society pages.'

'I have to sit in the dentist's waiting room same as everybody else. Sometimes I even have my hair done, and get to read *VIP* magazine.' Río took hold of a strand of her reddy-gold hair and examined the ends ruefully. 'I'm way overdue a cut.'

'W.B. looks as if he should have a wash and blow-dry too. What'll we do with him?'

'Maybe Mrs Murphy would like him as a memento of Dad.'

'I'm sure there are other mementoes she'd rather have. Maybe we should go take a look at our inheritance.'

'Our inheritance. A cat and a house. How much do you think this property's worth?'

'We should get a million for it.'

'A million! You've got to be kidding!'

'Think about it. It's right on the harbour. If you stuck a picture window in upstairs you'd have a stunning view of the sea and the mountains, and ditto if you stuck a dormer in the attic. Plus there's loads of room to extend.'

'Would you get planning permission?'

'Sure to. The precedent's been set. People have been extending their properties upward and outward all over Lissamore. Floor space here is as valuable as it is in Dublin 4.' Dervla knocked back her wine and got to her feet. 'Let's go take a look,' she said.

Chapter Three

Mrs Murphy had been busy upstairs. Frank's bedroom had been Mr Sheen'd and Shake-and-Vac'd and Cif'd. The bed linen had been stripped, and the curtains taken down. A glance through the window told Río that they had been Ariel'd in Mrs Murphy's machine, because they were billowing about brightly on the washing line in her back garden. Neither sister made a move to open the wardrobe door.

The attic, next. As Río climbed the stairs, she felt like a revenant. The ghost of her childhood self resided here, the little girl who had sat on the steps, hugging her knees to her chest and listening to the raised voices coming from the sitting room below. Looking back at Dervla, who was following her up the staircase, she sensed that her sister felt exactly the same way.

Neither of them had been in their attic bedroom since they had packed their bags and left Frank's house for the last time, full of hatred and rage. At the top of the stairs, the door hung off its hinges. As they passed through into the room, they reached for each other's hand.

The place was catastrophic. It was clearly a repository for everything Frank had decided he no longer needed. Trunks, boxes, old shoes, books, clothes, broken furniture – all lay as if they had been slung there by some giant hands. The beds had been dismantled, and dumped in a corner. Cobwebs big as mantillas hung from the ceiling, and a rather pretty fungus filigreed a section of wall. The glass in the skylight was broken, and the surface of a table that stood beneath was so blistering with damp it resembled a bad case of adolescent acne. The place smelled dank.

'OK,' said Dervla. 'I've just knocked a couple of hundred grand off the asking price.'

'We'll never get this sorted before the funeral!' wailed Río, looking around in dismay.

'You're right. But it's not as if we'll be inviting people into the attic. We'll just have to concentrate on the downstairs.'

'What are we going to do with all this *crap*?'

'We're going to hire a skip.' Dervla moved into the centre of the attic, stepping over a rusty fire guard and kicking a cushion out of the way. 'Look,' she said, stooping to pick up a velour elephant. 'It's Ella. Remember how you couldn't sleep without her, and Mama had to send a taxi to pick her up from some place once?'

'I'd left her behind at a birthday party, and Dad was too "tired" to drive.' Río took the elephant from Dervla and brushed dust from her ears. 'I wondered where she'd got to. I'll hang on to her now I've found her. She'll be useful for hugging when I'm feeling blue.'

'She's probably the only thing here worth salvaging.'

'She smells a bit musty. She'll have to go through the washing machine.' Río set Ella on top of a magazine rack. 'Poor darling. She'll hate that.'

Dervla raised an eyebrow. 'Don't you think you've reached the age where it's time to put childish things behind you?'

'It's never time to do that. Oh, look! There's my copy of *The Turf-Cutter's Donkey*.' She picked up a book that had a picture of two children on the front, perched on a cart drawn by a little grey donkey.

'It's mine, actually,' said Dervla. 'Grandma gave it to Mama, and Mama gave it to me.'

'She did, did she? Lucky old you. It's a first edition – with illustrations by Jack B. Yeats. It could be worth a lot of money.'

'It's mine,' repeated Dervla. 'You got the Arthur Rackham *Midsummer Night's Dream*—'

'That Dad ruined by spilling Guinness all over it.'

'And I got *The Turf-Cutter's Donkey*. Look at the flyleaf. It's got my name on it.'

Río looked. The words 'Dervla Kinsella' were there, all right, printed in Dervla's neat hand. She shrugged, and handed it over. 'I hope you get a good price for it.'

'What makes you think I want to sell it?'

'I dunno. I guess, when I visualise your penthouse, I picture a place that's not cluttered with books and keepsakes and stuff. Like a showroom kind of joint.'

Río saw Dervla stiffen. 'You don't have the monopoly on art and literature, Río, just because of your boho credentials.'

Ow. Río had clearly hit a nerve here, by labelling Dervla as some kind of philistine. She'd have to backtrack. She realised with sudden alarm that she didn't *want* to have Dervla revert to spiky mode. In the past hour they'd started to unravel a lot of tangled history – a cat's cradle of loose ends and missing threads and dropped stitches. Río had her sister back in her life, and she wanted to keep her there: she needed an ally to help her through this horrible time. Frank may have been an irresponsible and neglectful father, but he'd still been family. Now that Finn was on the verge of disappearing from her life, Dervla was the only family Río had left.

'I just – I'd just have thought you were the kind of gal who prefers minimalism.'

'But I also like to surround myself with beautiful artefacts. I embrace the aesthetic that decrees that one should have nothing in one's life that is neither beautiful nor useful. And I happen to consider this book rather beautiful.' Dervla hugged *The Turf-Cutter's Donkey* to her bosom. 'Mama used to read it to me.'

Río wanted to remind Dervla that Mama had used to read it to her too, but decided against it. She didn't want hostilities to resume at any second. Instead she started to root through a cardboard box full of old books and papers, and said: 'Whereabouts exactly in Galway is your apartment?'

'It's in the Sugar Stack development, by the docks. Do you know it?'

Río did. Privately, she thought the development was hideous. 'Oh – the Sugar Stack! Of course I know it. It's . . . astonishing.'

'Yes. It's been nominated for an award for best city-centre residential development.'

'How do you find city life?' Río was genuinely curious. The only time she had lived in the city had been in a kind of commune, with baby Finn and a load of arty vagabonds. She hadn't a clue how it might feel to be a high-flying achiever type like Dervla. 'I mean, I know you've lived there most of your life, but it's so different from this sleepy ville.'

'I love it. I love the buzz.'

'Isn't it stressful?'

'Luckily, I thrive on stress. Did you never feel the urge to leave Lissamore?'

'Never. I wanted to be somewhere I could put down roots for Finn, somewhere I knew people. I'd have hated him growing up as a latch-key kid in some inner city flat or commuter town semi.'

'What makes you think you'd end up living in a place like that?'

'Anything else would be out of my league, Dervla. Because I've no qualifications I'd have had to take some low-paid work and slog all hours of the day. Anyway, village life suits me – I love being part of a community. When Finn was growing up here there was always someone to mind him. And I couldn't ever live more than a mile from a beach. Can you blame me?' Reaching into the box, Río produced an out-of-date calendar that featured images of Coolnamara's beaches and the islands on the bay. 'I love to be reminded that we live on the most westerly stretch of Europe.'

'Hey!' said Dervla, peering at the calendar. 'I sold that cottage last year – the little pink-washed one on Inishclare. Got a good price for it too.'

Beneath the calendar was a once-glossy brochure with red wine rings on the cover. 'Look,' said Río. 'It's a PR puff for the Sugar Stack. I wonder what Dad was doing with this?'

There was a moment of silence, then: 'I gave it to him,' Dervla told her in a rush. 'I guess I wanted him to be proud of me. I wanted him to be able to show it to neighbours and say: "Look how my girl's made good. Look where she's living now." Pathetic, isn't it?'

Río shook her head. 'No. It's not pathetic. I always had a dream that he might look in through Fleur's window and see my paintings on the wall and be proud of me too. It's the same thing, really. You wanted him to be proud of your success, and I wanted him to be proud of my creativity. It's ironic, isn't it? We've no one to be proud of us now.'

'You have Finn,' Dervla pointed out.

'And you have me!' Río said with a smile.

Dervla gave her an uncertain look. 'Are you serious?'

'Yes. I'm really, really proud of you. Every time I drive past a property that has your name up outside it, I always get a kind of buzz. Have done, ever since I saw the first one – when was it? About fifteen years ago? You've come a long way, Dervla. Imagine being nominated as Entrepreneur of the Year!'

'It doesn't mean that much,' Dervla told her. 'I'm much prouder of the fact that I live in a penthouse at the top of the Sugar Stack. That's a real achievement, in my eyes.'

'It is incredibly exclusive, isn't it?'

'Yes,' said Dervla, with just a trace of smugness. 'It's probably the most exclusive address in the city. Adair Bolger was responsible for the development, you know.'

'The bloke who owns Coral Mansion?'

'Coral Mansion?'

'That's what the locals call it. He calls it the Villa Felicity.'

'Yes. That would be Adair.' Dervla set down the calendar, and opened her book. 'The turf-cutter's cottage,' she said, regarding the illustration on the first page, 'at the edge of the bog.'

'And the lights of home shining through the darkness,' added Río. 'I remember that picture so well.'

Dervla gave Río a level look. 'I am sorry, you know, Río. About Coral Cottage. But you know it would have been an absolute nightmare to restore – a complete money-pit. Knocking it down was the only viable option. And Adair had everything on his side. Money, contacts, influence . . .' She trailed off, and looked back down at the picture.

'I know.' Looking at her sister's downcast eyes, Río had a suspicion that the all-powerful Adair Bolger was not solely to blame for the destruction of her dream. Had Dervla been motivated too by a desire to get even with her sister over the Shane débâcle? Río pushed the thought away. That was all in the past now, and if she and Dervla were to resurrect their relationship they would have to work hard at letting bygones be bygones. 'I would never have been able to afford to put the joint right, anyway. It was just a silly dream.' She tossed the Sugar Stack brochure back into the box. 'Show me the picture of Seamus and the eagle!'

'When he steals the bird seed?'

'Yes. I love that one!'

Dervla leafed through *The Turf-Cutter's Donkey* until she found the illustration, and as they looked at it, memories came flooding back to Río of her and Dervla tucked up in bed with their mother reading to them, and how she'd pause now and then to show them the illustrations. And she remembered how safe she'd felt, and how fuzzy and warm with love for her mother and sister, and she decided there and then that she'd never let Dervla go again.

'Now start to work!' announced Dervla, echoing the words of the Wise Woman in the story. She laid the book down and put on her bossy big-sister face. 'We've stacks and stacks to do. You take that side of the room, and I'll get cracking on this half.' Negotiating her way past a broken clothes horse and a wire cat basket, Dervla set about untangling a Gordian knot of electric cable.

On the other side of the room, one door of a double-sided wardrobe stood half open, as if inviting Río to examine its contents. She crossed the floor on cautious feet, wishing she could take off her shoes, which were beginning to pinch. She knew it was unlikely that there would be mice lurking in the attic, but she had inherited their mother's fear of creepy-crawly things, and there could be lots of spiders. Stepping gingerly over a raffia basket that looked as if it might once have belonged to a snake charmer, she glanced at Dervla, who had finished twisting the cable into a neat figure of eight and was now busy pulling open drawers and delving into boxes and upending cartons. Río admired her sister's sang-froid, but then she supposed Dervla was well used to exploring old houses. It was funny. When they were growing up, Río had been the feistier of the two – the tomboy to Dervla's Barbie. Río had plunged into the sea with panache while Dervla shivered in the shallows. Río revelled in stormy weather, dancing in a garden lit by lightning, while Dervla hid under the bedclothes. But Dervla had always been the cleverer of the two, and that, Río supposed, was why Dervla lived in a penthouse apartment and drove a nifty little Merc while Río lived in a rented doll's house and drove a hackney cab.

The door of the wardrobe creaked spookily when Río tugged on the handle. This is like the scary bit in the movie, she thought, the bit where you put your hands over your eyes and tell the stupid girl to get out of there *right now* because—

'*Jesus Christ!*' came a screech from behind her. Río spun round to see Dervla clutching her hands to her heart. 'Jesus *Christ*, W.B.! You gave me such a fright!'

'What happened?'

'Bloody W.B. jumped out at me from behind a box.'

W.B. stalked indignantly towards a threadbare sofa that sagged like a sinking ship in a sea of junk. He leaped onto it and began to wash himself self-importantly, as if to reinforce his status as top cat in the household's hierarchy.

'That cat always did have a wicked sense of humour,' said Río, turning to resume her inspection of the wardrobe. Dervla's yell had fazed her not a little, and her heart was ricocheting against her ribcage as she pulled again at the handle.

Behind the right-hand door was a rail upon which hung a confusion of fabrics: the dresses, skirts, blouses and scarves that had belonged to their mother. Running a hand along the hangers, Río paused now and again to rub the collar of a chenille cardigan, a corduroy jacket, a merino sweater, remembering how the material had felt against her face when she had cuddled up with her mother on the sofa and leaned her head on her shoulder.

Mama had always smelled of vetiver, from the fragrance she favoured. Río hadn't been surprised when she'd learned from an aromatherapist that vetiver was renowned for its calming properties. She took a step closer to the wardrobe, hoping to get a trace of her mother's scent, but the clothes just smelled of mildew.

The door on the left-hand side of the wardrobe refused to yield when she tried the handle. She tugged and tugged, thinking it might be locked, when it gave abruptly, catching Río off balance. She stumbled backwards and fell clumsily onto the sofa where W.B. was grooming himself. Dust rose at the impact, and W.B. slanted her an indignant look.

'Sorry, puss,' she said, giving his ears a rub before turning back to face the wardrobe. There, behind a veil of dancing dust motes, suspended like ghosts of girls, were two kimonos. They were of fine foulard silk, patterned with birds and flowers. Frank had brought them back as presents for his daughters after a junket to Japan, and had instructed them how to wear them. The most important detail to remember, he had told them, was always to fasten them at the front with the left-hand side over the right. Right folded over left, he'd said, was bad luck, because that was the way the Japanese dressed their dead. One kimono featured a bird of paradise motif, the other, sprigs of cherry blossom. Below the kimonos on the floor of the wardrobe lay a small valise, the lid of which was open. It was crammed with letters.

'Dervla,' said Río, 'come here.'

Dervla looked up from the filing cabinet she was rummaging in. 'What's up?' she asked.

'Our kimonos. The ones Dad brought back from Japan.'

Dervla joined Río by the open wardrobe door, and stood looking at the wraithlike garments. They were both suspended from misshapen wire hangers, and as they swayed gently from side to side, it was plain to see that the one with the cherry blossom motif had been arranged to be worn by a living girl, while the one with the bird motif was arranged to be worn by a dead one. The kimono with the bird of paradise emblazoned upon it had belonged to Río.

Río shuddered. 'That's really spooky,' she said. 'That's horrible. Who could have done it?'

'I didn't do it,' said Dervla hastily. 'I didn't hate you that much.'

'Then Dad must have done it.'

'Don't be daft. It was probably somebody who came in to do housework for him,' suggested Dervla.

'No. None of the neighbours would ever have intruded as far as the attic. And anyway, who would have known the significance of the way they're folded? Look how neatly the sashes are tied. It had to be someone who knew what they were doing. It had to be Dad.'

'Making a drunken mistake.'

Río shook her head. 'No. This has been staged. This was done with intent. There's some kind of message here. A message from beyond the grave.'

'Get a grip, Río! This is no time for melodrama.'

'I'm not being melodramatic. We were meant to find this. And we were obviously meant to read those letters too.'

Río steeled herself, then bent down to pick up the valise. She recognised it as having belonged to her grandmother. It was one of those silly little cases lined with frilly-edged elasticated silk that had once contained manicure kit and hairbrushes and lotions and potions for personal grooming while travelling. But its function as a vanity case had become redundant once their grandmother had died, for Río and Dervla's mother, Rosaleen, had never had an opportunity to travel anywhere.

Río carried the case over to the bockety sofa and sat down beside W.B. Dervla brushed dust off the armrest before perching herself at an angle that would allow her to look at the letters over her sister's shoulder.

The first letter Río drew out of the case was in an unfamiliar hand. Because there was no envelope, it was not possible to tell who had been the recipient. '"Darling one,"' Río read out loud. '"It's only Tuesday, and already I miss you unspeakably."'

'Who could "darling one" be?' asked Dervla. 'Our father?'

'No,' said Río, scanning the page. 'This was written to Mama. Listen.

'I know what hell you are going through with Frank, my lovely, loveliest Rosaleen, and I wish I could help in some way. You tell me my letters help ease the pain of your joyless marriage, but any words I write seem woefully inadequate. I want to *speak* to you, so that I can feast my eyes on your beautiful face while I tell you over and over again how wildly, how besottedly I am in love with you . . .'

54

Río raised her eyes from the page, and regarded Dervla. 'Mama must have had a lover,' she said.

'A lover? Mama?' Incredulity was scrawled all over Dervla's face. 'No!'

'What else could this mean?'

'But . . . *Mama*? Mama was a kind of saint – she was such a *good* person! She was so wise and gentle, and she put up with Dad for all those years . . . Oh God. Maybe that's why?'

Río nodded. 'Maybe putting up with Dad was just too much.'

'But who might – the lover have been?'

Río looked down at the bunch of letters. 'Looks like we're going to find out.'

'Is there a signature?'

'Not on this one. It's just signed "P".'

'A date?' said Dervla, leaning over and taking a second letter from the valise.

'No.'

'There is on this one.' Dervla unfolded a sheet of pale blue vellum. 'October, 1970.'

'What does it say?'

'My love. I'm writing this letter on the beach, where I came to leave it in our secret place, and I saw you just now with Frank and baby Dervla. I didn't dare approach because there were too many people talking to you. Presumably they're all curious to know when the new baby will arrive. You looked blooming. Beautiful. I felt so jealous to know that everybody will imagine Frank to be the father—'

Dervla stopped short, and bit her lip. Río heard herself saying, in a peculiarly calm voice: 'Give me that letter.'

'I . . . I'm not sure that we should—'

'Give it to me.'

Wordlessly, Dervla handed it over.

'"I felt so jealous", murmured Río, '"to know that everybody will imagine Frank to be the father of our baby. If it's a girl, my lovely Rosaleen, I should hope that you might call her Ríonach . . ."'

Río let the letter fall onto her lap.

There was a pause, then Dervla rose to her feet. 'I think,' she said, 'that we should finish reading these letters over a bottle of wine. Come on.'

'I don't think I can stand up.'

'Come *on*, Río – we've got to get out of here. This attic is starting to do my head in. It's like the set of a scary movie.'

Dervla made a move to help Río up from the sagging sofa, and as she did so, Río noticed that she had a manila envelope in her hand. 'What's that?' she asked numbly.

'It's our father's will,' replied Dervla.

'You mean, it's *your* father's will,' said Río. 'I've clearly yet to find out who my father is.'

Chapter Four

In the kitchen, Dervla handed Río her cuddly toy elephant. 'Here's something for comfort,' she said, 'until the anaesthetising effect of the alcohol kicks in.' She refilled their glasses and set them on the table, where Río had upended the vanity case. Letters littered the pockmarked tabletop. There were about thirty of them. 'We should maybe try to sort them into chronological order,' Dervla added, really just for something to say to fill the dreadful silence that had reigned in the house since Río had made the discovery that Frank was not her natural father.

Río shrugged, then selected a letter at random. 'Let's get our priorities right,' she said, unfolding the pages and turning to the last one. 'We should first try to find out who wrote them.'

Another silence fell. Then: 'Well?' said Dervla.

'Patrick. His name is Patrick.' Río leaned back in her chair. 'Wow. That's helpful. My father happens to have one of the commonest names in all of Ireland.' Picking up her wineglass, she drained it in one sustained gulp. 'Yeuch,' she said, and belched.

'We don't know he's your father,' Dervla pointed out, without much conviction.

'Dervla – think about it. This Patrick geezer clearly swept Mama off her feet. It's like we said earlier: maybe putting up

57

with Dad was just too much for her. If you were married to a man like him, could you have kept faithful?' Río picked up another letter. 'Look, here's a love poem.

'Give me a thousand kisses, then another hundred,
Then another thousand, then a second hundred,
Then yet another thousand more, then another hundred.

'Sheesh. I wonder, did he write that?'

'It's Catullus,' said Dervla.

'What?'

'Catullus. He was one of the greatest Roman love poets.'

'You're kidding! *Finn* could write better poetry than that.' Río looked glumly at her empty glass. 'Dervla. Could you be a sweetheart and nip out to the shop for another bottle? I feel like getting very, very drunk.'

'Who could blame you?' Dervla reached for her bag. 'I'll be back in five.'

As she made for the front door, W.B. stuck his furry face out between the top banisters, looking like the Cheshire cat in *Alice in Wonderland*. Curiouser and curiouser, thought Dervla, shutting the door behind her.

Could it be true? she wondered, as she made her way along the main street of the village, which was still decked out in festive Christmas lights. Could it really be true that she and Río were half-sisters? She'd always been aware that they were quite different types – not just temperamentally, but physically too. Río had an unruly mass of red-gold hair, while Dervla wore hers in a sleek dark bob. Río had an unashamedly voluptuous figure, while Dervla's was lean and androgynous. Río's eyes were green, Dervla's conker brown. Río took after their mother, while Dervla favoured their father. *Her* father . . .

Who would know? Who in the village might possibly know the identity of Rosaleen's secret lover? For lovers they certainly had been – a cursory glance at a single sentence in one of the letters had told her that: 'My darling, my darling – I worship the place between your legs, and your buttocks, and your beautiful, beautiful breasts . . .' Dervla hadn't wanted to read on.

She thought of their poor mother, trapped in a wretched marriage, tied to a man who – while never physically abusive to her, as far as Dervla knew – had certainly inflicted massive emotional damage on Rosaleen. Dervla had sometimes wondered if the stress of being married to Frank had contributed to the cancer that had killed her. Perhaps the only joy she'd had in her life had been those snatched meetings with a man called Patrick. Where had they consummated their passion? In his house? Or in theirs, while Frank was comatose or ensconced in the pub? She pictured the couple exchanging covert glances, touching hands surreptitiously, stealing kisses. She imagined their mother making excuses to go to the beach, where the secret place was that Patrick left the letters that meant so much to her. *You tell me my letters help ease the pain of your joyless marriage . . .*

Why – *why* – if the marriage had been so joyless, had Rosaleen stuck it out? But even as she asked herself the question, Dervla knew the answer. She'd said it herself, earlier, when they'd cracked open the wine in Frank's kitchen. Rosaleen had done it for her daughters. Had she kept the letters for her daughters too? Had she held on to them so that some day in the future Río might know the truth of her paternity? It wasn't the kind of thing a mother could easily admit to; had this been Rosaleen's way of communicating with her daughter from 'beyond the grave', as Río had put it? Or had she held on to the letters simply because they were the most precious things she owned? Proof that she had been adored?

It did not cross Dervla's mind to be censorious. On the contrary, she was glad, so glad for her mother! Rosaleen deserved to have had some romance in her life, even if it had been clandestine. Dervla remembered the rare occasions on which her mother had laughed, and wondered had she laughed that way with Patrick, too. She hoped so.

Questions came crowding into her mind now. Had Frank guessed that Rosaleen had been having an affair? Or had he only learned about it after her death, through her written testimony? Where had Rosaleen kept the letters hidden? When had he found them? Dervla pictured her father hunched on the bockety sofa in the attic, reading the fulsome expressions of love for his wife that were written in another man's hand. How had he felt when he discovered that Río was not his daughter? Or had he always suspected it? How was Río feeling now? To find out on the day of your father's death that he was, in fact, not your real father must be some kick to the head. No wonder her sister craved alcohol.

In Ryan's, the local shop, Dervla responded to the expressions of sympathy that came her way, the offers of help, the solicitous enquiries. Everybody wanted to reminisce about Frank, and tell her what a 'character' he was. 'Character' was a very useful word to use about a deceased person, Dervla decided. A bit like the obituaries that referred to a stonking misanthropist as someone who 'didn't suffer fools gladly' or a roaring alcoholic as a 'bon vivant'.

She selected a pricy bottle of Châteauneuf-du-Pape for her and Río to share, then waited for ages at the cash register while Mr Ryan regaled the queue with a lengthy anecdote about Frank Kinsella's wit and wisdom. By the time Dervla left the shop, a glance at her watch told her that she had been gone fifteen minutes longer than the five she'd promised Río.

She hurried back down the main street, keeping her head low in the hope that her demeanour might discourage people from engaging her in conversation. But Tommy Maguire was at the door of his pub, and she couldn't pass by without acknowledging him. He spent five minutes offering his condolences, and ended by telling Dervla how much he would miss her father's custom.

You betcha, thought Dervla darkly, as she finally disengaged and hotfooted it back to the Kinsella family home. As she let herself in, she waved at Mrs Murphy, who was gazing through the window next door with her phone clamped to her ear, probably trying to get through to the radio programme to complain about the cost of funerals.

In the kitchen, Río was sitting at the table, perusing a document. Dervla saw at once that the stapled A4 typescript was their father's will.

Río looked up as Dervla came through the door, and gave her a mirthless smile. 'Do you want the good news or the bad news?' she said.

'Oh! I hate that question,' said Dervla, reaching for the corkscrew. 'Just bring it all bloody on.'

'Brace yourself. Frank divided his estate into separate entities – dwelling and land.'

'Well, that's probably fair enough,' said Dervla cautiously. 'With planning permission, the land could be worth almost as much as the house.'

'In that case, you'll be glad to know that you've inherited the lion's share.'

Dervla bit her lip. That clearly meant that Frank had bequeathed the house to her. 'OK,' she said. 'So you've inherited the garden.'

'No.'

'Oh. Did he . . . could he have left it to Finn, then?'

Río shook her head.

'So who *did* he leave it to?'

Río gave Dervla a mirthless smile. 'He left it to Mrs Murphy,' she said.

'The ironic thing,' Río said to Finn a couple of hours later, after she'd dried the copious tears she'd wept upon returning home, 'is that we'd thought it would be a nice gesture to let Mrs Murphy have a memento of Dad. Some memento, eh?'

'Maybe she'll do the decent thing and refuse to accept it.'

'Refuse to accept a prime wedge of real estate with development potential? Are you out of your mind, Finn? And even if she declined, her sons would be in like the clappers to claim it on her behalf.'

Frank had known full well the passion Río had felt for that garden. She had tended it for years, growing the kind of plants that her mother had told her would thrive beside the sea, in the inhospitable soil of Coolnamara. She had brought in topsoil and compost and mulch to nurture her plantlings; she had even gathered donkey dung, which was the best fertiliser she knew of, and seaweed to wrap around the roots of saplings to keep them cosy in winter. She'd kept the pond clean – even though the koi no longer swam there – and she'd pruned and weeded and mowed and strimmed.

She had done it because she knew Rosaleen would have wanted her to do it, and any time she spent in that garden, she felt as if her mother were smiling down at her beneficently from the blue-and-white-washed Coolnamara heaven.

And then one day around two years ago her father had told her that he'd lost the key to the back door.

'That's all right,' Río had reassured him, 'I'll get a locksmith in.'

'No,' Frank had said mulishly. 'I don't want to set foot in that garden ever again, and I don't want you going out there either.'

'But Mama would want me to take care of her garden for her,' Río had protested.

'What she wanted doesn't matter any more. She's dead, and her garden should be allowed to die with her. It's morbid, so it is, to keep it alive when she's not here to enjoy it.'

'But don't you want to be able to enjoy it, Daddy?'

'I never enjoyed it. I hated it, and I resented the time your mother spent looking after it. She took better care of that effing garden than she did of me.'

Can you blame her? Río thought, but didn't say. What she did say, with a stroppy toss of the head, was: 'Well, you've only yourself to blame if the place gets so overgrown you lose all your light.' Which was exactly what had happened.

And now Río wondered if perhaps it had been around that time that Frank had discovered the letters written to his wife by the man called Patrick. Had that been why he'd denied Río access to the thing he knew she loved best, and allowed the garden to become a wasteland? And had that been when he'd tampered with her kimono and drawn up his will so that she, the bastard offspring of his wife's lover, would not profit from his death?

She had never loved Frank. Now Río hated him. She had done her filial duty by him and looked after him without ever having received a word of thanks, and now she felt as though he'd shown her two fingers and slammed a door in her face as he'd made his final undignified exit from this life.

What was she to do now? What would become of her? She knew it was venal, but she'd always expected to inherit half of Frank's property, and hoped she might one day have enough capital to put a down payment on a place of her own. A place of her own! That dream was now as vestigial as the dream she had once woven around Coral Cottage and her orchard and her marmalade cat.

Money was at the root of her problems – of course it was. Money – or the lack of same – was always a worry for Río, and money was especially tight off-season when there were no tourists around to be ferried to and from the airport. There were fewer people too, clamouring for pints of the black stuff in O'Toole's bar where she worked so hard at charming them. And once Finn was off travelling she'd be hard-pressed to pay the rent on her house without his weekly contribution. Her landlord had hinted that a hike was due.

She shook the thoughts away. She wouldn't think about that stuff now; she'd think about it once the funeral was over and Finn was gone. In the meantime, she would have to put a brave face on things. She would have to play-act very hard indeed, because she knew that if she wept and wailed as she had done earlier in the evening, Finn would not leave Lissamore and set off on the adventure that was his life – he would stay here for her.

'Ma?' he said to her now. 'I've been having second thoughts about going away. I mean now that Grandpa's dead and – and all this stuff has happened, it wouldn't be fair on you if I upped and left. I think it's best if I hang around for a while.'

Oh God. He *was* thinking about staying for her! No, no – she refused to allow him even to consider that option. She would not become one of those needy mothers who clung on to their children and ruined their lives.

'Don't be daft,' she said smartly. 'You know me, Finn. I'm resilient. I bounce back – always have. I won't allow the bastard to get me down. I just won't.' She reached for the phone. 'Now that I'm all cried out, I'd better phone your father. Tell him about Frank.'

'I already did,' said Finn. 'He said he'd phone you later, and he said he was mightily sorry for your trouble.'

Río smiled. 'Begorrah, and did he now?'

'He did. It seems you can take the man out of the bog, but you can't take the bog out of the man, even after twenty years in Lala Land.'

'How is the fecker?'

'He seemed grand. He's working.'

'Let me guess. In McDonald's? Or Burger King?' joked Río, stapling on a grin. She'd smile and smile and joke and joke, and she'd get through the next couple of weeks somehow until Finn was gone from her, and then she'd launch herself into the fray again, because Río *was* resilient. She'd gone through tough times – name her one single parent who hadn't – but she'd always somehow emerged on the other side battle-scarred and weary, but otherwise intact.

'No, he's not waiting table this time,' responded Finn. 'He's got acting work.'

'He has?' Río was genuinely astonished. Shane had done nothing but wait on tables for at least two years now.

'Yeah. He's got a part in a pilot for a new TV series.'

'Oh. The title of which is presumably *The Series That Will Never Be Made*.'

Shane had appeared in numerous pilots for projects that had never got off the ground. He had played a cowboy in something called *Clone Rangers*, and a vampire in something called *Blood Brothers* and an alien commander in something called *Ace of Space*, which Río had renamed *Waste of Space*. She and Finn had dutifully watched the DVD he'd sent them and tried not to laugh, but after a couple of glasses of wine not laughing had proved impossible, and Río had guffawed so hard that wine had come spurting out of her nose. The pair of them had gone round quoting from *Ace of Space* for weeks afterwards, intoning such gems as 'Instruct the hyperdrive to convey us to Twelfth Warp!' and 'Planet Quatatanga is ours!'

'Well, you know what Dad's like,' said Finn. 'He's always convinced that whatever he's in will be the next *Lost*. He said to tell you how sorry he is that he won't be able to make it to the funeral. He's shooting all this week and next.'

'That's sweet of him to even think about coming over, but I wouldn't have expected him to travel all that way for Frank.'

'Sure, it'd be no problem for him with the auld Hyperdrive. That conveyed him to the Twelfth Warp in no time at all.'

'But the Hyperdrive exploded on Planet Quatatanga, taking Captain Ross and his crew members with it. And that was the end of that pay cheque. I got my winter coat and my Doc Martens out of that pilot.'

'And I got my Xbox.'

'I wonder what we'll get out of this one?'

'I know what I want.'

'What?'

'My scuba-dive instructorship.'

'Oh, Finn! It breaks my heart to think that if Frank hadn't left me out of his will—'

'Ma, Ma! Please don't beat yourself up over it! I'll find a way to get my certification, I promise I will.'

'But it's so expensive—'

'Please, *please* don't worry about me, Ma. That's the last thing I want you to do. You've enough on your plate.'

Río made a face. 'I just wish it was scallops and lobster.'

'I'll fetch you scallops on my next dive. I know where there's a big bed off Inishclare. Hey! Let's check the EuroMillions results.' Finn reached for the mouse and set sail on Internet Explorer. 'Maybe we'll be lucky tonight.'

There was a pause, then Río stapled on that grin again. 'Knowing our luck,' she said, 'Dervla's probably already won it.'

That night – after she'd said goodbye to Río, and driven the forty kilometres back to her penthouse in the Sugar Stack in Galway, and sipped a glass of chilled Sancerre, and performed her Eve Lom routine, and slid between her Egyptian cotton sheets – Dervla did something she often did after she'd recced a property. As she lay in bed, she walked through it in her head, retracing her steps in a kind of virtual tour.

The front of Frank's house would clean up well. White-washed walls, a new front door painted a tasteful shade of duck-egg blue, window boxes. Inside, the porch would have to be retained. Porches were important on this stretch of the Atlantic coast, not just as storage space for fuel and wellie boots and umbrellas, but because they acted as buffers against the wind that beat up against the fronts of the houses in wintertime. Beyond the porch, the hallway, the sitting room and the kitchen could be knocked through into one vast, L-shaped living space, with the kitchen housed in the extended foot of the 'L', and with the old scullery beyond serving as a utility room. The study could be converted into a spare bedroom.

Downstairs and up, huge, double-glazed picture windows could be installed to frame that panoramic vista of sea and sky and mountains. The front bedroom was sizeable enough to accommodate an en suite shower room if a section of the landing was annexed. The bathroom would have to be ripped out, and all fittings replaced with state-of-the-art sanitary ware. A home office could be fitted under the stairs, library shelves in the stairwell, and the spare room overhauled and fitted with storage units. A deck could be constructed on the roof of the downstairs extension that housed the kitchen and utility room, with double doors opening onto it from the landing.

The only conundrum was – what to do about the attic?

That night, after saying good night to Finn, Río poured herself a glass of rough red wine and took it into the bathroom to sip while she cleaned her face. Studying herself in the mirror, she searched for some physical manifestation of her paternal genes. Her nose? No, it was definitely her mother's retroussé. Her hair? That red-gold mass was her mother's legacy too. Her eyes held her mother's faraway gaze, and when she smiled, her mouth – with its slightly too-short upper lip – curved into something that men seemed to find a lot more lethal than a cupid's bow. Had Rosaleen smiled that way at her father? Oh, how Río hoped she had! She deserved to have had some fun in her life, and some romance too, even if it had been clandestine.

What she had learned today explained the dearth of family resemblance between her and Frank, and between her and Dervla. But while Dervla had inherited the dark Kinsella colouring, in effect, Frank had been no more father to Dervla than he had to Río. He'd neglected them both equally. Did she feel any less connected to Dervla now that she knew they had been fathered by different men? No. If anything, today's revelations could only have brought them closer. Having a half-sister certainly felt a whole lot better than having a sister from whom you were estranged. Any kind of sister was far, far better, Río decided, snapping the top back on her Simple night cream, than having no sister at all.

Chapter Five

'We'll need to have a long talk.'

'Oh God, will we?' Río turned towards Dervla, who was standing in the doorway of their father's study, looking business-like in a black suit with a little boxy jacket. Río didn't own anything black to wear to Frank's funeral. She had rifled through her wardrobe that morning and selected a chiffon and velvet skirt in saffron yellow, which she'd teamed with a woolly sweater and a pair of Doc Martens. She didn't care if it was inappropriate garb for a funeral. Frank had turned up drunk at their mother's funeral, and how appropriate was *that*?

'I've asked Mr Morrissey to stay on after the wake—'

'Who's Mr Morrissey?' asked Río, taking a sip from her wine-glass.

'Our father's – Frank's solicitor. He's in next door with Mrs Murphy now.'

'Delivering the glad tidings about the garden, presumably?'

'Yes.'

'It'll be all round the village soon.'

It was inevitable that word of Frank's will would get out. All of Lissamore had showed up at the church today, to listen to the priest's eulogy. Río had wondered idly what class of a sin Father Miley was committing, standing up there spouting platitudes about what a wonderful human being Frank had been. Ha! How had he fooled them all so consummately?

Once the lie-fest was over, she and Dervla had had to smile stoically as the parishioners stood in line to tell the sisters over and over how sorry they were for their trouble, before trooping down to the graveyard on the headland where they'd said prayers for the repose of Frank's soul under a blaze of blue sky criss-crossed with the wispy white lines of vapour trails heading west across the Atlantic. The day of the funeral had turned out to be one of those miracle days that you get in Coolnamara in midwinter, the kind of day that Rosaleen had used to describe as 'pet' days. And Río had put on her best downcast expression as she'd tossed a shovelful of earth onto Frank's grave and muttered, 'Bastard bastard wretched fucking bastard.'

Now the wake was underway, and Frank's spring-cleaned house was host to a throng of guests who had come bearing gifts for the girls, much as they had come bearing gifts for Frank when he was alive. The table in the kitchen was groaning under the weight of the food and drink that had been contributed, and W.B. was looking distinctly tubbier. He was patrolling the house proprietorially, clearly perplexed to see so many people invading his territory.

The doorbell went again.

'I'll get it,' said Dervla. 'And then I think I'll just leave the damn door open to all-comers.'

Dervla high-heeled off, leaving Río smiling wanly at yet another person who'd rolled up, glass in hand, to tell her how sorry he was for her trouble and what a character Frank had been.

She'd had enough. Muttering an excuse, she grabbed a bottle from the hall table, and hotfooted it upstairs. Plonking herself down on the bottom step of the staircase that led to the attic, she swilled wine into her glass and wondered if she was becoming an alcoholic. It was hereditary, she'd read somewhere. How ironic that the only thing she might have inherited from her father was his alcoholism. And then she reminded herself that Frank wasn't her real father, and the whole situation became more ironic still.

From downstairs, voices floated up to her, and she remembered how she and Dervla had sat hunkered here as children, eavesdropping on their parents' rows and clutching each other's hand.

There was Dervla's voice now, raised in greeting to some new arrival. 'So glad you could make it,' she was saying. 'And Isabella too. How are you, Adair?'

Adair? It could only be Adair Bolger, the man who owned Coral Mansion. Río hadn't seen him for yonks. The last time she'd had an encounter with him had been while swimming in the Lissamore estuary. Adair had sped by in his pleasure craft, cutting a swathe through the water and creating a wake that might have drowned a less able swimmer. Río had shaken her fist and yelled at him, but he had given no indication that he had either seen or heard her.

Curious, Río crept along the landing and peered down through the banisters. Dervla was air-kissing Adair warmly. He'd changed a lot since the day she'd first met him, when he'd reminded her of Sunday Supplement Man. He'd lost weight, and some hair too, having opted for a close-cut crop. Much savvier for a balding man than a comb-over, Río thought: it lent an edge, somehow.

'I'm good, Dervla,' said Adair, on finishing the air-kissing ritual. 'But I'm sorry for your trouble. Your father was a real character, by all accounts.'

Río scowled.

'I suppose one might describe him as a bon vivant,' said Dervla, diplomatically. 'Talking of bon vivants, thank you so much, Adair, for introducing me to Matt Flanagan at the awards ceremony. We had a most pleasant business lunch last week, and we've agreed to meet up for a round of golf when he's next in Galway.'

71

Awards ceremonies! Business lunches! Golf! What very different lives she and Dervla led.

'You're welcome,' responded Adair smoothly. 'I suspected you'd find him helpful. Matt and I go back a long way. When it comes to investment portfolios— Oh! Ha-ha. What a friendly little cat!'

Río craned her neck further to see W.B. winding himself around Adair Bolger's shins, and rubbing his muzzle against the expensive fabric of his trousers. How dare the cat welcome him, of all people, into the house?

'What *are* you doing, Ma?'

Finn had emerged from the bathroom, and was standing on the landing, watching his mother curiously.

'Ssh!' said Río. 'I'm spying.'

'On who?' asked Finn, taking a step towards the banister and looking down at the occupants of the hall. 'Holy moly!' he added in a stage whisper. 'Who's that?'

'It's Adair Bolger, the millionaire who owns Coral Mansion.'

'No, I mean, who's the hottie?'

'Hottie? You mean his daughter?'

'That's never Isabella? The little girl I took donkey riding? My, oh my, but she's some fox!'

Río allowed her eyes to roam in the direction of Adair Bolger's daughter. Uh-oh. Isabella Bolger *was* a fox – the kind of little vixen that would have the dogs of the village panting in hot pursuit if they ever plucked up the courage. Isabella was golden of skin and hair – that expensive shade of gold that comes courtesy of a team of colourists and beauty therapists – and she was dressed in something that could have stepped from the pages of *Vogue*. She had about her that air of composure that only the very rich wear – a kind of serene confidence that nothing can go wrong in their world.

'Hands off, Finn,' growled Río. 'You don't want to get involved with a girl like that.'

'As if, Ma! A girl like her wouldn't look twice at someone like me.'

Just then, Isabella raised her china-blue eyes to Finn's. Her gaze rested on him for a nanosecond before she was distracted by W.B., who was now winding himself around her lissom legs. But Finn was wrong about a girl like her not looking at him twice. Because after reaching down to give W.B.'s ears a perfunctory rub, Isabella looked straight back up at him. And smiled.

Chapter Six

Oh God oh God oh God, thought Izzy, tearing her eyes away from the vision that was Finn and fixing them on the lipsticked mouth of the woman called Dervla. You stupid, stupid girl. What did you mean by grinning flakily at someone who's just lost his grandfather?

Did he remember her? She knew she bore little resemblance to the kid he'd once hefted onto a donkey's back, the kid who'd ordered him off her land.

She cringed when she remembered the way she'd spoken to him that day, all puffed up with self-importance because her daddy had told her that the land she stood on – the pretty over-grown garden and the fairy-tale orchard and the stretch of beach beyond – belonged to them now. What a prissy, obnoxious brat she'd been! No wonder the people of Lissamore had 'taken agin' the Bolger family, big time. Today was the first time in all those years that anyone had invited them to anything.

Izzy had been having lunch with her dad in the seafood bar upstairs at O'Toole's, earlier in the day, when Dervla Kinsella had approached and invited them to attend the wake for her father. Izzy had known it was Dervla, because she'd met her while accompanying Adair to the Entrepreneur of the Year Awards in Dublin. Izzy hadn't wanted to go to the wake. She'd never been to one, and she wasn't sure how you were meant to behave on such an occasion, but her father had insisted. It would show respect to the Kinsella family, he'd said, and it would be noted with approval by their neighbours.

Izzy knew that her father was keen to curry favour with the people of Lissamore. Since he'd built the barnacle on the beach, the Bolger family had not been made to feel welcome here. They'd spent just a handful of summers in their 'country cottage' before Mummy had left Daddy, and the house had become one of those ghost houses that you see all over Coolnamara, boarded up for the best part of the year until the owners find windows of opportunity to descend for weekends.

Those summers had been one long stream of house parties, with guests arriving from Dublin in their Mercs and top-of-the-range SUVs. The grown-ups would spend the weekends drinking Pimm's and swapping gossip on the terrace while the kids played in the garden or in the pool. They weren't allowed to play on the beach because it was deemed to be too dangerous for the smaller children without their au pairs in tow (Izzy often thought that the real reason was because the yummy mummies didn't want the kids' OshKosh gear to get spoiled), although they were allowed to play on what Felicity called 'the Greensward' – the strip of lawn that she had had planted adjacent to the slipway.

Isabella had thought this stretch of land to be their own private property until it had been made clear by the Lissamore people that it was no such thing. The locals had taken to bringing picnics down to 'the Greensward' and playing ball games on it, and once the Bolger family had arrived down from Dublin to find some baby goats tethered there. Izzy had been delighted, wanting to keep them, but Felicity had nearly fainted when she'd seen the state of her lawn. That was the last time her mother had come near the 'country cottage'.

Izzy had come down a couple of times since with her father

– just the two of them – but they hadn't had much fun. Adair had encouraged Izzy to approach some of the local kids any time he'd seen them playing on the beach or on 'the Greensward' or swimming in the sea, but she hadn't had the nerve, and after a few such dismal weekends they had given up on the house in Lissamore altogether, and gone back to taking their holidays in the Caribbean instead. Separate holidays for Mummy and Daddy, of course.

Felicity's favourite haunt was the überposh Sandy Lane in Barbados, but Izzy hated going there because her mother treated the staff like shit, and the kids in the teen club nicknamed her 'Irish Potato Head'. She much preferred going on holiday with her dad because he didn't spend all his time in the spa, although he did disappear from time to time to do business – a.k.a. playing golf. Adair had told her that more deals got done on the golf course these days than in the boardroom.

So Izzy spent a lot of time on holiday swimming solitaire in the pool, or in the sea, scuba-diving: scuba was for her the ultimate escape from reality.

Then, a couple of weeks ago, when Daddy had announced that his best Christmas present ever would be the pleasure of his daughter's company in Lissamore, Izzy hadn't been able to say no. Her friend Lucy had spent some time with them, and her aunt and some cousins, but now it was just the two of them again.

She resumed her stoical expression as she listened to her father talking small talk to Dervla Kinsella. 'In estate agent's parlance, this house has a lot of character too,' he observed, looking round at the shabby entrance hall with the peeling wallpaper, the threadbare carpet and the cracked fanlight over the door.

'Actually, it's *oozing* with character,' Dervla corrected him with a smile. 'And damp.'

'As a property developer, all I see is potential,' said Adair. 'And this place has loads. Prime site too, overlooking the sea.'

Oh God. Now they were going to start talking property-speak – the most boring language in the world. How could Izzy escape? Through the open front door she could see a dog sitting on the sea wall across the road, smiling at her. Murmuring an excuse to her father, Izzy slipped away.

The dog on the wall was a bichon frise. Her mother owned two, but Felicity's bichons frises had been given those awful pompom hairstyles. This little dog looked more like a miniature sheep than a miniature poodle, and as Izzy approached, its smile grew broader and its tail began to wag.

'Hello,' said Izzy, sitting down beside the dog. 'What's your name?'

Because the dog looked so intelligent, she half expected an answer. So, taking the dog's paw in her hand, she introduced herself.

'I'm Isabella Bolger,' she said, 'Izzy for short. I live in a house just outside the village, by the sea – except I don't really live there, if you know what I mean. My dad bought the house because my mum wanted a holiday hideaway, except she didn't really want to hide away. She wanted to be able to show off her house to all her friends, and when people weren't that interested because they couldn't hack the drive down from Dublin she went into a sulk and decided she didn't want it after all, and then Dad told her that he couldn't afford the diamond she wanted for her birthday, so she decided to divorce him, and when she did that she took all their so-called friends with her.'

The dog's ears seemed to droop in sympathy, which encouraged Izzy to continue.

'And now my mum's living in our D4 house and dating the man who did buy her the diamond, and Dad's living in a penthouse in the financial district, in the same block as me, and he's dating no one because he's a social misfit on account of Mum taking all his friends away. And he's dead lonely, and I feel so sorry for him sometimes. And I wish he could get a girlfriend

– only not the kind of girlfriend that he's dated from time to time in the past, because I know for a fact that all those women were just after his money, and that they hated me, even though they pretended to like me and called me "darling Izzy". And, do you know what? I hate it here in Lissamore because it seems to me that everyone resents us because we're rich and because we took over the Greensward and the house is far too big for just me and Dad, and we feel like losers staying there, with not even any friends to invite for the weekend.'

'Would you look at yer wan! Talking to a feckin' dog!'

A voice somewhere to her left made Izzy stiffen.

'That's because nobody else wants to talk to her,' came the reply, accompanied by a snigger.

Izzy's peripheral vision told her that a group of lads had congregated on a corner diagonally across the road. Her instinct was to get up and walk back across the road into the Kinsella house, but she was damned if she was going to let them faze her. She kept her eyes fixed firmly on the middle distance, even as she felt her face begin to burn.

'I wouldn't mind giving her one.'

'Pah! I bet she's frigid.'

'Give her a pearl necklace, then.'

'She's already wearing one.'

'Not that kind of a pearl necklace, ya gom.'

'Maybe she takes it up the arse.'

'Like Posh Spice.'

'She's a great pair of tits on her.'

'Posh Spice?'

'Nah. The bitch sitting on the wall.'

'Wonder how much she paid for them?'

'Nothing but the best for a D4 princess. Sure Daddy would have paid for them.' A dirty laugh.

'Hey, sweet-tits! Were they worth the money? Make those baloobas bounce for us!'

Izzy couldn't take any more. She was just about to get to her feet and make as dignified a retreat as possible under the circumstances, when there came the sound of a new voice.

'Cut it out, lads. Go find someone your own size to bully.'

'Ooh. It's Finn Kinsella. We're quaking, Finny.'

'Go on. Get the fuck out of here.'

'It's a free country, Finny. We can shoot the breeze wherever we like.'

'Not here, you can't. I'll say it again. Get the fuck out of here, and stop abusing the lady.'

'You gonna *make* us get the fuck out of here, Finn Boy?'

'Not today, I'm not. That'd mean disturbing the peace. And I don't like the idea of doing that when there's a wake going on. I'm just after burying my grandfather.'

That did it. A silence fell, followed by a gruff: 'Forgot about that. Sorry for your trouble.'

'It'd be no trouble to kick the crap out of you if I hear you talking that way again,' came Finn's voice. 'Learn a bit of respect, lads.'

Out of the corner of her eye, Izzy saw the group disperse. She remained sitting motionless on the sea wall until she became aware of Finn's presence directly behind her. Then she turned, face aflame.

'Thank you for doing that,' she said.

'No problem.' Finn looked down at her, concern in his eyes. 'Are you all right?' he asked.

'Yes. I just hate Lissamore more than ever now. What a horrible, obnoxious bunch of people.'

'I'm sorry you were subjected to that. It was drink talking. They're normally scared shitless by girls like you.'

'Girls like me? What *is* a girl like me? What makes me different?'

'You have class. That's what makes you different, in their eyes.'

'And that makes them feel that they have the right to talk to me like that?'

'I guess it's a way of masking their insecurities.'

'My heart bleeds for them! What about *my* insecurities?'

'They probably don't think you have any.'

'Ha! Everyone has insecurities.'

The bichon frise looked indignantly up at her, and gave a little bark as if to say, '*I* don't!', and Izzy looked at her and smiled.

'Hey, Babette,' said Finn, reaching down to scratch the dog under the chin. 'How's it going?'

'Her name's Babette?'

'Yeah.'

'Cute!'

'A bit girly for my taste.'

'What's wrong with being girly?'

Izzy saw Finn's eyes go to her peep-toe shoes, and travel upwards to the floral print skirt, which she had teamed with a baby-pink cashmere cardigan. She saw him take in the pearl necklace, and the lapis lazuli-framed sunnies tucked into her neckline, and the chiffon scarf that she'd wound around her head, and she saw him smile as he said: 'Nothing much at all wrong with being girly, I guess. If you're a girl.'

Izzy felt herself go as pink as her cardigan, and said – to change the subject – 'Who does she belong to?'

'Babette? She belongs to Fleur, who owns the boutique up the road.'

'Fleurissima! Oh, that's a fabulous shop! I got these shoes there.'

'Yeah? I noticed them in the window. I was looking for a Christmas present for my ma,' he added, as if to explain what a macho bloke like him was doing checking out a girly emporium like Fleurissima.

She saw Finn's eyes go again to the patent leather peep-toes, and wondered – if he had noticed them in the shop – had he also noticed the obscene price tag of four hundred and ninety euro?

'What did you end up buying her?' she asked.

'A raffia basket.'

Izzy had seen the pretty little baskets in the bargain bin of Fleurissima, reduced to clear at twenty-five euro.

'Are you going to be around Lissamore much, later in the year?' Finn asked, sitting down beside her on the sea wall.

'No. I'm . . . going travelling.'

'Going travelling' sounded more streetwise than 'I'm going on holiday with my best friend and my dad'. Adair had promised to treat her and Lucy to a fortnight in a five-star resort in Koh Samui in Thailand at the end of the summer, if they performed well in their first-year exams. Izzy would secretly have preferred to have gone off backpacking with her mates, but she couldn't bear the idea of her dad staying in an island resort on his own.

'Me too,' said Finn. 'In a fortnight's time I'll be backpacking in Queensland.'

'Wow. How long for?'

'Till the money runs out. Where are you heading?'

Izzy shrugged in what she hoped was a nonchalant fashion. 'Haven't decided yet. Somewhere I can chill before I start the slog of a second year in college.'

'What are you studying?'

'Business studies. What about you?'

'I gave up on the idea of college.'

'So what do you do?'

'I work on boats.'

'In the marina here?'

'Yeah. And in the scuba-dive centre over on Inishclare.'

'Oh! You're a diver—'

'Finn!'

A voice from across the road made them look up.

'Hey, Ma! What's up?'

A woman whom Izzy took to be Finn's mother was standing in the doorway of the Kinsella house, arms akimbo. How different

81

she was to Izzy's mother, Felicity! Río Kinsella was statuesque, with turbulent red-gold hair. She reminded Izzy of the picture of Queen Maeve on the cover of a book on Irish myths and legends her father had given her once. She was barefoot and dressed boho style in tie-dyed chiffon and velvet, with heavy bangles around her wrists. Her stance may have been regal, but there was something mistrustful about the way she was eyeing the pair.

'We could do with some help here!' she called. 'There are glasses to be filled, and plates to be passed round.'

'Coming, Ma.' Finn turned back to Izzy. 'Gotta go,' he said.

'Thanks again for coming to my rescue,' said Izzy. 'My name's Isabella Bolger, by the way.'

'I know. We've met before. But I nearly didn't recognise you now you're all grown up.'

'Oh, I wouldn't have thought you'd have remembered.'

'I could hardly forget a girl who tried to order me off "her" land.'

Izzy registered the emphasis and felt herself blushing again. 'What a horrible brat of a child I was.'

'You got your comeuppance when you fell off Dorcas.'

'Yeah. You laughed like a drain at that.'

Finn smiled. 'I was actually quite looking forward to teaching you to ride.'

'Why didn't you?'

'Word got out that your mummy didn't want you associating with the local kids.'

Izzy bit her lip. Why did he call her mother 'Mummy' when he'd called his own mother 'Ma' earlier? Was he jeering at her? 'I can make my own decisions now,' she said with hauteur, 'as to whom I associate with.' And then she cursed herself for using the word 'whom' because she knew it made her sound prissier than ever, so she tried to change the subject again.

'Are the donkeys still there?' she asked.

'Pinkie is. But she's all grown up now too.'

'*Finn!*' came his mother's – his *ma's* – voice.

'Coming!'

He got to his feet and stretched, and Izzy was horrified to find herself studying the musculature of his chest under the cotton of his T-shirt and wondering how it would feel to run her hands over it.

'Goodbye, Isabella,' he said, saluting her with a relaxed hand before moving off. She watched his progress, aware that his mother was doing likewise, with a cross expression on her face. Halfway across the road, Finn paused, turned and gave her an appraising look. Then he smiled, and something elastic in Izzy's tummy tautened. 'I'd still like to do it,' he said.

'Do what?'

'Teach you to ride, of course, princess.' Finn's wicked smile broadened, his green eyes narrowed, and then he was gone.

Chapter Seven

Río had just said goodbye to the last mourner, a maudlin Mrs Murphy – who had been utterly mortified to find out that she, and not Río, had inherited her neighbour's garden – and now she and Dervla and Mr Morrissey, Frank's solicitor, 'needed to talk', and Río just felt like getting drunk and going down to the beach to huddle in the dunes and watch the waves.

'Glass of wine, Ma? Dervla?' Finn emerged from the kitchen with a bottle and fresh glasses, on loan from O'Toole's pub. 'Mr Morrissey, you'll have a glass of wine, won't you?'

'No thank you, young Finn. I'm driving.'

'I'll have one,' said Río, thanking God *she* wasn't driving.

'We'll take it into the study, shall we?' suggested Dervla.

Turning on her heel, Dervla walked briskly into the study, where she perched herself on top of the old partner's desk, which had belonged to Frank, and where their mother had used to sit crying over the household accounts. The way she crossed her legs and folded her hands in her lap reminded Río of one of her old teachers, and she felt as if she were back at school again. How had her sister become such a grown-up?

Finn poured wine and handed round glasses, and then he and Río and Mr Morrissey sat down on the kitchen chairs that had been borrowed from Mrs Murphy for the occasion. She'd also lent plates for the sandwiches she'd made, and teapots for the tea she'd brewed, and a cake stand for the cakes she'd baked. Mrs Doyle from *Father Ted* would have been lost in admiration for her.

'I hope you don't mind if I don't turn my phone off?' said Mr Morrissey. 'I'm expecting a rather urgent call from His Grace.'

'Not at all,' said Dervla. 'Shall we get down to business? Perhaps you'd like to outline my idea to Río, Mr Morrissey?'

'Certainly.'

Mr Morrissey took some papers from his briefcase, and shuffled them importantly. He wore the self-absorbed expression of an actor getting ready for his close-up, and Río couldn't help thinking of all those Agatha Christie novels where relations gather together to hear the will of some deceased family member. 'Oh, get on with it!' she wanted to say. 'I already know I've been cut out of the bastard's will!' She felt like reaching for a zapper and fast-forwarding him.

'As you know, Ríonach,' began Mr Morrissey, eyeing her over the rims of his glasses, 'your father left no provision for you in his will. However, your sister is keenly aware of the injustice of this, and is prepared to gift you a portion of the estate.'

Río turned to Dervla. 'Jesus, Dervla! That's bloody decent of you.'

Dervla shrugged. 'I can't claim that it's entirely for altruistic reasons. I have a professional reputation to safeguard, and it's a small town. It wouldn't do my credibility any good if word got out that I'd shafted my own sister.'

'You didn't shaft me. Our father did. Or rather, *your* father did. I take it that Mr Morrissey knows *why* Frank cut me out of his will.'

'I do,' said Mr Morrissey. 'And you may rest assured, Ríonach, that I shall not breathe a word of your – er – paternity to anyone.'

'That wouldn't be difficult,' said Río, 'since I don't have a clue about my paternity myself. How many men called Patrick were living in Lissamore in the early nineteen seventies?'

Dervla shot her a warning look, and Río remembered that Mr Morrissey's Christian name was Patrick. 'Oops,' she said. 'No disrespect intended, Mr Morrissey. I mean, I'm sure – um – you know – um. Sorry.'

Río was stifling an overwhelming impulse to giggle. This afternoon was turning out to be increasingly like something off a daytime soap. Maybe she'd wake up and find herself in the shower, like Bobby Ewing.

'No apology necessary,' burbled Mr Morrissey. 'No, no, no.' His ears had turned red, which made Río want to laugh even more. 'I'm sure, Ríonach, that if you were desirous to learn the identity of your real father, it could be done. With DNA testing, nowadays—'

'D'you know something, Mr Morrissey? At this moment in time – ' (it felt right to be saying 'at this moment in time' to Mr Morrissey) '– I actually *don't* want to learn his identity. I couldn't bear to find out that my real father was some salaryman with halitosis.' Oops. That was a pretty accurate description of Mr Morrissey. She'd better do some backtracking. 'I mean, I'd really rather think of him as some heroic adventurous type who swept my mother off her feet and then – um – left Lissamore for ever when he realised she was never going to leave my father. *Your* father,' she amended, turning to Dervla. 'Hey! I guess this means I can't call myself Kinsella any more. I'll have to be just plain old Río.'

'That could be pretty cool, Ma,' said Finn. 'You'd be like those famous one-name dames, like Madonna or Britney or Angelina.'

'You need have no worries on that account,' Mr Morrissey assured her. 'Your surname was always and always will be Kinsella. That you have legally inherited from your – er – stepfather.'

'Wow. At least he left me something other than destitute.'

'Let's get on with the matter in hand,' said Dervla. 'I'm sure Mr Morrissey has more pressing concerns.'

'Yes, indeed,' said Mr Morrissey, checking his watch. 'His Grace may phone at any minute.' He cleared his throat. 'Your sister, Dervla, Ríonach, is prepared to let you have a third of this house, on condition—'

'A third! A *third*!' Río turned shining eyes on her sister. 'Dervla, thank you, thank you! I can't tell you what a difference that kind of money will make to—'

'I suggest you listen to the conditions before you fall upon my neck, Río,' warned Dervla. 'You may not want to accept them.'

'Oh.' Río turned back to Mr Morrissey. 'In that case, bring 'em on.'

'It is not your sister's intention to sell the property—'

'What? Why not, Dervla?'

'Listen,' said Dervla.

'It is her intention,' continued Mr Morrissey, 'to convert this dwelling house into two apartments, and to offer you the uppermost one. I have drafted a contract, which I shall leave with you to peruse at your convenience. If you agree the terms and conditions of said contract, I shall require your signature to make it legally binding.'

Río took a swig of wine. 'Um. What are the conditions?' she asked.

'They are contained herein,' said Mr Morrissey, patting a manila envelope.

'You're making me nervous,' said Río. 'There's something about the words "terms and conditions" that always strikes me as dodgy.'

'There is nothing dodgy about the conditions in this contract, I assure you,' said Mr Morrissey, fishing his ringing mobile out of his pocket and studying the display. 'Ah. Excuse me, please. This is the call I was expecting. Your Grace! A pleasure, as always. Yes, yes. A most unfortunate occurrence . . .'

Mr Morrissey's voice faded away like the dialogue in a radio play as he left the room and moved down the hall towards the kitchen.

Río turned to Dervla. 'You've been busy,' she said.

'I took advantage of the seasonal lull to get my personal life sorted. Once I'm back in business, I won't have time for anything else, and right now, time is of the essence. It's important to get details like this nailed down before the shit hits the fan.'

'There's *more* shit on the way?'

'I'm reliably informed that before the year is out, the country will be in recession.'

'In that case, why don't you want to sell the house right now?' Río asked curiously.

'Simple. The market's about to hit an all-time low. Property isn't shifting.'

Río knew this. Her friend Fleur had had her house on the market for months, and had been so insulted when someone had offered her a hundred thousand less than the asking price that she'd withdrawn it.

'We could sit it out and wait until things start to improve,' continued Dervla, 'but we could be waiting a long time, and in the meantime this house will not only depreciate in value, it will deteriorate materially. The roof needs replacing, and a damp-course will have to be put in.'

Yikes. Río couldn't afford the luxury of sitting it out. Her bank statement had arrived that morning, and she had tossed it straight into the recycling bin without bothering to open it. She didn't want to know.

'The alternative would be to apply for planning permission to have the place demolished and rebuilt, but that'll take time and there's no guarantee that permission will be granted. Whereas we will almost certainly get permission to extend. And if we don't, we just go ahead and then look for retention. It's a no-brainer.'

A no-brainer for an estate agent like you, Río wanted to say. Instead she said: 'But, Dervla, there's nowhere *to* extend now we've no garden.'

'Yes, there is. We go up. We raise the roof.'

'You mean, like, put in a mansard?' asked Río.

'We'd be unlikely to get permission for a mansard because that would affect the skyline, and the planning department's very strict about that. But we could raise it enough to incorporate a mezzanine.'

'And you'll convert the downstairs for yourself?'

'No. I don't want to live here. I'm very happy in the Sugar Stack, thank you very much.'

'So if you don't want to sell your part and you don't want to live here, what do you want to do with the joint?'

'I want to turn my portion of the house into a holiday let. There's money to be made from holiday rentals. And I can't do it if the top storey isn't in good nick. So I'm prepared to invest money in the place. I spoke to an architect friend, and asked him to come up with a design for a one-bed loft apartment in the attic.'

'For me?' asked Río, feeling a bit uncertain.

'Yes.'

'Couldn't he design one with two bedrooms?'

'Not viable. There just isn't the space.'

'But what about Finn?'

'Ma.' Finn looked awkward. 'I really don't want you to worry about me. Once I get back from travelling, I think it's best that I find a place of my own. So write me out of the equation. I don't want you worrying about me – I just want you to be happy.'

'You mean you don't want to live with me any more?'

'It's not that I don't want to. It's just that it makes sense for you to grab the chance to have a home of your own.'

A home of her own. Those magical words! But did a one-bed apartment constitute a home? A one-bed apartment with no Finn to chat to when he came back from the boats, no Finn to share pizza with in front of a Bond DVD, no Finn to give out to for leaving the bathroom in a mess . . .

89

'Presumably if you're gifting Ma the apartment, Dervla,' resumed Finn, 'it'll be rent and mortgage free?'

'Of course. As long as we agree the conditions. I'm a business woman, not Lady Bountiful.'

'Giving your sister half a house—'

'*One-third* of a house, Finn.'

'OK – *one-third* of a house – is a pretty bountiful thing to do, I'd have thought.'

'I like to keep things simple. Think of the alternatives. For instance, if you decided to contest Frank's will, Río, things could get really messy.'

'Hello? I'm an illegitimate daughter. How could I contest it?'

'They don't use the word "illegitimate" any more. And, anyway, so-called "illegitimates" have the same rights as their natural-born siblings.'

'So that means Ma *could* contest it if she wanted to?' said Finn.

'Yes. But do you want to, Río?'

Río thought about it. 'No. You're right. It would be messy. And risky. I'd end up in *Stubbs Gazette* if the case was decided against me.'

'So what are the conditions, then?' asked Finn.

Dervla recrossed her legs, and gave Río a look of assessment. 'I don't want you to sell your share of the house within my lifetime, nor do I want you to rent it out.'

'Oh. Why not?'

'If I'm letting it as a holiday rental, it stands to reason that I have someone to keep an eye on the place. And who better to have ensconced in the upstairs apartment than my own sister?'

'So I'd be like a kind of caretaker?'

'I don't know that "caretaker" is the right word. It sounds rather menial, doesn't it?'

'I'm not proud, Dervla. I told you that. I've had a long history as a jack of all trades. I can turn my hand to most things.'

'Well. Let's use a rather more genteel euphemism. How about "resident supervisor"?'

'But I could be a complete liability, for all you know. I could throw wild parties and trash the joint and entertain unsuitable men and—'

'Ma!'

'Sorry, Finn.'

'But I know you won't do any of those things,' said Dervla. 'Because I know you've always wanted a home you can call your own. We both have.'

The sisters regarded each other for a long moment.

Finn broke the silence. 'Will Ma be consulted about the design of the place?' he asked. 'It seems only fair to let her have some say in what it'll look like.'

'Of course,' said Dervla, reassuming her brisk manner. 'You'll be glad to know that I've asked my architect to include a balcony to the front, Río, so you'll have a view of the sea. Subject to planning, of course.'

'Hm. This all sounds very good.' Finn reached for the wine bottle, and Río could tell by his expression that he was thinking that this all might be too good to be true. 'I hope you don't mind me saying this, Dervla,' he said, moving across the room to top up her glass, 'but I'd like to have a look at anything Ma has to sign, because she finds red tape a bit – well – intimidating.'

'That won't be a problem, Finn. Cheers.'

'Cheers.' Río gave her son a big smile as he refilled her glass. How sweet of him to look out for her! And he was right about the red-tape thing. Río had a fear of filling in forms and signing contracts that verged on the pathological. 'What will being "resident supervisor" involve, sis?' she asked.

'Turning the place around between rentals. Laundry, a bit of cleaning, making a note of meter readings, that kind of thing.'

'You mean skivvying,' said Finn.

He said it in a jokey voice, but from the detectable hint of steel,

Río could tell that Finn didn't like the idea of his mother doing Dervla's dirty work. Hell, she didn't mind! The prospect of living rent and mortgage free in exchange for doing a bit of housework was a heady one. She'd had worse jobs. She'd worked in a call centre once, where she'd been glad to be fired after she'd called a customer a dickhead (in her defence, he'd called her a cunt).

'Will I have to clean the loo?'

Dervla looked taken aback. 'Well – yes,' she said.

'In that case,' said Río with mock hauteur, 'I might have a few conditions of my own.'

'Shoot.'

'Can I keep a marmalade cat?'

'Yes,' said Dervla, with a laugh.

'Then I guess it's a done deal. W.B.'ll be glad to know that he's found a home. Have you got your Dalmatian yet?'

'No. I'll have to move into the Great House first.'

'With the Pierce Brosnan lookalike?'

'I've lowered my standards a bit since then.'

'What are you two on about?' asked Finn.

'We used to have a fantasy,' said Río, 'when we were little, that Dervla would marry a man who looked like Pierce Brosnan and live in a Great House with a Dalmatian and manicured lawns.'

'And where were you going to live, Ma?'

'I was going to marry a Pierce Brosnan lookalike too, and I was going to live in a cottage by the sea with an orchard and a marmalade cat. Ha! I'll have to forgo the orchard – unless I get a load of bonsais for my balcony.'

'Well, at least you got the cat bit right,' said Finn, as W.B. marched into the room, authority manifest in his ramrod-stiff tail. He was followed by Mr Morrissey, who was saying: 'Yes, yes, yes. I am, of course, Your Grace's most obedient servant.'

Mr Morrissey ended his call, and slid his phone back into the pocket of his suit. 'His Grace is ebullient as ever,' he announced with a self-satisfied smile. 'Now. Is everything settled?'

'We think so,' Dervla told him.

'Excellent!' said Mr Morrissey, with great enthusiasm. 'In that case, I'll be off. His Grace has invited me to cocktails at the palace.'

'As the actress said to the bishop,' quipped Finn.

'I beg your pardon?'

'Stop being facetious, Finn,' said Dervla, waspishly.

At the front door, they all shook hands, and Mr Morrissey said: 'May I just say again how sorry I am for your trouble. Your father was a real character.'

And Río and Dervla smiled and waved as he walked to where his Lexus was parked further down the street.

Río stooped to pick up a cigarette butt that someone had ground out on the doorstep. 'Time to clear up,' she said.

'I'll start on the dishes.' Finn retreated into the kitchen trilling, 'Where are my Marigolds?'

Dervla raised her eyes to heaven and retrieved her Hermès handbag from the hall table. 'We're nearly out of washing-up liquid. I'll nip up to the shop for some.'

'You might get some Solpadeine too. I feel a headache coming on.'

Río felt very tired suddenly. She shambled back into the study to begin tidying up the remains of the party. And as she started collecting plates and glasses and piling them onto a tray, she thought about what Finn had said earlier, when he'd told her he'd find a place of his own to live. She knew she could survive without him for a year, while he was off doing his round-the-world thing – especially now that there were loads of ways of checking that all was well via Skype and MSN and email. Keeping in touch wasn't what it had been when she was his age, when long-distance phone calls had been too expensive and letters too much of an effort. But she hadn't allowed herself to think about what it would be like once Finn left home for ever.

For ever! Río remembered what Dervla had said on the day

of their father's death, about putting childish things behind her, and she understood that that was what her son was trying to do. She supposed it couldn't be easy for him – a twenty-year-old man to be living with his mammy still. Maybe he got grief about it from his mates. Maybe he'd been angling to move out of their little rented house for years, but just hadn't had the bottle to tell her because he knew how much she'd hate to lose him, hate to find herself living life solitaire – a childless hackney driver who scraped by working in other people's gardens and part time in bars, and painting indifferent watercolours to sell like some old-time spinster. Hefting the tray piled with dirty dishes, Río moved down the hallway and kicked the kitchen door open with such force that Finn looked round as she came through.

'Ma? Are you OK?' he asked. The concern in his voice made her want to drop the tray and fling her arms around him and weep.

'Yes. I'm fine,' she said.

Stapling on a smile, Río looked at her son standing by the sink, waiting for the washing-up bowl to fill. He'd kicked off his trainers; they lay beside her Doc Martens on the kitchen floor, making them look like Barbie boots in comparison. He wasn't her little boy. He was a grown man; he was his own man. He didn't belong to her any more. And, as she'd said to him earlier that week, he never really had belonged to her. He'd only been hers to borrow for a couple of scarily short decades, and now she was counting down the days until he was no longer even on loan to her.

But what would become of her without him?

Chapter Eight

After Frank Kinsella's wake, Izzy and Adair had gone for a walk along Lissamore strand, Izzy swapping her heels for trainers. They'd spotted a seal making its way up the estuary towards the oyster beds, and Izzy had told her dad the legend of the selkies, those beautiful creatures who shed their seal skins in order to seduce humans. Legend had it that if a man could steal a selkie's pelt, he could prevent his lover from returning to the sea. Without her pelt, trapped on land, the selkie swims forever in the shallows, yearning to return to her ocean home. To Izzy's mind, it was one of the saddest and most romantic of all the Irish myths.

'Well, princess,' said Adair, taking a final look at the sea before sliding the cardkey into the ignition of his streamlined Mercedes coupé. 'That's probably the last beach I'll hit till Thailand.'

'But that's months away! Can't you take any time off between now and August, Dad?'

Adair shook his head. 'This year's going to be a tough one, sweetheart.'

It was going to be a tough one for Izzy too. She was finding Business Studies not a little boring. Izzy was bright and loved a challenge, but her degree course didn't supply her with many opportunities to stretch herself. She was beginning to wonder if she shouldn't have taken Film Studies instead. That had been her original subject of choice; but she'd allowed her dad to persuade her to go for the more practical option.

Adair startled the Scissor Sisters into action, and Izzy cringed despite herself. Why, oh why, couldn't he listen to something more appropriate to his age, she thought, like the Beatles or Bruce Springsteen or Elton John? She hated it when Adair picked her up from friends' houses with the soft-top down and Franz Ferdinand blasting out of the sound system. Why did middle-aged people these days insist on keeping up to speed with their teenage offspring? She loved her dad, but she wanted to die when he went 'Yo!' to her mates, and came out with awful phrases like 'Gotcha! and 'Coolaboola!' And the clothes he wore were dead inappropriate too. He had a leather jacket on today, and aviator shades. But at least he hadn't grown a paunch, like Lucy's dad, Izzy conceded and at least he still attracted admiring looks from women his own age.

And as for her mother! Talk about mutton dressed as lamb. She remembered one day watching her mother walking away from her down Grafton Street after a shopping session in Brown Thomas. Felicity had come away with two pairs of Jimmy Choos, a pair of vertiginous Christian Louboutins, an obscenely expensive Roberto Cavalli dress, and tons and tons of anti-ageing and 'age-defying' products that had cost her a fortune. As she'd sashayed off, Izzy had observed a couple of men eyeing her trim figure appreciatively, because from the back, with her expensively styled blonde hair swishing over her shoulder blades, and her gym-toned arse wrapped in Gucci, she really did look quite tasty. But when she turned round Izzy had noticed the expressions on the men's faces falter. Despite all the surgery her mother had had done and all the age-blasting products she'd splashed out on, and the St Tropez spray tan, there was no disguising the fact that this was a woman in her fifties.

Felicity and Adair had married very young, and because their only child had arrived comparatively late in their marriage, Izzy had always believed that she had been a mistake. She'd been delivered by Caesarean section, and this knowledge fuelled Izzy's paranoia. Had Felicity opted for a Caesarean for the safety of her baby, or had she been in the vanguard of the 'too posh to push' brigade? Izzy sensed that, while her father was perfectly happy with a single daughter, her mother would have preferred a boy. Sometimes she found Felicity looking at her with something akin to resentment, and Izzy figured that, as her mother aged, she couldn't handle the fact that her skinny little daughter with the braces was turning into a beautiful young woman.

Izzy knew she was beautiful because people told her so. Strangers came up to her in the street and told her so. Photographers at the glitzy events she attended with her father told her so. Her girlfriends' boyfriends told her so, especially after they'd had a few jars. Izzy believed the people who told her she was beautiful because she had no reason on earth to think that they would lie to her. But it did little for her self-esteem, whatever that was. Her mother had beaten that thing known as self-esteem out of her daughter years ago: Izzy had learned to her dismay that her very first word had been 'Don't!' Unsurprising, really, since 'Don't!' was Felicity's favourite admonishment: *Don't make a mess! Don't fiddle with your hair! Don't get your dress dirty!*

The only time that Izzy felt comfortable in her own skin was when she was in water. She reckoned that her passion for all things aquatic stemmed from the fact that her mother had forbidden her to swim in the sea at Lissamore when she was a child: yet another *'Don't!'* But her mother hadn't been able to keep her away from the pool on the terrace in the Villa Felicity, or the pool she'd had installed in the basement of their des res in Dublin, or the pools that the parents of their friends had on their rooftops and in their gardens. And she certainly hadn't been able to keep Izzy away from the 50 metre pool at the very exclusive boarding school she had attended.

Izzy reckoned that becoming a mermaid was her way of rebelling against her mother. While she hadn't been the most academically inclined pupil in St Sepulchre's, or the most gifted in the musical or artistic departments, she had been a star in the swimming pool. She didn't mind the five a.m. training sessions, or the permanent circles around her eyes that goggles imprinted; and she didn't heed her mother's dire predictions that the chlorine would ruin her hair. Izzy was a naiad through and through, and every time she won a medal, her dad would hug her and tell her she was his water baby and buy her a new charm for her gold bracelet. The bracelet now weighed so much she was surprised her right arm wasn't as muscly as Madonna's.

The Scissor Sisters wailed their last as the automatic gates on the driveway of the Villa Felicity swung open, and the Merc glided through and along the tunnel of trees that led to the house.

The Villa Felicity was a copy of an achingly hip hotel that Izzy's mother had used to frequent in Miami. It stood like a glass sentinel on its elevated position on the shore, and once inside, from wherever you looked the stunning views were framed by stark concrete or gunmetal grey steel or unyielding Perspex. In the architecture and design of the house, the theme was maritime. The floors were of quarried stone, the decks of teak planking, the structure ship-like. The lobby – which Felicity insisted on calling 'the atrium' – was a cavernous construction of timber and glass, its walls hung with massive blow-ups of navigation charts, and all the rooms were fitted in shades of navy, grey and white.

The woman who had designed the interior had been a protégée of Philippe Starck, and it showed. The furnishings were linear: square leather armchairs and rectangular leather sofas in the sitting room, and tall, triangular stools in the kitchen. Everything was controlled from a built-in panel of electronic buttons on a console in the atrium, including the entertainment and security systems, the underfloor heating, and the sliding shutters that covered the floor-to-ceiling windows like metallic eyelids when the family was not in residence.

Izzy hated it. The only things to recommend the Villa Felicity were the pool and the view.

Adair drew up outside the house, pulled on the handbrake, and aimed the remote at the oversized front door. 'Glass of wine, sweet pea?' he said, as he got out of the driver's seat and strolled into the house.

'Yes, please.'

'Open the doors, then, Iz, while I get the drinks.'

'Isn't it a bit cold to sit out on the deck?'

'I don't care. I'd rather be a part of the view than look at it from behind glass.'

On the deck outside the big sitting room, aluminium recliners faced the view. Izzy sat down on one, giving a little yelp as her arse made contact with the unyielding cold steel, and wound her scarf once more about her neck. She remembered the way Finn had taken her in earlier, allowing his eyes to travel from the pearls around her throat to the tips of her toes, and she wished now that she'd worn something less frivolous, something more suitable for a funeral. However, she wasn't sure she owned anything suitable for a funeral. Nobody seemed to be dying any more: all her friends had grandparents who were living in luxury nursing homes, being kept alive by gerontologists because if they died the families would sue.

'Here's your wine, Izzy Bizzy.'

'Thanks, Dad.'

Adair set a long-stemmed glass of white on the aluminium side table. It was Meursault, Izzy knew; not cheap at fifty-something euro a bottle. They'd brought a bottle to the wake as a gift, and Izzy had spotted Finn's mother sloshing it into a glass with abandon, without bothering to check out its bouquet. Her own mother, who had done a wine appreciation course, would have been horrified.

Izzy hadn't spoken to Finn after he'd been called away to help out. She'd seen him doing the rounds of guests, talking and laughing easily, keeping an eye on glasses and proffering canapés and amuses-bouches. Except they weren't canapés and amuses-bouches, she scolded herself. They were chicken skewers and cocktail sausages. Why couldn't she call a spade a spade? Why did she talk so posh? Talking posh meant that people didn't want to talk back to you because they assumed that you were stuck up and unapproachable. Or else they hurled abuse at you, the way those arseholes had done earlier that day.

Adair loosened his tie, and sat down on the recliner next to his daughter. 'Just look at that view!' he said with a contented sigh.

'Dad?'

'Mm-hm?'

'Have you ever thought about selling this place?'

'Why do you ask? Don't you like it here?'

'Well, of course I love the view,' she told him. 'But I have no friends here. And – well, *you* have no friends here either, Dad.'

Adair made an expansive gesture with his arm. 'Who needs friends when you have a view like this! And who says I have no friends, missy? I've invited Dervla Kinsella round for cocktails tomorrow, and I told her she was welcome to bring her sister along.'

'Her sister – Finn's mother?'

'Who's Finn?'

'He's the boy who was going round pouring drinks at the wake.'

'Oh, yes. He was very efficient. A very presentable lad.'

'I got talking to him—' Izzy had been about to say, 'I got talking to him when a crowd of local lads started slagging me

100

off,' but stopped herself just in time. Instead she said, 'I got talking to him on the sea wall.'

'What does he do?'

'He works on boats.'

'Is he trustworthy, do you reckon?'

Izzy didn't need to think twice about it. 'Yes,' she said.

'I wonder would he be interested in earning a few bob on the side?'

'Doing what?'

'Caretaking this place. Old boy Carvill's done his back in, and he's thrown in the towel. Says he's too long in the tooth to be lugging around garden furniture and strimming lawns.'

Old boy Carvill was the local odd-job man. Izzy had seen him at the wake, downing whiskey from a hip flask, presumably to anaesthetise his back.

'Well, there's no point in asking Finn to caretake, because he's going off travelling soon. And honestly, Dad, is there really any point?'

'What do you mean?'

'Well, we hardly ever come here any more. Where's the sense in employing a caretaker for a place that lies empty most of the year?'

'Because houses need airing and gardens need minding, and things need fixing from time to time.'

'It just seems such a *waste!*'

'Ah, but, Izzy, in a decade or so I'll be retired, and you'll be coming here to visit with your own children. I can picture it now – you in the pool with your very own water babies.'

'You're planning on retiring here?'

'Where else would I go?'

Izzy had a sudden image of her father rattling around on his own in this great steel and glass bunker with the Atlantic raging outside and the wind battering against the windows and the rain lashing down on the roof, and she felt such a surge of sorrow for him that she wanted to weep. She took a sip of wine to cover her emotion, and then she reached for his hand.

'I love you, Dad,' she said.

Adair Bolger turned to his daughter and smiled. 'I love you too, princess,' he said.

Chapter Nine

The day after Frank's funeral, Dervla swung by Río's house to drive them both to the Villa Felicity. Adair Bolger had invited them for cocktails to mark the start of a new year, and Dervla was dying to see what the interior was like.

Making the decision to gift a third of Frank's house to Río had not been a difficult one. Since the rift with her sister all those years ago, Dervla had had a recurring dream that she was living in Coral Cottage, and that Río had come to visit her, barefoot, with a baby in her arms. In the dream, Río asked Dervla if she could come in and shelter because there was a storm on the way. Dervla had said 'no' and then she had watched as Río made her way down the overgrown path of the garden and crossed the orchard where the fruit lay rotting on the ground. She heard the rusty creak of the old five-bar gate as Río passed through, and the crunch of her feet on the shingle as she started walking towards the sea. The dream always ended with Dervla calling, 'Come back, Río!', but Río just carried on walking because Dervla's voice had been snatched by the wind that had started to blow from the west. After these dreams, Dervla always woke up in a cold sweat, with the vision of her sister disappearing beneath the waves imprinted on her mind's eye.

Dervla hoped that by presenting Río with a home of her own,

the nightmares might stop, and with them the feelings of guilt that she'd harboured for so many years. Guilt that she'd over-reacted to the stupid Shane thing, guilt that she hadn't been there for Río when she was struggling to rear her baby, guilt that – being resident in Lissamore – Río had effectively borne the burden of caring for Frank. And now her guilt was compounded by the fact that Río had spent all those years caring for a man who was not even a blood relation. She also hoped that now that her sister was back in her life, they could be friends again. Frank may have been an irresponsible and neglectful father, but he'd still been family. Now Río was the only family that Dervla had left.

Dervla parped the car horn lightly outside Río's house and her sister came to the door wearing her usual hippy-dippy gear.

'Honestly, Río! Couldn't you have made a bit more of an effort? We're not going to Glastonbury.'

'I don't have anything smart to wear.'

'Don't you have a suit or something for when you're driving?'

'Yes. But I'm not putting on a suit to impress Adair Bolger. It's a horrible cheap old thing, anyway, and I hate wearing synthetic fibre.'

Dervla sighed. 'All right, then. Hop in.'

'You're not taking the car, are you? It's hardly any distance. Let's walk.'

'In these shoes?' Dervla raised an eyebrow and indicated her cream leather kitten-heeled mules. 'I don't think so.'

She started the ignition, and the car set off down the main street of the village, past the pub and the post office and the general store, past the fishermen's cottages and the holiday lets and the marina, past a millionaire's mansion and the old Protestant churchyard, past B & Bs and a five-star hotel and spa that was under construction. They passed Fleurissima, where the all-white window display had remained unchanged since the close of season, and the seafood restaurant, from which wafted a glorious smell of frying garlic, and the bottle bank, which was overflowing with empties after Frank's wake yesterday. Not far outside the village, they took the turn-off that led to the Villa Felicity, and the beach.

'I wonder will he rename it now that they're splitting up?' said Río. 'Maybe he could call it "Smugville".'

'I hope you're not going to wisecrack your way through the afternoon, Río. Adair Bolger is a very useful contact. You'd be unwise to offend him.'

'Is that the word you use to describe your friends, Dervla? "Contacts"?'

'I don't have many friends, Río. I'm too busy.'

'So it's all work and no play?'

'Mostly.'

'Don't you have any social life at *all*?'

'Oh, yes. I have a social life. I play golf and I work out in a gym. A very exclusive one. I attend corporate events and theatrical first nights and book launches and exhibition openings and fashion shows and golf classics and charity lunches. But that's work too. My social life is all about networking.'

'What do you do to relax?'

'I read the property pages.'

It was true. Dervla lived, breathed and dreamed property. She subscribed to every property periodical going, she recorded property programmes to watch late at night, she surfed the web ceaselessly, visiting other agents' websites to check out the competition and Googling developers to give her a handle on the market. This afternoon she'd be in a position to get some insider info from Adair Bolger, which she could use to her advantage. She was keen to find out more about what people had started to refer to as the forthcoming 'credit crunch'. Forewarned was forearmed.

In her capacity as an auctioneer, Dervla was ruthless – a Rottweiler. Every single person she had dealings with was a potential link to another person, and that other person might be in the market for a house. And if they weren't, they might know someone who *was* in the market for a house.

Dervla had asked Adair some questions yesterday, and had learned that the reason the Bolgers no longer spent much time in Lissamore was because Felicity's dream of hosting house parties had come to nothing after the first few summers they'd taken up residence. As the traffic on bank holiday weekends became more and more unspeakable, more and more of her Dublin 4 friends declined her invitations to visit the Bolgers' palatial summer home. In despair, Felicity had applied for planning permission for a helipad so her friends could fly to the west coast, but scandals involving property developments had rocked the country to Government level, and the new boys in Planning proved to be less compliant than their predecessors. When Felicity realised that her villa was no longer the stately pleasure dome that had been her heart's desire, she had turned her back on it, never to return.

At the gate, Dervla got out of the car and pressed the buzzer. Knowing that she'd be on video surveillance, she affected her most pleasant expression.

'Dervla!' came Adair's voice over the speaker. 'You're welcome! Come on in.'

The Merc glided smoothly through the big steel gates and joined Adair's coupé under the *porte-cochère* that protected its gleaming paintwork from the weather. The sisters got out of the car as their host emerged onto the massive slab of polished granite that was his front step. He was wearing a Ben Sherman shirt, Levi's, and deck shoes. He scrubbed down well, Dervla decided.

'Come in, come in,' he said. 'This way!'

'Thank you.' Dervla passed through the atrium, looking around in awe. Even for a seasoned professional like her – having handled sales worth millions – this was *impressive*!

'I feel like I'm boarding a luxury liner,' she said.

Adair turned to her and nodded. 'That's exactly the impression the architect intended to convey,' he said.

'Wish I'd taken a seasickness tablet before I left the house,' quipped Río under her breath, and Dervla narrowed her eyes at her.

They followed Adair into a vast living space, where a window that resembled a proscenium arch framed a priceless view. Beyond the expanse of sliding glass, a teak deck ran the length of the house. Dervla started doing mental arithmetic. To have a house like this on her books would lend her no end of prestige. She wondered if Adair was considering selling. Was that why he had invited her here this evening? To allow her an informal recce?

'Words fail me,' she said. 'It's magnificent, Adair.'

'Words fail me too,' said Río.

Dervla shot her sister a look to see if she was being sarky, but Río's expression was unreadable. 'I understand you have a pool,' she remarked.

'Yes.' Adair strolled to the other side of the room, where a second sliding door opened onto a vast patio that boasted pool, hot tub, changing pagoda and barbecue area.

'That was a feature of the original garden,' said Adair, indicating an ancient stone sundial on the raised area by the hot tub. 'We kept it for luck.'

'I remember it,' said Río. 'It used to be by the henhouse, where your barbecue is now.'

'There was a henhouse here once? How quaint!'

'Yeah. I used to come here with my mother to buy eggs. I suppose the only ones I could get here now would be of the Fabergé variety.'

'I've always liked the idea of keeping silkies,' said Dervla, keen to change the subject.

'What are silkies?' asked Adair.

'They're a breed of chicken.'

'I thought they were a brand of underwear,' said Río.

Dervla chose to ignore her sister. 'They're little fluffy bantams – awfully sweet.'

Río gave her a disingenuous look. 'It wouldn't be easy, keeping poultry in your penthouse.'

'Where's Izzy?' asked Dervla, by now wishing fervently that she'd left Río behind.

'She's on the phone to some pal in Dublin, so God knows when she'll deign to join us. You know teenage girls and their phones, ha-ha. Her last bill floored me, it was so astronomical. Now, what can I get you to drink, ladies? Champagne, martini, G&T?'

'Just water for me, thanks, Adair,' said Dervla.

'Are you sure I can't rustle up a cocktail for you? I know it's rather early in the day, but I'm still officially on holiday.'

'I'm afraid I can't join you, much as I'd like to,' Dervla told him. 'I've to drive back to Galway this evening.'

'How about you, Río?'

'I'd love a cocktail,' said Río, with a minxy smile. 'I'll have a Slow Comfortable Screw Up Against the Wall. Mexican style, please.'

'Um. Coming up,' said Adair. 'Just – er – let me check the bar to see that I've got sloe gin. That is one of the key ingredients, isn't it?'

'Yes,' said Río. 'Hence the pun on *slow*, although I can't say that I've ever had a screw against a wall that was even remotely comfortable.'

Once their host had disappeared on his cocktail-mixing mission, Dervla turned to Río. 'What the hell do you think you're at, Río?' she hissed. 'You may have a strong personal antipathy for the man, but please stop taking the piss.'

Río's eyes widened. 'I'm not taking the piss,' she said.

'Then what do you mean by asking for a Slow Comfortable Screw, for heaven's sake?'

'It just happens to be my favourite drink of all time. I've spent years as a bartender, remember? I know my cocktails.'

Dervla detected something prickly about Río's demeanour today, something slightly mutinous. Maybe her sister was still sore over the fact that she'd never been able to get her mitts on Coral Cottage, never been able to achieve her dream of living by the sea and cultivating her garden there. But, as Dervla had pointed out just last week, the past was another country. It was time for them to move on; and that included jettisoning adolescent flights of fancy involving Pierce Brosnan lookalikes and Dalmatians and marmalade cats.

'He's got a bar,' observed Río. 'How naff! Did you know that Aristotle Onassis had bar-stools covered with whales' foreskins on the —'

In her peripheral vision, Dervla saw Adair come back into the room. 'Yes, yes – you're right, Río,' she interjected adroitly. 'The pool *is* magnificent.'

'What?' said Río.

'The pool,' Dervla said, with emphasis, giving Río a meaningful look.

Thankfully, her sister copped on. 'Oh. Right,' she said. 'And so is the hot tub. And the barbecue. It's magnificent too.'

'We were just remarking on how magnificent your house is,' said Dervla, turning to Adair with a dazzling smile.

'Oh, yes? Thank you. Feel free to have a look around while I mix the drinks. You'll be glad to know that I do have sloe gin, Río, so I think I'll join you in a highball. Here's your water, Dervla.'

'Thank you, Adair.' Dervla accepted a tinkling Waterford glass tumbler of fizzy water and ice. 'Are you sure you don't mind us having a look around?' she asked. 'I don't want to seem like a nosy parker.'

'Be my guest!' said Adair. '*Mi casa es su casa*. The stairs are that way.' He indicated the door that led to the atrium, and disappeared in the direction of what Dervla took to be the bar. Yesterday he'd mentioned a games room as well as an entertainment suite.

As they climbed the impressive staircase, Dervla's mind segued into estate-agent speak.

An outstanding contemporary-style home with spectacular coastal views . . .

'Wow! Get a load of the chandelier!' said Río, gawping at the steel and glass confection that was suspended from the ceiling of the atrium. 'I wonder, has there been much swinging out of that?'

Situated directly on a beach, with a 180-degree panoramic view taking in the whole of Lissamore Bay including Inishclare Island plus several miles of the Coolnamara Estuary . . .

Displayed upon a long windowsill was a row of starfish.

'Have you ever seen starfish underwater?' asked Río. 'They're actually hideously ugly. They look like big, misshapen fish fingers. I'm always scared they're going to grab me.'

What was Río blathering on about? Dervla concentrated harder on her sales blurb in order to drown out her sister's inane remarks.

The Villa Felicity— No, that would never do. Río had been right when she'd said the name ought to be changed – but not to 'Smugville'. Something Irish would be good. How about *Teach na Mara* – the house by the sea? Yes. Perfect! *Teach na Mara provides a unique opportunity to acquire a truly splendid contemporary-style home. With a bold design statement that compliments*— No, no! She was always getting that wrong! She had to remember to spell it 'complements' with an 'e' . . . *that* complements *its sensitive coastal site and optimises natural light, this unique property works both visually and practically in a stunning coastal location . . .*

'Oh, look! A nautilus shell!' cried Río, pointing at a delicate, whorled shell in a glass case. 'They're *incredibly* rare. I wonder how much some dealer-in-endangered-marine-life palmed for that.'

But Dervla was too engrossed in her interior monologue to comment. *This two-storey building is on four split levels,* she resumed, looking up before taking a mental photograph of the view of the atrium from the top of the stairs. *The house has a balance between open-plan and private spaces, with the spacious ground-floor drawing room opening onto a deck that provides one of the most breathtaking vistas in the West of Ireland and . . .* And? Framed by the enormous picture window on the landing, the sun was gilding the line of the horizon . . . *and gives a private position to take in the beautiful sunsets out over the sea and Lissamore Bay.*

'Oh, wow!' breathed Río. 'Look at that seascape!'

'Yes. Isn't it stunning?'

'Well, yes – but I was actually talking about the one on the wall.'

Río was gazing at a painting hanging on the plain white wall of the landing. It was a representation in oils of a stretch of beach edged with a fringe of creamy wavelets.

'It's a Paul Henry, isn't it?' asked Dervla.

'Yeah. It must be worth thousands.'

Teach na Mara is a stroll away from the beautiful village of Lissamore, which is famous for its seafood restaurants and exclusive boutiques. There is a world championship golf links at nearby Coolnamara Castle Hotel, a marina, and a scuba-dive centre on accessible Inishclare Island. Teach na Mara is one of the finest seashore properties to come to the market in recent years.

Excellent! Now all that remained was to persuade Adair Bolger to sell.

The sisters wandered from balcony to balcony, from bedroom to bedroom, and from bathroom to bathroom.

'Look!' said Río. 'The ends of the loo roll have been folded into pointy shapes, the way they are in hotels. I remember having to do that the summer I worked as a chambermaid in Coolnamara Castle. It seemed to me the most pointless thing in the world, ha-ha – pun intended.'

Río's sense of humour really was incredibly juvenile, thought Dervla. Despite the pat denial, she suspected that her sister *had* been trying to wind Adair up earlier with her 'disingenuous' remarks about keeping poultry in a penthouse and slow comfortable screws. If Dervla had known that she was going to subject Adair to a barrage of infantile digs this afternoon, she'd have declined the invitation on her sister's behalf yesterday.

The last bedroom they entered was the master bedroom. The guest rooms were all fit for princes and princesses; this was fit for a fairy queen.

'Cor blimey,' said Río. 'It's clearly a *mistress* bedroom. There's nothing very masterful about this boudoir.'

It was an exceptionally pretty room, all white, with a spectacular view of the bay through sliding glass doors framed by yards and yards of wafty white muslin. The furnishings were French style, with white-painted armoires and a sleigh bed draped in white cotton piqué. Sofa and armchairs were fitted with loose covers in the same fabric, tied with grosgrain ribbon. A chaise longue had been positioned by the window, where the curtains lifted in the breeze that came in through half-open glass doors. Beyond the window was yet another balcony; Dervla had by now lost count of the number of balconies and buttresses that jutted out over the garden.

'It's a bit fur coat and no knickers, ain't it?' observed Río.

'What do you mean?'

'Think about it. The rest of the house is all impressively hi tech and minimalistic, but the sanctum sanctorum is like something Laura Ashley might dream up.'

'I guess you're right. Maybe his ex is a girly girl at heart.'

Louvred doors led from the bedroom to a dressing room and en suite bathroom. Dervla had lost count of the bathrooms too. Her expert eye took in a Grohe power shower, Catalano sanitaryware and a Villeroy & Boch Jacuzzi bath. There were no products scattered on shelves, and no clothes hanging in the dressing room. The lady of the house had left not a trace of herself behind. This was the way Dervla liked her houses – clutter free and screaming 'aspirational lifestyle'.

Moving back into Felicity's boudoir, she registered that there were no personal effects here, either – no photographs, no books, no ornaments. The space was as devoid of personality as a hotel room that had been turned around for the next guest. She wondered if Felicity had chosen the furnishings herself, or if she had employed an interior designer. The latter, in all likelihood. People – even very rich people – were rampantly insecure when it came to furnishing their homes. They liked to be told how to do it by an expert.

'He doesn't sleep here,' observed Río.

'No,' agreed Dervla. 'He must use one of the spare rooms.'

'The one with *GQ* magazine by the loo. He wears Acqua di Parma aftershave.'

'Maybe he never slept here,' said Dervla. 'It's such a quintessentially feminine space.'

'Did you ever meet her?'

'Felicity Bolger? Once. At a dinner party.'

'How did she strike you?'

'A bit neurotic. Manipulative too. Not averse to using emotional blackmail to get her own way, I'd have thought. She certainly got her own way as regards the property in Dublin.'

'Oh?'

'Yes. It's worth a cool fifteen mill.'

'Holy moly! How do you know, Dervla?'

'I had a long chat with Adair yesterday.'

'Adair! God – it's such a poncy name, isn't it?'

'His real name is Darragh. Felicity got him to change it. She thought Adair sounded classier.'

'What do you think of him?'

'I like him. He's a bullshit-free zone. And he's sexy.'

'Sexy? No man who wears Thomas Pink shirts can be sexy!'

113

'I beg to differ. And his shirt is not Thomas Pink. It's Ben Sherman.'

Río gave her sister a curious look. 'Would you make a move on him?'

'I told you, Río, I've neither time nor space for a man in my life.'

'Not even a really, really, *really* rich one?'

'He won't be really, really, really rich once the divorce goes through. He'll only be really, really rich.'

'So if his ex got the house in Dublin, where's *he* living?'

'He's bought a luxury apartment in a new docklands development. Correction – he's bought two.'

'Why does he need two apartments?'

'One of them's for his daughter.'

'No shit! I wonder how it feels to be a princess.' Río made a face. 'Why couldn't I have had a daddy who loved me enough to buy me a luxury apartment and shower me with gifts?'

'Because life's not fair, Río.'

'Maybe I should find myself a sugar daddy.'

'There's one downstairs.'

'Nah. I don't find him remotely attractive.' Río moved to the cheval glass by the window, and started running her fingers through her hair.

'So why are you checking out your hairstyle, sister?' Dervla asked.

'I'm wondering if I should get highlights.'

'Take my advice and don't. Highlights are high maintenance. My last session cost me two hundred euro.'

'Bonkers, isn't it? The girl in the local salon only charges forty for a cut.'

It was bonkers. To Dervla's eyes, of the two women reflected in the mirror, Río looked like the one who had forked out two hundred euro for her do. A mass of unruly hair surrounded her face like a halo in a Byzantine painting, while Dervla's meticulously cut bob appeared somehow to be trying too hard. She shot a look at her watch. 'Come on, we'd better make a move back downstairs.'

'There's another balcony to check out.'

'We've checked out enough balconies. It'll look rude if we stay up here any longer.'

Río shimmied away from the cheval glass, and executed a theatrical pirouette. 'Imagine what it would be like to live here, Dervla! Queen of all you survey!'

'I thought you hated this house? You said it was ostentatious.'

'It *is* ostentatious. Just like its owner.'

'I'd hardly call Adair ostentatious.'

'Hel*lo*? Mr Midlife Crisis personified, with his *Top Gear* car and his leather jacket and aviator shades? It wouldn't surprise me if he had a tattoo somewhere. I bet he'll help himself to a Harley next. You know what they say about middle-aged men who drive Harleys?'

'To make up for the fact that they've minuscule dicks?'

'Mm-hm.'

'Don't you think you're being a bit unfair?'

'You mean you've *seen* his dick?'

'Oh, grow up, Río, and stop behaving like the kid who lost out on pass the parcel!'

'What do you mean?'

'It's patently obvious that you're still smarting over something Adair did yonks ago.'

'Namely?'

'Pulling down your dream cottage.'

From the expression in her sister's eyes, Dervla could tell that she'd hit home. But then Río dismissed the remark with an airy shrug. 'Hey! Maybe even having to put up with a minuscule dick would be worth it if you could get out of bed in the morning and wander out on the balcony to get a load of the sunrise, then head off for a skinny-dip before breakfast.'

'Remind me to put that in the brochure copy if I ever get a chance to put this baby on my books,' quipped Dervla.

Laughing, Río danced ahead of her sister to the top of the stairs. 'Wow!' she called back to her. 'I'd love to slide down those banisters.'

A laugh floated up from the atrium below.

'Be my guest,' said Adair.

Chapter Ten

'I thought you hated this house? You said it was ostentatious.'

'It *is* ostentatious. Just like its owner.'

The words were shocking. Infinitely more shocking was the reply that followed some sentences later.

'Maybe even having to put up with a minuscule dick would be worth it if you could get out of bed in the morning and wander out on the balcony to get a load of the sunrise, then head off for a skinny-dip before breakfast . . .'

Río's voice faded away. It was just as well she hadn't gone out onto the balcony, Izzy thought, because if she had she would have seen Adair's 'princess' standing to the left of the sliding doors, fists clenched, listening to those two vile women as they bitched about her dad. Bitched? No. What Río had said was worse, much worse than mere bitching. She had cast aspersions on her father's masculinity, she had belittled him, she had written him off as a buffoon.

But – and, oh God, the knowledge pierced her to the quick – wasn't Izzy herself guilty of disrespecting her father? She herself was often mortified by his taste in clothes and music, by the fact that he was a dancing dad, an embarrassing oldie. But he was *her dad*. She was *allowed* to be mortified by him: disrespecting your parents was something all normal offspring did. But Río – this . . .

this *intruder* – had crossed a line. What she had said was unforgivable. It made Izzy sick to think about it; she couldn't think about it; she *wouldn't* think about it.

Where else in the house could the Kinsella sisters have gone snooping? Izzy wondered if they'd been into her bedroom. She wondered if they'd made disparaging remarks about her décor and sneaked into her walk-in wardrobe and checked out the labels on her clothes. She wondered if they'd scrutinised the contents of her bathroom and sniggered over her blemish bombs, or if they'd sneered at her *heat* magazine, the way they'd sneered at her dad's *GQ*. What kind of literature did she expect to find in a man's bathroom? Marcel bloody Proust? And what was wrong with a man taking care of his appearance? At least he bothered – unlike Río Kinsella, with her rag-bag clothes and her mad hair.

Izzy scooped up her phone from where she'd set it on the balustrade of the balcony, and jabbed redial. 'Lucy?' she said when her friend picked up. 'The most horrible thing has happened.' And she filled her best friend in on the bitchfest that had just gone down in her mother's bedroom.

'Ouch. Poor you, Iz! You must be hurting *bad*,' said Lucy when Izzy's tirade timed out.

'I am. I am. But I'm gonna get her.'

'How?'

'I don't know.'

'Spike her drink.'

'With what?'

'Um. Some of your mother's Xanax?'

'There isn't any. She popped the lot. Oh, Lucy, they were *vile*! And that Río woman really fancies herself. She was prancing around in front of the mirror, checking herself out and swishing her hair.'

'Uh-oh.' There was an ominous silence on the line, and then Lucy said, 'D'you know what I think, Izzy? I think she might be after your dad.'

118

'What?' Izzy was so appalled by this notion that her fist clenched harder than ever. 'But she said she didn't find him sexy! And she said she hates this house and everything it stands for!'

'What *does* it stand for?' asked Lucy.

'I suppose she thinks it's a symbol of plutocracy.'

'Um. Forgive my ignorance. What's plutocracy mean?'

Oh! There Izzy went again, using a big word when a small one would do. But at least her best mate was used to the fact that Iz talked kind of nobby. Anyone else night have thought she was showing off. 'Plutocracy means the power bestowed by wealth. She's probably an anarchist who despises anyone who earns more than she does. She wears kind of anarchist's clothes.'

'Hm. I wouldn't be so sure. Maybe she's just really bitter and twisted. People who are critical of other people's taste are usually eaten up with jealousy.'

'You reckon?'

'Yeah. So when she sneers at something, it means she secretly covets it.'

'*That's* interesting. She said my mum's bedroom was Laura Ashley.'

'In a disparaging way?'

'Yes. But then she said something about how lovely it would be to wake up in it.'

'She actually said that? She said she'd like to wake up in your mum's bedroom?'

'Yes.'

'Yikes, Izzy. She's after your dad's money. I'd keep an eye on him, if I were you.'

'Really?'

'Yeah. He's vulnerable right now, and ripe for rebound. It's a classic syndrome. When men are jilted, they're sitting targets for predatory types like this Río person.'

'Oh, I'm so glad I've a psychology student for a BF!'

'Just don't ask me about the Electra complex.'

'That's got something to do with fathers and daughters, hasn't it?' asked Izzy.

'Yep. You could be a case study, Iz. Joke.'

'And what's the one about mothers and sons?'

'That's Oedipus.'

'Hm. I wonder. You should have seen the look on her face when she spotted me chatting with Finn yesterday.'

'Whose face, and who's Finn?'

'Río's. Finn's her son. He's kinda cute, in a bogger way. He has the kind of floppy hair you'd like to push away from his face.' And the kind of face you'd like to study on a pillow, lying next to you, thought Izzy: then rapped herself mentally over the knuckles and told herself to *stop that*!

'How did she look at you?'

'The mother? Like, "Hands off my son", you know? All narrow-eyed and suspicious.' Izzy suddenly became aware of footsteps crossing the marble floor of her mother's bedroom. 'Oops – hang on, Lucy – there's someone coming.'

'There you are, Izzy!' Her father stuck his head round the sliding door that led onto the balcony. 'I've been looking all over for you. Come and join us for a drink.'

'Hang on a sec, Luce.' Izzy covered the mouthpiece of her phone with her hand, and adopted a pleading expression. 'Do I have to, Dad?'

'Yes, you do. I don't want word going round the village that my daughter has no manners. What are you doing on the balcony, anyway? It must be freezing out there.'

'I came out for some fresh air,' Izzy lied. She'd actually come out to hide from the snoopy Kinsella sisters.

'Well, if you're in need of fresh air, why don't you show Río round the garden? She said she'd love a tour.'

Adair withdrew, and Izzy sighed into her phone. 'I have to go now, Lucy,' she said. 'Dad wants me to join the she-wolves. He's worried that they'll think I'm being rude. Ha! They ain't seen nothing yet!'

'What do you mean?'

'After what they said about my father, I think I've every right to be as rude as I damn well please.'

'Are you going to tell him?'

'About the bitchfest in the boudoir?'

'Yeah.'

'No. He's had enough knocks recently. I couldn't bear to see the hurt on his face.' Laughter rose from the drawing room downstairs. 'I'd better go, Luce. Thanks for your advice.'

'No problem, darlin'. Let me know how things pan out.'

'Will do. Bye!'

Izzy depressed 'end call', and took a deep breath. She noticed that the palm of her free hand had little sickle moon shapes indented into it from where she'd been digging in her nails. In scuba sign language, Izzy remembered, narrowing her eyes, a clenched fist meant 'danger'.

Río was sitting on a leather rocker downstairs in the big room – what class of a room was it, exactly: sitting room, living room, drawing room, salon, lounge? She was chewing on Macadamia nuts and enjoying her Slow Comfortable Screw Up Against the Wall, Mexican style. Adair Bolger sure mixed a mean cocktail. The alcohol had gone straight to her head, and had bestowed upon her that lovely tingly feeling that was one of the more pleasurable effects of a stiff drink.

Adair and her sister had been talking boring property talk, so Río had tuned out. She had fixed her attention on the vista before her – the view that never failed to astonish her, whatever the weather. Its mood changed every minute of every day of the year; it was like watching a panorama in motion. Some days it danced before her eyes, sun bouncing off a diamantine sea; some days it threw a tantrum – wind and waves and sky railing against each other; some days it waxed melancholy, a blue moon reflected in its midnight depths. And sometimes, like today, it was dream-like, bathed in a blue-green mist. And there, far out in the bay – too far to wave to – was Seamus Moynihan's red and white fishing boat. She'd mosey down to the harbour later, to pick up some fresh fish for supper.

The gentle rocking of the chair combined with the alcohol made Río want to stretch out like a cat on the big leather cushions and go to sleep. How wonderful it must be to stroll out into your garden and be greeted by that view every day! How wonderful to know – because there were no other houses in the vicinity – that this breathtaking panorama belonged to you exclusively! It was shameful, really shameful, that this house was so seldom occupied, that it spent so many months of the year dozing behind its security gates, shuttered and forlorn.

Río knew that the granting of planning permission for the Villa Felicity had been based on the understanding that the house be lived in full time for a minimum of four years. What a daft proviso! How could it be enforceable? Was a spy from the Planning Department meant to lurk around the garden, making notes of the dates on which members of the Bolger family were in residence? Río had scant regard for the Planning Department. She knew it had once been run by penpushers with a proclivity for brown paper envelopes stuffed with cash, and she suspected that that was exactly how Adair Bolger had got the go-ahead to build his horrible blot on the landscape.

Still, she had to admit that sitting here with a cocktail to hand and that vista in front of her was a pretty damn fine experience.

'How do you do?'

Someone had strolled into the view. It was Adair's daughter, Isabella. She extended a hand to Río, and Río felt uncomfortable suddenly, lolling against cushions when a formal introduction was clearly expected of her. She stood up clumsily, the seat of the rocking chair banging into the backs of her knees.

'How do you do?' she echoed, setting her highball glass on a side table and taking Isabella's proffered hand. It felt stupid to be saying 'How do you do?' She didn't think she'd ever said it before in her life.

'Allow me to introduce myself. I'm Isabella Bolger,' said Isabella. 'Pleased to meet you. And you are . . . ?'

'Río Kinsella.'

As she said her name, a shard of Macadamia nut flew out of Río's mouth and landed on Isabella's cheek. Río was struck dumb with embarrassment, but she had to hand it to the girl: she didn't flinch. She simply raised a manicured hand and brushed the offending crumb away without comment.

'Río? What an unusual name,' said Isabella, lightly.

'It's short for Ríonach.'

'Really?'

'Um. Yes.' There was a pause, and Río felt obliged to elaborate. 'It's the Irish word for "queenly".'

'Cool!' said Isabella, cool as you like. She curved her mouth in a smile, then turned and observed the seascape. 'What beautiful weather for this time of the year!' she remarked.

'Yes,' said Río. 'But the forecast is for rain tomorrow.'

A silence descended between the two women. On the other side of the room, Dervla and Adair were oblivious, lost in property-speak. Río felt like a complete eejit, a goose. What else could she talk about, apart from the weather?

'Your garden is beautiful,' she managed finally. Wow! Inspired!

'Yes, it is. Daddy tells me you'd like to see around.'

'That would be delightful.' Delightful? Where had *that* come from?

'I'm happy to oblige. This way.'

The girl marched towards a side door, and held it open for Río. Steps led from the wraparound deck to a gravel pathway that ran adjacent to the west side of the house. Río trudged in Isabella's wake, feeling like a tourist being shepherded by a tour guide. She remembered that when the Bolgers had first built the place, this part of the garden had been open to the sea. Now it was enclosed by a high brick wall. It was necessary, she supposed, to protect the herbaceous borders from the elements, but the grey brick had a forbidding air about it. She was reminded of the Oscar Wilde story about the selfish giant, who had refused to allow children to play in his garden.

The path took them up a slope to where Felicity's yoga pavilion enjoyed a cracking view of the garden and seascape. Here, Isabella stopped and looked directly at Río, as if expecting some kind of response.

'It's – um – magnificent,' said Río. 'Do you practise yoga, Isabella?'

'No. But Mummy does. She finds it therapeutic.'

'Ah. Gardening is my form of therapy.'

'Really? Do you have a big garden?'

'No. I don't have a garden at all.'

'Oh? That must be something of a challenge.' And Isabella gave a laugh that reminded Río of the ice tinkling in Dervla's San Pellegrino earlier.

'I – er – look after other people's gardens for them.'

'I see. So you're a gardener.' Was she imagining it, or did she detect a hint of disdain in Isabella's voice?

'Well. I'm not exclusively a gardener. I have other jobs as well.'

'Oh?'

'Yes. I – er – paint.'

'Houses?'

'Sorry?'

'You're a house painter?'

'No, not that kind of painting.'

'Oh! So you're an artist! How fascinating. Daddy's a collector. He owns some fabulous artwork.'

'I saw the Paul Henry on the landing.'

'That's a copy. He doesn't keep the original here for security reasons. All his paintings are hanging in the apartment in Dublin.

Apart from the canvases that are on loan to the National Gallery, of course. What do you paint?'

'Landscapes mostly.'

'Might I know your work?'

'Some of my stuff's for sale in Fleur's shop in the village.'

'Oh, yes. I've seen it.'

Isabella's opinion of Río's work was made perfectly clear by the absence of any comment, and by the way she adroitly changed the subject by adding: 'I love your scarf!'

'Thank you. It was a present from Fleur.'

'That shop is beautiful, isn't it? Every time I go in there I just want to buy it all up!'

'Yes. She has a great eye.'

'Daddy got a fabulous nightdress there, in embroidered silk. Oh! He didn't get it for himself, in case you're wondering! Ha-ha, no! He got it for his girlfriend.'

Isabella's little jewel of a phone started to purr at her and she immediately checked out the display. 'Excuse me. I know it's so rude of me, but I have to take this call. Please feel at liberty to explore.'

Isabella held the phone to her pretty emerald-studded ear and said: 'Hello, Lucy! Calling for an update?'

Río stumbled off down the slope, feeling like a badly drawn cartoon character. That girl was not just a princess, she was a demi-goddess inhabiting some celestial realm where ordinary mortals could not tread. She had been perfectly polite, perfectly agreeable, but there was something so steely about the polite-ness that Río would have preferred open hostility. She had to admit to herself that she, Río, who was normally so easy-going and open, had been badly fazed by the encounter.

Sitting down on the edge of a raised flowerbed, Río took a couple of deep breaths, trying to reinstate the blissful sense of peace she had felt earlier, while reclining on Adair Bolger's leather rocker. Slowly her heart rate decelerated and the flush that she had felt creeping over her neck from the moment Isabella had introduced herself receded.

Río had never succumbed to the temptation she'd felt, while passing the Bolgers' gate on her way to the beach, to climb over it. She was sure she'd be caught on a security camera, and nicked for trespassing. Now she could admire the garden at her leisure. There was the spot where she had used to picnic with her mother, eating squashed tomato sandwiches and drinking MiWadi. There was the stretch of wall upon which she and Dervla had performed balancing tricks, pretending they were circus acrobats. And there was the apple tree, beneath the branches of which Finn had been conceived.

A yew hedge had been planted along the wall. It had not yet grown high enough to disguise the intrinsic ugliness of the grey brick, but it would do so in time. Trees – bay, myrtle and arbutus – were all thriving despite the salt wind that came off the Atlantic. Beyond the wall sprawled the orchard where Río had picnicked and robbed apples as a child. No flowers bloomed at this time of the year, but Río knew that in a couple of months' time it would be an Impressionist fantasy of blossom and spring bulbs.

It was, she decided, a successful garden, impressive in its own way, but unimaginative. Up on the yoga pavilion Isabella was standing poised as a prima donna, impervious to the cold, still talking on her phone. The watery sun had sunk lower on the horizon, and was now partially obscured by a eucalyptus. That shouldn't have been planted there, thought Río. It'll cast a huge shadow over the lawn when it's grown.

'You look very thoughtful,' came a voice from further down the garden. 'And I'd say they're worth far more than a penny.'

'I'm sorry?' Río turned to see Adair Bolger leaning against the trunk of a Scots pine, further down the path. His hands were in his pockets, he'd rolled up his sleeves, and he had about him the laidback demeanour of a man who was comfortable on his own territory.

'Your thoughts. I said I'd give more than a penny for them.'

'Oh!' Río managed an unconvincing laugh. 'I'm not thinking anything very profound.'

That was a lie. Because Río was wondering how long Adair had been standing there watching her, and how vulnerable she may have appeared stripped of her habitual wise-cracking façade.

'Ready for another cocktail?' he asked.

'I'd love one.'

She moved down the path and together they strolled back towards the house, where, beyond the expanse of glass, Río could see Dervla taking photographs of the view with her phone.

'Dervla tells me you're a dab hand at gardening?'

'I am.'

'Our usual caretaker's done his back in. Do you think you might be interested in looking after the garden here?'

If it had been anyone else, Río might have said, 'I'm sure I could fit you in'. But the idea of working in the garden of Coral Mansion – maintaining it for Adair Bolger's biannual delectation – made Río bridle. Who did he think she was? Some luckless countrywoman who'd be glad of an extra few euro to make ends meet? That was, in effect, exactly what she was, but Río had her pride.

'I'm afraid,' she said, 'there's a waiting list for my horticultural services.'

Adair looked taken aback. 'I didn't realise you were a trained horticulturalist,' he said.

'I'm not,' Río told him with an enigmatic smile. 'But I have a magic touch. Folk hereabout call me the plant whisperer.'

Adair looked impressed. 'The plant whisperer,' he repeated.

And if you believe that, Mr Bolger, thought Río, you're even more of an eejit than I first took you for.

Río and Adair's progress was monitored by watchful eyes. Up on the yoga pavilion, Izzy was giving Lucy a running commentary.

'There she goes, strutting her stuff back to the house. God, Lucy, you should have seen the way she was posing by the flowerbed, trying to look all pensive. And I could tell that she knew damn well that Dad was watching her.'

'Is she good-looking?'

'I guess so – in a kind of boho way. You know the arty Coolnamara type – all flowing skirts and hair.'

'In other words, the complete opposite of your mum.'

'Yeah. I wonder is that a good thing or a bad thing? The other sister's completely different. She's very nicely put together. One of those suckers who forks out fortunes for handbags.'

'Hello? And just how much did those new shoes you were telling me about cost?'

'If I'd known Dad was actually going to buy them, I'd never have admired them. I nearly died when he surprised me with them.'

'Face it, sweetheart. You're his princess.'

'And while that Río dame is about, I'm going to behave like one. I'm going to make it very clear that she's out of her league here, big time. I'll be so polite she won't be able to keep up, and she'll have to back off. Actually, it's quite good fun, pretending to be überposh. I even told her she was "at liberty to look around the garden"! Oh, and I let slip that Dad already has a girlfriend.'

'Does he?'

'No. But she doesn't need to know that.'

'Maybe you should do a bit of matchmaking when you're back in Dublin.'

'There's no one good enough for my dad. The D4 circus is full of Botoxed vampires, and he needs somebody fun. He's talking about retiring here, Luce, and I just can't bear the idea of him living all on his own.'

'That's years away! He's bound to have hooked up with someone by then.'

'Maybe. But not necessarily someone who'll want to come and live in the back of beyond. I read somewhere that prescriptions for Prozac go through the roof in Coolnamara off season. Uh-oh, Lucy, she's wandered out onto the deck to gaze wistfully at the sea. I'd better go put a spanner in the works.'

'Go get her, Machiavella!'

'Catch you soon!'

Machiavella was right, Izzy thought, as she slid her phone back into her pocket. There was a war to be won, and the best way to win it was through subterfuge, using guerrilla tactics. Izzy tossed back her hair, narrowed her eyes and prowled down the pathway, wearing her most panther-like smile. By the time she hit the deck, her demeanour had changed. The prowl had become a prance, and the smile was one Kate Hudson might have envied.

Later, standing by the hob in the kitchen, waiting for the milk for Adair's hot chocolate to warm, Izzy looked back on the afternoon with glee. Río's second Slow Comfortable Screw Up Against the Wall had turned out to be a very fast uncomfortable one. She had downed her cocktail in less than twenty minutes, and left the house reeling under Izzy's onslaught.

Izzy hadn't been rude, but she had been so determinedly polite that the atmosphere had become almost tangibly frigid. Every time Río had opened her mouth to make some banal observation about the house or the view or the weather, Izzy had fixed her with an expression of such intense interest that it could not but be unsettling for the woman. At one point Río had tried to lighten things up by telling a rambling joke, but by the time she'd reached the end, her audience was left looking bemused and laughing unconvincingly. Whereupon Izzy had told a dazzling story about the forthcoming nuptials of Nicolas Sarkozy and Carla Bruni that had left her father and Dervla helpless with laughter, and Río at a complete disadvantage. She clearly had not understood the punch-line, which Izzy had articulated in impeccably accented French.

Izzy stirred Green & Black's into a mug of hot milk, and

carried it through to her father in the drawing room. Sitting across from him, she tucked her feet underneath her.

'Aren't you having chocolate?' he asked.

'No. I'm thinking of my figure. I ate far too much over Christmas.'

Adair took a sip of his chocolate. 'What did you think of the Kinsella sisters?' he asked.

Izzy shrugged. 'I thought the one with all the hair a bit – well – *gauche*. She's not the kind of person I'd invite to dinner. She wouldn't have a clue.'

'What do you mean?'

'She'd probably use all the wrong cutlery and call a napkin "a serviette" and pudding "sweet".'

'Izzy! It's not like you to be such a snob.'

'Blame Mum for that. She's the one who was a stickler for good manners.'

'She used to host the most perfect dinner parties.'

'Do you miss them?'

Adair looked thoughtful. Then: 'I've a confession to make,' he replied with a smile. 'I used to dread those feckin' dinner parties. They were like an endurance test.'

'Really, Daddy?'

'Yeah. I'd have been happier sitting on the deck with a beer. But your mother was – well let's just say that the simple life wasn't for her. Open the window a little, Izzy. I'd like to listen to the waves.'

She did as he asked, leaning out to breathe the scent of sea air. On the beach below a heron took fright, launching itself upwards on ungainly wings, and from an island opposite came the ghostly call of a curlew.

'I love that sound,' said Adair, happily. 'Maybe I should come down here more often. I reckon I could cobble together a better social life in Lissamore than the non-existent one I have in Dublin.'

Izzy turned back to him. 'What makes you say that?'

'I run into too many of Felicity's crowd there. Ironic to think that I can enjoy a drink in any branch of the Four Seasons anywhere in the world, but I don't dare set foot in the one on my own doorstep.'

'I hate that place,' said Izzy, with feeling. 'It's full of plastic people.'

'You're right. The people in Lissamore are more . . . genuine, somehow.'

'I wouldn't say that,' Izzy put in hastily.

'Why?'

She could hardly tell her father that the two women he'd entertained earlier in the day had bitched about him in her mother's boudoir.

'Well, take that estate agent woman, Dervla, for instance. Estate agents are notorious for being fakes.'

'Actually, she was very helpful. She advised me not to put this place on the market right now because of the property slump, but said that she'd be glad to help me sell it in a couple of years' time, when the market bounces back.'

'So you really are thinking about selling up?'

'Just thinking. It's been on my mind since you suggested it yesterday. This house is too big for just me. When Felicity designed it, she designed it with house parties in mind.'

'It's more like a hotel than a house, really, isn't it?'

'Well, that's where the idea came from. From that joint in Miami that your mother loved so much. And it worked for a while. We had some good times here, didn't we?'

Izzy nodded, even though she had very few fond memories of time spent in the Villa Felicity. She remembered the crowds of people who had used to descend from Dublin to stay in what Felicity had called 'The Guest Wing' (the capital letters evident in her tone), and how they'd all pose by the pool or on the deck with their champagne flutes, and how the women had all been immaculately made up and coiffed – even at breakfast. However Izzy had rather liked the fact that they were too precious about their La Perla swim togs to get them wet, because it meant that she could have the pool all to herself, to pretend she was a selkie.

But Adair's words – 'when the market bounces back' – made Izzy feel something a little like fear flutter in the pit of her tummy. What if all the doom and gloom merchants and the headlines in the property pages were right, and nobody was buying houses any more? The Villa Felicity might never sell, and it would just sit here crumbling on the beach like a great white whale, its shutters closed for ever. Unless they got tenants in. But who would want to live here full time? Adair was right: the house had been built as a pleasure palace, and might not prove easy to sell. Izzy had always thought that it looked more like a clubhouse than a home. It was a soulless place. And then that vision came to her again, of her father as an old man, rattling around here all by himself. She swallowed hard.

'Finished your hot chocolate, Dad?' she asked.

'Yes, thank you, sweetheart. It was delicious. No one makes hot chocolate like you do.'

Izzy smiled at him, and carried his empty mug into the gleaming Poggenpohl kitchen, her face aching with the effort of trying not to cry.

Chapter Eleven

In Galway airport, just two weeks after she'd buried her father, Río watched her son move towards the departure gate. She watched him pass through security. She watched him make way for an elderly lady with a walking cane. She watched him reclaim his bag from the conveyor belt and sling it over his shoulder. And then he looked back at her, and Río didn't see a tall, fit dude at whom girls always looked twice; she saw a small boy heading off on an adventure, looking the way he had sixteen years ago when he'd walked away from her into school for the very first time. And then he smiled that fantastic Finn smile, raised a hand in farewell, and was gone, taking her heart with him.

A passing security guard laid a hand on her arm. 'Are you all right?' he asked, and Río realised that there were tears coursing down her cheeks.

'Yes. No.' She shook her head, unable to continue.

'Saying goodbye to somebody?'

'Yes.'

'I see it every day. It's hard. You should get yourself a coffee.' The man gave her arm a reassuring squeeze, and moved on.

Tears were streaming down her face in rivulets now, and people were staring, but she didn't care. She wanted to get to the safe haven of her car where she could howl out loud in anguish.

She was barely able to put one foot in front of the other as she negotiated the car park, doubled over in agony, walking like an old lady. When she reached her car, she slid into the driver's seat, slumped forward and laid her forehead on the steering wheel.

She'd always known – of course she had – that Finn wasn't hers for keeps. But she had never thought that the pain of letting him go was going to be such a sickening, visceral pain, and now there was a hole where her heart had been, and no joy in her soul.

In her bag, the strains of a melody began to play. Finn must have changed the ringtone on her phone: it was playing Duran Duran's 'Rio'. Río's sobs became even more ragged – she was hyperventilating as she fumbled in her bag. Get a grip! she told herself. You don't want him to hear you like this!

But the caller ID wasn't Finn's. Letting the phone drop, she allowed it to ring out.

When a love affair ends, you could talk about it. You could talk to a girlfriend or a sister or a mother and know that they would understand what it means to lose a lover. Losing lovers happens to every woman. Losing lovers is commonplace. But how could Río tell anyone that the only man she wanted to hold in her arms was her own grown-up son? If she let that slip, people would be aghast, or embarrassed, or repelled. They'd tell her to wise up and go get a life, or counselling, or both. How could she expect anyone to understand that Finn was her life, he was her *soul*?

Why, *why* did the smutty Oedipal thing have to rear its head when mothers spoke of the love they felt for their sons? She'd heard an actress on the radio recently talk about how she had spent the final day before her daughter went off on her gap year, lying in bed with her arms around her, swapping secrets and singing the nursery rhymes that she'd once sung to her at bedtime, and everybody had said: 'Ahhh . . .' and thought it so lovely that mother and daughter had such a good relationship. She could just picture Finn's face if she, Río, had gone up to his bedroom and suggested that they lie down and hug and sing nursery rhymes together.

But, oh! how jealous Río had been of that actress's relationship with her daughter! How she would love to have Finn confide stuff in her, and know that any opinions she proffered would be listened to rather than falling on deaf ears as they generally did. But you can't do that with boy children, once they start becoming men. When boys turn into men, they stop sharing secrets with their mothers.

Her ringtone sounded again. The number displayed meant nothing to Río. She dropped the phone back in her bag, then raised her head and saw a world that had no Finn in it, and what she saw was a bleak and ugly and wholly meaningless place.

It was official. She hated her life.

Dervla was kept busy issuing orders. She was issuing orders to her architect and to bloody bureaucrats and to construction companies, and because Dervla was so very good at issuing orders (and because she had contacts in the Planning Department), she was getting results. Her architect had come up with some excellent ideas for the conversion of the attic that was to be Río's eyrie – including a balcony to the front and a small cantilevered deck to the rear where her sister could grow a garden in miniature. Dervla was determined that Río should occupy as cosy a nest as possible, because she had an idea that she might be going through the doldrums a bit now that Finn was gone.

She'd done some research on empty-nest syndrome, and found out that it had an effect on some women akin to bereavement. For those in middle age, the knowledge that their function as child-bearers was over apparently made the grief even more intense, and while Río was hardly hitting the menopause yet, the fact remained that she'd had her tubes tied and would never be able to conceive another baby. Or maybe she *was* menopausal?

It was hard to tell. Dervla's online surfing had revealed all kinds of stuff that was news to her, including the fact that early-onset menopause was hereditary. However, because their mother had died so young she had no way of knowing if it ran in the family.

Her own menstrual cycle had been erratic recently, but, because it had been so long since she'd had sex, Dervla had put that down to stress. Times were bad in the property market, and she was working her ass off to sell houses that would once have sold themselves. She was using all the tricks of the trade to try to shift properties, but she couldn't be in two places at once and oversee every little detail, much as she'd like to. It made her heart sink sometimes when she'd open up a house for a viewing to see just how little care the owners had taken to make their interiors inviting. Some people didn't even bother to flush their loo, and Dervla now made a point of visiting every bathroom in every joint on her books, and flushing the pan before potential buyers showed up. She'd drawn the line at buying a pooper-scooper for the resident canines.

The only house that had sold in the past month had been an unprepossessing-looking two-up, two-down in Galway city. The front door gave no indication of what lay beyond, but once inside, the house was an Aladdin's Cave of unusual furniture and paintings and curios – a real home. The sellers had been clever, setting the table for dinner with gleaming silverware and crystal and a good bottle of wine, and baking bread before each viewing so that the house smelled glorious. Nothing ostentatious – just little touches that lent the interior an atmosphere that made viewers think, Ooh! I'd like to live like this!

In Waterstone's recently, Dervla had helped herself to a big, glossy coffee-table book called *The Way We Live – Making Homes / Creating Lifestyles*. It was crammed with images of dwelling places in different countries and cultures from all over the world: photographs of French villas and Irish cottages and Swiss chalets and English stately homes and Renaissance palaces and New York lofts. It was a treasure-trove of a book for anyone interested in property or interior design, and Dervla was pleased to observe that her own home compared favourably with any of those smart New York interiors.

And then one day she looked again at the title, *The Way We Live . . . Creating Lifestyles*, and she thought how weird it was that people these days really did aspire to live life *styles* – but not necessarily satisfying lives. Everything was for show. The dozens upon dozens of expensive, shiny magazines that lined the shelves in newsagents were testimony to that – magazines carrying ads for the latest must-have kitchen appliances or bed linen or garden furniture. What happened to readers of those magazines when they rushed lemming-like to max out their credit cards on handcrafted solid wood floors or three-door refrigerators or bespoke English bookcases? Did their extravagant purchases make them happier? What if a dog got sick on your fabulous Roberto Tapinassi sofa, or a toddler scribbled on it? What then?

Dervla loved her sofa, but then Dervla had neither dog nor toddler to trash it. As long as she remained living solo, her Corinthian leather upholstery was safe – as was the upholstery belonging to countless other singletons living in countless other exclusive gated communities all over Ireland.

Since Frank's funeral, Dervla had been spending more time in Lissamore village, prepping her father's house for its metamorphosis. She'd witnessed at first hand the community spirit at work there, and the laidback ambience that Río had told her she set such store by. Dervla had witnessed, too, the starring role her sister played in village life. People greeted Río on the street with beaming smiles; tourists gravitated towards her to ask for directions; even the local cats got off their arses and stretched when Río went by, as if inviting her to pet them. She'd seen Río in O'Toole's, pulling pints, flirting effortlessly with male punters and sharing secrets with the women. She'd seen her smile, laugh, blag and charm, and she knew that what Río had was more precious than handcrafted floors or three-door fridges or bespoke bookcases. Río had a life, not a life style.

How fine it must feel to be Río!

Río was lying in bed, trying to decide whether or not it was worth making the effort to roll over from her left side to her right. She decided against it. She didn't have the energy. The sheets felt horrible against her naked skin. She hadn't changed them in a week, and that was most unlike Río. She hadn't washed her hair for a week, either, and she hadn't had a shower for two days. One of life's greatest pleasures, in Río's mind, was to take a leisurely bath with a book and a glass of wine, and then slide into bed between freshly laundered sheets. Ironically, a website on empty-nest syndrome that she'd looked at shortly after Finn had gone travelling had recommended that she 'treat' herself by having a long lie in a scented bath. As if! Río didn't even have the energy to turn on the taps.

She'd tried cuddling her old velour elephant for comfort but that hadn't worked, so instead she'd wrapped one of Finn's T-shirts around her pillow, and cuddled that instead, saturating it with tears of self-pity. She was ugly, ageing, stupid, and she was sure she stank. Her eyes were red from constant crying, and from all the booze she was putting away. She was drinking far, far too much. She'd taken to buying wine boxes from the supermarket in Galway when she drove fares there, because empty wine boxes were easier to dispose of in a village where the bottle bank was situated directly opposite the church.

Hackney fares had been sporadic, which was good news for Río because she was pretty certain that much of the time she was over the limit from the amount of alcohol consumed the night before. Because the season didn't get underway until after St Patrick's Day, Fleur's shop was only open at weekends, so she had no window-dressing job, and only two evenings a week behind the bar in O'Toole's. She wasn't painting because her creative drive was non-existent – and anyway, hadn't Isabella Bolger been right? Her paintings were crap; they weren't even selling. And to top everything, her landlord had put the rent up, as he had threatened. So as well as being useless, ugly, ageing, stupid, smelly and a crap artist, Río was broke. Life really couldn't get very much worse. Not even the prospect of moving into the loft space in her former family home could energise her. She kept seeing herself through Dervla's eyes – the poor relation who was such a loser that she even needed someone to provide a roof over her head. She was fearful of moving, suddenly, she felt safer here in the familiar surroundings of her rented doll's house, even though she had done no housework for weeks and the place was looking neglected and uncared for.

Shortly after Finn had gone she had read all of the letters that the man called Patrick had written to her mother. They were so redolent with love that Rosaleen had written eight words in the margin of the very last letter she'd received from him. The words were in violet ink, in her mother's distinctive, swirly script, and they read: 'I know what it is to be adored . . .' Her mother had been adored. She may have had a tough life with Frank, but at least she'd been *adored* by somebody.

The only person who adored her, Río, was now off on the other side of the world, living his dream on a beach.

And there seemed to be no one she could talk to. Fleur and Dervla, being childless, would not understand. Shane would be sympathetic, but she didn't want sympathy. She wished she had a mother she could ask for advice, she wished she could pick up a pen and write 'Dear Mama, what would *you* do?' In despair, she consulted an internet site.

'Pull yourself together, you sad bitch,' had been the advice of some heartless contributor to the online forum she subscribed to. The contributor's nickname had been 'Virago', and Virago clearly had the emotional sensitivity of Anne Robinson or Pol

Pot. Virago had no time for men in her life: no time for sons, husbands or lovers. Men, Virago admonished her, were a waste of space, and Río should 'get a life, get a grip and get over it'.

Get over it? Get over *Finn*? It was way, way easier said than done. Getting over the kind of heartbreak that mere men divvied out was easy. Río had had her heart broken loads of times before in her misspent youth – and she'd broken her fair share too. After her mother had died and after she and Dervla had declared hostilities, and after she'd turned down Shane's proposal of marriage, Río had played men for fun, and run a little wild. Home for her and Finn in those days had been a squat, a kind of commune in Galway city. Home had been a big dilapidated Georgian town house where actors and artists and writers cohabited in an ambience that was more Gypsy King than Bohemian Rhapsody. The accessory *du jour* in those days had been a baby, and Finn, with his infectious laugh and dancing eyes, had been the accessory most beloved of the female members of the tribe, leaving Río free to paint and party and inspire poetry for as long as her baby was portable. But when Finn had ended up locked in a wardrobe at two years of age while one of his 'aunties' entertained a wandering minstrel-type with a penchant for Lebanese hash, Río had decided that it was time to return to Lissamore and a less liberal lifestyle. Since then, Finn had been the only man for her, despite expressions of interest and declarations of love from locals and holiday-makers alike.

Declarations of love! She, like her mother, had been adored once! Maybe . . . maybe now was the time for her to cast her net again, to think about finding a man who might fill the void that was her life without Finn? Maybe now she should aim to meet someone with whom she could share quality time: wandering hand in hand along beaches, and snuggling up to watch classic DVDs in front of the fire? But who would be interested in a useless, ugly, ageing, stupid artist? One who was not only penniless and smelly, but crap at painting to boot? A useless, ugly, ageing, stupid artist who didn't even know who her own father was . . .

Oh, what was the *point*?

The phone rang just as Río was debating again whether or not to roll over onto her other side. She reached out a slack hand for the handset, and saw that Dervla's name was on the display. Río didn't want to talk to her sister – she *couldn't* talk to her sister. Her *half*-sister, rather, who was so very savvy and erudite and stylish, her half-sister who worked out in an exclusive gym and attended theatrical first nights and book launches, her half-sister whose single bad habit was worrying her cuticles. Her all-singing, all-dancing, all-networking half-sister–

Oh! What was happening to her? People said that you get the face you deserve by the time you're forty, and if that was indeed the case, Río was going to have the face of a bitter and twisted old hag. Making a huge effort, she pressed the green button, held the phone to her ear, and heard her sister's voice greet her with a breezy 'Good morning!'

'Hello, Dervla,' replied Río, trying to match the brightness in her tone. But as she made to raise her head from the pillow, she got another trace of Finn's scent from his T-shirt, and immediately burst into tears.

'Río? What's wrong?' asked Dervla, and the note of concern in her voice only made Río cry harder.

'I can't bear it,' she wept. 'I just can't bear life without Finn. Without him, I'm nothing. I'm useless, Dervla. I just wish that something awful would happen to me so that I wouldn't have to go on living.'

For a moment there was silence on the other end of the line. And then Dervla said, 'Don't break open the safety catch on the Nembutal bottle just yet, Río. I know somebody who needs your help.'

'How could I help anyone with anything?' wailed Río. 'I've just told you, I'm useless.'

'You might be kind enough,' said Dervla, 'to help me.'

'*You?* But you're so self-bloody-sufficient, Dervla! You're the last person in the world who needs help with anything!'

'I'm going to prove you wrong. Are you at home? I'm coming over.'

'Now?'

'Yes. I'm just down the road, in our – in Frank's place.'

'But – but I'm still in bed,' said Río, feeling shame-faced.

'Good God! It's nearly midday, Río!'

'I know. But I don't care. I don't care about anything any more.'

Río heard an intake of breath, and then Dervla said, 'Stay there. I'll come over right away, and I'll bring some food. When did you last eat?'

'Um. I had something last night.'

'What?'

'A tin of tuna.'

'Uh-oh. It's got to that stage, has it?'

'What do you mean?'

'Staying in bed and not looking after yourself are classic symptoms of depression. May I ask you something personal?'

'Go ahead.'

'When did you last wash, Río?'

Oh God! 'I'm too embarrassed to tell you.'

'In that case, I'm on my way. I'll run you a bath and I'll pour you a glass of wine, and find something clean for you to wear. And then we'll sit down and have some decent food, and when you're feeling a bit better, I'll run something by you.'

'What does it involve?'

'It involves getting creative,' said Dervla.

A couple of hours later Río had had a bath, and rubbed herself all over with the Jo Malone body lotion that Dervla had brought her as a present. When Río had protested that this was too generous, Dervla had said that it was to make up for all the birthdays that they'd missed in the past. So, in return, Río had invited Dervla to choose a painting, and Dervla had chosen a view of Lissamore strand, worked in shades of ultramarine, Hooker's green, Indian yellow and Prussian blue. It was Río's favourite painting, and she was glad her sister had chosen it.

Dervla had also washed the dishes and vacuumed the floor while Río was in the bath, and then she had mixed a salad and set a dish of moussaka on the table and refilled Río's wineglass, making Río wish that she and Dervla had made amends years ago.

'Aren't you having wine?' Río asked. She was feeling better now that she had bathed and washed her hair, and the Jo Malone grapefruit body lotion was the most glorious thing she'd ever smelled in her life – apart from Finn's T-shirt.

'No,' replied Dervla. 'I'm driving.'

'But I'll feel like a pig sitting here and swigging back a whole bottle.'

'You don't have to drink the whole bottle, Río. You can always stick the cork back in.'

'I'm not very good at that,' confessed Río. 'When Finn was here, we always finished a bottle together. Now I tend to finish it by myself.'

'It's not a good idea. Alcohol's a depressant.'

'I know. But it numbs the bloody awfulness of life.'

Dervla gave Río a speculative look. 'I've been checking out empty-nest syndrome on the net,' she said.

'So have I,' said Río.

'What do you think?'

Río shrugged. 'Most of those websites offer advice like "establish date nights with your spouse", or "travel", or "get involved in church activities". Not much use to me since I don't have a spouse, I can't afford to travel, and I haven't believed in God

143

since Mama died.' Río took a sip of wine, then managed a wry smile. 'One even told me to repent my sins.'

'What sins?'

'Well, I bad-mouthed my father and barely spoke to my own sister for years.'

'I wouldn't have spoken to me either, if I'd been you,' replied Dervla, matter-of-factly. 'Have you thought about seeing your GP?'

'No. I'd be scared he'd prescribe antidepressants, and I hate the idea of filling my body with chemicals.'

'What about counselling?'

'Lying on a couch and having some shrink nod sagely while I twitter on about myself? No thanks. Anyway, shrinks are expensive. I can't afford weekly one-on-ones. My dreams tell me all I need to know about my psyche.'

'What do you dream about?'

'Being homeless. I have recurrent dreams where I'm always packing to go off on some journey, and the packing always goes wrong. Cases fall open and boxes split and all my bags have big holes in them. And I keep losing stuff – keys, wallet, passport, phone; my sketchbook. I dream that Finn has left me and then I wake up and realise that that's not a dream. It's a nightmare, and it's real. I'm actually *living* the dream – ha-ha.'

'So what do your dreams tell you?'

'That I'm lost, alone, abandoned.'

'OK. Let's have a serious think about this. You're a creative person, Río, and right now you're being creatively stymied. The fact that you're not painting is symptomatic of that.'

'I can't paint. My painting's crap.'

Dervla indicated the canvas that Río had given her and said, 'I beg to differ.'

Río slumped. 'I can't paint now, Dervla. I just can't. I'd want to take a knife to the canvas.'

'Then listen up. I have a job proposition for you.'

144

'You want to employ *me*? As an estate agent? Dervla, I'd be *beyond* crap at that!'

'Not as an agent, no. Remember how I told you that I needed someone to "stage" homes for me? I want you to be my stylist.'

'A *stylist*? Me! Is this some kind of a joke?'

'No. Listen up. I don't mean the kind of stylist who works on glossy photo-shoots or with celebrities. I need someone with a lot of imagination, who knows how to make a house look like a home.'

'That's easy. You live in it.'

'Or you *aspire* to live in it. Look at what you've done with this place.' Dervla's gesture took in a mosaic splashback, an elaborately branched chandelier, a *trompe-l'oeil* mural and a ceramic Dutch stove. 'Who do you think would aspire to live here?'

'Nobody I know. Except for me and Finn.'

'I have plenty of clients who would aspire to live in a place like this.'

'You do?'

'Yes. I know a writer who would give anything to be able to downshift and spend the rest of her life here. I know a retired guard who would kill – that's a joke, by the way – to become part of a village community and live in a house full of such charm and character. And you're the gal who has invested this house with said charm and character. I'm assuming that this is all your own work?'

'Well, yeah. The place was a bit soulless when Finn and me first moved in.'

'You've made it your own, Río. And presumably you did it on a pretty tight budget.'

'I do everything on a tight budget. The chandelier came from a junk shop. And I found the stove on a skip.'

'You see? You have a great eye. And you have experience.'

'Experience?'

'You trained as a theatre designer. And you know about gardens. The exterior of a house is as important as the interior.'

Río looked thoughtful. 'Hm. Gardens I *could* do.'

'And you could bring your window-dressing skills to bear. You're fantastic at telling stories with images. Remember that window you did for Fleurissima last summer? The one that featured in *Galway Now*?'

'Oh, yes! I had fun with that.'

Fleur had asked Río for something provocative, that would make people want to stop and look. It had worked so well that *Galway Now* magazine had run an article on it. The display Río had come up with had featured a trail of clothing that appeared to have been discarded by a showgirl: a flirty hat followed by a pair of elbow-length satin gloves; just-kicked-off cherry-red heels; a dress left lying in a pool of silk; two half-full champagne saucers abandoned on a rococo column next to a casket spilling diamanté jewellery; a single red rose; silk stockings draped over the back of a boudoir chair, a bra in humming-bird hues and matching directoire knickers. The narrative had been self-evident, the inference clear.

'You could have fun with this too,' Dervla told her. 'What I have in mind is . . .'

And Río listened carefully as Dervla outlined her ideas, and as she listened, her imagination began to go into overdrive. She was impressed by the story of the Galway couple who had staged their home, and she began to think of other things that might help to sell a property. All five senses would have to be engaged – the look of the place, obviously, was the first thing to be taken into consideration when fabricating an aspirational lifestyle. The look would depend upon the individual house: no Arts-and-Crafts ambience in a modern apartment, for instance, and nothing neo-Gothic in a suburban semi. Smell? The aroma of baking bread or roasting coffee was commonplace – a trick that everybody knew by now. Jo Malone was a savvier option. Then there was touch – a sofa swathed in a soft chenille throw and piled with cushions could look fantastic; crisp linen on a bed, fluffy towels in a bathroom. And sound: something gentle on the CD player, or maybe a fountain in the garden, or even a recording of birdsong? The sound of ocean waves in a house by the sea . . . Taste? Why not? A glossy cookery book left open at a photograph of an exotic stir fry, chopsticks and rice bowls laid out on Japanese mats, a bottle of sake – oh, this could be fun!

And when Dervla had finished outlining her ideas, Río realised that she had not thought of Finn for a whole ten minutes. Dervla's peculiar brand of diversion therapy seemed to be working already. She looked at her sister and smiled, and then she raised her glass in a toast. 'I'd be so *good* at this!' she said.

Chapter Twelve

Dervla loved showing houses after Río had worked her magic on them.

Over the course of a few months, her sister had equipped herself with what could only be described as 'inventive' tools of her new calling. She made her own furniture polish from linseed oil and turpentine, claiming that nothing beat the smell of fresh polish. She had accumulated a plethora of props with which to 'dress' properties after the cleaning people had been in – old Chanel No. 5 or Jo Malone bottles filled with coloured water, second-hand coffee-table books, her own paintings, some beautiful clothes on loan from Fleur: an embroidered lawn dressing gown to drape casually at the foot of a bed, a pair of designer shoes positioned to look as though they'd just been kicked off, a theatrical sunhat that she'd leave on a garden table next to a Gucci sunglasses case (empty) and the current issue of *Vanity Fair* magazine. For another house, *New Statesman* might be more appropriate, for yet another, *GQ* or *Vogue*, or *Elle Decoration*.

'It's fun!' Río told her sister. 'First I go in and wander round and think about the type of person who might like to live there. If the house is near the sea, I think "maritime", so the coffee-table books will all be about fishing, or yachting. Or if it's a city-centre apartment, I think "city chic", and dress it with edgier, more modern stuff – all a snip from Dunnes homeware. And auction-room or car-boot-sale finds are great for older houses – I got some beautiful china tea cups, and a lacquered fire screen and a sterling-silver dressing table set. It's amazing what you can find for half nothing if you look hard enough.'

'Where on earth do you keep it all?'

'Mrs Murphy's allowed me to use her garage. She's still sick with guilt about the garden.'

'I noticed the big bowls of fruit and the baskets of vegetables—'

'They're nearly as important as fresh flowers. But you have to choose only misshapen veg, otherwise they don't look organic.'

'You've been busy,' Dervla told her. 'That's good. It's so important to keep busy when you're trying to fight off the blues.'

'Gardening's the best therapy of all,' pronounced Río.

'Clearly. You've done great work on the Whelans' garden.' Río had transformed a nondescript yard into a fabulous patio with the help of half a dozen bags of golden gravel, half a dozen paving slabs, and some bedding plants in urns and baskets. 'And by the way, did I spot hollyhocks in the garden on Eaton Terrace?'

'Yep.'

'How did you manage that?'

'They were leftovers from the previous viewing. They were nearly finished, so I just whipped them out of the vase and stuck the stems in the flowerbed. I did that with the tulips in the Grantham Street place too. And I was thinking of dropping shop-bought apples around the trees in Norton Row, except it's the wrong time of the year. I'll have to wait until autumn before I can pull that stunt.'

'Um. Why fallen apples?'

'Well, just think how nice it would be to wander out into your garden and pick up a load of apples to juice for breakfast. People are really aware of that sort of stuff now that it's hip to be frugal. If I had the time, I could do a to-die-for vegetable patch. Oh, another thing I've come up with is postcards.'

'Postcards?'

'To stick under fridge magnets. Finn's been sending me post-cards from all the exotic places he's been, and if I stick them on the fridge, it makes people think that the people who own this house must be really popular, because of all the postcards they get, and maybe if they bought the house, some of that popularity might rub off on them. And, Dervla, please don't get rid of any of your invites to your posh social events. I've got an idea for them too.'

So Dervla furnished Río with all her party invitations, and the next time she visited one of her properties, she was amused to see that the pin board in the home office was covered in invites to exhibition openings and fashion shows and golf classics and charity lunches. And there were memos too, written in Río's beautiful, flowing italic script that read: 'Buy birthday cham-pagne for the Hamilton-Stewarts' and 'Send flowers to Naomi' and 'Email Joneses – thanks for the garden party.' And once, when Dervla had been showing a couple round, she heard Río's voice come over the speaker on the answering machine saying: 'Hello! Hope you're well! Just to say thank you so much for dinner on Sunday. We had a wonderful time, and I have to say that your house is looking divine! Thanks again – and looking forward to seeing you at the premiere next week!'

'You might start leaving love letters lying around too,' said Dervla, the next time she spoke to Río on the phone.

'Not a bad idea!' said Río.

'I was joking.'

But Río did indeed start to leave billets-doux peeking out from under books and magazines, written on beautiful handmade paper, and bearing such affirmations as 'I said yes!' and 'Love, love, love you!' and 'Beauty is truth, truth beauty . . .' until Dervla drew the line when one puzzled viewer said: 'I may be going mad, but didn't I see that notepaper in the house we looked at last week?'

Still, Dervla had to admit that her sister's unorthodox approach was bearing fruit. Who wouldn't want to live in a house with good karma, a house that smelled of Jo Malone and furniture polish, where the women lounged around in embroidered white peignoirs over breakfast in the garden reading *Vanity Fair*, and the men left their bow ties casually flung on a bedside table beside a book on quantum physics, and the children played with old-fashioned building blocks and zoo animals, and read traditional storybooks instead of slumping over computer consoles, and where everybody ate fresh fruit and vegetables instead of junk food, and drank vintage Bordeaux and San Pellegrino instead of Blue Nun and Sunny Delight?

Thanks to Río's flights of fantasy, Dervla's houses started to sell themselves again. She was keeping her head above water in what was a barely buoyant market. And one day she realised that, although the news on the radio was all doom, gloom and bye-bye boom, she was feeling A-OK. It was good to have a sister.

The weather was fantastic too, which helped lighten her mood, and – while sales were still down – the fact that she was selling more houses than any other agent in the Coolnamara region was music to her ears. The restoration of Frank's house was going smoothly; building work was easy to come by, and cheaper than it had once been, and together the sisters had overseen the construction of Dervla's rental apartment, and of Río's eyrie. The downstairs duplex was designed as a typical holiday let, fully fitted and furnished with hard-wearing pieces from Ikea and an entertainment system for rainy days. The entertainment system comprised HD television, hifi and Xbox, and Dervla thought wryly of past Sunday afternoons playing Cluedo or Monopoly in front of the fire in the old sitting room. The rear of the kitchen had been replaced with a wall of glass brick, to allow light into the room, and to preserve the privacy of Mrs Murphy in the garden that was now hers, and all the regulation fire alarms and extinguishers and blankets had been installed.

Upstairs, accessible via a separate staircase, Rio's apartment was full of light from the Veluxes that had been built into the roof. It was one long, wide open space, with a bathroom adjacent and a mezzanine under the eaves that housed a sleeping platform. Río had painted this alcove chalky blue, and hung it with gauzy drapery to create a private place for dreaming.

In the main space, the colour scheme was similar – the floorboards limewashed, the tongue-and-groove walls sponged in duck-egg blue. Río had set up her easel and a trestle work table in a corner next to the door that led onto the small deck, and screened it off with white-painted lattice-work. The kitchen was separated from the main living space by a blue-tiled counter, and glass-fronted cupboards housed Río's collection of blue and white china. In the sitting area two sofas covered in loose white linen covers sat on either side of her pretty ceramic Dutch stove, and a big cosy armchair had been positioned by the door that led out onto the balcony – from where Río could observe the comings and goings in the harbour below. There was space for a pull-down chaise longue where Finn could sleep when he came to visit.

The move hadn't even been that stressful for Río. Every time she visited from her rented house just down the road to chat with the painters and the carpenter, she had brought with her a box of books or a crate of paintings or a bin bag full of rugs, and Dervla watched as, bit by bit, her sister's nest began to take shape. A cushion here, an embroidered throw there, a jug of daisies – just so! All combined to make a home 'oozing' – in estate agent's parlance – 'with charm and character'.

And as soon as everything had been completed to her satisfaction, Dervla contacted an outfit that specialised in holiday lets, put her name on their books, and sat back waiting for her first tenants to arrive.

Río was looking round Mrs Murphy's garage, trying to rationalise the space. Mrs M had recently replaced an old bureau, a Formica-topped table and a plush eighties-style armchair with trendier items that she had asked Dervla to pick up for her from Ikea. The redundant furniture had been relegated to the garage, awaiting the arrival of a van that would take them to the recycling depot.

Río had shifted the table and armchair to one corner of the garage, and was wondering where best to stow the bureau. It was a pretty little rosewood thing, but badly scratched. Looking at it now with a critical eye Río realised that if sanded and French-polished, it might be worth keeping. Hunkering down, she inspected it for woodworm. There were no telltale signs on the exterior, and the drawers all seemed worm free.

The interior was nicely fitted with cubbyholes, and a 'secret' drawer. Río's grandmother had had something similar in her house in Galway, and had used to leave sweets inside for Río and Dervla to discover. Pressing the mechanism that opened the drawer, Río peered inside. There was no trace of woodworm here either, but there was a letter. Mrs M must have forgotten about the hidden drawer while clearing out the contents. The envelope was addressed to 'Anne-Marie', which Río knew was Mrs Murphy's Christian name.

She was just about to pocket it to hand back to her neighbour when something made her stop. The writing on the envelope was identical to the writing on the letters that the man called Patrick had written to Rosaleen. Río's stomach did a somersault; her mouth went dry. Her hands began to tremble as she did the thing she knew was wrong, the thing she could not stop herself from doing. She opened the envelope and took out the letter.

'Dear Anne-Marie,' she read, in her father's hand,

I am leaving tomorrow. Will you make sure that Rosaleen gets the enclosed? I know that she will be too weak after the baby to be able to get to the beach for some weeks, and I dare not risk leaving a letter in the usual place for such a long time, in case someone might find it.

You have been a real friend to us. I know that it went against all your moral principles to help us the way you have, and I am sorry to have vexed you in that regard. Yet I will always be grateful for your all-too-human connivance. It made Rosaleen and me very happy. But you are right. I can no longer stay here, especially since the arrival of little Ríonach.

Please, please keep your promise to never breathe a word of what you know to anyone. I dread to think what might become of Rosaleen and our baby if Frank were to find out.

Also, please find it in your heart to wish me well, Anne-Marie, and to pray for me. My heart is so very, very heavy as I write this. I will not know such love again. May God bless you.

Yours,
Patrick

Río put the letter back in the secret drawer. She stood there for many moments, lost in thought, then shook herself out of her reverie. Now that she looked again, she decided that the rosewood bureau was not worth restoring. It would look silly and old-fashioned next to Mrs Murphy's spanking new Ikea furniture, and Mrs Murphy would not thank her for returning it to her. Río would instead put it in the back of the van that would transport it to the recycling depot, taking its secret with it.

Chapter Thirteen

Because Izzy and her mate Lucy had done so well in their exams, Adair had organised an überluxurious holiday for them in a resort in Koh Samui. Izzy hated to admit it, but she was bored witless by the joint. It was too ostentatious, too grown-up, and too up its own arse. The description in the brochure had been full of words like 'majestic', 'magnificent', 'luxurious', 'refined' and 'epicurean'. The bedrooms, the brochure told them, were 'a fusion of continents and periods' (a.k.a. bad taste, decided Izzy) and were furnished with stuff like Louis XV-style armchairs, lacquered Chinese cabinets, Lalique-style vases, an African lamp on a buffalo-horn base (Izzy found this particularly offensive), an 'ormolu mounted' (whatever that was) boulle (whatever that was) kneehole desk and furnishing fabrics with Indian designs.

As soon as the three of them arrived, they were offered iced tea by a smiling waiter, and greeted by the smiling manager. Their luggage was magicked away by a smiling porter, and unpacked for them by a smiling butler, who introduced himself as Asish, and for whom, he told them, with a bow, nothing would be too much trouble. Every evening Asish would come to their suite with the various tools of his trade – ylang ylang to rub on the teak furniture, and scented candles and rose petals and sandalwood oil for the baths he would insist upon pouring.

The couple of times Izzy told him not to bother, he had actually looked so stricken that she began to wonder if she had a serious personal hygiene problem.

The dress code in the dining rooms was 'smart casual', and every night the diners all tried to outdo each other by wearing a different outfit. Every evening smiling waiters unfurled pristine linen napkins for them, and topped up their wineglasses and lifted the domed silver lids on their plates to reveal 'exquisite' and 'divine' food. Everywhere you went, staff bowed and smiled. Izzy and Lucy began to avoid them and hide from them because they really didn't like being bowed to.

No one applauded the pianist in the piano bar, and Izzy felt so sorry for him – tapping away on the ivories with no one paying him any attention – that she took to clapping loudly every time he finished a tune, and insisted that her father and Lucy join in. He rewarded them with a big smile, and – when he found out their names – played a very mellow version of 'Lucy in the Sky with Diamonds' for them. Except Lucy and Izzy were probably the only two gals in the joint who weren't wearing diamonds.

The beach was divine, of course – all raked white sand and palm-tree-fringed – and the swimming pools were divine, and the marine life was divine. But really the joint was aimed at folks who were dripping with gold and sagging with middle-age spread. However, in spite of all the luxury – the spas, the shopping, the staff (who seemed by far to outnumber the guests) – nobody looked particularly *happy* apart from the hawkers on a nearby beach, touting everything from jewellery to tattoos to hair extensions. They smiled and joked and sang, cajoling passers-by to try their wares and spreading their palms philosophically when the dripping-with-gold types strolled on by as if they were invisible. The hotel had warned guests to be wary of these beach vendors, but because Izzy and Lucy were determined to break a few rules, they made it a matter of policy to buy sarongs and sunhats and sandals from this alternative source, instead of frequenting the obscenely overpriced resort boutiques, with their chichi crap.

'Tattoo, pretty lady?' a smiling boy solicited them one morning as they ambled along the sand.

Izzy smiled back, indicating that she already had a tattoo, a little Japanese kanji on the inside of her elbow. She'd had it done a couple of years ago to piss off her mother.

'Another tattoo – here!' suggested the beautiful boy, touching the hollow beneath his collarbone.

'No, thank you,' said Izzy.

'Or here!' The boy pointed at his ankle.

'No, no,' said Izzy, more firmly. 'But, hey, why don't you get one, Luce?'

Lucy shook her head violently. 'Are you mad?' she said. 'You know I have a pathological fear of needles.'

It was true. Izzy had had to accompany Lucy to the GP for her shots before coming away on holiday.

'Hair extensions?' suggested the boy, as they moved off. 'Thai massage?'

This time it was Lucy's turn to indicate that she already had hair extensions.

'You, pretty lady,' the boy importuned Izzy. 'You get long hair like your friend. Like a beautiful mermaid!'

Izzy hesitated. She had to admit that, while her Agyness Deyn crop was easy to manage, Lucy's extraordinary Rapunzel locks attracted a lot of compliments. Underwater her extensions looked divine, like a heroine in a Pre-Raphaelite painting, while Izzy looked as boyish as Saint-Exupéry's Little Prince. She wondered if she shouldn't have a go. If she didn't like them, what would it matter here on Koh Samui, where there'd be nobody she knew around to see them? And once they were back in Dublin she could just whizz into her stylist and have them removed. What the hell – live dangerously and all that. She had nothing to lose.

'I think I'll go for it,' she told Lucy.

157

'Get hair extensions?'

'Yeah. I wouldn't have the nerve to have them done in Dublin. Might as well experiment here.'

'Go, girl!' said Lucy. 'Do you want me to come with you and hold your hand? Or maybe I should get a massage.'

'Go for it! I bet you'd get a proper hard-core Thai, not that namby-pamby stuff you get in the resort spa.' Izzy turned back to the beaming boy. 'Me – hair extensions; my friend – massage. In same place?'

'Yes, yes,' said the boy enthusiastically. 'Hair, massage – nail art too?'

'No. No nail art,' Izzy told him. 'How much?'

The boy did some brief mental arithmetic. 'Fifteen hundred baht,' he pronounced.

'Cool,' said Izzy, and the boy looked gobsmacked.

'Come – come with me,' he said quickly, before she could backtrack. 'Beautiful hair extensions and massage this way.' He turned and beckoned them to follow him.

Lucy gave Izzy an incredulous look. 'You're meant to haggle, Iz! We could have got ourselves a deal for half that!'

'C'mon, Luce. Just think what they'd charge us at home. These people are desperate for money. I'm not going to haggle over a couple of thousand baht.'

'Well,' said Lucy, dubiously. 'Let's just hope it's worth it.'

It was worth it. A couple of hours later, Lucy emerged from the Beach Diva Beauty Parlour in slooow moootion, having been massaged to within an inch of her life; and Izzy emerged sporting tresses that Goldilocks might have envied.

'Let's break out of here,' Izzy suggested to Lucy later that evening, after they'd returned from a night dive. Even the diving in the resort was posh, with St Tropezed divas sporting Pucci-print exposure suits and colour co-ordinated accessories, and men convinced they were the ultimate macho heroes with the contents of an entire dive shop strapped to them: state-of-the-art dive computers and pony bottles, and enormous knives and torches, and the latest in hi-tech camera equipment.

'What do you mean, break out?' asked Lucy. They were sitting disconsolately by the edge of the pool, dangling their feet in the water, and eating oversized slices of watermelon.

'Let's pay a visit to Koh Tao.'

'Koh Tao?'

'Yeah. Tao's the ultimate dive destination. Didn't you know? Koh Samui's the family island, Koh Pha Ngan's the rave island, and Tao's the dive island.'

'But what about your dad? He won't want to go there. He's dead happy here.'

This was, indeed, the case. Adair had met a couple who were golf fiends, and they spent most of the day on the spanking-new golf course, and most of the evening chatting over drinks in the piano bar.

'He won't miss us for a day or two,' said Izzy. 'I'd just love to live like a beach bum for twenty-four hours. This place is beginning to get to me.' She set down the rind of her watermelon, which was instantly scooped up by a smiling flunky, then turned anguished eyes on Lucy. 'Oh God, Luce! I must sound like a totally ungrateful spoiled brat. Dad went to so much trouble and expense to do this for us.'

Lucy shrugged. 'He just wants the best for you, Izzy. He loves to pamper you. I told you before, you're his princess.'

Izzy drooped a little, then jumped to her feet. 'Come on,' she said. 'Even princesses have to take a break. Let's go check out Tao online.'

Back at the suite, sitting at the ormolu-mounted boulle kneehole desk, Adair was working on his BlackBerry. Izzy had tried to persuade him to ditch it before they left Ireland, but he'd been adamant that he couldn't survive without it for a fortnight.

'Da-ad?' she said, in the cajoling voice that she knew always worked.

'Yes, princess?'

'Could we check something out online?'

'Sure. What do you need to know?'

'We were thinking about taking a day trip to Koh Tao.'

'Where's that?'

'It's an island not far from here.'

'Oh, Iz. You know I just want to stay put and chill. I really don't want to go gallivanting around islands.'

'Well, actually –' Izzy started playing apprehensively with a strand of her brand-new hair – 'I meant just me and Lucy.'

'Oh.'

'You wouldn't mind, Dad, would you? It's just that it's got the reputation of having some of the best diving in Asia.'

Adair looked up at her, clearly crestfallen. 'Isn't the diving here any good, sweet pea?'

'It's fine. But it seems mad not to dive in Koh Tao when it's right on our doorstep.'

Adair looked uncertain. 'I'm not certain that I like the idea of letting you two girls go off together to some island by yourselves. What if something happens to you?'

'Like what?'

'Like – I dunno – falling into the hands of white slave traders—'

'*Dad!*'

'Or – or having somebody sneak drugs into your bag. I hear that happens all the time. Traffickers target innocent-looking people and use them as – um – donkeys.'

'They're called "mules", Dad.'

'Whatever. And remember that I'm *in loco parentis* for Lucy. I'm not sure her parents would like the idea.'

'I'm pretty sure they'd be cool with it,' said Lucy.

Izzy tried not to smile. Lucy's parents were Trustafarian dope

160

heads, who grew their own marijuana and couldn't understand why Lucy never joined them in a toke.

'*Ple-ease*, Dad,' said Izzy, putting on her most winning expression. 'Let's just have a *peek* at the island online.'

'OK, then.' Looking mulish, Adair twinkled his thumbs over his BlackBerry. 'There it is.'

'Oh! It's so *pretty*!' exclaimed Izzy, swishing her hair back over her shoulder as she leaned in closer to the screen. 'Oh, I'd *love* to go there! Isn't it gorgeous, Lucy?'

'Yes,' said Lucy, giving her friend a catlike look that said, 'I know exactly what you're up to – go, girl!'

'And it's so *near*! Only an hour on the ferry.'

'I'd lay on a speedboat for you.'

'No, no, Daddy! If we do this, we've got to do it the proper way, like all the backpackers do. And look – we could sleep in a beach hut! Yay!'

'You mean you're thinking of staying overnight? I'm not sure—'

'But, Dad, if we have to spend two whole hours travelling, that'll give us hardly any time there at all. And we'd only be able to fit in one dive.' Izzy gave him the benefit of her most beautiful bewildered look, her eyes wide, her brow furrowed, her mouth pouting in a perplexed *moue*.

'What about a helicopter?'

'No! Could you imagine the effect that would have on our street cred? Helicopters may be fine and dandy here, Dad, but not on a laidback joint like Koh Tao. That would be a bit like going to Burdock's for fish and chips in a chauffeur-driven limo.'

'I've done that, actually,' said Adair, with a touch of nostalgia.

'Yeah, but you have no street cred at all, Dad.'

'I'll have you know that I was dead streetwise when I started out in the property business, Isabella. You had to be a cute divil to get anywhere in those days.'

'And I bet you were the cutest of them all!' Izzy clapped her hands and did a little dance, setting her hair extensions jumping like skipping ropes. 'So, Daddy, what do you say?'

Adair gave a great sigh. 'I suppose I can't keep you wrapped up in cotton wool for the rest of your life. When do you plan on going?'

'Tomorrow?' she hazarded.

Adair heaved another sigh. 'Tomorrow, then.'

'Oh, Daddy – thank you!' Izzy stooped to give her father an enormous hug and a kiss on the end of his nose, and Lucy went 'Yay! Thank you *so* much!'

Then, setting aside his BlackBerry and reaching for his wallet, Adair took out a wad of baht. 'Have fun, princess' he said.

On the ferry, Izzy and Lucy looked just like all the other back-packers who were heading to Tao. The decks were crammed with golden kids from all over the globe, all good-looking, all loose-limbed, all disenfranchised. Izzy finally felt that she belonged – that she'd found her niche in life at last. Giddy with delight at having been sprung from their gilded cage, she and Lucy laughed like drains with two New Zealanders for the hour-long journey, and impressed the boys no end by lapsing into Irish from time to time, when they wanted to make private observations about which of the two was the hotter.

The sun was hot too, and Izzy had forgotten her hat, though she'd taken care to slap on buckets of factor 50. But as she tossed her head in response to some jokey remark by a New Zealander, she realised with dismay that one of her hair extensions had detached itself and gone flying out into the Gulf of Thailand. What the hell! Nobody else seemed to have noticed, so she kept shtoom, and desisted from flinging her hair around as much as she'd been wont to since having the false locks put in.

They parted with the Kiwis in Mae Haad, and made the short journey to Sairee Beach by motorbike taxi along dusty dirt tracks. As Izzy whizzed along, the wind tugged at her hair, and she felt as if she was starring in a bio-pic of someone with a fabulous life. She wished she could be this girl all the time – a carefree, sun-kissed beach babe with Kate Hudson tresses.

There was to be a big party to celebrate the full moon later that evening, they learned when they arrived at the dive outfit, with an international DJ spinning 'fresh and funky' sounds, but before the party started, there were bubbles to be blown.

They'd booked two dives over the internet. The first took them and half a dozen other divers by cabin cruiser to Shark Island, where their dive master took them down twenty metres to visit a fairy-tale city of hard coral surrounded by gardens of multicoloured soft coral, where starry pufferfish gaped at them and titan triggerfish headbutted them, letting them know in no uncertain terms that if their nests were disturbed, they were in for it. A leopard shark lay basking on the sandy bottom, looking like a pasha being cooled by coral fans, and Izzy got a breath-taking glimpse of a spotted ray, soaring high above her like a blue angel.

Back on board, Izzy and Lucy and the other divers disman-tled their equipment before speeding back to Sairee, where they lugged their gear up to the dive shop, and hosed it down. On Samui, all this had been done for them by dive masters. Here, everything was hands-on, and Izzy revelled in the sheer hard physicality of the work. This was what diving should be about, not having your kit donned and doffed and disappeared by a team of dive masters behaving like footmen. But as Izzy went to hose down her mask, she saw that another of her hair exten-sions was wound around the rubber strap. She felt a flutter of panic.

'Lucy?' she said *sotto voce*, as they queued to have their logbooks signed. 'Is there something wrong with my hair? I think I've lost a couple of extensions.'

Lucy took a look, and shrugged. 'It's hard to tell while it's still wet,' she said. 'I'll have a proper look when it's dried off.'

A beach-side café beckoned for supper. They ordered slurpy Thai noodles, fish cakes and a bottle of Tiger beer – no somme-lier to proffer wine for tasting here, or maître d' choreographing a host of waiters with 'exquisitely presented' fusion food on silver salvers.

'Wouldn't it be bliss if we could stay here for the rest of the holiday?' Lucy said. She took off her sunglasses and slid them onto her head, the better to observe a beautiful boy who was setting up for a night dive.

'I couldn't do that to Dad, Luce. The very most I could push it without feeling guilty would be one more day.'

'Why not phone and run it by him?'

'He'd probably freak. He'd think that I was making the call under duress, with some white slave trader holding a Luger to my head.'

'You're lucky to have a dad who cares so much about you. Mine probably doesn't even know where I am right now.'

Izzy shrugged. 'It can be a real pain. I dread the first time I'll have to bring a boyfriend home to meet him. He'll be like Robert De Niro in *Meet the Parents*.' Izzy picked up the bill and scanned it. 'Shit. Can you believe it? This entire meal cost what you'd pay for the cheapest starter in that joint on Samui.' Extracting baht from her bum bag, Izzy handed the banknotes to a passing waiter. Then she reached up, shook out her hair, and ran her fingers through it. 'It's dry now, Luce. Will you take a—'

Izzy froze suddenly, eyes fixed on her hands. Hanks of hair were dangling limply from her fingers like strands of seaweed. She turned stricken eyes on Lucy, who had clamped her hands over her mouth, hiding what might have been an expression of horror, or one of guilty amusement.

'Ohmi – ohmi*god*, Lucy! My hair! Ohmigod! What am I going to do?'

'Oh,' said Lucy. 'Oh dear. Oh. Dear.'

And then Lucy started to laugh.

164

Izzy shook her hands to rid herself of the offending hair extensions, and fixed her friend with a hostile look. 'Well, thanks a bunch. That *is* helpful.' Yanking her sarong from around her shoulders, she draped it over her head. 'It's that bad, is it?'

'Um. It's pretty bad, all right,' said Lucy, clearly making an effort to contain herself.

'On a scale of one to ten, how bad?'

'Um . . . seven?'

'Seven? Oh, *fuck*! I'm a laughing stock. What'll I do?'

'Don't worry about it, Izzy. We're going on a dive now. Nobody's going to see your hair underwater. Chill.'

'Chill yourself. It's easy for you to say. You're not the one who looks like Worzel Gummidge.'

At this, Lucy laughed so hard that she'd actually went, 'Haha hee hee hee,' like Taz in *Looney Tunes*.

'It's not *funny*,' said Izzy.

'Worzel Gummidge! That's it! That's exactly who you remind me of! Hee hee ha-ha-ha!'

'Shut up, Lucy.'

'Sorry.' Lucy looked contrite, and then spoiled the effect by letting rip a great snort of mirth. 'Sorry,' she said again.

A couple with whom they'd dived earlier raced past them, heading for the dive boat, which was moored some eighty metres down the beach. Lucy threw a look at her dive watch and made a face. 'Yikes. We're late.'

'I don't care.'

'What do you mean, you don't care? If we don't get going now, Iz, we're going to miss the dive.'

'I'm not going on the dive.'

'What?'

'I can't go, looking like this.'

'Oh, don't be daft! It's not that bad, really.'

'You said it was a seven.'

'I meant more of a six. Please, Iz. It's a beautiful night for

diving. We *can't* miss it. Look, why not grab a hat from that stall.'
Lucy got to her feet and headed towards a beach vendor who
was selling souvenirs and novelties. 'C'mon, Iz!' she threw back
over her shoulder. 'We're running out of time. Look, they've
nearly all boarded.'

Further down the beach, the divers were congregating on
board the boat. Even at this distance, Izzy could hear laughter,
and get a sense of the buzz that was beginning to build. She
wanted to be part of it, she wanted to be down there, weightless in water. Hell! What did it matter what she looked like?
Impulsively, she followed Lucy over to the souvenir stall.

'A hat, please – no, not for me, for my friend,' Lucy was
saying.

'A beautiful hat for a beautiful lady!' said the smiling vendor.
'This one is good, yes?' He took a wide-brimmed sunhat from
a hook, and brandished it at her. Izzy could hardly wear a floppy
sunhat on a night dive. She shook her head and pointed at an
assortment of baseball caps.

'This one?' said the vendor, waving a cap at her. 'Or this one?'

'That one,' said Izzy, pointing randomly as she pulled baht
from her bum bag.

'Quick, quick, Izzy!' Lucy started legging it down the beach.
'They're doing a head count.'

Izzy handed over the requisite amount of baht, took the cap
from the vendor, and jammed it on her head. Then she raced
off after Lucy, feeling the flap flap flap of the rubbish hair extensions – or what was left of them – as they bounced off her
shoulder blades.

Their hire gear was on board, waiting for them. There were
more divers on this trip, so a little confusion reigned as people
stepped over piles of equipment, trying to identify what belonged
to whom. Izzy pulled on her neoprene shortie and made her way
to the port side, where Lucy had started to fill in details of the
morning's dive in her logbook. She glanced up as Izzy joined

her, and Izzy registered at once the taken-aback expression on her friend's face.

'What is it now?' she demanded.

'It's – um – it's just . . . what on earth made you choose that hat?'

'I could hardly go for a sunhat. I know baseball caps are a bit naff, but—'

'It's not the cap,' Lucy told her. 'It's the slogan on it.'

'It has a slogan?'

'Yes.'

Glancing to left and to right to make sure no one was looking, Izzy whipped the cap off her head. Another hair extension came with it, and she threw it overboard with a vexed 'Get off!' before turning her attention to the slogan on her cap. It read: 'I Like 2 Dyke.'

'Oh, no!' cried Izzy, slamming the cap back on her head. 'Oh, no!'

Beside her, Lucy started to laugh again.

'Some friend you are, Luce,' Izzy told her crossly. 'How can you laugh? This is beyond mortifying.'

'You're telling me. Everyone will assume I'm your girlfriend, girlfriend.'

Folding her arms and legs in an attempt to make herself look smaller and thus less conspicuous, Izzy started casting surreptitious looks from under the peak of her baseball cap at all the dudes and dudettes who were diving with them this evening. Nobody was wearing headgear, apart from a hot black guy who was sporting a green, white and gold bandanna. Izzy's naffness stuck out like a sore thumb, and the worst thing in the world was that she could not take the cap off. On the starboard side, two stunning girls were whispering and giggling together, and she was convinced that they were giggling about her 'I Like 2 Dyke' cap.

'Good evening,' Izzy heard an Australian accent say, as she

glowered down at her toes. 'I'm Howard Hanna, and I'll be leading this evening's dive along with my assistant dive masters, Lee from China, and Finn Byrne, who hails all the way from Ireland.'

Ireland? Izzy glanced up from her toes, and snuck a peek stern-ward at the Irish dive master.

'Yo, Finn!' came a call from aft. 'Great name for a diver.'

'Not as good as my mate, Muff's,' came the ready reply.

There was much laughter, and as Finn's eyes scanned the faces of the assembled divers, Izzy lunged for the sunnies on Lucy's head, and jammed them on.

'What are you *doing*?' asked an indignant Lucy.

'Shut up!' said Izzy. 'Sh, sh, sh! Ohmigod!'

'What's wrong?'

'It's him! Finn!'

'Who?'

'The bloke I told you about. The cute bogger from Lissamore.'

'No! The one whose mother is after your dad?'

'Yes. Oh, oh – what am I going to do, Lucy?'

'What do you mean?'

'I just – I just don't want him to know it's me.'

'Why not?'

'Why do you think? Not only am I wearing a baseball cap that says "I Like 2 Dyke", I've got the worst hair in the world.'

Lucy started to laugh again. 'So here you are, trapped on a boat with him. How do you intend to keep your identity secret? You can hardly go diving in your current disguise. Or are you going to keep my sunglasses on under your mask?'

'Shut *up*, Luce. Let me think.' Izzy pulled her sarong up around her face, and thought. Then: 'Listen,' she said. 'When we're donning fins and masks, be sure to keep yourself between me and him, will you? Once we're in the water, he won't have a clue who I am.'

Izzy had a point. With regulators in their mouths, and masks obscuring most of the face, it was virtually impossible to recognise people underwater.

Howard had set up his whiteboard, and was preparing to draw a map of the dive site. 'OK. Listen up, people, while I outline the plan,' he said in his authoritative Australian accent, and Izzy and Lucy shut up at once. They could be in for a thrill at White Rock, according to Howard. Word around the dive outfits was that a whale shark had been sighted there, and if they were very lucky, it might still be in the vicinity.

'Y'all know the hand signal for shark?' he asked.

As one, the divers raised their hands to their foreheads, fingers together, representing a shark fin.

'Good. When you see Finn or me or Lee making that hand signal, you'll know there's a once-in-a-lifetime treat in store. Sightings of whale sharks at night are extremely rare.'

Izzy could feel her heart pitter-pat a little faster in anticipation, and tried to slow it down by taking deep breaths. As the boat dropped anchor, she adjusted the strap on her mask, slid her feet into her fins, and stuck her reg in her mouth. On the command, she stepped off the dive platform into the sea, loving the surge and fizz of the warm water as it churned around her in an explosion of bubbles and refracted, silvery light. Then she was at the surface, bobbing next to Lucy, and the next diver into the water was . . . She waited until he'd resurfaced after entry, then steeled herself to look into his eyes behind the mask . . . Finn.

Finn Byrne, the instructor had called him. Funny, she'd always thought his name was Kinsella. But then she remembered that that was the surname of his mother and aunt, which must mean that Byrne was his father's surname. Who might his father be, she wondered. Probably some local Lissamore hippy type, if the mother was anything to go by. He didn't look much like Río. His black hair was slicked against his skull, his eyes behind the mask were fringed with dark lashes, and on each of his earlobes, a bead of water hung, like diamond droplets. Sheesh, he *was* übercute, and – having copped a load of him clad in surf shirt and shorts – Izzy was more aware than ever that he was pretty damn fit too.

Finn showed not a flicker of recognition as his eyes met hers, and Izzy knew that, once underwater, when her features would be even more indistinct, her anonymity was guaranteed. She and Lucy looked at each other and gave the OK signal, and Izzy could see that behind the mask Lucy was still smirking as they switched on their torches and descended.

The dive was as near to heaven on earth as Izzy could ever aspire to: the reef came alive at night, like a red-light district in some Gothic metropolis. They negotiated swim-throughs and peered into caves and under rocky outcrops where murderous morays glared back at them, disturbed by the light of their torches. They somersaulted, they played peek-a-boo with anemones, they communed with the jewel-like inhabitants of the big blue, and finally they were rewarded with every diver's dream: they finned alongside the biggest fish on earth. The whale shark emerged from sapphire depths and cruised past them, and Izzy understood at last the real meaning of the words 'majestic' and 'magnificent'. She felt as if she were in a cathedral, and the words of the world's first great diver, Jacques Cousteau, came back to her: 'Underwater, man becomes an archangel.' Oh, Izzy so adored being an archangel that when Finn finally made the signal to ascend, she wanted to take her regulator out of her mouth and shout: 'No, no, no!'

But up they went. Slowly Ascend from Every Dive, thought Izzy, repeating one of scuba's many mantras while scrutinising a novice above her who was evidently having problems with his buoyancy. This boy was more hippo than archangel, ascending in fits and starts, and clearly giving Finn cause for concern. As he tweaked his protégé's fin to attract his attention, the boy executed an awkward kick – and got Finn directly in the face. In the beam of her torch, Izzy saw Finn sweep his right arm out

170

to the side, a sure indication that his regulator had been dislodged. As had his mask, Izzy realised. Finn made no attempt to grab it as it drifted downward – his priority was to reinstate his breathing apparatus – but Izzy knew that a diver without a mask is effectively a blind diver. She had lost her mask once during a training session in a flooded quarry, and the sense of vertigo she'd experienced had completely disoriented her: for several terrifying moments she hadn't been able to work out which way was up and which down, and she'd suffered from nightmares for weeks afterwards.

Keeping her torch trained on the runaway mask, Izzy tucked her knees against her chest, exhaled, and swooped down after it, scooping it up before performing a nifty upward jackknife and finning back to where Finn was continuing to ascend with remarkable sang-froid. She touched his hand, then wound his fingers around the strap of his mask and watched as he clamped it back on and cleared it. His lovely green, upward-tilting eyes smiled at her as he took hold of her hand to high-five her. Are you OK? she asked, putting thumb and forefinger together in an 'O', smiling back at him when she received a corresponding 'OK' to indicate that all was well.

'Smug cow,' Lucy said when they were back on deck, and Izzy had reverted to her disguise of 'I Like 2 Dyke' cap, shades and sarong. 'Trust you to be the one who saves the dude. I suppose your log will read, "Saved dive god on ascent".' She reached for her logbook. 'Did you get a load of that pipe fish?' she added. 'Ugliest one I ever saw.'

'That wasn't a pipe fish,' said Izzy. 'That was another of my hair extensions.'

'Hell, you really are moulting, aren't you?'

'Maybe I could start a funky new trend. My real hair's full of sticky bits where the glue has melted in the sun. They must have used really cheap stuff.'

'Hi.'

Izzy peered up through her wraparound sunglasses from under the peak of her cap. Finn was looking down at them, smiling.

'Which of you girls was responsible for retrieving my mask? I owe you a drink.'

Izzy didn't hesitate. 'It was Lucy,' she said, giving her friend a dig in the ribs with her elbow. 'Wasn't it, Luce?'

Lucy gave Izzy a nonplussed look. 'Um . . .' she began.

'Yes, it was,' insisted Izzy.

'Oh yes, then,' said Lucy, 'that would definitely have been me.'

'You're Irish?'

'Yeah. Dublin.'

'I'm from Lissamore, in Coolnamara.'

'I know.'

'Oh?'

'I can – er – tell by your accent.'

Finn smiled down at her. 'That manoeuvre took some pluck, as well as skill,' he told her. 'You're definitely dive master material, Lucy. How many dives have you notched up?'

'A hundred and fifty-seven,' Izzy told him, for Lucy's benefit.

Finn looked impressed. 'Then go for it. Maybe you should aim for certification while you're here.'

'I'd love to,' said Lucy, batting her eyelids and clearly enjoying her role as heroine. 'But we're leaving tomorrow. Or the day after.'

'Definitely tomorrow,' Izzy corrected her.

'Shame,' said Finn, looking at Lucy with interest. 'Will you be going to the party in the AC bar later?'

'Wouldn't miss it,' said Lucy, with her best smile. 'And just in case you're wondering, *I'm* not gay.'

'Glad to hear it,' said Finn, flicking an amused glance at Izzy's cap, and returning the smile.

As he moved away along the deck, Izzy turned an outraged face to her friend. 'What do you think you're *doing*?' she said.

'I'm flirting. You're right. He is very, very cute.'

'But I found him first!'

'Then you shouldn't have pretended not to know him.'

'What was I meant to do? Take off my cap and reveal my gummy hair extensions?'

'Well, at least if you'd done that he wouldn't have thought you were a dyke.'

'Bummer. *Bummer!*' Izzy's outraged expression turned into one of anguish. 'I've dug myself into a big hole, haven't I?'

'Looks like it. You can hardly turn round and say, "Oh, I made a mistake! *I* was the one who came to your rescue, actually, not her."'

'*Oh!* Why am I such a *loser*?'

'You're not a loser, honeybun. But you do tend to complicate things unnecessarily sometimes.'

And as Izzy turned to stare morosely at the navy-blue horizon, she realised that, as usual, Lucy was absolutely right.

After they'd dumped their gear, they had to queue for their logbooks to be signed. Izzy's face was swathed in batik'd cotton, and even in the comparative gloom of the dive shop, she was still sporting shades and baseball cap.

'Sunburn?' Finn asked, looking at her with sympathy as she handed over her log.

'Yes.'

'What a bitch. Have you tried aloe vera?'

'Mm-hm.'

'Well. Take care.' Finn signed her log, then turned his attention to Lucy. 'Hi, Lucy! I should really sign this "With thanks"!'

Lucy gave a little tinkling laugh. 'My pleasure!' she said.

'There should be plenty of Irish at the party. You'll have a blast.' Finn set Lucy's log on the counter and scribbled his signature. He was just about to hand it back to her when he hesitated, looking puzzled. 'Where did your tattoo go?' he asked.

'What?'

'Your tattoo,' he repeated, indicating the inside crook of Lucy's right elbow. 'I was sure I saw a tattoo there, on your arm, when we high-fived. I noticed it because it was unusual.'

Lucy and Izzy exchanged glances, and Izzy immediately folded her arms tightly across her chest.

'It was just a temporary peel-off tattoo,' said Lucy. 'It was the – um – the Japanese symbol for – um –'

'Water,' provided Izzy. 'And it's a kanji, not a symbol.'

'Cool. You should have it tattoo'd on permanently.' And Finn gave Lucy the benefit of his great smile before handing back her logbook, and moving on to the next doe-eyed dive girl.

He looked just like a film star signing autographs, Izzy thought. Damn and blast! Why, why, *why* hadn't she just come clean about who she was? But what could she have told him? This isn't my real hair, and I'm not really a lesbian? And then she remembered the vile things that his mother had said about her family, and she decided that it would be a bit like fraternising with the enemy if she ever became chummy with Finn Kinsella. Finn *Byrne*. Maybe it was just as well that she'd stayed incognito.

Once outside the dive shop, Izzy and Lucy moseyed down to the beach, heading for the hut they'd booked themselves into.

'Well, there's no way I'll be boogying over to the AC bar tonight,' said Izzy.

'Don't be stupid, Iz,' Lucy told her. 'Have a shower, and I'll work on getting rid of the rest of those extensions. Then we'll go get something to eat. After you've had a couple of beers, you'll feel better. We can't miss out on a full moon party!'

Twisting a soggy strand of hair around a finger, Izzy reflected. Lucy was right. It really wasn't fair of her, Izzy, to put a dampener on things just because she had messed up. 'OK, then,' she said. 'We'll go. And if I run into him I'll just make a joke of— *Ow!* What the *fuck*?' A stabbing pain shot through Izzy's foot. It felt as though the sole had been pierced by a white-hot blade. Lunging for Lucy's arm, she clung on for support, and started hopping up and down on one leg. 'Ow, ow, *ow!*' she gibbered.

'Hey!' said Lucy. 'What's wrong?'

'I've stood on something,' whimpered Izzy. 'Ow, ow, *ow*!'

'Sit down. Let me see.'

Izzy sat down on the sand and Lucy took her foot between her hands and examined it, before turning pale.

'*Ohmigod!* Help!' she cried, jumping up and waving her arms. 'Can anyone help?'

Indeed they could. Within seconds, Izzy and Lucy were surrounded by a bevy of beefcake, and within minutes, they were being transported on the back of a couple of motorbikes to the nurses' station in a nearby resort.

'Tch, tch,' said the nurse, shaking her head. 'That is a nasty wound. I can clean and bind it for you, but you must get to a hospital as soon as possible.'

'Where is the nearest hospital?' asked Izzy, blinking back tears of agony.

'Koh Samui,' said the nurse.

'*Nooooooo!*' wailed Izzy.

'Go straight to gaol,' said Lucy, with a resigned shrug. 'Do not pass Go . . .'

And within the hour, Izzy and Lucy were on a speedboat heading for Samui, just as the full moon was making a tantalising entrance from behind a curtain of tangerine-coloured cloud.

Chapter Fourteen

Towards the tail end of the summer, Dervla had a response from the letting agency she'd engaged to say they might have a tenant for her, on one proviso. Was she prepared to accommodate pets?

Was she? Hm. She wasn't sure. She'd have been perfectly happy for Río to hang on to W.B., but because the garden now belonged to Mrs Murphy, the cat had transferred his allegiance to her, and was now living next door.

'Not more than one,' Dervla hazarded back, trusting that the pet in question was not a python or a Komodo dragon or a Vietnamese pot-bellied pig.

Her duplex was booked the very next day.

A week later, Dervla was sitting on the sea wall opposite 'her' house. Río had invited her for supper, so that they could celebrate their mother's birthday together in the home in which they had been brought up. Because Dervla was early and the evening was so lovely, she decided to loiter for a while and shoot the breeze with whoever should happen by.

Lissamore was looking especially pretty today, decked up as it was for a forthcoming arts festival. There was bunting strung all along the main street, and fairy lights festooned from lampposts.

Above her, Río's balcony was so riotous with pinks, poppies and petunias that it could have been an entry in the Chelsea Flower Show. Dervla was glad she'd managed to wangle planning permission for its construction: permission for the deck at the back of the building had been no problem because it was out of sight, but the balcony had been less of a dead cert because it overlooked the street. Thankfully, her architect had been clever – if it weren't for the fact that Río's balcony was a virtual hanging garden, you almost wouldn't know it was there.

Dervla's eyes travelled from Río's balcony down to the first storey of the house. Her tenant had evidently arrived – the blinds on the bedroom window had been raised. It must be seventh heaven, Dervla thought, to wake up in the morning and be faced with that view. Putting the picture windows in had been a smart idea: the prospect was south-east, and watching the sun rise over Lissamore could only be good for the soul. Maybe she'd been wrong to let the house? Maybe she should have swapped her city-girl heels for Río-style espadrilles and downsized to the stress-free zone that was village life? But then the vision that was Dervla's gleaming penthouse arose before her mind's eye, and her view over the bright lights of Galway city, and her Zen roof terrace, and the hot tub on the balcony of her bedroom, and she said to herself: 'No, no, no!'

There was movement going on behind the window on the ground floor, and Dervla tensed, hoping that whoever was in there wouldn't think she was spying on them. But then, her tenant wouldn't have a clue that she was the landlord, so it didn't matter. She didn't look much like a landlord today anyway, dressed as she was in faded denims and T-shirt. She could be just another tourist taking her ease, soaking up the end of the glorious Coolnamara summer, and watching the world go by. But something made her reach into her bag and slide her shades on anyway, for that added touch of anonymity.

As she did so, the front door opened and a dog came bounding out. It was lean and sleek, with an alert look and the air of a thoroughbred. Spotting Dervla on the other side of the road, the dog made for her instantly, wagging its tail, clearly keen to make a new friend. It was a female, about two years old, with the kind of coat Cruella de Vil would have killed for. It was a Dalmatian, and the man who followed it through the door onto the footpath was the spitting image of Pierce Brosnan.

On her balcony, Río was watering her little bonsai tree. The aroma of roasting garlic wafted through to her from the kitchen, making her hungry. She had invited Dervla to supper this evening, to celebrate what would have been their mother's birthday.

Río's miniature gardens were both looking good. The deck at the rear of her apartment accommodated two recliners and a collection of terracotta troughs, in which she'd planted several varieties of geraniums. Here on the balcony there was room for a table, two folding chairs, some urns and hanging baskets, as well as specially constructed ledges for lots of smaller pots. There were nut feeders and a nesting box for her resident bluetits and robin, a preposterously kitsch miniature fountain, strings of fairy lights, and other bits and pieces of whimsy – a tiny Tibetan monk worshipping at the foot of the bonsai, a small zoo of carved wooden animals prancing the length of a shelf, a rather rude Síle na Gig, and a piece of driftwood in the shape of a mermaid complete with tail, flowing hair and smiling face painted on by Río.

The sound of a familiar laugh from the street below made Río look down. There, sitting on the sea wall, looking rather fetching in a spaghetti-strapped cotton T-shirt and jeans, was her sister. She was smiling up at a man whom Río did not recognise, and a Dalmatian was dancing attendance, leaping up to put her forepaws on the sea wall so that Dervla could better pay her attention. It seemed she was bestowing most of her attention upon its master, because they were eyeing each other in that boy-meets-girl manner, body language quite openly flirtatious. Dervla held her head at a coquettish angle, and she kept pushing a strand of her (newly coloured) hair behind her ear, while the man's stance was one that combined easy grace with courtesy – an alpha male with manners!

Well, this was interesting! For a woman who had said only a few months previously that she had no room for a man in her life, Dervla was putting out all the wrong signals. Río watched as her sister got to her feet, checked her watch, then extracted a card from her bag and handed it to her swain, who in return handed over a card of his own. The pair said their farewells, and Dervla bent to scratch the Dalmatian's ears before crossing the road without a backward glance. If she had looked back, Río was amused to notice, it would have been to see alpha-male-with-manners regarding her retreating rear with considerable interest.

The doorbell rang. With a smile, Río set down her watering can and went to let her sister in.

'Yo! Welcome to my crib!' she sang in mock hip-hop as she threw open the door. Dervla had taken her sunglasses off, and her eyes, as she climbed the final flight of stairs to Río's loft, held a look of private amusement. 'Who was the *dude*?'

'You've been spying on me!' Dervla passed through the door and dropped her bag on a sofa. 'Wow! Fantastic smell. What are we having?'

'We are having,' said Río, in the manner of a maître d' announcing the evening's specials, 'chicken baked in a lemon and garlic vinaigrette, with saffron roast potatoes and French beans, a side salad of rocket, red onion and roasted peppers followed by choc—'

'No, no! Don't tell me what's for dessert. I'll only want it, and I'm trying to lose weight.' Dervla handed Río a hand-tied bouquet of country-garden-style blooms. 'These are for you. A bit coals to Newcastle, to judge by all the green-fingered activity that's been going on since I was last here. Your balcony looks like a display in a florist's window.'

'Thanks,' said Río, accepting the flowers and admiring them. 'They're beautiful. Hey, they'd look good in the bedroom of four Lauderdale. They're the exact same colour as the painting I hung on the wall there.'

'Don't you dare! I bought them as a present for you, not as set dressing.'

'So,' said Río, selecting a fluted white vase in which to display her bouquet, 'who *is* the dude?'

'Is that vase Parian china?'

'Yeah. I got it in a car boot sale, and stop trying to change the subject.'

'The dude,' said Dervla, settling herself on a sofa, 'happens to be the tenant from downstairs. Didn't you meet him when he came to pick up the key?'

'No. I was out doing the Bradshaws' garden. I left the key with Mrs Murphy, and stuck a note on the window telling him he could get it from next door.'

'Isn't that a little rash, Río? Any chancer could have applied to Mrs Murphy for the key and carted off the entertainment system that cost me an arm and a leg.'

'Phooey. Sure didn't I leave my car door unlocked the other night, and my wallet on the passenger seat, and nobody went near it. That's the beauty of living in a village like Lissamore, Dervla. You can leave your front door on the latch all day. And you're still trying to change the subject.'

'His name is Christian Vaughan.'

'Cool moniker!'

'And he's taken the place for a week because he's thinking about coming to live here. I told him I'd be only too delighted to help him, and gave him my card.'

'Serendipity!'

'Serendipity?'

'Serendipity's when fate intervenes and good things start to happen.'

'I know what serendipity means. I'm just trying to work out what's so serendipitous about meeting a potential client and passing on my card.'

'Well, he's your man, isn't he? The one with the Dalmatian who looks like Pierce Brosnan. I mean *he* looks like Pierce Brosnan, not the Dalmatian.'

'I suppose he does rather,' said Dervla. But Río noticed that there was something a little too studied about the casualness with which she made the observation.

'What kind of house is he looking for?' asked Río. 'A big one with manicured lawns and topiary?'

'Well, I don't know about the manicured lawns and the topiary, but he is looking for something spacious – preferably with a granny flat or studio attached that could accommodate his mother.'

'Uh-oh. A mummy's boy? Is he gay?'

'He is most emphatically *not* gay,' said Dervla, and Río almost laughed at the affront in her sister's tone, as if the virility of her putative dream man was somehow in question. 'He's divorced, with a daughter at boarding school in England.'

'What does he do?'

'He's a wine importer, in Dublin. He and his business partner have decided to branch out, and he's made an offer on a shop in Ardmore.'

'So why's he looking for a house here if his business is going to be in Ardmore?'

'His preference is for Lissamore. It's prettier, and the commute's only fifteen minutes. And his mother was brought up here. He says he'd love her to spend her final years in the place where she enjoyed a happy childhood. She's been living in London for years.'

Río gave her sister a look of admiration. 'You got a lot of gen on him in a short space of time, Dervla. You could be a chat-show host.'

'People skills are part of my job, Río. You don't sell houses if you don't show a bit of interest in your clients.'

'He's not your client,' Río pointed out.

'Not yet, he's not,' agreed Dervla, with the narrow-eyed smile of a seasoned speculator. 'But I can guarantee you that he'll be checking out my website later on this evening. Can I have a glass of wine, please?'

'Sure.'

Río poured two glasses, handed one to her sister and said: 'Here's to Mama.'

'To Mama,' echoed Dervla. She took a thoughtful sip, then wandered towards the window to look out at the view. 'I wonder what she'd make of us now. I wonder if she'd approve of how we've turned out.'

'She'd approve of *you*,' said Río. 'Who wouldn't approve of a daughter who turned out to be such a high-flying achiever?'

'Maybe. But you produced the grandson, and reared him all by yourself. That's no mean achievement. We've both worked hard, in our own ways.'

'I wonder who we inherited the work ethic from?'

'Well, I certainly didn't inherit it from Frank. Do you ever wonder about your – about the Patrick person?'

Río shook her head. She hadn't told Dervla about the letter she had found in Mrs Murphy's rosewood bureau. She had told no one about it. She felt that she owed it to her neighbour not to compromise her, and she felt that, in a way, she owed it to her father too. Abandoning Rosaleen and his baby daughter had clearly not been easy for Patrick, but it had been the right thing to do at the time. Back then, life in a rural village would have been hell for a married woman with children fathered by two different men.

Río had wondered – of course she had – about the final letter her father had written to Rosaleen, the one he'd enclosed in the envelope addressed to 'Anne-Marie'. It was impossible to know

182

if Mrs Murphy had delivered it, because there had been no evidence of any farewell letter amongst the others her mother had stowed away in the battered vanity case. Río had resigned herself to the fact that it was something she would never find out. Maybe that was just as well. The past was another country, after all, and she had no wish to disturb the people who lived there still, who might finally have found some kind of peace.

She had also wondered – if Frank had found out that his neighbour had connived at her parents' affair – would he have included Mrs Murphy in his will? It was doubtful, Río decided. He would probably have left the garden to the cat.

'Do you think he might be here still, somewhere in Coolnamara?' asked Dervla.

'No. I shuffled his letters about and tried to put them in chronological order. They come to a kind of abrupt end. I think he probably hotfooted it out of town shortly after I was born.'

'And you still haven't made any effort to trace him?'

'No. I'd be too scared he might be a waster, Dervla. From the way he writes, you can tell he's a hopeless romantic. I met lots of men like him in the days when I was living with Finn in that commune in Galway – the kind of men who'd pass through and fall in love and then scarper if things got too heavy. Loads of girls ended up having babies by men they knew they were never going to see again. I was one of the luckier ones. At least Shane cared enough to send money when he could, and made an effort to see Finn from time to time. Still does. At least Finn knows his father's on his side.'

'And his aunt. If he ever has any worries that he can't talk to you about, tell him he can come to me.'

'Thanks. It'll be good for him to know he has family apart from me and his dad. Shane's folks never wanted to know. They couldn't handle the idea of a bastard in the family.'

Dervla made a sympathetic face. 'It must have been lonely sometimes.'

'It was. It's funny – because I'm so outgoing and sociable people always think I'm doing grand. You're the only person who knew how bad things had got that time after Finn left.'

'How are you feeling now?'

'Much better, thanks to you.'

It was true. Since Río had started to work for Dervla and 'got creative', things were on a more even keel. Now that she'd moved into her new home and no longer had so many money worries, life without Finn was more bearable. She'd even started painting again. The bad dreams she'd suffered from – the ones where she trailed through the night like a vagabond, losing things all over the place – were less frequent, and every time she turned the key in the lock and shut her front door behind her, the sense of contentment that suffused Río made her feel as aglow as a Ready Brek kid.

'Oh, I nearly forgot,' said Dervla, setting down her glass, 'I brought you a house-warming present.' She reached into her leather tote and took out a rectangular object wrapped in hand-made paper.

'As well as flowers? Dervla, you've got to stop being so generous.'

Río was reluctant to take the parcel that Dervla was holding out to her. Her sister had gifted her her home, she had found her a job, she had restored her self-esteem. It made her feel uncomfortable sometimes to contemplate how indebted she was to Dervla, and she fervently hoped that some day she would be in a position to repay her.

Beneath the paper – in a simple wooden frame – was a sampler, hand-embroidered in silk thread. Birds and bees and butterflies worked in French knots and featherstitch and herringbone en-circled a motto that read 'Home is where the Heart is'. Río smiled. It was the most perfect house-warming present she could have asked for.

'You do like it?' asked Dervla. 'You don't think it's too kitsch?'

'I absolutely love it,' Río told her. 'I'm going to hang it in pride of place, above my Dutch stove. Where on earth did you find it? Samplers like this have real scarcity value.'

'I drove a hard bargain,' she said. 'It cost me ten euro in a car boot sale.'

Río crowed. 'Well, doesn't my sister rock! An antique dealer would have charged you ten times that!'

Dervla dimpled a little. 'There's a lot to be said for austerity chic,' she said, 'and I'm lucky to have the best mentor going.'

'Oh, yeah? Who might that be?' asked Río.

'My sister,' said Dervla, holding out her arms for a hug.

Later, after a second helping of the chocolate mousse, which Río had twisted Dervla's arm into eating, and after many reminiscences about their childhood that had them in fits of laughter rather than in floods of tears ('Remember the time Dad came back from the pub when he'd sold his business for cash?' 'Yes! And he had tenners spilling out of his pockets and he gave us each a handful and told us to go and buy something nice to wear!' 'And d'you remember the time he recited the lines along with the actors when we went to that Yeats play?' 'Yes! And then he fell asleep and started snoring. And d'you remember the time . . .') – much later, when Dervla checked on her BlackBerry for the second time that evening, there was, indeed, mail from C. Vaughan.

'Result! Listen to this. "Dear Dervla,"' Dervla read out loud, '"It was –" wait for it! – "serendipitous to meet you earlier this evening. I should be extremely interested in viewing a number of properties on your books. Perhaps you could give me a call at your convenience? In case you may have mislaid my card, my number is –" blah blah blah.'

'Show me, show me!' said Río, reaching for the BlackBerry, and feeling a flutter of excitement for her sister. Scanning the screen, she scrolled down and widened her eyes. 'Wow,' she said. 'Did you get a load of the way he signed off?'

'No,' said Dervla. 'You grabbed the BlackBerry before I got a chance.'

'Give me a thousand kisses, then another hundred, then another thousand, then a second hundred, then yet another thousand more, then another hundred,' said Río, deadpan.

'Ha-ha,' said Dervla, with a laconic yawn. 'What did he really say? "Best wishes", "All best", or "Best"?'

'None of the above,' said Río. 'He said "Warmest".'

Dervla looked thoughtful for a moment, and then she gave a little smile. 'The cheek of him!' she said.

'There are three properties I'd be interested in viewing,' Christian Vaughan told Dervla over the phone the next day. 'One is the converted church.'

'That's definitely worth a look,' said Dervla.

'The other is the Victorian hunting lodge.'

'An absolute must-see.'

'And, thirdly, I'd like to have a look at the Old Rectory.'

'Oh.'

'Don't tell me it's gone?'

'No. In fact, it's been on our books for some time.'

'So why hasn't it sold? Is there some problem with it?'

'No, no. It's – it's beautiful. It's just that the owner has refused to drop the asking price, and buyers these days are looking for bargains.'

Dervla had had mixed feelings when the owner of the Old Rectory had refused to budge on the price. It had put prospective buyers off even bothering to view the property, which was, of course, bad news for her, professionally. But while the Old Rectory remained unsold, Dervla allowed herself to dream that one day it might be hers.

It was, of course, a complete pipe dream. Dervla was a registered member of IAVI – the Institute of Auctioneers and Valuers in Ireland – and was bound by a strict code of ethics. While the property was on her books, there was no way she could even think about putting in a bid for it. There were ways that other, less ethical, agents got around this rule. They would keep the price unrealistically high and make viewings as difficult as possible for prospective buyers, and then – when the vendors were on the verge of despairing that they would never sell – the agent would put in a low offer, a kind of 'sympathy' bid. Once the contracts had been signed and the property was legally theirs, they would scarper, cackling up their sleeves like pantomime baddies. It wasn't just the code of ethics that Dervla felt bound by; she had her own fairly strict moral code, and liked to think she was a person of integrity. It was for these reasons that she made a point of never allowing herself to become emotionally entangled with her properties. It was just too dangerous.

The Old Rectory, however, was an exception. The house so resembled the one of her childhood dreams that she had fallen in love with it at first sight. It was a small double-fronted Georgian manor, approached by a winding, tree-lined avenue, which curved graciously up to the front entrance before serpenting round to the back. Here, a large courtyard housed the kind of outbuildings that were crying out for conversion. The main house had retained all its original features. Dervla could repeat the list like a mantra: original cornices, coving, ceiling roses and bas-relief panels; original stone flag flooring, fireplaces, recessed windows and wooden shutters.

'What about the Mill House?' suggested Dervla, trying to expand Christian Vaughan's horizons. 'It's a rarity, and an absolute beauty.'

'Too much hard work,' said Christian. 'The thatch would be a bitch to maintain, and I don't have a clue how a mill wheel works.'

'The Old Schoolhouse? It's in turn-key condition.'

'Too small.'

'No worries!' said Dervla, sounding a lot more upbeat than she felt. 'I'll put in some phone calls, and hopefully all three properties will be available to view tomorrow.'

Dervla knew they would be available: none of the owners was resident, and she had keys to all three houses. But it was a matter of professional courtesy to let those concerned know that a viewing was on the cards, whether they were in situ or not.

She made the phone calls. The converted church? Check. The hunting lodge? Check. The third call was long distance to Mr McKenzie, vendor of the Old Rectory. He had bought it as a holiday home a decade ago, and visited it only twice. 'Sure – go ahead,' said McKenzie. 'And tell whoever's interested that I'm prepared to negotiate downward.'

'Downward?' echoed Dervla. 'I thought you were determined to stick to your original asking price, Mr McKenzie?'

'Sheesh. I've been waiting over a year for that baby to shift. If you can't beat 'em, makes sense to join 'em at this stage, dontchathink?'

'Well . . .' Dervla thought quickly. If McKenzie was prepared to drop his price, and the house still didn't sell, then that could be good news for her because he would, in all likelihood, decide to switch agents. In which event there was nothing to stop her, Dervla, from entering the bidding. 'Well, Mr McKenzie, perhaps you'd like to think about the kind of figure you have in mind?'

'Nah. See what the sonofabitch is prepared to offer, and get back to me.'

'Certainly,' said Dervla, adding, 'Good morning, Mr McKenzie.'

It was actually afternoon here in Ireland, but only ten a.m. in New York where McKenzie was receiving calls in his brownstone overlooking Central Park. But Dervla was a stickler for accuracy, and had trained her receptionist to say 'Good afternoon' if she picked up the phone just one minute after midday. First impressions were *so* important.

She got straight back to Christian Vaughan.

'Well, Mr Vaughan—'

'Christian, please.'

'Christian. Since all the properties are within a few minutes' drive of Lissamore, I suggest we kill three birds with one stone. We could schedule the viewings for tomorrow morning, if that suits you?'

'I have business in Ardmore, I'm afraid. But I should be through by midday. How about meeting up then?'

'Certainly.'

'I'll pick you up in Lissamore. That means we can halve our carbon footprint by using just the one car.'

Dervla hesitated. Since the disappearance of estate agent Suzy Lamplugh over twenty years ago, women auctioneers knew the importance of being vigilant. Dervla had completed a self-defence course, and her oversized Hermès handbag was not just a fashion accessory. It contained a personal attack alarm, a spray can of Mace, and a digital voice recorder, which she discreetly switched on any time she felt uneasy during a viewing. Her speed-dial numbers included her office, a private security firm, and half a dozen garda stations.

But in this instance, she had no worries. All Christian Vaughan's details – including his passport and credit card numbers – were on record with the agency responsible for letting the house that was now known as 'Harbour View'. If her tenant had any ulterior motives for viewing her properties – such as rape, abduction or murder – he wouldn't get very far.

'Sounds like a good idea,' she said. 'Tomorrow, midday, outside Harbour View?'

'Perfect,' said Christian. 'I look forward to it.'

On putting the phone down, Dervla picked it up again to Río. 'How are you fixed for casting a critical eye over some properties? I have to warn you, it's pretty short notice.'

'That's OK. Which ones?'

'The church, the hunting lodge, and the Old Rectory. No. Wait a minute. You don't have to bother about the Old Rectory. But I might ask you to take a look at the other two and make sure they're presentable? Just in case anyone's been staying there?'

'Sure,' said Río.

Dervla was reasonably certain that both properties were in good nick, but she'd made a point of double-checking after she had learned a salutary lesson. On one occasion, a vendor's son and a crowd of his friends had arrived down to Coolnamara from Dublin for a bank holiday weekend, and had either not been warned or hadn't given a tinker's that there was a viewing scheduled for the following Tuesday.

Dervla had gone into the house to be confronted by a smell that could only be stale Parmesan cheese or vomit, and which had proved to be both. Red wine had been spilled on the sitting-room carpet, unwashed plates were stacked in the kitchen sink, and half-empty bottles and glasses had been abandoned in every room in the house, including the downstairs loo. Dervla had found not one, but two pairs of discarded panties in an unmade bed under which lurked a couple of used French letters and a pornographic DVD.

It was the only time she had ever been relieved to receive a call from the prospective buyer to say that their car had broken down, and might it be possible to postpone the viewing until another day.

The following morning, Río called Dervla back to say that all was well. She'd laid fires in the sitting rooms of both properties, positioned plants strategically (orchids always looked fantastic in bathrooms) and laid out fresh towels and soap.

Midday found Dervla sitting on the sea wall opposite Harbour View, this time dressed in her work uniform of charcoal-grey suit, crisp white blouse and sensible shoes.

'Hey,' said Christian, when he rolled up bang on time. 'I very nearly didn't recognise you in those duds. Hop in.'

He was sitting behind the wheel of a Saab convertible, with leather-lined interior, sat nav and übercool sound system. Dervla was impressed, and impressed too by the way he handled the car once they hit the winding roads beyond the village. Christian had the air of a man who was totally in control, yet relaxed with it. It felt good to ride in a passenger seat. Dervla couldn't remember the last time she'd been driven anywhere, except by taxi.

'Where's the dog?' she asked.

'I took her for a long walk on the beach this morning, before I hit Ardmore. She'll likely spend the rest of the day sleeping off the effects of all that sea air. Being a city girl, she's not used to it.'

'Somebody once told me that the air in Coolnamara has the same effect on city people as a pint of Guinness,' Dervla told him.

'Pity you couldn't bottle it,' he returned with a smile.

'Some enterprising local did, once. Bottled Coolnamara air, and sold it to Yanks.'

'Maybe I should think about stocking some in the wine shop.'

Their first stop was the Victorian hunting lodge.

'Do you ride?' Dervla asked, as they pulled up outside the stable wing. 'There are some lovely hacking trails nearby.'

''Fraid not,' said Christian. 'What interests me most about this house is the potential for converting the stables.'

They got out of the car, and Dervla produced a key. 'The place has been extensively renovated in recent years,' she told him, as she pushed open the front door, 'to exceptionally high standards.'

Seguing effortlessly into estate-agent speak, Dervla led Christian through the hall to the kitchen, utility, sitting and dining rooms, the cloakroom and the office. Upstairs there were four bedrooms, two of which incorporated en suite bathrooms. Río had been thorough. The place looked loved.

The stable block next. Here there was no whiff of Jo Malone

grapefruit, but Dervla was convinced that clever Río might have wielded a room spray that suggested the scent of freshly mown hay.

'Perfect for conversion to a studio apartment or granny flat, don't you think?' With a smile, Dervla launched into her spiel, but when she finished, Christian just murmured a polite 'Thank you. That was very interesting. Shall we move on to number two?'

Shit, thought Dervla. Either Christian Vaughan was totally unimpressed, or he was an excellent poker player.

On they drove to the converted church.

'As you can see,' began Dervla, 'this was once a Gothic church. The extension was built less than ten years ago, and was designed to blend into the style of the existing building. The whole incorporates many gorgeous features, including this very impressive teak staircase with decorative rails and banister.'

Leading Christian upstairs, Dervla continued her eulogy. Actually, she wasn't mad about this property. She thought the refurbishment not entirely successful, and there were too many folderols, like canopied beds and chandeliers. The place felt as if it was trying too hard. She could tell that Christian was as unmoved by it as she was, because, after a perfunctory look around he said, 'Thank you. How about property number three?'

'The Old Rectory,' said Dervla, almost as an afterthought. 'Oh, yes.'

As they drove through the gates, Dervla found herself fighting the temptation to say: 'Bit of a waste of time, viewing this one. I'm sure it isn't the right property for you.' But of course, she didn't.

They got out of the car and stood looking up at the rose-coloured brick façade.

'It's a handsome building,' remarked Christian.

'Yes.' Dervla climbed the steps and unlocked the front door. Inside the front hall, light flooded through the fanlight onto the stone-flagged floor. Dust motes had been sent dancing by the sudden draught, and cobwebs swayed overhead. There was no smell of Jo Malone here, no gleam of polish on woodwork.

'As you can probably tell, the house has not been viewed for some time,' said Dervla.

'Clearly not,' said Christian, looking around with a smile. 'She's like the Sleeping Beauty.'

'I'll show you—' began Dervla, leading the way towards the cantilevered staircase.

But Christian cut her off. 'Thank you, no. I'd prefer to explore on my own, if that's all right with you?'

'Of course,' said Dervla. 'I'll wait outside.'

She spent half an hour sitting on a wrought-iron bench by the front door with the sun on her face, admiring the view, and feeling guilty that she wasn't using the time to send emails on her BlackBerry. It was perfectly silent in the overgrown garden of the Old Rectory, the only sound being the lazy buzz of a bee in the shrubbery.

As a child, when she and Río had shared their daydreams, this was the kind of house that Dervla had had in mind when she'd pictured her future. She'd imagined herself dressed in white linen, drifting around a garden with a basket on her arm, plucking flowers that she would arrange later in the kitchen with the help of a rosy-cheeked housekeeper. Together they'd go over the plans for the evening's menu, and later friends would arrive and they'd have aperitifs on the terrace before going in to dine at the polished mahogany table in the dining room, and she would sit at one end, and her husband would sit at the other, and the repartee would ring round the table until it was time for their guests to drive off into the night, leaving their hosts to enjoy a nightcap by the dying embers of the drawing-room fire before extinguishing the candles and putting the dog out and, finally, climbing the stairs to bed.

Dervla had been a sucker for romance in those days. She'd

read Mills & Boon books by the dozen, and pinned Pre-Raphaelite posters on her walls, and wept at mawkish movies. Now there was no room for romance in her life. Romance was a dream peddled by PR people and media consultants and cynical, jaded advertising executives. And estate agents.

So why was she still harbouring a dream about one day swapping her penthouse for a place like this, where there would be no concierge to help things run smoothly, and no nearby trendy florist to deliver her weekly arrangements, and no smart facilities to turn on her lights and her heat and her entertainment system at the touch of a button on a remote control?

It was stupid of her to entertain notions of McKenzie taking his business elsewhere so that she could put in a bid for this property. It was stupid to think that she could make the switch from city to country living without the kind of major, major stress that would have her importuning her GP for Xanax. And imagine the commute! No matter how much she loved her nifty little Merc, forty kilometres to Galway every day would do her head in.

Hearing the sound of feet crunching on gravel, Dervla got to her feet. Christian was rounding the corner of the house, looking up at the rooftop with a hand shading his eyes. When he reached her, he turned to regard the view, and remained silent for a long moment.

'Well?' said Dervla pleasantly. 'What do you think?'

Christian smiled down at her. 'I love her,' he said.

His expression said it all. She'd seen that look before on the faces of those prospective buyers who had found 'The One', and Dervla knew at once that she might as well forget her dreams of ever being châtelaine of the Old Rectory. Once a man started referring to a house as 'her', there was no going back. It looked like Sleeping Beauty had landed Christian Vaughan hook, line and sinker.

'I can just picture Kitty racing through that landscape,' he continued, his gaze taking in the meadows that ran down to a river below, and the rolling blue hills on the horizon, and the glint of the sea beyond. 'She would be so happy here.'

'Who's Kitty?'

'The dog.'

'So,' said Dervla, taking a deep breath, 'you think this might be the house for you?'

'I don't think so,' replied Christian, turning to look up at the stone pediment over the front door. 'I know so. Isn't it a bitch when you fall in love with a house?'

Dervla slid her shades on, and extracted her bleating BlackBerry from her bag. 'Yes,' she said. 'It is.'

Chapter Fifteen

Río was busy sewing on nametapes. 'You can't go travelling without nametapes on your clothes,' she told Finn. 'And because I know you'll be subsisting on junk food, I've packed a lunchbox for you with fresh fruit and cottage pie and a can of Guinness as a treat. Now, just let me answer the phone. It'll be your father – he promised to send you some money.' As she reached for the phone by her bed, she half expected it to turn to putty in her hand, the way it always did in her dreams. But the handset was solid, and the voice in her ear real: real and familiar.

'Ma! Hey, it's me!'

She was awake instantly, sitting up in bed, clutching the phone to her ear.

'Finn! What is it? What's happened?'

'Nothing, nothing, Ma – no worries. Listen, are you hooked up to satellite in your new gaff?'

'What? Yes. Why?'

'Quickly, go and turn the television on.'

'Oh, oh, hang on.' Río slid out of bed and grabbed her robe before negotiating the captain's staircase that would take her down to the main body of her living space. Oh Christ, she thought, struggling with the sleeves. What could be going on?

Some disaster – an earthquake, a tsunami, a coup? Where was Finn now? Koh Tao? Or had he left for Bangkok? Casting wildly around for the remote, she finally found it under a cushion. 'Which channel, Finn? What am I looking for? Sky News? NBC?' she said in a rush, aiming the device randomly at the screen.

'No. Go to iSpy.'

'iSpy? Never heard of it.' After several botched attempts, Río located the channel. 'What's up?' she asked. 'It's just an ad break.'

'Hang on. You'll be interested in what happened next.'

The jingly music announcing an ad for shower gel came to an end, followed by more jingly music announcing the resumption of a chat show. The bling legend on the screen told Río that she was watching a programme called *Celebrity Chat with Charlene.*

'Finn,' she said tiredly, 'it's half-past three in the morning here. Why have you woken me to watch some piece of crap on the telly? Are you buzzing on Thai grass or something?'

'No. I've just come in from an early morning dive and Carl happened to have the telly on. Wait.'

On the screen, the blonde woman called Charlene was smiling to camera with improbably white teeth. 'And now,' she was saying, 'will you please welcome my next guest – star of the surprise sleeper of the season – *Faraway*'s Mr Shane Byrne!!!'

'Look, look, Ma! There he is! There's Dad!'

'Holy shit.' Río let the handset drop to the floor. She stood there motionless for a moment or two, watching as Shane emerged from behind a glittering Perspex screen and strolled towards the over-stuffed couch upon which Charlene – all cleavage and legs – sat waiting for him. Then she picked up the phone again. 'I'll call you back,' she told Finn.

Transfixed, Río sank down on the sofa. The camera had panned to the inanely grinning studio audience, most of whom were women, all of whom were cheering and clapping wildly – cheering for Shane Byrne. *Shane!* Former love of her life and father of her child! How had this happened?

Charlene asked the question for her. 'What we all want to know,' she mock-chided him, 'is how did this happen so suddenly? Where have you been hiding until now, Mr Shane Byrne?'

'Hiding?' said Shane, with a quizzical smile.

'Yeah. You've gotta be Hollywood's best-kept secret. You say you've been living and working here for almost two decades. But how come we didn't hear of you until *Faraway* burst onto our screens?'

Shane gave a self-deprecating shrug. 'I've always been a very private individual,' he said. 'I didn't go into the business with a view to becoming rich and famous.' Oh, no? thought Río. 'I look upon acting as a craft – a vocation – and I've been happy right up till now to ply my craft in relative anonymity.'

'So this overnight success has taken you by surprise?' beamed Charlene.

'Absolutely. When I was cast in *Faraway* I never dreamed that it would go beyond the pilot stage – and I don't mean that as any criticism of the creative team. It just seemed to me that the series was too . . . I guess the right word is "maverick", to become mainstream.'

Shane crossed one long leg over another, and draped his arm over the back of the velvet-upholstered couch. Río had to admit that he looked good. He was wearing faded denims and a shirt of soft chamois leather. His hair was a lot longer than when she'd last seen him, and he'd clearly been working out. He was tanned – but not too tanned; and his teeth were white – but not too white. Río wondered if he'd employed a stylist to help him achieve this cool, understated look.

'You're already on your way to becoming a major sex symbol,' Charlene told him, raising a provocative eyebrow. The ladies in the audience yelled their approval, and Shane shook his head and gave them a look from under his eyebrows that translated as *Sheesh!* 'I understand that no fewer than seven fan sites have been set up since the first episode of *Faraway* was aired. What's the secret of your appeal?'

'I have no idea,' replied Shane.

'Well, *we* do, don't we, ladies?'

'Yesss!!!' came the enthusiastic response from the audience.

'Would you like to see a clip of Shane in action?'

'*Yesssss!!!*' This time the reaction verged on frenzy.

With a catlike smile, Charlene gestured to the giant screen behind her. 'Ladies and gentlemen,' she said, 'I give you . . . *Shane Byrne!*'

And now Shane was on Río's television screen in larger-than-life close-up, glowering moodily into the middle distance, green eyes narrowed against an apocalyptic sunset. The camera drew back to reveal him in all his glory, bare of torso with a gleaming six-pack. Some class of a leather kilt was slung round his hips, and his hair fell in dreadlocks to beyond his shoulder blades. His exaggeratedly accented Irish brogue provided the voiceover.

'In a faraway place, in a faraway time,' Shane intoned, 'a great calamity befell the earth. Few humans survived, and those who did were the unlucky ones . . .'

Río couldn't help it. She started to laugh. Picking up the phone, she speed-dialled Finn. 'Is this for real?' she asked.

'Yeah,' said Finn. 'I'm checking out one of his fan sites as we speak. Well, they've got his date of birth wrong, for starters. Dad's managed to shave four years off his age. Listen to this: "Shane Byrne is a dangerous Scorpio, so to all you besotted ladies out there – watch out for the sting in his tail!" Holy moly. It's weird to think that that's Dad they're talking about, isn't it?'

'Yeah,' said Río, smiling at the image of Shane striding across the apocalyptic landscape in his kilt. 'It really, really is. Send me links to the websites, will you?'

'Sure,' said Finn. 'Hey, whaddayouknow – *I'm* on here! "It is said that Shane – who is currently single – was involved in a tempestuous relationship early on in his career, which resulted in a love child born in Ireland." Get that! I'm famous, Ma!'

'You'd better get on to *Hello!* mag, and sell your story right away. Oh, look, he's back shooting the breeze with smarmy Charlene. Talk to you later, Finn, and thanks for the call. It was *so* worth getting up for.'

Río depressed 'end call', booted up her computer, then returned her attention to the television. Who would ever have dreamed that her ex would wind up as a Hollywood player? Admittedly, he had both looks and talent, but he had never had the drive. Like her, he had drifted through life, accepting the good times and the bad as they came in equal measure. She remembered his reaction when she had told him she was pregnant – how solicitous he'd been. He'd even volunteered to marry her! But Río had known that Shane was not the marrying kind any more than she was, and she sensed that he was relieved when she'd declined his very sweet, very generous offer. They had been far too young to marry, anyway. Their union would have ended up on the rocks in jig time.

'Tell me about your relationship with your co-star, Holly Matthews,' Charlene was saying. 'Can you put your hand on your heart and tell me that things are strictly platonic between you?'

Shane didn't supply an answer to the question. He simply put his hand on his heart and smiled, causing the audience to go, 'Oooooooh!!!'

'She's a very beautiful woman,' said Charlene, slanting him a meaningful look.

'Yes, ma'am, she is.'

'I understand that you and Holly have been approached by *Vanity Fair* to do a photo-shoot?'

'Well, yes, that's correct. But the shoot involves the entire cast of the series, not just Holly and me. There's no star hierarchy involved in *Faraway* – we're just a bunch of jobbing actors who got lucky.'

'So stardom really isn't important to you?'

'No. Not at all. I mean, at the end of the day the work is about survival, it's not about getting up to the top rung. It's about the adventure of doing different gigs and working with different people. And suddenly I've been elevated for something that was none of my doing. It just had to do with circumstance, timing, and somebody's choice, you know. Suddenly I'm in a hit show, working with a company of twenty-three, twenty-four people – working with an ensemble who are all as astonished by the success of the series as me, and that's a mind-blower. And then when you finally come to terms with it, you just sit back and think, What a jammy job.'

My God, thought Río. How on earth did Shane get to be so confident, so articulate – so grown up? Did this mean that she was going to have to start taking him seriously?

Charlene turned to the studio audience. 'I'm sure a lot of you gals have questions that you'd like to ask our guest. Those who do, just put up your hand.'

There was a lot of giggling and squirming as hands were raised, and fingers twinkled to attract attention. 'Yes!' said Charlene. 'The lady in pink angora! What do you have to say to Shane?'

'Hi, Shane! I'm Candy.'

'Pleased to meet you, Candy.'

'Can you tell us how you like to relax?'

'Well, I like to ride. It's always been a dream of mine to own my own horse. And that just may be about to happen. I'm in the process of buying a house with a stable yard and paddocks.'

'Um. What about indoor pursuits?'

The 'gals' in the audience squirmed and giggled some more.

'I like to play chess,' said Shane. 'And I also like to relax with a glass of wine and a good book. I'm currently rereading *Ulysses* by James Joyce, who was, of course, the most famous writer Ireland ever produced.'

What? thought Río. Riding? Chess? *Rereading Ulysses*? Had Shane been taken over by an alien?

The questions started coming thick and fast. *What's your favourite kind of music, Shane? Where do you like to go on holiday? What's your favourite food? Do you enjoy cooking? What, in your opinion, is the best film ever made?*

Finally, Charlene took the floor again. 'Shane Byrne,' she said, 'I'm sorry to have to say that our time's up. It's been a real pleasure meeting you.'

'The pleasure was all mine, ma'am,' replied Shane, returning her meaningful look.

Turning to the camera, Charlene smiled her white, white smile. 'I'd like to end our chat this evening by playing another scene from *Faraway*,' she said. 'And I may mention that this particular scene was specially requested by our audience. Don't forget, folks, *Celebrity Chat with Charlene* is where *you* call the shots and *you* ask the questions!'

Río reached for her water bottle. The *Faraway* theme music came thundering through the speakers, and an equally thunderous cheer rose from the studio floor as Shane appeared again, shimmering onto the screen. A woman's hand came into shot. Shane allowed her briefly to trace the line of his jaw with an index finger, before abruptly grabbing her wrist. 'No!' he said in an authoritative voice. 'You know it is forbidden for us to engage in the act of love, Pandora.'

The next shot was a close-up of Pandora, who Río guessed to be Holly Matthews. Golden of skin and lissom of limb, Holly resembled a young, pre-*Baywatch* Pamela Anderson.

'Rules are made to be broken, Seth.' *Seth!* Río spluttered on her water. 'And I, for one, hold in contempt any rule made by the warlord Xerxes.'

'I could not countenance it if any harm came to you,' said Shane/Seth.

'No harm can come to me if I am safe in your arms. Hold

me, Seth.' Holly/Pandora wound her beautiful arms around her co-star's neck, and there was a moment when you could see Shane/Seth engaged in an internal struggle. Then he was returning the embrace, pulling Pandora against his bare chest, crushing her lips with his, tangling his fingers in her hair. The clinch went on for ages before the camera tracked back to include the obligatory blasted landscape, and there – on a cliff top – a solitary caped figure was gazing down upon the star-crossed lovers. That had to be the warlord Xerxes, Río speculated. Well, hell! This was epic stuff!

The sound of an email landing in her inbox distracted her from the Technicolor vision that was Shane. It was from Finn, with a list of links to his father's fan sites. Río clicked on one at random. Oh! There was a photograph of Shane, gazing straight at her with a mean and moody expression. 'Welcome,' she read, 'to Shane Byrne dot com.'

Río clicked on 'Welcome' then scrolled down to find the following: 'About Shane . . . Photos & Videos . . . Fan Fun . . . The *Faraway* Quiz . . . Fans' Forum . . . Fans' Fantasies . . .'

Fans' Fantasies? Río *had* to go there! She clicked on something called *An Irish Interlude*.

'"Begorrah, Colleen – and 'tis beautiful you are looking this fine spring day with the shamrock blazing green as your eyes on the heath." Shane cut a fine figure of a man as he stood on the hummock, looking down upon me as I made my way along the boreen with the milk pails. "Thank you, Master Shane," I breathe, lowering my eyes. "Let me help you with those pails, lass," he says, taking them from me without a bother on him. I see the muscles bulging under the fine linen fabric of his rolled-up billowing shirtsleeves—'

Jesus! thought Río. What are these women on?

Another random click produced the following: '"Please, Sir Shane, do not harm me!" I cower half-naked on the floor of the dungeon while Sir Shane towers above me, menacing in his leather trews. He raises the hand with the whip in it and growls: "Nay, I will not harm thee if thou grantest me a favour." I quail. "What mightest that be?" I stammer, trembling. "This," he says sternly. He unfastens the thong on the crotch of his trews and—'

Ew! Río leaped back to the comparative safety of the home page, where her saturnine ex was eyeballing her, and found herself echoing the question that had been posed earlier on the iSpy Channel by flirty Charlene. How – *how* – had this happened so suddenly? There was really only one person to ask. Río did some mental calculations and worked out that it was eight o'clock in the evening, LA time. Picking up the phone, she dialled Shane's number.

'Shane?' she said when he picked up. 'It's Río.'

'Río, *acushla* – love of my life and mother of my first-born! How's it goin'?'

The intimacy of his voice in her ear had the effect on her that familiar music did. It made her feel warm, syrupy, a little fuzzy round the edges.

'Mother of your first-born?' returned Río. 'Does that mean you've had more sprogs since?'

'Nah. I just love to speak in the flowery lingo of my native isle. What's up, Río?'

'I just saw you on the telly.'

'On Charlene's gab fest?'

'Yeah.'

'But it's only four o'clock in the morning in Ireland! What has you up and about so early in the day?'

'Finn rang to tell me. He was watching you in Koh Tao.'

'So that's where the gobshite is. Last I heard from him he was in Australia.'

'That was months ago.'

'How's he getting on?'

'He's diving. What more can I say?'

'OK. So he's in heaven. How about you? Have you moved into your new gaff yet?'

'Yes. I sent you a change-of-address email, Shane.'

'Um. Sorry. I haven't been keeping up to speed lately. There's been so much going down here.'

'So it would seem. How does it feel to be a star overnight?'

'Very, very, *very* weird. People who wouldn't normally have looked twice at me in the studio commissary are now suddenly blazing a trail to my table. And actresses are twinkling at me and blowing kisses all over the place. It's as if— Hey, sweetheart, this is your phone bill! You can't be wasting your money on calls to LA. Let me call you right back.'

He was as good as his word.

'Tell me all about you, and life in Lissamore,' he said.

'Come on, Shane! You really want to hear about my boring life in the sticks?'

'Nothing would give me more pleasure. I mean it. I'm an ex-pat, remember, and ex-pats get awful homesick.'

So Río did. She told Shane all about her new apartment, and her new job, and how life was a lot rosier now than it had been since the last time they'd communicated. That had been a brief flurry of MSN over six months ago, Río realised, before she'd got her life back on track.

'Is there anything I can do for you, Río?' he asked. 'You know, I'm making a fair amount of money now.'

'No, Shane. It's sweet of you to offer, but I'm managing OK.'

'Are you still working in the bar?'

'Occasionally, if they're stuck. But now that I'm working for Dervla and I don't have to fork out for rent, money worries aren't as pressing.'

'Still driving?'

'Again, not as much as I used to. But it suits me now that we're heading into autumn. I've always hated driving in the dark.'

'I remember how you used to be scared of the dark. I'll never forget having to comfort you when you woke up from nightmares, calling for the light to be turned on.'

'Oh! Yes.'

There was a pause over the phone line, and then Río said, 'Tell me all about your new life, Shane. Do you do all sorts of starry things like strolling up red carpets and signing autographs? And are you really going to do a *Vanity Fair* photo-shoot?'

'Yeah.' From the tone of his voice, Río could tell that the prospect did not fill him with glee. 'It'll be one of those wanky pull-out covers where the whole cast poses in character and looks soulfully to camera.'

'So you'll have wear your leather kilt?'

'Yeah. God, it's embarrassing. I've had extras deliberately drop things as they go by so that they can bend down and take a gander.'

'So what *do* you wear underneath?'

'A Victoria's Secret confection of satin and lace.'

Río laughed. 'I'll post that nugget on one of your fan sites.'

'Oh, *no*! Don't tell me you've been checking out the fan sites, Río?'

'Sure have. Finn put me on to them.'

'Oh, *fuck*! This whole thing just gets more and more embarrassing.'

'Take the money and run, Shane. But beware the warlord Xerxes.'

'He's actually a transsexual. He used to be a beauty therapist called Suellen.'

'In real life or in *Faraway*?'

'In real life. But don't tell anyone I told you.'

'I could sell that tidbit to the *Enquirer*.'

'And have Xerxes lose his job next season? That would be uncharitable of you, Río.'

'So there's going to be another series?'

'Yep.'

'And it really was a complete sleeper? *Faraway* took you completely by surprise?'

'Not just me, Río. It took all of LA by surprise. There's no accounting for the tastes of the great American viewing public.'

Río became aware of a faint beeping noise on the line. 'Hey, you've another call coming in, Shane. You'd better take it.'

'Yeah. I better had. It's my agent. But listen, Río, it was really good to talk to you. Good to be back in the zone, you know?'

'The zone?'

'The bullshit-free zone.'

Río smiled. 'Take that call, Shane,' she said. And then she put the phone down, unfurled herself from the sofa, stretched and yawned.

Wandering onto her balcony, she watched the sun climb above the mountains to the east, tracing golden brushstrokes over the topmost peaks. How strange to think that in LA, Shane's day was about to end – probably with dinner in some nobby restaurant. And on Koh Tao, Finn had already spent half the morning underwater, checking out marine life. What should she do now? Go back to bed? No, she was too wide awake. She'd hit the beach – that's what she'd do. Four thirty a.m., with the sun rising and the tide high and the curlews calling – there was no better way in the world to greet the dawn than by diving into the Atlantic and emerging under a sky bluer than a teal's wing.

Down in the lobby, her bicycle was waiting. Río wheeled it through the front door, mounted it, and set off through the village, humming as she went.

It was only when she was in the water, floating on her back and gazing up at a cloud shaped like a dolphin, that she realised that the tune she'd been humming had been the ominous theme from *Faraway*.

Chapter Sixteen

Izzy had decided to surprise her dad by treating him to a home-cooked meal. She wasn't much of a cook, but she'd got herself some ready-prepared stir-fry ingredients and a pre-washed salad and a bottle of wine from Marks & Sparks. Izzy was a bit worried about her dad. He'd been losing weight since they came back from Koh Samui, and was looking haggard. She'd seen something on the news recently about stress-related heart attacks, and had felt a flash of fear for him.

At seven o'clock, she texted him to say that she was on the way up to his apartment. Being Friday, she was reasonably – although not altogether – certain he'd have finished work by now. Sure enough, the reply that came bouncing back read: 'Izzy bizzy dying 2 c u come strait on up.' So Izzy gathered together all her bits and pieces of shopping, switched off her phone, and took the elevator up to the penthouse.

Adair opened the door, and gestured to her to come in. He was talking on his BlackBerry, and Izzy could tell by his demeanour that it was business talk, as usual. It wasn't fair! It was after seven now, and the bastards still couldn't leave him alone.

She dumped the bags in the kitchen, poured two glasses of wine, and took them through to the living area. Handing one to her father, she moseyed over to the vast window that overlooked Dublin's docklands. Glinting glass, gleaming steel – God, how samey it all was, how very identikit! If she could Google Earth in close-up now, she knew what she'd see: city dwellers in developments all over the world gazing out at identical views from identical apartments, all furnished with identical décor. Girls like her with identical hair wearing identical clothes listening to someone talking identical corporate-speak on identical phones.

Flopping into an armchair, Izzy picked up a magazine. *GQ*, again. She made a *moue* of exasperation. When was her dad ever going to grow up? Still, at least he didn't subscribe to *NME*, like Lucy's parents. She leafed through the glossy pages, scanning text and photographs with unseeing eyes. Gadgets. Grooming. Gear. Yawn.

Since Tao, Izzy had grown restless. She had taken a long look at her life, and she hadn't much liked what she'd seen. Every day she spent hours stuck in traffic, commuting to college. Every day she listened to her Business Studies lecturers banging on about profit margins and market economy and investment portfolios. And every day she wondered if she was doing the right thing. *Business* Studies? What in the world had made her apply for the course in the first place? Did she want to become a clone of one of those Alan Sugar wannabes, living, breathing and sleeping accountancy and marketing and finance? Did she want to go into property development like her dad and end up stressed out and working twenty-four/seven? No, no, no!

What other role models had she? Her mother? The last time she'd visited Felicity, she'd had a look at her organiser. It read like this: 'Mon: gym, a.m.: man, ped, p.m. Tues: gym, a.m.; hair, facial, p.m. Wed: gym, a.m.; private view, p.m. Thurs: gym, a.m.; charity lunch p.m. Fri: gym, a.m.; psychotherapist, p.m. Sat: gym, a.m.; personal shopper p.m. Sun: gym (personal trainer reassessment) a.m. . . . The space reserved for 'Sun p.m.' activities had been blank.

'What do you do on Sunday afternoons, Mum?' Izzy had asked her.

'Sunday afternoons?' Felicity had to think about it. 'On Sunday afternoons I take to my bed, darling, suffering from exhaustion.'

'No,' Adair was saying. 'It's the wrong time to invest in commodities. Profit margins are down, and the economic structure's unstable.'

Izzy looked over at her father, and gave him a look of enquiry. 'How much longer?' she mouthed. 'Five minutes,' he mouthed back. Ha. That meant at least another ten. Reaching for her wineglass, she took a sip and returned her attention to *GQ*.

A full-page ad for vodka showed a wide-eyed, dim-witted-looking beauty applying her lipstick while hunkered down next to a man's crotch. The message? Buy this product and you might get a blow job. Is this what Business Studies was going to teach her? If so, then she needn't bother finishing her degree. Q: What sells product? A: Sex sells product. End of.

Flicking idly through the pages, looking for more stupid ads aimed at even stupider men, Izzy stopped abruptly, arrested by a black-and-white portrait of the Man of the Month. 'Introducing Shane Byrne,' went the headline. Hm, thought Izzy. Man of the Month was not an exaggeration. Shane Byrne was some dude. The photograph showed him looking directly to camera, connected, engaged, receptive – and yet with a vague air of *noli me tangere*. He was dark, sculpted and dangerous-looking, sporting the obligatory designer stubble and narrow-eyed smile. He was, Izzy learned, as she ran her eyes over the text, also old enough to be her father.

The three-hundred-word piece of puff journalism told her that he 'hailed from' County Galway in Ireland, and that he had struck lucky when he'd landed the role of Seth Fletcher in *Faraway*, a hit US television series due to hit screens all over Europe. The usual adjectives featured. Shane Byrne was self-deprecating, humorous, amiable, laid-back, down to earth, considerate and – of course – charming. Izzy yawned, and was just about to send the magazine skidding across the surface of the coffee table, when something made her stop and look again at his photograph. There was something about him – about the eyes especially – that reminded her of some man she'd met in the recent past. Who, exactly? And where and when had she met him? At a party? In the student bar? In a dream? It had to have been in a dream because men like that didn't exist in the real world, and they definitely did not exist on campus.

'Izzy!' At last her dad was off the phone. 'I'm sorry, baby, to have kept you hanging on. That's definitely the last call I'm taking this evening, I promise.' His BlackBerry shrilled again, and Izzy saw his eyes go to it, shiftily, as if he was trying to resist the impulse to pick up.

'It's OK, Dad. Take the call if you need to,' she said.

'No!' said Adair. 'In fact, I'm going to turn the damn thing off!' From his defiant attitude, you'd have concluded that he was committing some act of anarchy. 'There! And good riddance!'

'Sit down, Dad. Have some more wine.'

'I will. I'd like that.'

Adair collapsed against the cushions on the sofa that ran the length of an entire wall, then turned the corner and went on for several more feet. It could have seated fifteen, easily. And Izzy found herself wondering if had ever seated more than just two people – her dad and herself.

'Here.' She refilled his glass and handed it to him, then sat down next to him and curled her feet up underneath her. 'You look awful tired, Daddy,' she said. 'I'm worried about you. Even that break in Samui doesn't seem to have done you any good.'

'Two weeks isn't enough for me to recharge the auld batteries any more, Iz.'

'What would help you recharge them?'

'If I cut back my workload to four days a week, and took more time out in Lissamore, I'd be happy.'

'And can't you do that?'

Adair laughed, but there was no humour in the laugh. 'No. If anything, I'm going to have to start working six- even seven-day weeks.'

'Daddy, no! You can't! You'll drive yourself into the ground.'

'It's the way of the world once recession hits, sweet pea. It's a jungle out there – red in tooth and claw – and you know what the first rule of the jungle is, don't you?'

Izzy shook her head. She didn't want to be hearing any of this.

'It's "Survival of the Fittest". And I'm not as fit as I once was, Iz. It's a young man's game. You and your peers are the next generation of young turks. The world is your oyster. Grab it while it's hot.'

If Izzy hadn't been feeling so worried about her dad's fitness level, she'd have teased him about his mixed metaphors. He was always getting things wrong – song lyrics, famous quotes, aphorisms. And he always laughed at himself when he tried to keep up with fast rap or mimic Lily Allen's accent. But this evening Izzy wasn't finding anything very funny.

'Maybe we could go down to Lissamore again? Just you and me? There's a long weekend coming up, and we haven't been for – what? Nine months?'

'That's sweet of you, Izzy. I know Lissamore isn't your favourite place in the world.' He looked away from her towards the window that framed the view of the glittering cityscape, and added, 'In fact, I was thinking of going down there soon. I could do with a fix of that view. I just want to sit in the hot tub and gaze at mountains and sea and sky.'

'Yay! Let's do it, Dad!' Right now she'd do anything to make her dad happy, even if it meant trailing down to that arse-end of nowhere.

'The thing is, sweet pea, it's not just the view I want to go for. I need to go for business reasons too.'

212

'Not *more* business, Dad! Lissamore is your escape. You can't be dragging business down there. Look, I'll even go round the golf course with you, if you like. I know I'm not very good at it, but—'

'Izzy. I'm going to have to sell up.'

There was a horrible, horrible silence. Then Izzy said, in a very small voice, 'Sell the Villa Felicity?'

'Yes. I've been in denial for too long, Iz. The place is like a big white elephant around my neck, and it's been bleeding money. I can't afford to maintain it any longer.'

'But, Dad, it's your dream home! It's where you were going to retire to!'

'Correction. It was Felicity's dream weekend retreat. It wasn't designed as a retirement home. If I sell it, I can afford to buy somewhere smaller – somewhere you might like to come and stay when I'm a barmy old git, and bring my grandchildren to visit.'

'Oh, Daddy, don't talk like this! Everyone knows that the recession is just a hiccup. In no time at all, everything will be right as rain and you'll be sitting pretty again.' Somehow, Izzy felt that her father might find it comforting if she spoke to him using the clichés he was so fond of.

'I don't know, sweetheart. I feel as if the fight has gone out of me. I kind of feel the time really has come for me to take up pipe-smoking and slippers. Maybe I'll get a dog when I cash in my pension. I could call him "Rover", and I could call my retirement cottage "Dunroamin".'

Izzy managed a laugh. 'If you've really done roaming, then the last thing you'll want to call your dog is "Rover".'

Adair smiled back at Izzy, and her heart wanted to break when she saw the tired lines around his eyes, and the hollows under his cheekbones and the way his mouth was starting to droop at the corners.

'Let's go down there together,' she told him. 'Then, when you've soaked yourself to a prune in the hot tub and got yourself a fix of your view, we'll go for long walks and play Scrabble and toast marshmallows. I might even let you win, to cheer you up.'

'I had a pet rat called Scrabble when I was a kid.'

'Cool! I'd love a pet rat. Maybe I could get one for Mum for her birthday. I wonder do they have posh carriers for rats, like the ones she has for her pooches? And maybe she could dress them in little rat clothes and find bejewelled collars for them, and hats and . . .'

And Izzy's flight of fancy rambled on and on, until finally she had her daddy laughing again.

'Dervla Kinsella speaking.'

'Dervla. It's Adair Bolger here.'

'Adair! How good to hear from you.' Dervla opened her electronic organiser, pressed 'B', scrolled down until she found 'Bolger, Adair', then double-clicked for 'Notes'. There she had filed the following: 'CEO: Keyline Group. Ex: Felicity; one daughter Isabella (Izzy for short).' Other details included info that she had bookmarked diligently over the course of the past eight or nine years, including Adair's estimated net worth, his business affiliates, and the approximate value of his house in Lissamore. Hm. She'd have to readjust that downward, that was for sure. 'How are things in Dublin, Adair? Or are you calling from Lissamore?'

'I'm calling from Dublin, but I'll be heading to Lissamore this weekend. I was hoping we might meet up.'

Uh-oh. It was always tricky when a potential client used this line. One was never entirely sure whether the agenda behind the meeting was business or pleasure.

'Certainly,' said Dervla smoothly. 'When might suit you?'

'No, no – when might suit *you*?' insisted Adair. 'I know you're a busy woman.'

Dervla was glad that Adair wasn't looking over her shoulder at her organiser. The appointments page was virtually blank.

'When do you arrive?'

'Friday evening.'

'Well, I have a couple of viewings on Saturday morning,' lied Dervla, 'so perhaps we could meet up on Saturday afternoon? Have you a venue in mind?'

'Yes. The Villa Felicity. I'd like to know your assessment of its value.'

'I see,' said Dervla, feeling a flutter of excitement. 'Have you a particular reason for wanting an evaluation?'

'I do,' said Adair. 'I'm putting the house on the market.'

Yes! 'Well,' said Dervla. 'I'd be glad to drive over to you at, say, two o'clock?'

'Two o'clock sounds good. The place should be well aired by then.'

'Doesn't your caretaker usually do that for you?'

'I never got round to replacing him. I did ask your sister if she might be interested, but she told me she had a waiting list for her plant whispering service.'

'She did?' What mischief had Río been up to? 'Well, if you're putting the place on the market, Adair, you'll want it looking presentable and well cared for. You might think about approaching Río again. She's staging my properties for me, and she does an excellent job.'

'Sounds good. Perhaps she could come along on Saturday and let me know what she thinks?'

'I'll put in a call to her. I'm sure she'd be delighted to have a look.'

'Thank you. Say, why don't I do lunch for you gals?'

'There's really no need, Adair.'

'It would be my pleasure. Really.'

'Well, that's very generous of you.'

'Consider it done. I look forward to seeing you again, Dervla.'

'Likewise, Adair. Have a good journey.'

When Dervla put the phone down to Adair, she picked it up again to Río.

'How would you feel about putting some manners on a garden, Rí?'

'Whose garden?'

'The Villa Felicity's.'

'It's hardly the right time of year for planting.'

'I think it's major tidying that's needed here. Nobody's been near the place for nearly a year.'

'But that's criminal! That garden needs masses of TLC if it's to thrive.'

'And I'm hoping you're the gal to do just that.'

'Hm. Tell me more.'

Dervla filled her sister in on Adair's plans for the Villa Felicity.

'So he's hoping to sell it? Yikes. Who'd want to buy a monstrosity like that?'

'Let's not be negative, Río. We've got to concentrate on all the pluses.'

'I suppose you've written the blurb already?'

'Río, I wrote it months ago.'

'Oh, yeah? What do you have to say about the frilly bedroom?'

'Exquisitely decorated.'

'And the oversized deck?'

'Ideal for entertaining.'

'So who's on your mailing list? Elton John?'

'Río, are you interested in the job or not?'

'Of course I'm interested. Times are hard. The recession lost me two gardening jobs last week.'

'In that case, I'll pick you up at one fifty on Saturday. He's going to give us lunch, so please look presentable.'

'I'll wear my French maid's outfit. Will I get to style the house too?'

'If Adair Bolger is as insecure as most people, I'm sure he'd be glad of your advice.'

'Torch the joint, would be my advice. Torch it, and rebuild Coral Cottage with the insurance money.'

Dervla sighed. 'That's hardly helpful, Río.'

'C'mon, Dervla. It's clear that his taste is chalk to my cheese.'

'You mean Felicity's taste. That house was designed to her spec.'

There was a pause on the other end of the phone. 'It was?'

'Yes. It was her pet project. All Adair cared about was the view.'

'Some pet project. Ha! I know just what to put in them thar closets.'

'Let me guess. Skeletons?'

'Spoilsport! How did you *know* I was thinking skeletons?'

'I'm pretty familiar with your sense of humour, Río. Just draw the line at putting fake poo in the loo, will you? I might as well warn you that I check *everything* out before a viewing.'

'Sheesh,' said Río. 'I'd better cancel that order to the online joke store, so.'

Chapter Seventeen

On Friday afternoon, Río got a call from the hackney company to ask her to pick up a fare from Galway airport. The fare's name was Sharkey, his destination was Lissamore, and, as ill luck would have it, she learned too late that his flight was delayed by an hour and a half. 'Sure, no matter!' said the girl in dispatches, as Río negotiated the Galway ring road. 'Take yourself into town and treat yourself! Lucky you, to have time off for a bit of shopping!'

Río couldn't understand the girl's ebullience. She had never been much of a one for shopping. She wasn't easily intimidated, but department stores were, for her, amongst the scariest places on earth. How some women viewed shopping as a 'leisure activity' was beyond her. She hated having to ask advice of the snooty-looking girls behind the cosmetic counters with their immaculate *maquillage*, and she hated it when she shuffled out of changing cubicles, shaking her head apologetically at the sales-girls because the clothes that looked so gorgeous on the rack looked like shit on her.

But sometimes you had to be brave and just do it. Having finally found a place to park, Río slouched into a posh empo-rium, feeling shabby in her polyester suit. It looked all right from the waist up, she supposed, but the bum had gone shiny from all that sitting in the driver's seat. She ventured first into the cosmetics section, and was immediately set upon by an army of girls wielding perfume sprays. No, no, *no*! There was nothing worse for a fare than being stuck in a hackney with a driver who smelled like an air freshener. Río ducked and dived like a resistance fighter, and finally drew up at a counter where there was a promotion on. She found herself being suckered into parting with a nauseating sum of money for a night cream that the salesgirl promised would eliminate free radicals (whatever they were) and a cleanser that would calm her stressed skin.

Upstairs, she made her way to the discount rail, where a nondescript mackintosh caught her eye. It stood to reason that if the coat looked unappealing on the hanger, it might look quite good on her, and she was right. Because she badly needed a coat now that autumn was on the way, she bagged it, and then she bagged a pair of jeans that had been marked down from 250 euro to 50 (who in their right mind would pay 250 euro for a pair of jeans?), as well as a plain black dress with elbow-length sleeves that was very un-Río but looked pretty stylish, and a pair of heels that she knew she'd never be able to walk in. A cardigan! Why not?

Río was feeling reckless, now – so reckless that she thought she might even pluck up the nerve to infiltrate the lingerie department. It was Fleur's birthday soon, and she wanted to buy her friend something special. On Río's last birthday, Fleur had presented her with the most beautiful coffee-table book of underwater photographs by David Doubilet. Río wanted to return the compliment by giving Fleur something she knew she would love, and Fleur was passionate about underthings. In the lingerie department, she helped herself to a pair of darling knickers, polka-dotted and trimmed on each hip with a miniature geyser of scarlet ribbons, and a matching bra with teeny bows on the straps.

What was she doing, she wondered, as she handed over her credit card. She had never spent this kind of money in her life, ever! As she keyed in her PIN, her palms were sweaty and she was practically hyperventilating – and then two things happened that made her wish that the ground would open up and swallow her and her glossy carrier bags in one big gulp.

The first thing that went wrong was when the salesgirl murmured: 'I'm sorry, madam, but there appears to be a problem with your card.'

'A problem?' stammered Río to the assistant, whose name tag told her she was Kirsty. 'Surely not! I've made several purchases already with my card.'

'I'm sure it's just the usual gremlin in the works,' said Kirsty, with professional politeness, 'but I will have to phone the bank to get clearance. Liz –' this to a fellow salesgirl – 'could you serve the gentleman, please?'

'Certainly!' said Liz, joining her colleague at the cash desk.

And this is when the second awful thing happened. Río heard a man's voice from behind say: 'If I'd known that you were going shopping for girly stuff, I wouldn't have come with you. I always feel like a perv in these places.' And then she heard a girl's voice say: 'Put your wallet away, Dad! I will *not* have you paying for my underwear.' Río knew that voice, that imperious Dublin 4 accent.

She started to sidle unobtrusively away from the cash desk, but as she did so, she heard the man's voice say: 'Río! Hello! What a coincidence. I believe you're joining us for lunch tomorrow?'

'Hello, Adair. Yes, I believe I am.' Río turned to him, agonisingly aware that her face was now redder than the ribbons on her new purchases.

Isabella was looking at her with an expression of ill-concealed affront, and Río knew that it was because she had clocked the items of underwear that Kirsty had left on the counter when she'd gone off to phone the bank. They were, Río realised now, identical to the ones that Isabella herself was purchasing. Oh, God! This was awful, *awful*!

'I'm sorry,' said Kirsty, putting her hand over the mouthpiece of the phone, 'they've put me on hold.'

'Oh, look,' said Río, 'it doesn't matter. I'll come back another time.'

'I don't mind holding,' said Kirsty.

'No, no, really.' Río was now desperate to get out of there. 'I'm running late for an appointment. Please give me back my card.'

'Well, if you're sure . . .' said Kirsty.

'Sure, I'm sure. Thank you.' Río snatched back her card and jammed it into her wallet.

'Can I help?' asked Adair.

'No. No, thanks. Really.' Río's wallet hit the deck, and a load of coins came tumbling out of her change purse.

'It's just that the bank's taking ages to respond,' Kirsty told him, helpfully.

Oh God, she must have assumed that she and Adair were shopping together, thought Río, as she scrabbled around on the carpet for fifty-cent pieces.

'Please allow me,' said Adair, turning to Liz, 'to add Ms Kinsella's purchases to my bill.'

'Certainly, sir.' Liz reached for the pile of ridiculous frippery and helped herself to a length of tissue paper.

'I can't allow you to do this, Adair!' protested Río, getting to her feet. She was now so frazzled that she thought she might start snivelling.

'Why not? Sure, won't we be seeing each other tomorrow? I'll allow you to pay me back then, for the – um . . .'

Liz had started to wrap each of the flimsy items carefully in tissue paper, and as she did so, a terrible silence descended, as everyone registered exactly what Río was buying. The silence was broken only by Kirsty, who had started singing along to 'Greensleeves' down the phone.

'Thirty-six C?' Liz trilled at Río, holding up the polka-dot bra with the scarlet bows. Río nodded.

221

Then: 'Thirty-two C?' she trilled, turning to Isabella. Isabella said, 'That's right,' in that perfectly modulated voice of hers, and just gazed serenely into the middle distance. Oh! The wretched child didn't seem at all fazed by the fact that the two women had opted for the same underwear, and Río went redder still when she thought of shapely little Isabella sporting scanties that would make Río in comparison look like a wobbly chunk of fatty mutton masquerading as lamb. She suddenly remembered the dancing hippos in Disney's *Fantasia*, pirouetting in their tutus, and she couldn't help it – she started to laugh and cry at the same time.

Adair looked at her with concern. 'Is something the matter?' he asked, and Río managed to shake her head. How she'd love to be able to explain that the underwear wasn't for her – that it was actually for her very girly girlfriend – but she had a suspicion that an explanation would make her look as if she were protesting too much. 'I'm – I'm just remembering a joke,' she said, 'that makes me laugh, but because – because my son told it to me, it makes me cry at the same time.'

Oh God, oh God. Any minute now Río was going to wake up and laugh when she realised that the past ten minutes had been just a crazy nightmare! But no such luck. The next thing she knew, her phone was alerting her to a text, which read: 'Sharkey's flight landing in ten.'

'Oh, yikes – yikes – I've gotta go,' she whimpered. And she grabbed up her assorted carrier bags and fled the lingerie department. If all the hounds of hell had been hot on her heels, Río couldn't have fled it faster.

'Was she *drunk*?' Izzy asked her father, who was looking after Río with a bemused expression.

'I don't think so,' said Adair. 'I didn't get a smell of drink off her.'

'Maybe she's mad,' said Izzy.

'A little scatty, maybe,' conceded Adair. 'She's a bohemian. You expect bohemians to be a bit eccentric.'

'What was that you said about seeing her tomorrow?'

'She's coming with her sister, to have a look at the house.'

'Why does she have to look at it?'

'I'd value her opinion.'

Izzy gave him an incredulous look. 'Is that wise, Dad? You just admitted yourself that she's batty.'

Adair shrugged. 'Apparently she's excellent with gardens. She whispers to plants.'

'That makes her officially mad. And look, she left her stuff behind.' Izzy indicated the carrier bag that Liz had packed with such care.

'Sir?' Liz was looking at Adair expectantly.

'Oh, I beg your pardon,' he said, pulling out his wallet.

'No, Dad.' Izzy laid a firm hand on his arm. 'I told you you were *not* to pay for my stuff.'

'What about Río's stuff? I said I'd pay for that.'

'I'll pay for it. Knowing you, you'll be too embarrassed to ask her for the money back. And I don't imagine she'll be beating a path to your door to offer it to you on a plate.'

'What do you mean?'

'It's just a hunch. If she's an eccentric bohemian she's probably an anarchist too. And since anarchists believe in the equal distribution of wealth, by inveigling you into footing her bill, she's doing her bit to redistribute it.'

'When did you get to be so cynical, Izzy? Is this what they're teaching you in college?'

'I'm not cynical, Dad,' said Izzy, jabbing her number into the chip-and-pin machine. 'I'm just a realist. You're the big softie in our family.'

And I'm not going to allow that cow Río, with her coy blushes and her big blinking bovine eyes, to take advantage of you, Izzy vowed, as she waited for the transaction to go through. She wondered how much of today's chance meeting had really been down to 'chance'. Had Río spotted them and followed them to the lingerie department, and then staged it so her credit card didn't register? It would be an easy thing to do: just enter the wrong pin a couple of times, and hey presto! Suddenly you're a damsel in distress, in need of a knight in shining armour to rescue you. She wouldn't put it past that Kinsella woman to have lots of con-artist tricks up her polyester sleeve.

'Thank you so much,' she told Liz as she swung the pair of carrier bags off the counter.

Her father was regarding his watch with a dismayed expression. 'I knew we shouldn't have stopped off in Galway,' he said. 'It's nearly four o'clock.'

'We needed to stock up on food,' Izzy pointed out. 'You've invited people for lunch tomorrow. I hope we have enough for four.'

When Adair had told her he'd invited Dervla for lunch, he hadn't mentioned that her evil sister was part of the equation.

'We could always eat out tonight.'

'No. I'm going to make sure you eat properly. That's why I got all that fruit and green vegetables. You haven't been looking after yourself, Dad, and if you carry on working at this rate and eating out all the time, you're asking for trouble. At least when you and Mum were together, you had a healthy diet.'

'Nag, nag, nag.'

Izzy smiled up at her father, and linked his arm as they made their way towards the escalators. 'Somebody has to do it,' she said.

It was true. Somebody had to nag him and cook for him from time to time and give him shoulder rubs. Izzy was doing her best, but she couldn't be there for him for ever. It was definitely time, she decided, that Adair got himself a new life partner. Preferably one of Izzy's choosing.

* * *

Río was still whimpering as she manoeuvred the hackney into a space in the airport car park. How had it happened, she asked herself. How had she managed to make such a spectacular eejit of herself in front of Adair Bolger and his ice-princess daughter *again*? She felt like a circus clown – not the pretty Pierrette type, but the big bungling one with the outsized feet and the fright wig and the red nose, the one that all the other clowns jeered at.

But what bothered her more than anything was that she actually cared. Río – who normally didn't give a toss about people's opinion of her – actually *cared* what the Bolgers might think of her. How had this happened? When had she decided that she wanted to be accepted by Adair and Isabella, who stood for everything she despised?

Had her change of heart happened that time she'd seen Isabella and Finn sitting together on the sea wall, during Frank's wake? They had made such a beautiful couple and looked so at ease with each other that Río had felt a weird sense of shame. What if they decided to become friends – or even more than just friends? Finn would hardly want to bring a princess like that home to meet a mother who might be dancing round the place singing along to her iPod, or sitting crying in front of a DVD of Disney's *Dumbo*, or gazing out to sea with a joint between her fingers.

Or had the change of heart happened when she'd seen that Adair could take her petty wisecracks on the chin? Or when he had made her laugh that time he'd invited her to slide down his banister? Or when she'd learned it had been Felicity, not him, who had been responsible for that monstrous villa? Or even today when—

Hell! Now was not the time to indulge in speculation about her relationship with the Bolgers. Now was the time to get her arse over to Arrivals and look out for Mr Sharkey. The noticeboard told her his flight from London had arrived, and as she scribbled 'Mr Sharkey' in block capitals on an A4 sheet, the first of the passengers began to straggle onto the concourse. Río held the sign aloft, scanning the weary faces of the emerging travellers. Nobody looked twice at her. They were all too busy gawping at the dapper chauffeur who was holding up a sign that read: 'Mr Flatley'.

'OK,' an American voice hissed at her suddenly, as a man strode by. 'Let's drive. Go, go, *go!*'

'Mr Sharkey?' But the man was already moving fast across the concourse. Río legged it after him, trying to keep up. Sharkey was dressed in a black leather jacket and black jeans. He had on a baseball cap that screened his face and wraparound aviators that screened his eyes. A black leather rucksack was slung across one shoulder, and a suiter was draped over his arm. Once outside the automatic doors, he stopped and half-turned to her.

'Where's the car?'

'Um. Follow me.'

Río led the way across the car park. As she took the keycard from her bag, she reached for her phone and punched in the number of the hackney company. If this guy turned out to be some criminal on the run, she wanted to know that all she had to do was press 're-dial', and someone would be on her case. She aimed the card at the door, and Sharkey got into the front and tossed his bag in the back. Río slid into the driver's seat, and started the ignition.

'Please put your seat belt on, sir,' she told him, as she put the car into gear. 'I'll be liable for penalty points if you don't.'

'And isn't that the last thing I'd wish to be after happening?' said Sharkey. 'That a lovely girl like yourself would get hit with a great big fine on account of a divil like me.' Río stopped the car and turned to her fare. With a broad grin, he doffed his cap and shades. 'And isn't it a grand soft day that greets my return to the Emerald Isle?' he said, in a voice she recognised.

'Shane Byrne,' replied Río, deadpan. 'What the hell do you think you're playing at?'

'I'm not playing at anything,' he said, looking aggrieved. 'I'm a fugitive.'

'From what?'

'From the paparazzi, of course.'

'Oh, *them*! The ones who were yowling like jackals to get the first shots of you arriving into a provincial airport.'

'Less of the sarcasm, Río. Just pick up a copy of this week's *National Enquirer* and you'll see what I mean. Since *Faraway* hit the screens in the US it's been open season on me and the rest of the cast.' He slanted her a smile. 'Especially on me,' he added.

'Well, hot-shot, welcome home.' Río leaned over and gave him a kiss on the cheek.

'Thanks, mavourneen.'

'If I'd known it was only you I had to pick up,' she remarked, looking into her rear-view mirror and pulling out, 'I wouldn't have bust a gut to get here. Where to?'

'Lissamore.'

'Lissamore? Why Lissamore? I'd have thought you'd have booked yourself into somewhere trendy like the G Hotel in Galway.'

'What? And have the paparazzi parked outside the door once word got out that I was staying there? No, no, sweet Río. I have come here for peace and quiet. That's why I booked your services under the pseudonym of Sharkey.'

'You asked for me specifically?'

'I did. I said I wanted the driver with the red-gold hair and the laughing green eyes and the fantastic baloobas.'

'Pity they got it so wrong, then. They should have sent Anita.'

'Who's Anita?'

'A colleague of mine who happens to have red-gold hair and laughing green eyes and fantastic baloobas. She also happens to be about fifteen years younger than me.'

'Arra, acushla! For me, you will be forever young.'

'Shut up, and tell me if I'm clear on that side.'

Shane looked to the left. 'You're clear,' he said.

'You still haven't told me what brings you to Lissamore.'

'My agent suggested a break,' Shane told her. 'Somewhere far away from the razzmatazz and stress of Lala Land. And I figured that Lissamore was about as far away as it gets.'

'And you'd be right. Lissamore out of season may as well be renamed Zed-Ville. Where are you staying?'

'Dunno.'

'You mean you haven't booked a rental?'

'No. I thought I'd just stay in a hotel.'

'Shane! You dozy lummox! There's no hotel in Lissamore.'

'You're kidding me! Not one?'

'Well, there's one under construction, and there's Coolnamara Castle – but you'd have to get yourself a hire car because it's too far to walk. You might get a room in a B & B in the village—'

'A B & B? Are you out of your mind?'

'Oh. I forgot you're Hollywood royalty, now.'

'It's not that, Río. It's just that I've always had the heebie-jeebies about B & Bs since that landlady tried to ride me when I was on tour once.'

'What? You never told me that!'

'Ach, it was years ago when I was touring with some bloody awful schools' production of *Macbeth*. We were all put up in this B & B with pictures of the Sacred Heart on the wall, and didn't I wake up in the middle of the night to find the lady of the house wrapping her arms and legs round me and whispering into my ear about how I was a fine strong lad and wouldn't I like to have a hoult of her.'

'Wow! What did you do?'

'I lay there and pretended to be asleep until she gave up and went away. And then I packed my bags and was out of there like Roadrunner.'

228

Río laughed. 'I guess you're fighting off celebrity babes now, not landladies decked out in pink nylon.'

Shane shrugged. 'I don't have the time to meet any babes. All I do is work and sleep. It ain't glamorous being a commodity, Río.'

'A commodity?'

'That's all I am. I'm under no illusions that if the powers that be decide to axe the series I'll be back to waiting tables. Stardom is as ephemeral, acushla, as the last fading ember of turf in the hearth, or the glint of the sun on the curlew's wing as it skims across the bog, squawking its plaintive melody—'

'If you don't shut up, Shane, I'll feck you out of the car.'

'OK. I'll change the subject. What'll we talk about?'

'Quantum physics.'

'You have two minutes on quantum physics, starting from now.' Shane's pronouncement was followed by exactly two minutes of silence, and then he said: 'Hey, couldn't I stay with you, Río?'

'No, you could not. I've no spare room.'

'I could sleep on the couch.'

'No.'

'Why not?'

'Because I like having the place to myself, Shane. I do not want it compromised with someone else's stuff scattered around the joint and a big man stretched out snoring on my sofa.'

'I could stretch out in your bed, instead.'

'No!'

'Not even for old times' sake?'

'Jesus, Shane! If you really wanted to get into my bed, you'd have to come up with a better line than that.'

'I could talk to you in Italian. You used to love it when I did that.'

'"Used to" being the key words.'

'*Vorrei mettere la mia mano sotto la tua gonna e farla salire su*

229

per la tua gambo fino alla pelle morbida, morbida in alta sulla tua coscia.'

'Shut up, Shane. It's not going to work.'

'E poi vorrei fare l'amore con te.'

'We are now entering the Gaeltacht. Please revert to your native tongue.'

'Pah!' said Shane, folding his arms crossly. 'You know I don't speak Irish.'

As they approached a red traffic light, Río was distracted by two women in an adjacent car waving wildly at them, signalling to them to pull down the window.

'What's wrong with them?' asked Río. 'Is there something the matter with my car?'

'Must be,' said Shane, lowering the passenger seat window. 'Hi! Is there some problem—'

But the driver wasn't listening. 'Seth! Seth!' she called. 'We love you! *We love you!* Can we have your autograph?' Reaching out an arm, she handed over a scrap of paper and a Biro. Shane signed with good grace, and handed the autograph back with a smile.

The woman kissed the paper, and waved it in the air as if she'd just won the lottery. 'Thank you! Thank you!' she yelled, while behind them car horns honked irritably at them to get a move on.

Río put the car into gear, and shot Shane a curious look. 'How does that feel?' she asked.

'Pretty damn stupid, to tell you the truth. They never have a clue who Shane Byrne is, so I always have to put "a.k.a. Seth Fletcher" as well.'

'But it must be dead flattering, all the same?'

'Nah. It's not me they're interested in, Río. It's just the character I play. People go to bed with Seth Fletcher and wake up with Shane Byrne. Hey!' He turned to her suddenly with an eager expression. 'If I can't share your bed, maybe Seth could?'

'Have you got your leather kilt in there?' Río indicated the bag that Shane had slung onto the back seat.

'Are you mad? No.'

'Then all I can say is – nice try but no cigar.'

'You mean you'd only sleep with me – I mean with Seth – if I wore that leather yoke?'

'Me and a million other gals,' said Río. 'I told you I'd visited your websites.'

'Brave of you. I don't dare go there.'

'I'll take you by the hand and give you a guided tour some day.'

Río's phone rang.

'Hey!' said Shane. 'Our song!'

Duran Duran's 'Río' was still her ringtone: she hadn't changed it since Finn left. She and Shane had used to play it on his cassette player during the time of their passionate affair. She smiled at him, then glanced at the display. 'Hi, Dervla,' she said.

'Hey, Río. Just to say that Christian left Harbour View this morning.'

'Oh, right. So you want me to turn the place round?'

'There's no hurry. I've no one queueing up to get in there. The season is well and truly over.'

'I might have someone for you. I've just picked up a fare from the airport and he's looking for somewhere to stay.'

'Great. Thanks, Río. I'll see you tomorrow.'

'Tomorrow?'

'We've been invited to Adair's, remember? For lunch.'

'Oh. OK. Shit.'

'What do you mean "shit"?'

'I saw him in town earlier. He has his spooky daughter with him.'

'What's so spooky about her?'

'I dunno. She reminds me of one of the classmates in that film *Heathers*.'

Dervla sighed down the speaker. 'Don't be daft, Río. I'll pick you up tomorrow. One fifty.'

'Yes, Dervla.' Río made a face, and cut the Bluetooth connection.

'Yikes,' said Shane. 'Dervla hasn't changed much.'

'She's actually mellowed, believe it or not.'

'Why didn't you tell her that I'm her new tenant?'

'I – I don't know. I guess I was scared of reopening old wounds.'

'Is she still beautiful?'

'Yes. Very.'

There was a pause, then, 'Do you remember that pastiche of the Yeats poem I made up about the pair of you?' Shane asked.

'Erm . . . no,' lied Río.

'I do. It went like this.

> 'The light of morning, Lissamore,
> Sash windows, open to the south,
> Two girls in silk kimonos, both
> Beautiful, one I adore.'

'You could make a fortune recording poetry for the Yanks,' said Río, trying to sound careless. The recitation in Shane's dark-chocolate voice had been meltingly beautiful. She remembered how she had used to lie in his arms as he recited passages from the play he was working on, the better to fix the lines in his head, and how she would never let him finish because his voice was so sexy she just *had* to kiss him.

'My agent's on my case,' he told her. 'I've already contributed to a couple of anthologies. Anyway – tell me. What's Dervla's place like?'

'Lovely. She's done a terrific job on it. State-of-the-art kitchen, and all.'

Shane gave her a puppy-dog look. 'I guess I'd better stock up on tins of baked beans and frozen pizzas from the corner shop, then. My culinary skills still aren't the best.'

'It's OK, film star. I'll cook for you this evening. As long as you're not expecting Pacific Rim cuisine or whatever's *de rigueur* in LA these days.'

'Thanks. Believe it or not, Irish stew is quite trendy in LA right now. Anything Irish is trendy there. That's probably why I got lucky.'

There was silence for a moment or two as Río negotiated a treacherous bend, then Shane started beating a light tattoo on his knees. 'Who's Adair, Río?' he asked.

'Adair? Oh, he's the millionaire who knocked down Coral Cottage and built a mansion.'

'Coral Cottage, where we made Finn?'

'Yes.'

'And you're having lunch with him tomorrow?'

'Yes. Well, it's more kind of business— Oh, you *wanker*!'

'Jesus, Río, that was close!'

'Yeah, this stretch of the road is chequered with accident black spots, and I bet half the cars using it would never get past their MOT. You'd better let me concentrate on driving.'

Shane pulled the 'recline' lever on his seat and slid his shades back on. 'In that case, I guess I'll just lie back and enjoy the ride.'

'Do you want the radio?' said Río, flicking a switch. On a live music programme, someone was playing the fiddle.

'Oh, no,' said Shane. 'Turn it off. Please.'

'What's wrong?' asked Río.

'That tune,' said Shane. 'It's the theme of *Faraway*. It seems to haunt me wherever I go. There's a bar on Sunset that I can't go into any more because the pianist plays it every time I walk through the door.'

'Well, buster,' said Río, shooting him an amused look, 'didn't I always tell you to be careful what you wished for?'

'I never got what I wished for.'

'Poor Shane! What did you ever wish for apart from fame and fortune?'

'*Ti. Ti ho sempre amato, sciocchina.*'

'What are you on about now?'

'It's an old Latin proverb.'

'What does it— Oh! You stupid fucking *idiot*!' As yet another boy racer did his damnedest to involve them in a multiple pile-up, Río slammed on the brakes. 'Sheesh! How does it feel to be back in the land of saints, scholars and psychopaths?' she asked, smoothing her hair before shifting down a gear.

'Dangerous,' said Shane. 'It feels very, very dangerous indeed. I'm beginning to think that I shouldn't have come home at all.'

Because he was regarding her through the black lenses of his aviators, she couldn't read his expression, so Río just laughed. 'Sounds like a line from your television series,' she said.

Chapter Eighteen

That evening, Dervla got a call from Christian Vaughan.

'Dervla. I'm calling to say thank you so much for everything. For the use of your charming apartment, for your professionalism, and for locating what could very well turn out to be my dream home. You'll be glad to know that I'll have a surveyor on the case very soon.'

'No thanks are necessary,' said Dervla smoothly. 'But it's very courteous of you to call, Christian. How was your journey back to Dublin?'

'It was fine once I hit the motorway. But that road into Galway is a nightmare. All the cars that passed me seemed to be driven by lads swigging out of beer cans and jabbering on their mobile phones.'

'I saw one of those lads the other day,' said Dervla. 'He was wearing a T-shirt that said, "I like my cars fast, my beer cold, and my women hot". My calculated guess was that he wasn't much more than thirteen years old.'

Christian laughed, gratifyingly. Then he said, 'There's something I'd like to ask you, Dervla.'

'Yes?'

'I'm going to be back in Galway next week, on business. A convention of wine importers is being held at the Hamilton

Hotel, and I'd very much like it if you could join me there one evening for dinner.'

Dervla hesitated. And in that moment of hesitation she thought three things. She thought: I am hitting my 'best before' date, and my diary is blank. She thought: There is something about this man that I like very much. And she thought: maybe – just maybe it's time to live life a little more dangerously ... She took a deep breath. 'I don't very often mix business with pleasure, Christian,' she said. 'But I guess there's a first time for everything, and in this instance I'm prepared to make an exception.'

'I am very glad to hear it. Would Monday suit?'

Dervla didn't bother to pretend to check her BlackBerry. She didn't bother to say, 'Well, actually, Tuesday would suit me better.' She decided to throw all those stupid goddamn dating rules and that silly-bugger game-playing out of the window, and instead she just said, 'Yes, thank you. Monday would suit me very well. It's a bank holiday, isn't it?'

'Yes. I decided to drive down from Dublin the evening before the conference begins. What time suits you?'

'What time suits *you*? You're the one doing the driving.'

'Let's say I book a table for seven thirty?'

'Seven thirty is fine.'

'I look forward to seeing you again, Dervla.'

'Likewise, Christian.'

And as Dervla put the phone down, she started to plan in minutest detail what she was going to wear for Christian Vaughan on Bank Holiday Monday evening.

Río was standing in front of her wardrobe, planning what she was going to wear for lunch at Adair Bolger's place tomorrow. The last time they'd visited the Villa Felicity, Dervla had sneered at Río's boho look, and she was damned if she was going to be a target for her sister's criticism again. So she unfurled her smart

236

new dress from its tissue paper nest and teamed it with her new cardigan and her new shoes. Teetering into the bathroom to check herself out in the full-length mirror, her reflection looked back at her with an astonished expression. The effect was one of effortless elegance – especially when she draped the cardigan casually around her shoulders and discarded her ankle chain. To complete the look, she knotted her newly washed hair into a loose chignon, hooked on a pair of pearl earrings (six euro from Claire's Accessories), and squeezed a spot.

She was playing around with the complimentary make-up that had come with her expensive potions earlier, enhancing the fullness of her mouth as per the directions by adding a smudge of gloss to her lower lip, when the doorbell rang.

'Who is it?' she asked through the security phone.

'A murderer,' came the answer.

'Come on up, Shane.' And Río headed for the kitchen to switch on the kettle.

'I really could have been a murderer,' Shane said cheerfully, as he pushed open the door of her flat. 'Remember that film where— Holy moly! What are you wearing?'

'A dress,' said Río, reaching for a packet of tagliatelle.

'Well, yes, I can see that. But it's – it's a kind of grown-up dress.'

'Shane, I *am* a grown-up. I am the mother of a twenty-year-old son.'

'Ach, you know what I mean, Río. It's not *you*.'

'Don't you like it?'

'Well, yes, I do.'

'That's enough, then. I'm going to an important business lunch tomorrow, and I wanted to check that this outfit ticked all the boxes.'

'You want it to tick all the business boxes, yeah? Ergo, you *don't* want to look sexy.'

'God, no.'

237

'Well then, you'd better wear something else, Río, because that dress is sexy.'

'What? Don't be daft, Shane!'

'It's sexy. It's sexy in a classy way – like Grace Kelly.'

Río wandered across to the fridge, trying to think of some witty riposte. None came to her, so, 'I'm just throwing something together from store cupboard staples,' she said. 'Nothing fancy, so you won't have to mind your manners.' Taking a bulb of garlic from the vegetable basket, she set it on the chopping board and selected a knife. 'Peel me a few cloves, will you, Shane? I'm going to get out of these threads before they start to reek of kitchen smells.'

'Where's the corkscrew? I brought some wine.'

'In the top drawer.'

Río kicked off her heels and climbed the captain's ladder to the mezzanine. Here, she hung her smart new clothes in the wardrobe, donned a baggy pair of sweat pants and an oversized surfer dude T-shirt, and took off her earrings.

Back downstairs, Shane was pouring red into two wineglasses. He handed one to her as she crossed into the kitchen.

'Mm,' she said, taking an experimental sip. 'Rioja?'

'What else?' said Shane, with a smile.

An hour and a bit later, Shane was clearing away plates and stacking the dishwasher, and Río was draining her wineglass.

'D'you want coffee?' she asked him.

'No, thanks. Coffee'll just mess up my body clock even more. It hasn't a clue what time it is.'

'If you stay up a little longer you won't suffer so much tomorrow. I know, let's uncork another bottle and do a little surfing.'

'At this hour of the night?' Shane looked dubious. 'I know Lissamore's got some of the best surfing in Europe, but—'

'Not that kind of surfing, you eejit,' said Río, booting up her computer. 'We're gonna check out some websites. Will you open the wine?'

'Sure.' Shane uncorked a second bottle and finished clearing away dishes.

By the time he'd done that, Río, said, 'Da-dah!' and patted the cushion next to her on the sofa. 'Come and have a look at this, film star.'

'What are you up to, Río? You have that minxy look on that used to scare me shitless.'

'It did? Why?'

'Because it meant that you were going to do something insane like surfing – *real* surfing – at midnight, or skinny-dipping in the rain, or making out in somebody's garden.'

'We never made out in anyone's garden!'

'Yes, we did. That's how Finn happened, remember?'

'That was an orchard, not a garden.'

Shane sat down beside her and refilled their glasses. 'What's this?' he asked, looking at the computer screen. '"Introducing . . . Shane Byrne." What the fuck!'

'It's one of your fan sites,' Río told him.

'What? Who dreamed this up? Oh, *Jesus* . . .' Shane clamped his hands over his mouth and his eyes grew wide with horror as Río clicked, and clicked some more. 'Oh, sweet mother of Jesus! See that? That go-see pic is *ancient* – it must be at least twenty years old! And there's me as Hamlet and – oh God – look at that! I was so drunk when that was taken. How did they get their hands on this stuff?'

'I sent all those pix,' said Río. 'I got good money for them.'

'You *what*? You—'

'Joke. *Joke!*' Río interjected, registering Shane's outraged expression. 'I don't have a clue where they got them. You'd have thought they'd have sunk below the radar years ago, wouldn't you? I guess there must be an archive somewhere.' Returning her attention to the screen, she clicked again.

'Hey, what's that pic doing on some random chick's blog? That's not archive.'

'It seems it was taken at Los Angeles airport,' Río told him, scanning the text, 'day before yesterday.'

'*What?* Does this mean I can't go *any*where without somebody papping me with a camera phone?'

'I guess not.'

Shaking his head, Shane gave her a bemused look and said, 'I have only one question. *Why?*'

'It's the price you pay for being famous, you eejit. Get a load of this!'

Río clicked again, and as the strains of Prince's 'Kiss' came over the speakers, a montage of video footage glimmered into view, of Shane sharing screen kisses; Shane slow dancing; Shane tumbling around between tangled sheets with some nubile young thing . . .

'Enough! Enough!' he yelled, clutching his head. 'I can't bear watching this stuff, Río. Knock it off – please, please, knock it off. Let's look at pictures of Finn, instead.'

Río brightened. 'Oh, yes – let's.'

She accessed her photo album, and together they scrolled through the pictures and video clips that Finn had sent her from New Zealand and Australia and Thailand. Some showed their son larking about on a beach or a boat; some showed him underwater against a shimmering background of jewel-coloured coral; some showed him relaxing with his mate Carl in a variety of palm-thatched bars. In nearly all the photographs, a different girl featured.

'He's a good-looking kid,' Shane remarked.

'He takes after his daddy,' said Río, generously.

'Ah, but he has your beautiful soul. And wicked eyes.'

They smiled drunkenly at each other and gazed some more upon the vision that was their son, until Shane's head flopped onto Río's shoulder. It felt comfortable, the weight of him there, and she automatically reached up a hand to smooth his hair. How many women the world over would kill to be her now! To be curled up on a sofa with Seth Fletcher falling asleep in her arms! But he could never be Seth Fletcher to her. To her he would always be plain Shane Byrne.

'Time for bed, Mr Sharkey,' she said.

'Mm. Can't we just snuggle down here?' he said, with a yawn.

'No, we can not. Come with me.'

Río pulled Shane to his feet, led the way down to his apartment, took off his boots and tucked him into bed. And then she kissed him on the forehead and whispered, 'Night, night,' and climbed the stairs back to her own place.

And all that night, her dreams were fabulously full of Finn.

Shane rang the doorbell again, just before midday the next day.

Río let him in, then moved into the kitchen and reached for the cafetière. 'How did you sleep?' she asked, as he shambled into her apartment.

'I slept well, thanks. That bed's very comfortable. But my circadian rhythms are still syncopated, big time.'

'Do you still take milk and sugar?' Río asked, pouring coffee into a mug.

'No. I take my coffee black now. I have to. The camera adds four kilos.'

'So you suffer for your art?'

'To hell with art. It's my career I have to think about. The money men aren't going to keep me on if I turn into Mr Blobby.'

'What are your plans for the day?' she asked.

'I thought we might take a walk along a beach.'

'You forget I have a lunch to go to.'

'Bummer. Then I'll take a walk along a beach all by myself. Can I buy you dinner tonight?'

'In O'Toole's?'

'Yeah.'

'I thought that, being a fugitive from the paparazzi, you wouldn't want to show your face anywhere.'

'There won't be any paparazzi in O'Toole's.'

'There'll be people with camera phones.'

'Yeah, but they'll be locals, mostly, won't they? Lissamore folk are too cool to be bothered to take photographs of arriviste television stars like me.'

It was true. Stars of stage and screen turned up in Lissamore on a regular basis, trying, like Shane, to escape the stress of city life. Bono had strolled into a local pub once, and nobody had batted an eyelid apart from a drunk who had greeted him with, 'Found what ye're lookin' for yet, Bonio?'

'Remind me what time you're going out,' Shane said.

'Dervla's picking me up around two. But don't feel you have to scarper. You could have lunch on the balcony, if you like.'

'Thanks. Lunch on the balcony sounds good. I could do with a blast of sea air.'

'Just remember to leave the door on the latch, if you're coming and going between the apartments.'

'Aren't you worried about security?'

'In Lissamore? Are you mad? Every second front door in the village is left on the latch.'

The faint strains of Duran Duran sounded from somewhere, and Shane cocked an ear. 'There's your phone,' he said.

'Bugger! The damn thing always ends up some place I can never find it.'

Río located the ringing phone under a cushion on the sofa and her face lit up when she saw the number on the display. 'Finn!' she said into the receiver. 'What a coincidence! We were just talking about you last night.'

'We?'

'Your dad and me. He's here in Lissamore, far from the madding crowd.'

'Hey!' said Finn. 'In that case we'll be a family again real soon.'

'We will?'

'Yes. I'm at Heathrow. I'm flying in to Galway tonight.'

'What? What are you doing at Heathrow, Finn?'

'Didn't you get my email?'

'No. I haven't looked at my mail since yesterday.'

'Well, check it out, Ma. I can't talk for long because my phone's nearly out of juice.'

'But – hang on a sec, Finn! Are you really coming home tonight?'

'Yeah, yeah.'

'That's so fantastic! What time'll I pick you up?'

'There's no need, Ma. Carl's dad's gonna collect us. We should be in Lissamore by around nine o'clock.'

'OK. Oh God – this is *fantastic* news! But, Finn, everything's all right, is it? You haven't had an accident or anything?'

'No, Ma, my phone's about to go. Check your inbox. There should—'

And Finn's phone went dead.

'That was Finn?' asked Shane, looking up from the bread he was slicing.

Río turned shining eyes on him. 'Yes, he's on his way home!'

'What? I thought he wasn't coming home until after Christmas.'

'That was the original plan, but something's happened. He said he'd sent an email.' Reaching for the laptop on the coffee table, Río booted it up, and steeled herself as she heard the sluggish drone that announced that the machine was emerging from hibernation. 'Agh! This dozy thing is going to take for ever,' she said. 'Dammit, why didn't I check my mail last night instead of waltzing around your stupid fan sites?'

Shane stretched, then wandered over to the French windows, munching on a hunk of baguette. 'That morning sun smacks you right between the eyes,' he said, sliding back the glass panel and stepping onto the balcony. 'Hey. This is a swell spot for being a nosy neighbour, isn't it?'

'Mm,' replied Río abstractedly, willing her laptop to lumber into life.

A low whistle came from the balcony. 'Wow,' said Shane. 'Who's the hottie?'

'What hottie?'

'The toothsome chick who's just come out of Fleur's shop.'

Río scampered across to the balcony and peered over the balustrade. 'Oh, *her*!' she said dismissively. 'That's Isabella Bolger, Adair's daughter. She's the most stuck-up little princess on the planet.'

'Hm.' Shane's eyes narrowed in appreciation.

'Stop that, Shane! She's young enough to be your daughter.'

'So are most of my co-stars,' said Shane. 'Once a gal hits twenty-four in LA she's past it.'

'Oh, yeah?' said Río indignantly. 'What about the Wisteria Lane ladies? What about Carrie and co?'

'They spend a fortune to keep themselves looking like that, Río. They're just commodities, like me. It's all to do with smoke and mirrors.' He nodded towards Isabella on the street below. 'She's the real thing.'

For some reason, Río felt miffed by this remark. She flounced back to the coffee table, where her laptop was finally beginning to show signs of life.

Amongst the spam in her inbox – Legendary Tales of Your Sausage; Put More Flesh on Your Pole; Erotic Maidens in Costume – was a message from Finn: 'Subject: Coming Home'.

Hugging herself with delight, Río clicked, and the following appeared.

Hey – Ma. d'you want the good news or the bad news? the good news is that I'm on my way home. I'm typing this in an internet cafe in bangkok. the bad news is that I have to come because Carl broke his leg and can't travel alone – well not without a lot of difficulty, and another reason is that i've run out of money. I haven't been flaithiulach, honest. i decided in the end that rather than carry on travelling i'd do my instructor training in Tao and you know it costs a LOT of money plus the gear but not half as much as i'd have had to fork out for it if i'd done it in Ireland. so here I am coming home a FULLY CERTIFIED DIVE INSTRUCTOR!!!!!!!!!! i'll fone from Heathrow.

    your loving son, the DIVE INSTRUCTOR Finn
    XXXXXXXXXXXXXXXXXXXXXXXXX

'Wow. He's certified.'

'Hm?'

'Your son has certified as—' Looking over at Shane, Río was aware that he was still mesmerised by Isabella Bolger on the street below. 'Hello? *Hello!* Earth calling Shane Byrne.'

'Yeah? What do you want?' he replied absently.

'I'll only tell you if you can manage to tear your eyes away from princess posh.'

'Sorry.' Shane ambled back into the sitting room. 'What's happened?'

'Your son has certified as a scuba-dive instructor.'

'No shit! No *shit!*' Shane's face spread into a broad grin. '*Wow!* Do you know what kind of respect those guys are held in, Río? They are the coolest dudes on the face of the planet! They're – they're courageous, they're Zen, they're tough, they're fit, they're laid-back, they're – um – cool . . .'

'Yes. You've already said that. I get your gist.'

'No *shit!*' Shane punched the air, then looked a bit sheepish when he realised how uncool *he* looked. 'Wow. This has made me one very proud parent. When's he due back?'

'This evening, around nine o'clock. Carl's dad is picking them up in Galway.'

'Then he can join us in O'Toole's. I'll ask them to put champagne on ice. Good idea, yeah, Río? Río?'

'Sorry?'

'Hey! What has you looking so pensive, mavourneen? Don't you feel like celebrating?'

'Yeah – yeah, of course. I was just wondering ... um ... whether Finn would want to crash here or in Carl's.'

'He can crash downstairs with me. My roomie – my main man – the dive god!'

'Good idea. I'll make up another bed.' Río got to her feet and stood looking undecided for a moment. 'But first I'd better go and get ready,' she said. 'Dervla'll be beeping her horn any minute, badgering me to get a move on.'

'Shoo, then,' said Shane. 'Can I read Finn's email?'

'Be my guest.'

Upstairs in the mezzanine Río got into her new outfit, hooked on her earrings and twisted her hair into a chignon with mechanical hands. This was good! This was all good news. But one thought kept tugging at her. She knew that job opportunities for dive instructors in Ireland were scarce. However, the scuba journals that Finn used to leave around the house were full of vacancies for English-speaking instructors in countries as far flung as Vietnam, Egypt and Russia. If Finn was going to get work in his chosen profession, he was going to have to look for it further afield. He was going to have to look for it a world away, on another continent.

Chapter Nineteen

Izzy had prepared lunch with the help of the *Avoca Café Cookbook*. On the glass-topped dining-room table in the Villa Felicity she had laid out platters of grilled vegetables, buffalo mozzarella, prosciutto, artichoke hearts, figs and a selection of salamis. She had opened red Bordeaux and left it to breathe, and she had chilled white Burgundy to the correct temperature. She had set four places with gleaming Newbridge silverware and John Rocha glassware. She had arranged flowers in a centrepiece (actually, they had been arranged for her the previous day in Galway), and she had put together an exotic fruit salad. (That too had been put together for her. Izzy had no qualms at all about cheating when it came to things culinary.)

In effect, Izzy had thrown down a gauntlet. She was sending out a message to her lunch guests that said, 'Try competing with that, gals! Nobody can look after my daddy better than *I* can!'

It had worked. Throughout the course of the afternoon, Izzy had played a blinder as the consummate hostess, refilling glasses, passing around dishes, offering second helpings, clearing away plates, and brewing coffee. Any time she shimmied off into the kitchen, she took care to keep within earshot of the conversation, which was – it had to be said – pretty unilluminating. The awful Río woman seemed a bit subdued – probably because she hadn't partaken of Slow Comfortable Screws Up Against the Wall this time – and Dervla and Adair were all business. After coffee, the sisters took themselves off to do a recce of the house and take photographs while Adair returned all the calls that had come in while his phone had been switched off during lunch.

Izzy loaded the dishwasher, and helped herself to another glass of wine. Hardly anyone had touched the stuff during lunch. Izzy had hoped that that dipsomaniac Río might have got drunk and made a few good gaffes, but any time Izzy had tried to force wine on her, the woman had put her hand over her glass and said, 'No more for me, thank you,' as if she were a model of abstinence. Izzy guessed that she was on her best behaviour now that the Villa Felicity was on her sister's books. Dervla had said something about how Río's flair for 'staging' had helped sell properties that might otherwise have lingered on the market, and Izzy had felt indignant. Even though Izzy hated it, she knew the Villa Felicity was easily the most stylish residence in Coolnamara.

Swigging back wine, Izzy wandered outside and took the path up to the yoga pavilion. The pavilion was looking a bit sorry for itself. In fact, the whole garden was looking sorry for itself, she saw now. She hadn't been able to check it out last night because their priority had been to get the house aired and beds made, but today the sun shone on woefully unkempt flowerbeds and overgrown lawns, and trees that looked like the Whomping Willow in *Harry Potter*. Ms Río Kinsella would have her work cut out.

The sound of feet crunching on the shingle below made Izzy look down. A man was walking along the beach. He was dressed in black, hands thrust deep into the pockets of his leather jacket. When he reached the Greensward – which was now as sadly neglected as the rest of the garden – he paused and looked around. Izzy set down her glass and, doubling over, guerrilla fashion, so that she could not be seen, skittered towards the sea wall. A section of the masonry had been undermined by the roots of bramble bushes, and what had crumbled away provided a niche in which she could curl herself up and observe, unobserved.

The man remained motionless for some time, watching a cormorant dip in and out of the waves, and then he turned and looked up at the walls of the Villa Felicity. When Izzy saw his face, she nearly fell out of her niche. It was the star of that new television series *Faraway*! She had seen his picture just last week, in her father's *GQ* magazine. What was his name? Shane something. And then Izzy remembered that the article had mentioned that he hailed from Galway. So here he was, probably back on a sentimental journey to the auld sod! How *intriguing*!

As his eyes scanned the sea wall, Izzy froze. But his gaze passed over her hiding place and continued on until it came to rest upon the old orchard gate. People seldom used this gate now, and because it was hidden behind a curtain of some droopy green stuff, nobody who wasn't a local would even guess that it was there. But Shane – Shane Byrne – that was his name she remembered now! – moved directly towards it, laid a hand on the latch, and pushed. The gate didn't give, nor did it budge when he pushed it a second time, more forcefully. And then Izzy watched in astonishment as he set both his hands on the topmost bar, and vaulted the five bars easily. He was standing in her garden now. He was standing in the garden of the Villa Felicity, looking as if – looking as if he owned the place!

Izzy shrank back further as he gazed around proprietorially, but then he turned his back on her and proceeded along a rabbit trail that meandered through the orchard. There he stopped under an ancient, gnarled apple tree and raised his face to the sky, and Izzy saw a beatific smile curve his mouth, heard his voice mutter some kind of incantation. He was singing something – Izzy strained harder to hear – something about a bird of paradise dancing on the sand. Oh shit. Was this man completely barmy? Should she make a run for it back to the house, and alert her father to the fact that there was a mad film star trespassing in their garden?

But then Shane Byrne stopped singing, and stood again looking out to sea, and Izzy saw that this time there was something nostalgic in his expression. Oh, how she wished she had her phone with her to record the moment! Lucy would never in a million years believe that one of the sexiest men in the world had vaulted a gate into *her* garden!

Now Shane was on the move again, swinging back over the gate, striding along the shingle the way he had come. His phone was in his hand, and she heard him say, as he passed directly beneath her, 'Hey, it's me, Shane, leaving a message at around four o'clock. Just to say I visited our orchard. Did you know the apple tree's still there? I felt I should have done something that might have lent the moment significance – you know, said thanks to whoever's up there for bestowing such a cool kid on us. But instead I just looked up at the sky and sang your song. I reckon that was enough. Don't you?'

And Izzy watched as Shane Byrne slid his phone back in his pocket and disappeared around the headland.

Río felt lacklustre. Isabella Bolger had made her feel even more woefully inadequate than she had done last time they'd met. The lunch that she claimed to have 'thrown together' had looked like something you'd see in the pages of a foodie magazine. She had been an impressively attentive hostess – in fact, Río had decided that there was something almost intimidating about the way Isabella had hovered over her guests, refilling glasses and offering second helpings. Any time Río entertained, the affair was a kind of scrum, with guests helping themselves to food and drink amid much shouting and laughing and telling of jokes, and often – at the end of the evening – rambunctious singing. Río wondered what would happen if she volunteered to sing her favourite Björk ditty as Isabella passed around the porcelain coffee cups.

She also knew that she'd made a big mistake in wearing her new black dress, and the heels she could hardly walk in. She felt like a female impersonator – and not a very good one, at that. Everyone else was wearing smart/casual, while Río wouldn't have looked out of place at a nobby cocktail party. She was also out of her league when it came to most of the topics under discussion. Dervla, she knew, was an expert on practically every subject under the sun. She had made it her business to bone up on politics and sport and books and music because it meant that she could hold her own in any social setting. Her sister should go on *Mastermind*, Río conjectured; she'd be genius at General Knowledge, with her specialist subject being, of course, the property market.

'Río? Are you all right?'

It was Dervla's voice.

'Yes. Yes, I'm fine thanks. I – I just have a bit of a headache.'

'Maybe we should go,' said Dervla. 'Heavens! It's after four.'

'Are you sure you wouldn't like some more coffee?' said Adair.

'No, thanks very much, Adair. They say that if you want to get a decent night's sleep you shouldn't drink coffee after four o'clock in the afternoon. Although I can't say I'm not tempted. That was exceptionally good coffee. Jamaican Blue Mountain, if I'm not mistaken?'

'You'd have to ask Izzy that. Izzy! Izzy?'

There was no reply from the kitchen.

'I saw her go out into the garden earlier,' said Río. 'And by the way, Dervla, Jamaican Blue Mountain has been bested by that Indonesian stuff that comes out of cat poo.'

'I must add that to my list of fascinating trivia,' said Dervla crisply, draping her taupe cashmere cardigan around her shoulders. 'Thanks so much, Adair, for a most enjoyable lunch. And please say thank you also to Isabella. She made it all seem so effortless!'

'Her mother taught her well. Can you believe that at one stage Felicity was considering sending Izzy to Le Rosey?'

'The finishing school in Switzerland?' queried Dervla.

'Yes. But Izzy quite correctly pointed out that she wouldn't learn anything at Le Rosey that her mother hadn't already taught her. Actually, I think it was just the little minx's way of getting out of going!'

Dervla laughed politely, and Río felt obliged to join in. Ha-ha-ha! What a clever little refusnik that Izzy was!

As they moved into the atrium, Adair said, 'Oh, hang on, Dervla. I'd better let you have a key to the house. And you'll need one too, of course, Río.' He dived into the study, and emerged with two large envelopes, which he handed to Río and Dervla respectively. 'There are keys in each of those, as well as instructions on how to operate the security system, and any other details you might need to know. It's all pretty straightforward, I think, but if you need any more info, please don't hesitate to get in touch. All my contact details are in there.'

'Thanks, Adair,' said Dervla. 'I'll get the copy for the brochure off to you a.s.a.p. I'll need your appro on it, and the photographs too, of course.'

At the door, the air-kissing ritual was observed. Río would have preferred to have shaken hands, but the more formal option was hardly valid after Adair had kissed her sister robustly on both cheeks. As he brushed the side of her face with his, Río was aware of his scent – the citrusy notes that were, presumably, the signature ingredients of Acqua di Parma.

He had just taken a step back from her when Isabella danced into the hall, swinging a carrier bag by its silken handles. 'Don't forget your underwear, Río!' she said chirpily. 'I wouldn't want you disappearing without it *again*!'

'Oh, thanks.' Río took the glossy carrier bag from her sweetly smiling hostess. 'Clever of you to remember. I – um – I don't have any cash on me right now. But I'll send a cheque, if that's all right?'

'Sure. Send it care of Daddy.'

With a little wave of farewell and an odd look at Río, Dervla passed under the *porte-cochère* to where her car was parked, and zapped the locks.

'What was *that* about?' she asked, as Río clambered into the passenger seat, longing to kick off her shoes.

'Oh, it's too boring to go into. I told you that I met Adair and Izzy while I was shopping, yesterday? Well, he helped me out when my credit card started giving me grief because otherwise I would have been way late for my airport fare.'

'Oh. I meant to ask you who your fare was, by the way. Presumably that's the tenant you've ensconced in Harbour View?'

'Yes. It's Shane.'

'*Shane?*' Dervla looked at her in astonishment. 'Not Shane Byrne?'

'Yes. He's come back to Ireland on a kind of sentimental journey.'

'Really? Why didn't you tell me?'

'I did try to earlier, when we were on our way to lunch, but you were rabbiting away so much on your hands-free that I didn't get a chance.'

'So Shane is staying in my holiday let?'

'Yes. You – you don't mind, do you, Dervla?'

'Mind? No. Why should I mind? I imagine his money is as good as anybody else's.'

'Better, probably.' And Río filled her sister in on Shane's recent success.

'Hm. That's interesting to know,' said Dervla. 'So your ex is now a man of some wealth and influence? I'll have to get him to sign my visitors' book.'

'Guess who else'll be staying, Dervla – Finn!' And Río filled Dervla in on even more recent developments.

'What fun!' remarked Dervla, as the car pulled up outside Harbour View. 'The three of you can play at being happy families together.'

'Play? We *are* a happy family. Not a particularly orthodox one, admittedly.' As Río opened the passenger door, her sister's phone rang.

'Bye, Río. Talk soon,' said Dervla, blowing her a kiss. Río saw her check out caller ID, and then, just as she went to close the passenger door, she heard her say, 'Hello, Christian.'

Christian? It had to be Christian Vaughan. What was he doing, phoning Dervla out of office hours? Sly-puss Dervla! She remembered the body language that had gone on between the two of them outside Harbour View on the evening Dervla had come to dinner, and wondered if things might have progressed since then.

Rummaging in her handbag for her key, Río let herself in. Upstairs, Shane was fast asleep on her sofa. She set her carrier bag down on the coffee table, and headed towards the kitchen. The sound of a cupboard door being opened didn't rouse Shane, but the sound of a cork being popped did.

'Gah,' he said, shaking himself awake. 'Jet lag sucks. What are you doing, Río, opening wine at this untimely hour of the afternoon? Or is it past six already?'

'I want to allow it to breathe,' Río told him. 'I thought that I'd do a home-cooked dinner for the three of us this evening, and then we can book a table in O'Toole's for tomorrow night instead.'

'Sounds good – so long as you don't mind going to the bother of cooking.'

'It'll be no bother at all,' said Río. 'There's home-made cottage pie in the freezer. Finn's favourite.' She smiled to herself and started humming 'Lullaby of Broadway', something she'd used to sing to Finn when he was little. 'What did you get up to this afternoon?' she asked Shane.

'What did I get up to?' said Shane, drowsily. 'I tried on your clothes and read your private email.'

'Yeah? What did you think of the mail?' asked Río, reaching for a jar of teabags.

'That's what sent me to sleep. God, you have a dull life, Río.'

'I'm very glad you think so. You clearly didn't access the encrypted files to do with my double life as an undercover agent.'

'For whom?'

'Ann Summers. D'you want a cup of tea?'

'Yes, please. I'd love one.'

Shane reached for the carrier bag on the coffee table and looked inside. 'Hello? What's this? Are you *really* an Ann Summers agent?'

'Excuse me!' said Río with hauteur. 'That stuff is *way* classier than Ann Summers.'

Shane looked uncertain. 'So, did you go shopping today as well as have lunch?'

'No. That was just some stuff I'd left behind.'

'Left behind where? At the Villa Felicity?'

'Well, no. Well, yes. Oh, it's too complicated to go into.' Río filled the kettle and switched it on, then moved to the cupboard to fetch mugs. One of them bore the legend 'I ♥ MUM'. It had been a present from Finn for her thirtieth birthday. The other mug had the Celtic logo on it, and was chipped. Río imagined serving builder's tea in mugs to Isabella Bolger, and found herself laughing.

'What's so funny?' asked Shane.

'Oh, nothing really. I'm just comparing the perfection of the Bolger household to my slum.'

'It's not a slum, Río,' Shane told her. 'It's a real home. LA is full of soulless palaces – the kind you'd see on *Second Life*. You've got yourself a very cosy little nest here.'

'I guess I have, and I'm grateful for it, really. I just wish I had a garden.' She handed Shane the Celtic mug. 'Still, I guess gardening by proxy's the next best thing. I can't wait to get my hands on the garden of Coral Mansion.'

'You're doing Adair Bolger's garden for him?'

'Yes. I'm getting the house ready to go on the market.'

'He's selling up?'

'Yep.'

Shane gave her an interested look. 'I was there this afternoon.'

'Where?'

'Coral Mansion. Didn't you get my voice mail?'

'No.'

'Have a listen.'

Río retrieved her phone from her bag, and accessed her mail box. When she'd finished listening to the message, she looked at Shane and smiled. 'So while I was sitting in Coral Mansion having lunch, you were standing singing in the orchard?'

'Yeah.'

'How did you get in?'

'I vaulted the old gate.'

'Yikes. Just as well Miss Isabella didn't see you. She'd have had the law on to you before you could have said son-of-a-gun.'

'I wonder what old Bolger would do if he knew we used to make out under his apple tree?'

'Less of the old, Shane. Adair Bolger can't be that much longer in the tooth than you.'

'Hm.' Shane took a thoughtful sip of tea.

'What are you thinking?' asked Río.

'I'm thinking that the next time I trespass, I should change my tune. Maybe instead of singing Duran Duran, I should sing the old Glenn Miller classic.'

'Which one?'

'"Don't Sit Under the Apple Tree (With Anyone Else but Me)",' said Shane.

'Sit?'

'Oh, all right. Make out.'

'We didn't just make out,' she told him with a smile. 'We made Finn.'

Later that evening, Dervla picked up the phone to Río.

'Hi,' she said. 'Just to say that I've Jpegged the pics of the Villa

Felicity to you. The interior shots are all fine, but I don't want to put any of the garden ones up on the website until you've appro-ed them.'

'OK. I'll have a look in the morning.'

'Has Finn arrived yet?'

'No. He should be here any minute. Oh, by the way, Dervla, we've booked a table in O'Toole's for dinner tomorrow night. Would you like to join us?'

Dervla hesitated. 'By "us", I presume you mean you, Finn and Shane?'

'Yes.'

'Hell, why not? It would be an experience to have dinner with a real live movie star – even if he is only Shane. What time?'

'Eight o'clock.'

'I'll see you there.'

Dervla put down the phone, picked up her glass of chilled Sancerre, and moseyed onto the roof terrace that overlooked Galway city. The notion of seeing Shane again after all these years intrigued her. How people changed! She had been so gauche, so naïve, so *young*! After Shane, Dervla had grown up very fast. Having had her heart broken at such a tender age, she had taken to wearing a tough emotional armour, and had never allowed herself to fall in love since. Unless you could describe as love the feelings she harboured for the Old Rectory . . .

Below her, the streets were teeming with people on their way to pubs and clubs and cinemas. The sky was darkening, but instead of that rich, dark, velvety blue that would now be descending over Coolnamara, a jaundiced night sky was draped slackly over the cityscape. Instead of the call of curlews, the sound that rose up to Dervla's twelfth-storey penthouse was a cacophony of traffic.

Leaning her elbows on the balustrade, Dervla allowed her mind to go back over the events of the day. It was a real feather in her cap to have acquired Adair Bolger as a client, she knew.

However, upon recceing the Villa Felicity a second time, she was even more uncomfortably aware that the property might not prove easy to shift. She had asked Río for her thoughts, but Río had been uncharacteristically glum, saying that the place had about it all the hallmarks of an aesthetic that was alien to her. Well, those weren't her exact words. She had actually said that Coral Mansion (as she insisted on calling it) had been so self-consciously designed that it had disappeared up its own arse, and there was nothing Río could do to make the house feel like a home that any sane person would want to live in. There was absolutely no point in her bringing any of her vision to bear on the interior, she insisted, and her remit could go no further than the garden.

Dervla wondered now if it hadn't been a mistake to offer to sell the Villa Felicity for Adair. She already had several overpriced properties on her books, some of which had not attracted a single viewer. Celtic Tiger Ireland had lost all its teeth and been declawed and was moulting like something diseased. Every day she heard rumours of other estate agents downsizing or going under or suffering nervous breakdowns. Just how was Dervla going to get through the recession that was forecast to run for at least another eighteen months?

Christian had come up with an interesting idea today. He had phoned to say that he had been singing her praises to a friend of his who worked in publishing, and his friend had asked if Dervla might be interested in writing a book. 'Don't knock it!' Christian told her, when she'd laughed at the idea. 'Everyone wants to know how to go about making their property saleable. If you pitch an idea to a publisher, you could win yourself a book deal.'

So, since this afternoon, Dervla had been thinking about it. It wasn't the first time that she'd been approached about writing something on the Irish property market. An editor of one of the major property supplements had asked her, at the height of the boom, whether she'd be interested in penning a weekly column for him, but at that time Dervla had been just too busy. Now she'd have given anything to be able to while away the time waiting for no-shows by jotting down ideas for newspaper articles.

Dervla eased into a stretch, took another sip of Sancerre and headed back inside, where her laptop with its Taj Mahal screensaver was shimmering on the breakfast counter. Setting her glass down and going to 'My Documents', she opened a file and stared at the screen for a minute or two, rallying her thoughts. Then she typed in: '*Selling Your Home – What Every First-Timer Needs to Know*', and pressed 'Save'. 'Save To?' the computer prompted her. And instead of automatically saving the file to her documents, Dervla clicked again and opened a brand-new folder upon which she bestowed the moniker 'My Bestseller'.

Chapter Twenty

Izzy was sitting on the sea wall, where she had joined the only friend she had in Lissamore, Babette, the bichon frise. She was filling the dog in on where she'd been on her holidays, and lamenting the fact that she'd ended up in hospital in Koh Samui after stepping on a shard of broken beer bottle in Tao, when she became aware that someone was standing too close to her, looking directly at her. Immediately on the defensive, thinking it might be one of those horrible local boys who had jeered at her at Frank Kinsella's wake, Izzy looked up with a supercilious expression.

'Hi,' said Finn. 'Why are you looking so cross?'

'I'm not cross. I'm – um – thinking.'

'Thinking about what?'

'About what I'm going to have for dinner this evening. I'm meeting my dad in O'Toole's in half an hour.'

'What a coincidence. So am I. Eating there, obviously,' he amended, 'not meeting your dad.' Sitting down beside Izzy, he reached over and scratched Babette under her chin, making her close her eyes and smile ecstatically. 'Hello, Flirty-Paws,' he crooned. 'Have you missed me, Babushka?'

'You've been away?' Izzy asked.

'Yep. Just got back yesterday.'

'Where were you?'

'New Zealand, Australia, Thailand. Where did you end up? I remember last time we met, you told me you were going travelling later in the year.'

Izzy was just about to tell a lie about not having been away anywhere, when she remembered that her dad had already told the Kinsella sisters that they'd taken a holiday to Thailand together; what would happen if Río twittered about it to Finn? So she took a deep breath, and said with affected casualness: 'Oh, I was in Thailand too.'

'No shit! Where?'

'Koh Samui.'

'Just south of me. I spent most of the summer on Tao.'

'Nice.'

'Very nice. Do you dive?'

'Yes.'

'To what level?'

'Master scuba-diver.'

'I'm impressed.'

For form's sake, the question had to be reciprocated. 'You – erm – you dive too, do you?' asked Izzy, feeling ridiculous.

'Yes. I'm a master instructor.'

'Oh! So you certified while you were over there? Congratulations!'

'How did you know that?' asked Finn, looking puzzled.

Izzy thought fast. 'Er – Mrs Ryan in the corner shop told me,' she lied.

'Oh God. I suppose my ma has been blabbing her mouth off all over the village about it. Even the dogs in the street will know by now. Did you know, Babushka? Did you know that Finn was now officially a fish?' And taking both of Babette's little ears between his hands, he started to tickle them, whereupon the dog looked as though she might swoon with rapture. 'If you were in Samui, it would have made sense to get your arse up to Tao,' resumed Finn, as Izzy cast around wildly for some way of changing the subject. 'I actually had a close encounter with a

261

whale shark there – even got a photograph to prove it. Some of the best diving in Asia is off—'

'Oh, look!' said Izzy, abruptly. 'There's that film star. I *thought* I saw him on the beach earlier! I wonder what he's doing in Lissamore.'

Shane Byrne had just come out of Ryan's corner shop, and was standing shooting the breeze with one of the village elders.

Finn tore his attention away from Babette's ears. 'Oh,' he said, dismissively. '*That* arsehole. Shane Somebody or other.'

'Shane Byrne. There's a feature about him in this month's *GQ* magazine. Do you really think he's an arsehole?'

'Anybody who features in *GQ* magazine has to be an arsehole. He's in some new television series, isn't he?'

'Yes. It's called *Faraway*. I've seen a couple of podcasts, and he's actually very good.'

'Why don't you take a photograph of him?'

Izzy shrugged. 'I wish I could. I left my phone in Dad's car.'

'I'll take one for you, if you like.'

'Oh, would you? I'd love that! My mate Lucy'll be *so* jealous. She got a picture of herself standing next to Johnny Depp once.'

'Hm.' Finn gave her a speculative look. 'How about if you go one better?'

'What do you mean?'

'How about if you get a picture of Shane Whatshisname with his arm around you? I'll ask him for you if you feel too shy.'

'You wouldn't! Would you?'

'Sure. But it'll cost you. How much would you be prepared to pay for a picture of you in a clinch with this Shane Thingy?'

'Um. Say – five euro?' hazarded Izzy. Five euros would be worth it to see the expression on Lucy's face.

'Ten.'

'Seven fifty.'

'OK,' Finn conceded with a shrug. 'It's a deal. How about if I ask him for an autograph, too? How much would that be worth?'

'Um. Another five?'

Finn gave her a scornful look. 'Get real, princess! Have you any idea how much autographs go for on eBay these days? You could double that, no problem.'

'OK, then. How about twenty, all in?'

'Done deal. Show me the money.'

Izzy reached into her bag and produced her wallet. Sliding a crisp twenty-euro note from it, she handed it to Finn.

'Thanks, Isabella,' he said, grinning at her and getting to his feet. Then he put his fingers to his lips and blew. The whistle could have stopped traffic. A couple of women gossiping on a doorstep broke off mid-sentence and Shane Byrne looked up from his conversation and raised an interrogative eyebrow.

'Hey, Dad!' hollered Finn. 'There's someone here I'd like you to meet.'

As Shane began to stroll down the street towards them, Izzy turned to Finn and gave him an incredulous look. 'Is this some kind of joke?' she asked.

'No. He really is my dad,' said Finn.

'What? You're telling me that an überdude like him just happens to be—' And then Izzy remembered how Finn had signed her logbook in Tao: 'Finn Byrne'. She clamped her hands over her mouth. 'Oh. Oh God. This is totally embarrassing.'

'What's so embarrassing about it?'

'I don't know. The fact that he's your dad is – it just makes things different. It makes me feel like even more of a tool.'

'I wouldn't worry. The novelty of being an overnight success hasn't worn off yet. Sure, he'd love to have his photograph taken with a fox like you.'

There was no time for further protest. Shane was within earshot.

The film star greeted his son with a mock punch on the arm and a 'Hey, Finn,' before turning his attention to Izzy. She felt herself blushing as he looked down at her and said with a smile, 'Introduce me.'

263

'Dad, this is Isabella Bolger—'

'Izzy,' said Izzy.

'Izzy,' amended Finn. 'And this is my father, Shane Byrne.'

'Pleased to meet you, Izzy,' said Shane.

'Likewise.'

'Izzy was hoping to get a picture taken with you, Dad,' said Finn.

'What? No, I wasn't!' The 'Hello?' look that Finn bestowed upon her obliged Izzy to backtrack fast. 'I mean, I certainly didn't mean to intrude or cause you any inconvenience . . .'

'What's inconvenient about posing with a pretty girl?' asked Shane. 'Fire ahead, Finn. Where do you want us?'

'Against the sea wall would be good,' said Finn, taking his phone from his pocket.

'Like this?' Shane slung his right arm around Izzy's shoulders.

'Yeah. That's good.' Finn took aim. 'Smile, Izzy!'

Izzy forced a rictus smile as Finn happy-snapped away. 'Good, good, *good*!' he exclaimed. 'Hey, Dad, you've become a real pro at this. Izzy, d'you think you could look a bit more relaxed? Put your arm around Dad, or lay your head on his shoulder or something.'

Izzy cocked her head and smiled some more, hoping she looked carefree and spontaneous, and feeling like a klutz. As soon as Finn lowered his phone, she took a step backwards and said: 'Thank you very much, Mr Byrne.'

'Shane!'

'Shane.'

Izzy practically genuflected in gratitude, and made to move away, but Finn stopped her in her tracks: 'Hey! You've forgotten the autograph.'

'Oh, it doesn't matter,' said Izzy, wishing she'd never made the stupid deal with Finn. 'I don't want to take up any more of your time—'

'I'm a man of my word,' said Finn, rummaging in his jacket

pocket and pulling out a crumpled flyer. 'You paid me good money for an autograph, and an autograph you shall have. Here, Dad. Sign that.'

Shane produced a pen and was just about to sign, when Finn snatched back the flyer and said, 'No, wait. I've a better idea. Hang on a minute.' And he tore off up the main street, leaving Shane and Izzy looking at one another.

'What did he mean, you paid him good money? I hope the little shyster hasn't been fleecing all and sundry by promising them autographs?'

'Oh, I'm sure he wouldn't do that!'

'I'm sure he would,' said Shane.

A passing tour bus rumbled past, and Shane saluted the passengers, who were all plastered up against the windows, gawping at him.

'You could become a tourist attraction. Do you come from Lissamore originally, Shane?' Izzy asked, seguing smoothly onto another subject.

'No. I was born and reared in Galway. But I used to spend a lot of time hanging around here in my misspent youth. You're from Dublin, right? Do you come down a lot?'

'No. My dad would love to spend more time here, but it isn't really feasible.'

'I understand he's thinking of selling up?'

'How – how did you know that?'

'Finn's mother told me. You know each other, I think. Río Kinsella.'

'Oh, yes. She and her sister had lunch with us yesterday.'

So. Río Kinsella was in all likelihood spreading the news round the village right now that the Villa Felicity was up for grabs at a bargain price, and that the garden was a shambles. And there Río was now, wafting into Ryan's corner shop in her hippy threads, arm in arm with Fleur, doubtless looking forward to a good old yak. And then – yikes! – Izzy remembered that she had told Finn earlier that the corner shop was where she'd heard about his certification, and – oh double yikes! – what if the shop-keeper *didn't* know about it, and was just now hearing the news from the horse's mouth, a.k.a. Río? And what if Finn was in there going, 'But Izzy Bolger said she heard it from you, Mrs Ryan,' and . . . oh God, oh God, this was awful – like an episode in an afternoon soap. How right Lucy had been that time she'd told Izzy that she tended to complicate things.

Shane was smiling down at her, and she remembered how, when she'd first seen his photograph in *GQ*, he'd reminded her of someone. She knew now, of course, that that someone was Finn. And she thought that she'd never seen a more attractive smile in her life, and she couldn't help but return it.

And now Finn was back, brandishing a copy of *GQ*. 'Here, Dad – sign this!' he instructed, before turning wicked eyes on Izzy. 'A much classier option than an autograph on the back of a pizza parlour flyer, don't you think? Although I'm afraid I'm going to have to add an extra six euro something to your bill. That rag is scandalously expensive.'

'You *have* been charging people for my autograph, you little shit!' said Shane, mock-punching him again, but this time more forcefully.

Finn looked injured. 'Hey! What's a man to do?' he said. 'I'm just back from Thailand, penniless after forking out all that money for my training and my kit. I've got to earn a few bucks somehow. I've a loan to pay off.'

'Well, I won't have you paying it off by suckering people.'

'I only suckered Izzy.'

'How much for?'

'Twenty euros.'

Shane pulled a wallet from his pocket, peeled off a twenty, and handed it to Izzy. 'Please allow me to apologise for my son,' he said.

'No, no, I can't take your money!'

'I insist.'

'No, *I* insist.' Izzy knew she was turning puce.

'OK, then,' said Shane, directing a black look at Finn and sliding the banknote back into his wallet. 'In that case, you might do me the honour of joining me for a drink?'

'Oh! I'd love that,' said Izzy. She was suddenly feeling very glad indeed that she had accompanied her father to Lissamore this weekend.

Shane crooked an arm and extended it to Izzy, who linked it and beamed up at him.

Loping ahead of them across the road, Finn pushed open the door to O'Toole's. 'Mine's a pint, Dad,' he threw over his shoulder.

'Get lost, buddy,' said Shane. 'I don't drink with con artists. What'll you have, Izzy? Champagne? Yes, of course you will. Michael! A bottle of your finest champagne, please.'

'Finest?' said the bartender, ambling in from the back room. 'We only run to one brand.'

'Whatever. I'm sure it'll be grand. Take a seat, madam.'

Izzy hopped up onto the barstool he pulled out for her, and then Shane sat up on her right while Finn straddled the stool on her left.

'Wouldn't you love to have a shot of you and my dad quaffing champagne together?' said Finn in an undertone. 'Special price. Ten euros.'

'Con man, hie thee hence,' said Shane.

'OK. I'll hie off up to Dervla's and put some new pics of you up on the internet.'

'What pics?'

'I got some great ones of you this morning while you were still fast asleep. I thought they'd come in handy for blackmail purposes.'

'What are you on about?'

'Well, you were snoring, so your mouth's wide open and there's some drool—'

'OK, OK,' said Shane. 'You can stop right there, buster. Michael?'

'Yep?'

'Make that a bottle of champagne and a pint of Guinness, please.'

'Coming right up,' said the bartender.

Río was sitting at a table in the first-floor restaurant of O'Toole's, gazing unseeingly at a menu, trying to ignore the sounds of laughter that came floating up from the bar below every time the door swung open. Shortly before eight o'clock, Dervla arrived.

'Where are your beloveds?' Dervla asked, kissing her sister on the cheek and sitting down opposite her.

'They're downstairs in the pub, slugging champagne,' said Río, testily.

'So why aren't you down there, slugging champagne with them?'

Río looked around the restaurant and lowered her voice. 'Because they're with that spooky Isabella.'

Dervla raised her eyes heavenward. 'Honestly, Río! I don't know why you've taken so agin the girl.'

'It's she who's taken agin me. Every time I open my mouth she gives me the evil eye.'

'I've never seen her be anything but perfectly polite to you. You're being completely paranoid, you know.'

'You can smile and smile and still be a villain,' said Río, tapping her nose. 'Shakespeare said that.'

'And Thomas Jefferson said that the happiest moments of his life had been the few he passed in the bosom of his family. You should welcome the opportunity to celebrate this reunion, Río. How often do you get a chance to drink champagne with your son and his father? If you carry on in a big strop you'll ruin the evening and regret it in the morning.'

'Who says I'm in a strop?'

'It's perfectly obvious that you're in a strop. You can't bear the idea of Finn and Shane having fun without you, and you're too miffed to join in.'

'I wouldn't want to intrude,' said Río.

'Oh, act your age.'

'Act my age?' Río returned indignantly. 'Act my *age*? Just what age do you think Shane is acting – flirting with a girl who is young enough to be—'

Just then a waitress approached their table. She was carrying a bottle of champagne, an ice bucket and two flutes, and Río immediately stapled on a dazzling smile. 'Hi, Miriam!' she said. 'What's this? Did you order champagne, Dervla?'

Dervla shook her head. 'No.'

'Compliments of Mr Bolger,' Miriam told them.

'Mr Bolger? You mean Adair?' said Dervla. 'How kind! Where's he hiding?'

'He's in the alcove table, around the corner.'

'Oh, you must ask him to join us!' said Río, brightly. 'Please do, and bring an extra glass!'

'You'd better make that three extra glasses,' said Dervla.

Río raised an eyebrow at her. 'Three?'

'Finn and Shane are about to join us,' Dervla reminded her.

'They don't deserve any more champagne.'

Miriam hovered, looking uncertain. 'One glass or three?' she asked.

'Three please, Miriam,' Dervla said categorically, skewering her sister with a look.

Río shrugged, and Miriam sashayed off.

'I thought you said you had no time for Adair?' remarked Dervla, leaning her elbows on the table. 'What makes you so keen to invite him to join us?'

'What's sauce for the goose,' remarked Río, airily.

'And by that you mean . . . what, exactly?'

'If Shane can sit and flirt with Princess Isabella over a bottle of champagne, I don't see why I can't flirt with her father.'

Dervla struck her forehead with the heel of her hand. 'Dear Jesus, Río! You're even more juvenile than I thought!'

'Well, if you'd seen the way Shane was leaning over my balcony ogling her arse yesterday, *you'd* want to get back at him too.'

'Why should you want to get back at Shane for ogling a pretty girl's arse, for God's sake? It's not as if he belongs to you.'

Río thought about it. What Dervla said was true. Shane didn't belong to her. And yet, and yet . . . since he'd become famous as a Hollywood big shot and all those creepy web women had been posting their comments and weaving their lurid fantasies online, Río had felt increasingly that actually, yes, Shane *did* belong to her. He certainly belonged to her more than to any other woman: he was the father of her son, after all, wasn't he? He had sired Finn, the famous so-called 'love child', born of a 'tempestuous relationship' early on in his career in Ireland. Ha! Río had to admit that when you looked at it that way, it sounded quite intriguing – almost as intriguing as an episode of *Faraway*.

Her musings were brought to an abrupt end by the arrival of Adair Bolger – all smiles and compliments and solicitous enquiries after their health – and no sooner had he arrived than Shane and Finn came roistering up the stairs, preceded by a visibly glowing Isabella.

Uh-oh, thought Río. Dervla had been right. She *had* been a bloody eejit to invite Adair to join their table, because now, of course, his daughter would be part of the equation. What a complete wuss she had been, not to have deduced that father and daughter would be likely to be dining *à deux* in O'Toole's!

And now everyone was making room and small talk, and new places were being set at the table for Adair and Isabella, and another champagne flute – and, indeed, yet another bottle of bubbly – was on its way, and menus were being handed round.

Río observed the way the seating arrangements were shaping

up, and was delighted when Adair elected to sit next to her at the top of the table, where she could flirt with him as outrageously as she liked and piss Izzy off. And maybe even Shane, too. Shane chose the seat on her right, while Izzy sat facing her father, with Shane on her left, and Finn on her right-hand side. Dervla, meanwhile, after greeting Shane with an elegantly executed air-kiss, resumed her seat directly opposite her sister, regarding her with an inscrutable expression.

'Shane! You'll have mussels to start, I know you will!' sang Río. 'You never could resist them. And Adair? Let me see . . . scallops for you? How did I guess! And for me, Miriam? I think I'll have oysters. Half a dozen, please. No, wait! Since Shane's paying, I think I might just manage a dozen.'

And Río looked across at Dervla with a catlike smile, as if to say, 'How could you ever have imagined that I was in a strop? I'll be Ms Congeniality personified tonight!'

At the end of the table, with Shane on her left and Finn on her right, Izzy felt as if she were sitting between two very attractive bookends. Father and son were really ridiculously alike, with the same lopsided smile, the same wicked green eyes, and the same preposterous cheekbones. Their mannerisms were identical too, and they even spoke in a similar timbre, which Izzy found bizarre, considering that they had lived apart for most of their lives. The rapport between them was unmistakable.

She had learned from Finn that his mother had brought him up single-handedly, and made many sacrifices for him – including her career. She could have been a huge success as a theatre designer, he told her. Even though she had never formally trained, she had served as a kind of apprentice to a highly acclaimed international designer while she was still in her teens. And for a number of years she had worked in the fashion business as well, as Fleur's partner. Had Izzy seen the lovely watercolours on display in Fleur's shop? Well, they were his mother's!

271

Izzy had listened and smiled and nodded. The watercolours were gorgeous, she agreed. She thought she might even buy one for her father for Christmas (and hide it away in a drawer). Poor Finn was clearly deluded about his mother, as so many only children were. She was lucky that she suffered no such delusions about her own mother, and she was fortunate too that she had a father who was the most generous and understanding and lovable in the whole world, and who adored her unconditionally.

At the other end of the table, she couldn't help noticing that her dad was spending a lot of time leaning to his right, engaging Río in conversation, and laughing a fair bit at her 'repartee'. Pah! Couldn't he see through the bohemian, hippy-dippy façade to the gold-digger that lurked beneath? Wasn't it obvious that here was a woman hitting a certain age, who was using all the ammunition left to her disposal to bag herself a man before it was too late? She'd clearly been pulling out all the stops yesterday, when she'd worn that black dress to lunch. It had been elegant, certainly – even sexy in an understated way – but entirely wrong for the occasion. The woman had no social nous whatsoever.

This evening she was back in hippy garb, sporting some cobwebby ensemble with bangles and trailing scarves that made her look like a Celtic version of Mystic Meg. Izzy found herself wondering if she was wearing her recently purchased underwear, and immediately slapped a mental health and safety no-go-area sticker on *that* particular idea.

Izzy herself was wearing her new polka-dotted bra and knicks combo under jeans and a pretty, long-sleeved Alberta Ferretti T-shirt. She'd checked herself out in her mother's cheval glass earlier, and was relieved to see that she'd lost most of the weight she'd put on in Koh Samui. After she'd injured her foot on Tao at the end of August, she'd been out of action exercise-wise, and had spent the rest of the holiday slumped on a sun lounger, feeling glum and stuffing her face with paninis because there'd been nothing else for her to do in paradise if she wasn't diving.

Back in Dublin, Felicity had offered to wangle her membership of her very exclusive gym, but the idea of exercising alongside her mother made Izzy go weak at the knees. She knew for a fact that her mother actually exercised like a demon *before* she went to the gym, so that when fellow gym bunnies marvelled at the fact that she kept so trim simply by performing a couple of effortless yoga poses, Felicity could turn to them and say: 'Oh, I'm just naturally slender, you know. I even burn calories while I do sudoku!' Of course, the added bonus for Felicity was that, because her brand of yoga was sweat-free, she could keep her make-up and jewellery on.

This evening Izzy was a make-up-free zone, with the exception of a touch of mascara and a smear of lipgloss. She wondered what it must be like for a dude de luxe like Shane Byrne to be surrounded by such ordinariness. He must be used to dining in fabled eateries like Spago and the Hotel Bel-Air in the company of the world's most glamorous women. She felt incredibly privileged to be sitting here now, the sole focus of his attention. He certainly was an accomplished flirt: he knew how to listen, he knew how to make her laugh, and he knew how to make her blush.

It was warm in O'Toole's, and the champagne (and the compliments!) had made Izzy flushed and muzzy. As Shane refilled her glass she thanked him, and pushed up the sleeves of her T-shirt. At the other end of the table she could hear Río's voice saying, 'I had no idea that the islands were so close, Adair! If you'd hooked up with Finn, he could have taken you diving on Tao.'

'I'm not a great one for diving,' said Adair, 'but Izzy is. She did go diving on Tao, actually – had a close encounter with a whale shark, no less! – but she had to leave the island the same day because she injured her foot.'

And as Izzy was registering this exchange in one part of her brain, another part was registering Shane's sonorous voice saying, 'Hey! What an interesting tattoo! What is it?'

'It's a Japanese kanji,' responded Izzy automatically. 'It

means . . .' And then she and Finn turned to each other at exactly the same moment and said simultaneously, 'Water'.

'Speaking of which,' said Shane, 'we could do with another bottle. What's the waitress's name, Finn?'

'Miriam.'

'Miriam! Could you bring us another bottle of still water, please?'

'Sure,' said Miriam. She swooped down between Finn and Izzy and started to clear away plates, but as she made to move away, a fingerbowl slipped and water and prawn tails landed all over Finn's jeans.

'Oh! I'm so sorry!' said Miriam, reaching for a napkin. She dropped to her knees, and began to mop ineffectually at the spill. 'Oh, Finn! I can't believe what I've done! You're soaked.'

'No worries, Miriam,' said Finn, looking uncomfortable. 'It's only water.'

'But I can't allow you to sit there in wet jeans!' Reaching for his hand, Miriam pulled him to his feet. 'Come with me. I have an idea.'

And as Miriam led Finn away, ignoring his protests that he was fine, and to stop making such a fuss, Izzy decided to grab this opportunity to get out of there before he came back and started interrogating her about the kanji.

Feeling even muzzier, she rose from the table with a vague, 'Excuse me.' Then she turned and fled for the sanctuary of the loo as if a school of tiger sharks was in pursuit.

The loo was downstairs, but Izzy didn't need to pee. She just stood there fidgeting and fretting, wondering if Finn had put two and two together yet. If he had, what was he going to think of her? She had gone to extraordinary lengths that day on Tao to keep her identity secret just because of her stupid hair extensions, and she now wished fervently that she hadn't, because she fancied the arse off Finn Byrne. Sorry – what? Rewind. Replay. *Because she fancied the arse off Finn Byrne . . .*

Oh God. Izzy looked at herself in the mirror and would have blenched if her face wasn't so red and shiny. Her roots needed doing, she had a spot that even her blemish bombs hadn't been able to blast, her lipgloss was half chewed off, and her mascara was smudged. What was she going to do? She had two choices. She could do some remedial work on her face and go back upstairs as if nothing had happened, or she could beat a hasty retreat, phone her dad, tell him that she wasn't feeling well and that she'd decided to walk home.

Oh – walk, walk, yes! She wanted to walk and clear her head and figure out what kind of mess she'd got herself into. And, more importantly, figure just how she was going to get out of it. Except, she reckoned, as she slung her backpack over her shoulder and escaped through the door of the pub, she actu- ally *didn't* have to figure out how to get out of this particular mess. Come next week, the Villa Felicity would be on the market and she'd never need to come here to Lissamore again, would never need to see Finn Byrne and his maddening smile, and – best of all – she'd never need to see that obnoxious Río Kinsella again.

Outside, the main street of the village was deserted, apart from here and there the spectral shadow of a cat. Izzy pulled her phone from her bag and jabbed speed-dial. Adair sounded concerned when he picked up, saying, 'What do you mean, you're walking home by yourself, Isabella?'

'Don't worry, Dad. I'm fine. I just need some fresh air, and the walk will do me good. Don't even think about leaving on my account – *please* don't. I *promise*! I'll have hot chocolate waiting for you – just give me a bell when you're leaving. Yes, yes, yes – love you, too! See you later. Mwah!'

Izzy continued walking, phone tucked snugly in her hand like a gun, just in case. But of course, she hadn't reckoned on the fresh air getting fresher as she walked, or the rain starting to come down, and before she was halfway along the village street she was wet and freezing, and wishing that she hadn't left her jacket behind in the restaurant, hanging on the back of her chair.

And then she heard a voice behind her calling her name and saying something about her jacket, and thank God, thank *God*, it was Finn! And thank God she *had* left her jacket behind because otherwise he might not have come after her.

Izzy turned, and pushed a strand of hair away from her face. But as the dark figure striding up the road towards her became more distinct, she realised that it wasn't Finn. It was Shane.

'Hey!' he said. 'You forgot your jacket, gorgeous.'

Chapter Twenty-one

Dervla was enjoying her evening. Shane was looking good, she thought. Success clearly agreed with him. And why wouldn't it? After years spent at the rockface, suffering setbacks and rejections, he deserved to reap some reward for all his hard work. Few people in the restaurant were crass enough actually to approach him, but Dervla noticed how the eyes of most of the women diners kept sliding in his direction, and little Isabella Bolger was clearly smitten. She'd laughed immoderately at his jokes all evening, and her body language had been pretty flagrant too. Maybe it was the champagne, or maybe, thought Dervla, it was a ploy to keep Finn on his toes, because there was something – some kind of a connection between the two young people – that positively *shimmered*.

There seemed to be something shimmering between Adair and Río too, and as Dervla sat back in her chair sipping coffee, she realised that what was going on was a none-too-subtle gavotte. Río was flirting with Adair to make Shane jealous, and Shane was flirting with Izzy to make Río jealous, and Izzy was flirting with Shane to make Finn jealous, and Finn was flirting with Miriam to make Izzy jealous, and oh! how glad Dervla felt not to have to be involved in any of this silly-bugger game-playing!

277

Then suddenly the evening was winding up, and there seemed to be some confusion as to Shane's whereabouts because the manager was keen to give him back his platinum card, and Finn – wearing a pair of blue-and-white-checked kitchen porter trousers – was standing laughing with Miriam, and Adair was distributing the last of the champagne.

Dervla stood up from the table, twinkled her fingers unobtrusively at Río and mouthed, 'Talk to you soon.' Then she slipped out of the restaurant and walked to her car.

On the street, all was silent but for the wet silk sound of the wavelets in the harbour as they slapped against the keels of the fishing boats, and the drip drip drip of rain from gables. Once Dervla reached her car, she lowered the driver's side window and sat motionless behind the wheel, listening for a minute or two before switching on the ignition and the windscreen wipers, and turning the car in the direction of Galway city, and home.

There were two new additions to the flotilla of 'For Sale' signs up on the main street of the village. A lot of the houses that had come onto the market in recent times were second homes being sold by wealthy Dublin 4 types, desperate to get rid of their holiday cottages. Dervla's vocabulary had expanded as she'd searched for ever more flowery language to describe the properties in an effort to attract buyers. Views had become 'staggeringly beautiful', 'bijou' ousted 'cosy', gardens were 'luxuriant' and 'verdurous'.

Agencies were letting staff go, or asking them to take salary cuts. Breaking even was an achievement. It was not a good time to be in the property business.

Dervla suddenly felt weary. The game didn't excite her any more. The cut and thrust had become tedious, the competition too intense. Instead of going home to navigate myhome and daft.ie, how she would have loved to curl up with hot chocolate and a good book. The last time she had escaped from real life with a novel had been on holiday three years ago in Mauritius. She couldn't afford a holiday now.

And the rain was coming down in torrents.

Izzy and Shane had been clinging to each other, using Shane's leather jacket as a makeshift umbrella, but a passing motorist skimming through a puddle had sent water sluicing over them, and there was no point in trying to stay dry any longer. Shane dropped his jacket, and the pair of them stood there in fits of laughter, rivulets of rain cascading down their faces, hair plastered to their skulls.

Once they'd managed to stop laughing, Izzy gave him a rueful look. 'Your jacket is ruined!'

'No worries. It was a gift from the designer.'

'One of many perks?' said Izzy, teasingly.

'Not really. You'd be surprised how sniffy their PR people get when you tell them that you don't like their gear.' Shane adopted a bogus accent. '"You mean you are telling us zat you vill not vear ze T-shirt with ze nipple holes? Zen Sven will have to scratch you from his list."'

They'd reached the boreen that led to the gates of the Villa Felicity.

'This is your turn-off?' asked Shane.

'Yes. Yikes. It's a quagmire. Don't you even think about walking me to the gate in those shoes, Shane. I bet they were a present from a designer too.'

Shane looked dubious. 'I can't not walk you to the gate.'

'Well, *I* am going to put my foot down.' Izzy did just that, stomping a foot into the mud. 'Look! This is no place for Italian leather footwear.'

'Well, OK . . . If you're sure, sweetheart?'

'Sure I'm sure. I'm nearly home – look, you can see the lights of the house from here. And you've really got to get yourself back to your flat so you can get out of those wet clothes. Why don't you make yourself some hot chocolate? That's what I'm going to do.'

'Good idea.' Shane took a step backward.

Bummer. He wasn't going to kiss her. For the past ten minutes, Izzy had been speculating how she might react if he *did* try to kiss her. After the way Finn had behaved this evening, virtually ignoring her at the dinner table and then skulking off with that waitress, she had felt that it might just have served him right if she'd stolen a kiss from his father instead. An additional plus, it would be something to wind Lucy up with. She'd even composed a text in her head: 'Scored Seth from Faraway ☺' But now it didn't look like it was going to happen.

'Thanks a lot for walking me home, Shane,' she said, stalling for time. 'But I feel guilty that you got so pissed upon. Might I see you around the village tomorrow?'

'I'll make it my business to run into you. You owe me a pint.'

'Done deal. Well, thanks for a lovely evening.'

'You're welcome, ma'am.'

'Good night, then.'

'Good night.' Shane took a step towards her and gave her a brief hug. Then he leaned down and placed a chaste kiss on her cheek before turning and heading back in the direction of Lissamore. The sodden hems of his jeans made a swishing noise as he trod through puddles, and she could hear him whistling.

Yay! He *had* kissed her! She could send that text after all! Izzy blew an extravagant kiss of her own at his retreating back before returning her attention to the boreen. She frowned as she wondered how best to negotiate it; then decided that – hell – if she didn't want to ruin her own shoes, she'd just have to go barefoot. She took off her trainers, rolled up her jeans and ploughed on, relishing the squelch of the mud between her toes, before realising that, *shit*, she had no keycard to the gate because her father had let Río Kinsella have it. Still, she had her house keys and she could access the garden via the beach. She wouldn't go via the short cut, though. She'd disturbed a badger once, in the orchard, and it had given her the fright of her life. She'd go the long way round.

The path that led down to the shore was like an obstacle course – steep and slippery – and once there, she had a stretch of shingle to cross. 'Ow, ow, ow!' mewed Izzy, as she crossed on tiptoes like a cartoon cat on hot coals, sharp pebbles and flints digging into the soles of her feet. She remembered the agony she'd gone through in Tao when she'd trodden on glass, and she prayed that she'd make the journey between here and the gate without inflicting further damage upon herself.

As she drew near the tangle of brambles that had grown up and over the sea wall of the Villa Felicity, she thought she saw a shadow move. Was it her imagination, or a trick of the light? She paused momentarily, aware of her heart fluttering like a bird behind the cage of her ribs, and then she took a step sideways, inching closer to the wall, hoping that whoever – or whatever – was down there hadn't spotted her. It could be a sheep, she knew, or a goat. But she'd seen too many horror films in her life to think that a girl on her own approaching a nondescript shadowy thing on a dark, rainy night was a good idea.

She was off the shingle now, treading over a bed of seaweed that had been washed up by the tide as far as the base of the wall. Suddenly she was up to her ankles in it, slipping, losing her balance. She dropped her shoes, reaching out blindly for something to steady herself, and whatever it was she grabbed made her squeal as pain knifed through her. Son of a *bitch*! She had plunged a hand through brambles and was clinging on to barbed wire. With a yelp, Izzy let go, sliding on the seaweed and landing on her back, and as the shadowy thing by the gate moved again she ordered herself not to faint . . . And then she realised that she might actually have fainted because a kind of gap happened, like a DVD jumping forward, and the next thing she knew someone was crouching over her and a voice was saying: 'Izzy! What's happened? Are you all right?'

It was Finn.

'No!' she wailed. 'I'm not all right!'

'It's OK, it's OK. Stay calm. I can help you. I'm an emergency first responder.'

Izzy started to laugh and cry simultaneously. 'So am I.'

'Well, you obviously can't help yourself. Is it your foot?'

'No. My hand. But now you mention it, I think I might have banjaxed my foot too.'

'Let me help you sit up.' Finn levered her into a sitting position, and she felt seaweed tumble from her hair onto her shoulders. 'Can you move it?' he asked.

Izzy tentatively wiggled her toes. 'Yeah.'

'Let me have a look at your hand.' Finn reached for it, and angled it one way, then another. 'OK. I can't see too much in this light, but we'll have to clean you up. Let's get you into the house.'

'I'm not sure I'll be able to walk very far. Hang on – I'd better grab my shoes.'

'Got them?'

'Yeah.'

Finn hunkered down lower. 'I'll give you a fireman's lift as far as the gate. Just grab on to me and lean forward, over my shoulder. Can you manage? Good – that's it.'

Finn stood up, shouldering Izzy, his left hand grasping her right forearm, his right arm hooked around her thigh. She heard the shingle crunch under his feet as he made his way along the foreshore, and then he was carefully lowering her over the five-bar gate. Once her good foot made purchase on the lowest bar, she waited for Finn to climb over.

'Thank you,' she murmured.

'We're not there yet. Now, sling your left arm around my neck.

Don't worry, I'll bear most of your weight if you think you can hobble the rest of the way.'

'I'll manage.'

Between them, they crossed the leafy floor of the orchard, then emerged from under the trees onto the lawn. Except the lawn was so overgrown that their progress wasn't as easy as it might have been, and as Izzy limped towards the house, she was fearful that they'd both end up sprawled in the long grass.

'Which way?' asked Finn.

'Left onto the path – we'll go in by the utility room,' said Izzy.

Once there, she leaned against the doorjamb, unhooked her keyring, and handed it to Finn. The alarm started to bleat as he turned the key in the lock and the door swung open.

'Three five nine zero hash,' said Izzy, watching Finn key the number into the pad by the door. 'I'd do it, but I don't want to get blood everywhere. Light switch is on the left, first-aid kit's on the wall over there.'

'OK. But first let's get you sitting down. Is the kitchen that way?'

'Yes.'

Finn steered Izzy across the floor and pulled open a door. Beyond the utility room glimmered the hi-tech sanctuary of the kitchen, all burnished pewter and polished concrete. Staggering across to the stainless-steel table, still leaning heavily on Finn, she collapsed onto one of the dining chairs.

Finn hunkered down next to her. 'Show me your hand.'

She obliged. Taking her hand between both his own, he examined her palm from a couple of different angles. 'Hm. It's not as bad as all that. I thought by the shriek you let out that you might have severed an artery, but there are just a couple of small puncture wounds. Was it barbed wire?'

She nodded.

'I take it you've had a tetanus shot?'

'Yes.'

'One less thing to worry about. You'll be glad to know I won't have to call an ambulance.'

'Bummer. I rather like the idea of whizzing along roads with a siren blaring and *ER*-type interns saying stuff like, "Bring on the CPR."'

'You're hardly a candidate for CPR,' Finn said. 'And you wouldn't like it once you were dumped in A&E. You can see the local doctor tomorrow if necessary, but in the meantime, let's try and take care of this in the comfort of your own home. Where can I find paper towels?'

'Over there.'

He crossed to the kitchen counter and tore off a length of kitchen towel. Then he swung a stool out from under the counter, carried it over to Izzy and laid her leg across the seat.

'You'll need to keep your foot raised,' he told her, as he swathed her hands in paper. 'Where'll I find proper towels?'

'There's an airing cupboard next to the washing machine in the utility room.'

'Don't move. I'll be back in a minute.'

Izzy sat there obediently, watching raindrops chasing each other down the window until Finn returned, pushing a housekeeping trolley. On board the trolley was a basin of water, a roll of bandages, a box of dressings and another of antiseptic wipes, a pack of disposable surgical gloves, a pile of towels and a picture of a kitten.

'Why the kitten?' asked Izzy.

'It's to distract you while I poke around. You can gaze upon it.'

'Thanks. Where did you find it?'

'It's the Kitten Soft one, off a calendar.'

'Shouldn't I be having a cup of hot, sweet tea while I gaze upon the kitten?'

'Patience. You can have a cup in a minute. Let's see to your wounds first.'

Finn snapped on a pair of rubber gloves, and Izzy looked at him admiringly. 'You've done this before,' she said.

'Yes, ma'am, I have.'

Dipping a hand towel in water, he set about cleaning Izzy's hands and forearm. 'The cuts aren't deep, so that's good. Hang on, there's a nasty thorn . . .' Reaching for a tweezers, he nipped, pulled, and dropped the offending thorn onto a cotton wool pad. Then he helped himself to an antiseptic wipe. 'This'll sting a little. Be brave.'

'Ow,' said Izzy automatically. She watched Finn's fingers as he deftly cleaned and dressed and bandaged her wounds. When he finished, he sat back and assessed her.

'You're soaked to the skin,' he remarked.

'So are you. Why are you wearing different trousers?'

'Miriam lent them to me, after she spilled the fingerbowl over my jeans.'

'Water, water everywhere,' said Izzy. 'What were you doing, sitting by the gate in the rain?'

'I wanted a word. We have unfinished business.'

'Unfinished business?'

'To do with a Japanese kanji.' He brushed her arm with his thumb.

Nooooooo! Izzy didn't want to talk about that right now. And then she remembered what an expert she'd been at changing the subject earlier in the day, so she did it again. 'How come you got here before me?' she asked.

'I took a short cut across the fields. Do you want that hot sweet tea, now?'

'To hell with tea. I'd prefer a brandy.'

'You're going to have to get out of those wet clothes first.'

'So are you.'

They looked at each other levelly. Something in the air between them crackled and fizzed: a metaphorical gauntlet hung there like Macbeth's dagger. *Challenge*, thought Izzy. *Adrenalin. Danger.* Words from her dive manual that made her tingle. And she remembered the blurb on the cover. 'Experience intense adventure. Take it to the edge . . .'

'I saw robes in the airing cupboard,' said Finn.

'Robes seem like a good idea.'

'OK. I'll get them.'

Finn disappeared back into the utility room. He was gone for several moments, during which time Izzy watched more raindrops run down the window and did some thinking. She was going to have to come clean about that day on Koh Tao, or she was going to have to make up more big fat fibs, and she knew that her current state of mind was not conducive to making up big fat fibs. She was too buzzy, too distracted.

When Finn came back, he was wearing a towelling robe, and carrying another. 'I took the liberty of dumping my clothes in the dryer,' he told her. 'That's the second pair of trousers I've had to discard today. I feel like some loser out of *Jackass*. Now, Little Miss Bolger, how can I help you undress without embarrassing you?'

'I don't embarrass easily,' said Izzy.

'Divers don't, generally.'

Izzy's bandaged hand meant that she was having problems with her fly.

'Can I help you with that?' asked Finn.

'If you don't mind.'

'Not remotely.' Finn unzipped her jeans for her, and she shucked them down over her hips. He took hold of the hems and pulled.

'Pretty knicks,' he observed.

'I can manage them myself, thanks,' she said, with mock hauteur. 'Will you get the brandy?'

'Sure. Where'll I find it?'

'There's a bar. Second door on the left in the atrium.'

'The what?'

'The hall.'

'Why didn't you just call it a hall, then?'

'Because my mother decided it was more upmarket to call it an atrium.'

286

Finn quirked an eyebrow, smiled and left the room, where-upon Izzy peeled off the rest of her clothes, dumped them in a pile on the floor and shrugged herself into her robe. Then she reached for her phone and – holding it carefully between finger and thumb – speed-dialled her dad.

'Oh, darling, I'm so sorry!' said Adair when he picked up. 'I'd lost all track of time. I'm leaving now.'

Her dad was having to raise his voice to be heard. In the back-ground, Izzy could make out the distinctive rasp of bow against strings, and the drone of uillean pipes.

'What's that noise?'

'It's a load of musicians, tuning up. There's going to be a session.'

'A trad session?'

'Yes.'

'Hey, Dad, you mustn't miss that! You've always said it was your dream to catch one of those gigs.'

The impromptu traditional music sessions that took place in O'Toole's were the stuff of legend. Adair had often bemoaned the fact that, while they'd been coming to Lissamore for nearly a decade, their visits had never once managed to coincide with one.

'Stay on, Dad, why don't you?'

'I can't, Izzy. I can't bear the idea of you sitting there drinking hot chocolate all by yourself.'

'I'm not by myself. Finn Byrne's here.' Izzy started peeling little strands of seaweed away from her décolleté.

'Oh. Um, what's he doing there?'

Izzy decided a white lie was called for. 'I left my jacket behind in O'Toole's. He very kindly brought it round, so I asked him in for a drink.'

'Oh. And everything's . . . all right?'

'Yes, Daddy. Everything's fine.' There was no way Izzy was going to tell her father that she'd injured herself again. He'd have her hoisted immediately onto a private helicopter and transported to the Blackrock Clinic.

'Well, as long as you're— Hey! It's— Wow!' Her dad's voice on the phone sounded like a big kid's who's just opened his best Christmas present ever. 'Wow! I can't believe it, Izzy! Guess who's just come in? Donal Lunny and that gorgeous fiddle player – what's her name? Zoë you-know-who.'

'Zoë Conway? Well, hell, Dad, you've landed yourself in the middle of trad royalty there. Don't even *think* about coming back here any time soon.'

'Are you sure, Izzy-Bizz?'

'Sure I'm sure. Have fun. Just text me when you're heading home, will you?'

'Why?'

Izzy thought fast. 'I'll worry otherwise,' she said.

'Darling, I'm a grown man—'

'And I'm a grown woman, and I *always* pay you the courtesy of texting you when I think you might be worried about me. Promise me you'll do it?'

'Promise.'

'Good Daddy.'

Izzy put the phone down, calculating how long Adair was likely to be an absent father. The session would go on until past midnight, and then there'd doubtless be one for the road, and, of course, the fifteen-minute walk home because he'd left the car behind this evening in anticipation of having a few jars. There was plenty of time.

Finn came back into the kitchen. 'I was going to bring the brandy in here,' he said. 'But I thought we'd be more comfortable in the sitting room. Or do you call it the "salon"?'

'Sitting room will do,' said Izzy, levering herself off her chair.

'Are you sure you can walk by yourself?' asked Finn.

Izzy was just about to say, 'Yes, I'm sure', and then she remembered how nice it had felt to have Finn's arm around her waist earlier, so she changed it to, 'Oh – actually, I'm not so sure.'

'Maybe you should put on an elasticated bandage?' Finn suggested.

'No!' said Izzy emphatically. Those bandages were hideous to behold, like orthopaedic socks. 'I don't need one. They make my feet feel claustrophobic.'

'OK.' Crossing the floor, Finn helped Izzy to her feet, then manoeuvred her across the gleaming atrium and into the vast sitting room. He had lit the fire, and set a bottle of Remy Martin VSOP and two brandy balloons on the hearth. As Izzy dropped into one of the deep leather armchairs and pulled up the collar of her oversized robe, Finn looked at her and laughed.

'What's so funny?'

'You look like something out of an advertisement for one of those posh spas,' he said, handing her a glass.

'With seaweed in my hair?' she said, plucking a strand of the feathery green stuff from her damp curls. 'I don't think so.'

'You had seaweed in your hair the night we dived with the whale shark.'

Finn sat opposite her, and they looked at each other for a long moment.

Izzy said nothing. He had put two and two together. He wasn't a fool. 'That wasn't seaweed,' she said finally. 'That *was* my hair.'

'So you're the girl who rescued my mask in Tao.'

'Yes.'

'Why did you pretend it was your mate?'

'Um. She fancied you, and wanted to big herself up?'

'You're lying, Izzy.'

'How do you know?'

'You're a diver. Because you speak with your eyes, it's dead easy to tell when you're lying.'

Izzy looked down at the rug.

'What was the real reason you wanted to remain incognito on Tao?' Finn asked.

'The real reason,' said Izzy, feeling very stupid, 'was because my hair extensions were falling out.'

She waited for him to hoot, but he didn't even smirk. 'That was it? That was the only reason?'

'No. The other reason is that you thought I was a lesbian.'

Now he did laugh. 'What on earth would have made me think you were a lesbian?'

Izzy didn't want to compound her embarrassment by reminding him that she'd been wearing a cap with I Like 2 Dyke on it. So instead she said: 'Babette is jealous of me. She is the Perez Hilton of Lissamore. She's been spreading lies all over the village about my sexual orientation.'

Finn sighed. 'She'll have fun holding court on the sea wall tomorrow, spreading the latest gossip, so.'

'What might that be?'

'That Shane Byrne, star of the cult television series *Faraway*, was seen flirting outrageously in O'Toole's seafood eaterie with a beautiful Business Studies student before escorting her to her beach-front home.'

'How do you know he escorted me home?' said Izzy indignantly. 'Were you spying on us?'

'No. I heard you talking on the road above.'

'He – he just wanted to make sure I got my jacket.'

'Oh, yeah?'

'Yeah. I'd left it behind on my chair—'

'That old trick!'

'– and your dad was chivalrous enough to return it to me and make sure that I got home all right.'

Finn gave her a sceptical look. 'That doesn't explain why you spent the entire evening flirting with him.'

'Who else was there to flirt with?'

'I suppose I am not worthy?'

'You! You couldn't keep your eyes off that Miriam one—'

'I've known Miriam all my life! She's like a sister to me!'

'– and then you went skulking off into the storeroom with her at the first opportunity.'

'What do you mean, the first opportunity? My jeans were soaking!'

'After she'd *accidentally* poured water all over them.'

'It *was* an accident!'

There was a pause. Izzy reached for her brandy glass, then made a face, and put it down. 'Ick,' she said. 'I'd forgotten that I don't really like brandy.'

'There's Baileys.'

Izzy was just about to say that yes, she'd love a Baileys, when she remembered the old television ads for the liquor that featured loved-up couples just about to do it. So instead she said, 'Thank you. But maybe I should steer clear of alcohol.'

'Hot sweet tea, then?'

'No, thanks. I don't like tea much, either.'

'What would you like?'

Izzy thought about it, tracing the kanji on the inside of her elbow with a forefinger. *Water . . .*

'I'd really, really love a bath; I feel a chill coming on.'

Finn took a taste of his brandy, made an appreciative face, then moseyed over to the window. 'D'you know what would be much better for you than a bath?' he said.

'What?'

'A Jacuzzi. I've just spotted the hot tub on your deck.'

Izzy clapped her hands. 'Oh! A Jacuzzi in the pouring rain! I can't think of anything more blissful.'

'Then let's go for it,' said Finn.

'Do you need me to show you how to operate it?'

'No, ma'am, I do not. I spent a summer working in Coolnamara Castle Hotel, where Jacuzzis are as much a part of the furniture as emperor-sized beds.'

Finn moved to the doors that opened onto the deck, then paused. 'What time is your dad due home?' he asked.

'Not for a while. There's a session starting in O'Toole's.'

'A session? No shit! Who's playing?'

'Um.' Izzy thought fast. If she told Finn that Donal Lunny and Zoë Conway were playing, he'd be back down the pub in – well, in jig time. 'A baroque quartet,' she improvised.

'A baroque quartet? In O'Toole's?'

'Yes. They're trying to raise money to study at the Conservatoire in Paris.'

'I wish them luck with their fund-raising. I'd say your dad'll be the only one in the audience.'

Finn dropped his bathrobe, stepped naked into the rain, and made for the Jacuzzi. Izzy watched as he raised the lid and reset the motor. Oh! He was fitter than Beckham and Nadal and Ronaldo rolled into one.

Rising from the armchair, Izzy moved to the window. Finn straightened up, and turned to face her. He pointed an index finger first at her, then at himself, and then he made the 'OK' signal with forefinger and thumb. Izzy smiled. He was communicating in scuba language.

'Shall we?' he signed, raising an interrogative eyebrow.

Izzy demurred. 'You go ahead, I'll follow,' she told him with both hands – a little shyly.

He climbed the steps to the hot tub, then lowered himself into the water, and drew a big smile across his face. Izzy stepped through the door, and stood there, hesitating.

Finn said something, but the thrumming of the rain against wood meant that she couldn't hear him. She indicated that she might have a problem.

'Is something wrong?' he queried with an eloquent hand.

She nodded, holding out a clenched fist to warn of potential danger.

He pointed a finger at his chest. 'Me?'

Nodding again, Izzy raised her hand to her forehead, fingers together in the shape of a dorsal fin. 'You could be a shark,' she was telling him

He laughed, then placed his hands on either side of his head, and wiggled his index fingers to tell her that, really, he was a pussycat.

Izzy stalled some more, then gave an exaggerated shiver, and hugged herself. The signal she was sending indicated that she was cold, or frightened, or nervous, or all three.

'Take it easy,' he told her with a movement of his right hand. Then he put both palms prayerfully together, bowed his head, and gave her a beseeching look from under his eyebrows.

She looked at him, deliberating, then laughed out loud as she watched him place his fingertips against his mouth, stretch out a bronzed arm, and blow. The invitation proved irresistible. He was a master scuba instructor, after all – a dive god. And you *never* flouted the authority of a dive god. His wish was her command. Izzy caught the kiss. Then she untied the sash of her robe and let it fall.

Chapter Twenty-two

Because Shane didn't call to her door the next morning, Río decided to call on him.

He answered the door bare-chested, in loose cotton pyjama bottoms.

'Good morning!' said Río brightly, trying to overcompensate for her hangover. 'Where did you get to last night? You missed a great session in O'Toole's.'

'There was a session in O'Toole's? Why did nobody tell me?'

'You disappeared off the face of the planet clutching Isabella Bolger's jacket to your heart. I figured you might have other things on your mind.' Río smiled sweetly at him as she passed through into the living room.

'Jesus, Río! You didn't think—'

'I will not condemn you, Shane, and I will not criticise you. What you do with your private life is none of my business. Where's Finn?'

'Finn didn't come back here last night. I guess he ended up staying with Miriam.'

'Miriam? Never! He's always looked on her as a sister.'

'You could have fooled me, the way they were carrying on last night.'

Río's eyes took in the empty cafetière on the coffee table, the mug with dregs, the script covered in scribbled notes, the orange highlighter pen, the open laptop. 'Looks like you've been up for a while,' she said. 'It seems an awful shame to be working on a bank holiday when everyone else is in leisure mode.'

'I didn't know it was a bank holiday,' said Shane.

'All you needed to do was look through the window at all the miserable holiday-makers dripping in the rain.' Río flopped down on the sofa, and picked up the script. 'You been studying lines? Hey! You get to snog someone called Akasha. "Seth presses his lips against Akasha's. She resists at first, but Seth's expertise proves irresistible and the kiss grows passionate." Hm. Is this Akasha hot?'

'They're all hot. I work in Hollywood, remember?'

Río gave him a curious look. 'What's it like, having to snog strange women?'

'Embarrassing. It's no fun at all. I only enjoy snogging women I adore.'

'You must have adored plenty in your time.'

'"In my time?" Are you implying that my time for adoring women is over?'

'Not likely. Sure won't they be forming a queue to be adored by you, you gorgeous ride?'

Shane gave her a cynical look. 'They don't want to be adored, Río. They just want to screw a star, so they can boast about it from the rooftops, or stick it in their blog. Hardly anyone in the film business screws around these days. It's too dangerous.'

'Because of STDs?'

'STDs, hell. If you're really unlucky, you might end up in Rip-Off Report.'

'What's Rip-Off Report?'

'An online site that's meant to be for consumer complaints, but where you can – conveniently enough – post any kind of scurrilous shite you like.'

'Such as?'

'Such as: "Shane Byrne is, like, totally crap in bed. He has the smallest dick I have ever seen, he can't get it up, and he is a beyond lousy kisser."'

'But that's totally untrue!' Río leaned over and kissed him on the cheek.

'Thank you, sweetheart! If it ever happens, I'll ask you to write a rebuttal.'

Shane's laptop pinged, to indicate that an email had come in.

'Bollocks,' he said, checking it out.

'What is it?'

'A questionnaire from my agent. It's for *Variety*.'

'Hey, let's fill it in! I love questionnaires.'

'Be my guest. I hate them.' Shane stood up and stretched, then ambled towards the kitchen.

'Don't be a spoilsport!' Río angled his laptop so she could scan the text. 'All you need to do is come up with some makey-uppy shite, and I'll type it in for you.'

'Go ahead, then,' said Shane, with a manifest lack of enthusiasm.

Río hummed the *Mastermind* theme tune as she clicked and scrolled. 'Question One: "What is your idea of perfect happiness?"'

'What kind of a dumb-ass question's that to ask a red-blooded male?'

'I'm sure you can come up with *something* that doesn't have to do with sex,' Río told him archly.

'OK. How's this? My idea of perfect happiness is dining in O'Toole's seafood restaurant with my family and friends.'

Río raised an eyebrow at him.

'It's true. Last night was the best fun I've had in ages. I just wish I hadn't missed out on that session.'

'It was a good one, all right.'

'It must have been a great welcome home for Finn. I hope you got maudlin enough to sing "Wild Rover" for him.'

'Finn wasn't there.'

'Oh? So, who all ended up downstairs?'

'Just me and Adair. And about a hundred locals.'

'Adair? Baldy Adair, the boring millionaire?'

'He's not boring, actually.'

'OK. Baldy Adair the charismatic, fascinating, scintillating and nimble-witted millionaire.'

Río shot him a look, and Shane said: 'Well, to judge by the way you were laughing at his remarks last night, he must be all that and then some.' Sending her an urbane smile, he turned his back on her, and busied himself with something at the kitchen counter.

'We'll carry on with the questionnaire, shall we?' said Río, resisting the impulse to retaliate with some sarky remark about the millionaire's scintillating daughter.

'Question two: "What is your greatest extravagance?"'

There came a sound of a champagne cork popping, and Río looked up. Shane was standing with a bottle of O'Toole's finest in his hand. 'My greatest extravagance,' he said, 'is opening bottles of champagne on random occasions.'

'Good answer!' said Río. 'Except I shouldn't really indulge. I still feel a bit drunk from last night.'

'Good. That means you'll be drunk again after a glass.'

'Why do you want to get me drunk?'

'So that I can seduce you, of course.'

'Ha.'

Shane poured, then strolled back into the sitting area, and handed Río a glass. 'To family reunions,' he said.

'Well, I can't not drink to that.' Río smiled up at him, and chinked his glass.

'Bring on the next question,' said Shane, settling back on the sofa.

'Next question is . . . "What do you consider your greatest achievement?"'

'That's easy. My son, Finn, the dive god.'

Río smiled. 'What a coincidence! That happens to be my greatest achievement, too.' She typed in the answer, then said, 'You're going to have to think a bit harder about this one. "Which talent would you most like to have?" And you're not allowed to say "Acting".'

'I don't have to think about that at all. The answer is, I'd like to be able to lie.'

Río gave him an interested look. 'Would you really, Shane?'

'Yes, I would. Hollywood is full of liars, all out to shaft you. I'd love to be able to shaft some of them back. Which talent would *you* most like to have?'

Río considered. 'I suppose being able to lie *would* be pretty useful. Dervla's magnificent at it. You have to be able to lie really well to be a successful auctioneer. Think of all those works of fiction that are estate agents' blurbs. I'm surprised one of them hasn't won the Booker prize.'

'Maybe Dervla will, one day. I heard her say something to Finn last night about some book she was working on.'

'She's writing a book? Sly-Boots, Dervla! Any idea what it's about?'

'Nope.'

'Knowing her, it's probably a memoir called *My Brilliant Career*. Or else she was just telling yet another one of her lies.' Río returned her attention to Shane's computer. 'Next question. "What is your most treasured possession?"'

'A photograph,' Shane replied, without hesitation. 'It's my screen saver.'

Río typed in 'A photograph', not bothering to ask what the photograph was of. Knowing Shane, his screen saver probably featured some nubile centrefold. She ploughed on. '"Who are your heroes in real life?"'

'My son and his mother.'

'Clever. "What or who is the greatest love of your life?"'

'Ditto.'

'Even cleverer! "What is your greatest regret?"'

'That I didn't marry the mother of my son.'

'Ha! Nice one! You're great at answering questionnaires, Shane. Even I couldn't make up that shite.'

Shane reached out a hand and brushed something away from the side of Río's neck.

'What was that?' she asked.

'A fruit fly.'

'At this time of the year?'

'They're not seasonal any more.'

'It's funny about seasonal stuff, isn't it? I used to love peaches, but now I can buy them any time I want, I can't be arsed with them.'

'I guess that's a metaphor for life. As soon as people get the stuff they once only ever dreamed about, they don't want it any more.'

'Ow. That observation's a bit too profound for a tipsy gal with a hangover. Next question. "What is your current state of mind?"'

'Let me think about that.' Shane took a slug of champagne. 'Horny.'

'Horny? Hm. Maybe it's not such a good idea to put that in. The readers might think you're looking at porn.'

'But I told you earlier, I'm crap at lying.'

Something about the way Shane was looking at her made Río feel unsettled suddenly. 'What are you saying, Shane?'

His eyes didn't leave hers. 'I guess I'm telling you in a very roundabout way that I want to go to bed with you, Río.'

'You do?' said Río. 'Um. Why?'

'Because I adore you.'

'Oh God! For a minute there, I thought you were serious.' But there was no corresponding smile. 'Um. Are you serious?' she asked.

'I am.'

Río stood up from the sofa, grabbed her glass and moved to

the window. 'Don't be *stupid*, Shane! How could you possibly adore me?'

'I've always adored you.'

'But we were disastrous together from the word go. We were way too young to be in a relationship.'

'You weren't too young to be a mother.'

'That's beside the point.'

'Is it? I've always thought of Finn as a genuine love child.'

'He was. I mean, he *is*. But things could never have worked out between you and me.'

'They could now.'

Río turned to him. 'What do you mean?'

'I have money now, Río. I know I offered to marry you before Finn was born, but you were right to say no, because in those days I was a waster with no future. And I always hoped that one day you might meet somebody who would be able to provide for you better than I ever could. But that didn't happen, and I'm glad it didn't, because I couldn't bear to think of you married to someone else. You're the only woman I've ever really loved, Río Kinsella. And now I *can* provide for you. That's why I came back here.'

'You're not . . . you're not asking me to *marry* you, Shane?'

'Yes. I am.'

'Oh! Oh God – that is so sweet of you! That is really, *really* so sweet of you! But I can't do that. I can't marry you.' Río took a great gulp of champagne.

'Why not? Is it because of that baldy git?'

'No.' Río couldn't help it. She started to laugh.

'Because it wouldn't surprise me if it was because of him,' continued Shane. 'I saw the way he annexed you last night, Río, all smarmy smiles. He clearly fancies the arse off you.'

'Shane. It's not because of Adair.' She moved back to the sofa, and sat down next to him. 'It's because I'm finally in a place where I'm as content as I imagine I will ever be. I don't need to be married.'

'But if you married me—'

'Listen to me. I have somewhere to live, I have no money worries – well, no *serious* money worries – I have reared my son – *our* son – and I think I've made a pretty good fist of it.' Río drained her glass, then held it out to him. 'Oh God. Give me more drink. This is starting to sound like the kind of dialogue you have to spout in *Faraway*.'

'"You're right, Akasha. We definitely need more drink."' Shane moved across to the kitchen counter, saying, as he went, '"Seth moves to the bar, grabs the bottle by its neck. He sloshes champagne into both their glasses, hands one to Akasha, then slumps back onto the sofa."'

'That was very good!' said Río admiringly. 'Is that what you call method acting?'

'No. It's the Spencer Tracy school of acting. It's called knowing your lines and not bumping into the furniture.' Shane sighed. 'Christ, I'm an eejit, Río.'

'Sure, I've known that for years.'

'No, I mean I'm eejit the way I handled this. I played my cards all wrong.'

'It doesn't matter how you played your cards, Shane. You know there's no way things could ever work out between us. We're two completely different people from the ones who made Finn. I'm a bogger from Coolnamara and you're a Hollywood hottie.'

'I used to be a bogger from Coolnamara too.'

'But you've had twenty years to learn how to pretend to be someone else. Could you imagine me turning up with you at some red-carpet do, trying to make small talk with studio executives and starlets? What a joke!' Río took another gulp of champagne, then leaned back against the cushions and turned to face him. 'How *were* you going to play your cards, incidentally?'

Shane tapped his nose. 'You'll never know now, will you?'

'You could tell me.'

'It's hardly worth telling you if you don't want to come out and play.'

'Oh, go on!'

'Let's just say that it involved a candlelit dinner in a deluxe suite overlooking the lake in Coolnamara Castle Hotel with champagne and presents.'

'Presents?'

'Specially couriered over from Paris. It's a shame. I'll have to give them to somebody else now.'

'Why can't you give them to me?'

'You don't want to play. You won't even allow me to buy you dinner.' Shane sighed and reached for his phone. 'I'd better cancel the booking.'

'No!'

'Why not? Have you somebody else in mind who might want to have dinner with champagne and presents in a deluxe hotel suite?'

'Well . . . me.'

'You wouldn't be able to drive. You told me you were still drunk from last night, and you've had a glass of champagne.'

'You could drive us.'

'But you don't want to come with me.'

'Oh! Shane Byrne, you are a bastard. Can't I at least *see* the presents?'

Shane stood up and looked down at her with a smile. 'Sure.' He disappeared into a bedroom and re-emerged with a big, glossy cardboard box, which he set on the coffee table in front of her. 'Be my guest.'

Pulling away the tulle ribbon that bound the box, Río lifted the lid, feeling – like Pandora – a little apprehensive. Inside, nestled in scented tissue paper, was a treasure trove of silk: chiffon, foulard, crêpe de chine. Río looked at Shane in astonishment.

'It's beautiful,' she breathed.

'Better than the stuff Baldy bought you?'

'I keep telling you—'

'"He didn't buy me anything."' Shane finished the sentence for her, mimicking her vexed tone. Then he smiled, and nodded at the frippery that was clamouring for her attention. 'Go ahead,' he said. 'Have a look.'

No one had ever bought lingerie for Río before in her life. With reverent hands, she lifted item after item of exquisite underthings from the folds of tissue paper, and as she did, rose petals drifted onto the carpet. A scalloped bra trimmed with layer upon layer of ruffled baby-blue satin; another in ebony watered moiré: both with matching French knickers. A baby-doll nightie in barely-there mousseline, a pair of high-heeled mules with marabou feather pompoms. An assortment of embroidered garters, a dozen gossamer stockings, a butterfly's wing of a camisole.

When she'd finished marvelling at the gauzy articles, Río laid them carefully back in their tissue paper nest, and placed the lid back on, firmly – as if it were a fabulous confection of chocolate and she was on a diet.

'Well?' asked Shane.

'Well what?'

'Don't you want to keep them?'

'Of course I do!'

'Then they're yours.'

Río gave Shane an uncertain look. 'No strings attached?'

'Strings? Ribbons might be more appropriate.'

Río gazed at the box as if she could hear little siren songs emanating from it. Then she reached for her champagne glass and drained it. 'I'm definitely over the limit now,' she stated.

'Whereas I have been a model of restraint. I could still chauffeur you to the Castle, where a deluxe suite awaits with champagne chilling and dinner already paid for.'

'No ribbons attached?'

'No ribbons attached.'

'How many beds are there?'

'Alas, there is just the one. But it measures at least nine feet by nine. We could put a bolster down the middle to designate our sleeping areas.'

Río did a little muzzy thinking. The notion of a night in a five-star hotel – not having to cook or clear away or wash up, and being waited on hand and foot instead of doing the waiting – was enormously seductive. Maybe she could have a massage or some kind of spa treatment – the spa in Coolnamara Castle was the last word in luxury. Fleur always raved about the hot stone treatment, and had promised to treat Río to one for her next birthday. Looking down at the box that contained the fairy-tale lingerie, Río decided that she *could* go to the ball – this once.

'If we're going to do this,' she said slowly, 'I'd better get into something a bit smarter than pyjama bottoms and T-shirt.' She rose to her feet, cluching the box to her bosom.

'How long will that take you?' asked Shane.

'Give me fifteen minutes,' said Río.

Fifteen minutes later, Río and Shane were standing in the hallway of Harbour View, looking through the open front door at the rain. Underneath Río's smart new dress she was wearing the ebony silk bra (she'd discovered that its clasp was a tiny red rosebud!) with matching knickers and a pair of sheer silk stockings. There was no room for a toothbrush in her teeny tiny purse, so she'd stuck it behind her ear.

Shane was wearing a suit (the first time Río had ever seen him in one) but no tie; French cuffs, but no cufflinks. He had the air of a dapper vagabond, and Río realised, as she caught a glimpse of their reflection in the hall mirror, that they made a damn fine couple. They smiled at each other, and then Shane jacked up a big black umbrella and said: 'Let's make a run for it.'

They piled into the car, and Río strapped herself into the passenger seat, then went to turn on the CD player.

'Wait,' said Shane, laying a hand over hers. 'I've something here I want you to play.'

And as they took off down the main street of Lissamore, the strains of Duran Duran's 'Río' could be heard thrumming over the stereo speakers.

In Coolnamara Castle, a porter led them to their suite. It overlooked the lake, as Shane had promised, and was sumptuously furnished with antiques, paintings, ornate mirrors and a vast four-poster bed swathed in rich brocade. Logs were set in a fire basket ready to be lit, and a wide French window opened onto a balcony ablaze with Virginia creeper. If ever such a property were to come under her remit, this is just how Río would have staged it. Champagne was waiting for them in an ice bucket, and in the en suite bathroom Molton Brown products were lined up on glass shelves, pleading to be pilfered.

'Yay!' said Río, ducking into the bathroom and cramming soaps, gels, shampoos and body lotions into a Coolnamara Castle laundry bag before shimmying back into the sitting room and setting upon the sewing kits and notepads and pencils. 'And look, chocolates, heart-shaped shortbread! They've thought of everything. Fresh fruit – check. Books, flowers, candles – check. Hell, I suppose I can't take *all* this stuff home with me. Music – check. Binoculars – check! But where's the television?'

'There isn't one,' said Shane. 'It's a television-free zone. You're meant to look at the view instead. That's why they provide binoculars.'

Río wandered out onto the balcony as Shane stripped the foil from the champagne bottle. It felt a little unreal to be alone in a hotel bedroom with her ex, especially in such quintessentially romantic surroundings. When they'd conducted their whirlwind affair all those years ago, they'd had no money to spend on luxurious hotel rooms. They'd snatched precious hours in Shane's dingy flat in Galway, or backstage in his

305

dressing room or – as in the instance when Finn had been conceived – alfresco. The sound of the champagne cork popping made her turn. Bubbly was fizzing over the neck of the bottle, and she darted back into the room before any could be wasted.

'*Sláinte*,' said Shane, when he'd finished pouring.

'*Sláinte* back.'

They raised their glasses and looked at each other over the rims. Then Río took a step back, set her glass down on a side table, and picked up a book, just for something to do. It was a volume of erotic verse, she realised too late as she opened it randomly at a page upon which she read the following:

> I was content to serve you up
> My ballock-full for your grace cup.

Her eyes took in the words 'cunt', 'arse', 'fuck' and 'frig' before she realised that the author of the poem was none other than Rochester, the debauched earl who had been played by Johnny Depp in some film she'd seen on DVD.

'Oh, this is very rude stuff!' she exclaimed.

'Yeah? Show me,' said Shane.

Swiftly, Río turned to another page and handed the book to Shane, hoping that the verses were less lurid than the ones she'd just read.

'Well, whaddoyaknow!' said Shane. 'I know this. It's from *Carmina Burana*.'

'Oh? Read it to me,' said Río.

'No. I'd feel like an eejit, standing here spouting poetry.'

'Oh, please! It means that I can e-mail one of your fantasy websites to say that Shane Byrne read me an erotic poem in real life.'

'OK. But you're not to snigger.' Shane cleared his throat. '"Innocent breasts",' he began.

'Hmm. There ain't anything very innocent about these breasts,' remarked Río, looking down at her cleavage.

Shane gave her a pissed-off look. 'I'm not going to do this, Río, if you're going to interrupt.'

'Sorry.'

'I'll make it "beautiful breasts" instead, OK?'

'OK, OK. "Beautiful breasts" is good.'

'"Beautiful breasts", resumed Shane, '"when I have looked upon them,

Would that my hands were there,

How I have craved, and dreaming thus upon them,

Love wakened from despair.

Beauty on her lips flaming,

Rose red with her shaming,

And I with passion burning

And with my whole heart yearning

For her mouth, her mouth, her mouth

That on her beauty I might slake my drouth.'

Río was speechless. The poem, as read by Shane in his dark velvet voice, was astonishingly erotic. And even though she hadn't a clue what 'slake my drouth' meant, he'd made it sound like something devoutly to be wished for. 'Oh,' she managed finally.

Shane put the book down. He looked at her from under his eyebrows, and then he allowed his eyes to travel downward. 'Would that my hands were there,' he said, slanting her a smile. 'You're in great shape, Río. I remember you always used to go braless. It was very sexy.'

'That was back in the days when my breasts *were* innocent,' said Río ruefully. 'I needs must wear a bra now. Gravity has a way of creeping up on a girl.'

'Tell me it's the present I gave you.'

Oh, God. Something about the way Shane was looking at her made her know that he knew it was the present he had given her. And not only that – that he knew that *she* knew he knew. 'It's the present you gave me,' she admitted.

'The blue one or the black?'

'The black. To go with my stockings.'

'Stockings, too?' He sucked in his breath. 'With the suspender thingy?'

'I thought they called them garter belts in America?'

'I don't know what they call them in America. I've never bought underwear for a gal before.'

'In that case, I feel privileged to be the first.'

'Did I get your bra size right?'

Río hesitated, then gave him a challenging look. 'Maybe you should check for yourself.'

'I think,' said Shane, taking a step closer, 'that that's a very good idea. Did Baldy get the size right?'

'How many times do I have to tell you—'

Shane laughed. 'You sure look beautiful when you're angry, Miz Kinsella.' Reaching out a hand, he put a finger under her chin and tilted it. '"Beauty on her lips flaming",' he murmured.

'You know the poem by heart?' She wanted to hear it again. His voice always did it for her.

'Yes, I do. I recorded it for an audio anthology of love poems for next Valentine's Day.'

Río bit her lip, then lowered her eyes. 'Remind me how it goes again?'

'"Beautiful breasts",' murmured Shane, '"when I have looked upon them, Would that my hands were there . . ."'

And as he trailed his fingers from her mouth to her shoulder, Río found herself wishing, too, that his hands were there. But Shane was taking things slowly. She remembered how in the past, she had felt as if under the spell of a master musician when Shane took charge of their love-making. He'd control proceedings adroitly, plucking at one invisible string to make her sing, stroking another to make her sob. Now his touch indicated that she turn her back to him, and she complied, feeling his fingers brush against her skin as he drew the zipper of her dress slowly from the nape of her neck to the very base of her spine.

'"How I have craved",' Shane breathed, running his hands back up from tailbone to shoulder blades, '"and dreaming thus upon them, love wakened from despair".' Río could not prevent a give-away shudder. The corresponding smile in his voice made her feel more shuddery still, as a knuckle skimmed her ribcage and he asked: 'May I?'

'Yes.'

Unhooking the rosebud clasp of her bra, Shane gently tugged at the ebony silk so that he could cup her breasts. '"And dreaming thus upon them, love wakened from despair",' he repeated, retracing the contour of her back with a finger. '"Beauty. Beauty on her lips flaming, rose red with her shaming . . .".' Río pressed herself closer into him and found that while she might be trembling, Shane was hard with arousal. 'And?' she prompted weakly, as the palms of his hands travelled over belly and breasts and buttocks.

'"And I with passion burning . . ."'

Shane scooped up the mass of her hair to drop kiss after kiss on the nape of her neck, and Río half-closed her eyes in a virtual swoon, before turning to him.

'"And with my whole heart yearning",' he crooned, lowering his mouth to her collarbone and sliding the sleeves of her dress along her arms. She heard the fabric fall to the floor with a sigh, and felt an artful finger slip under silk. Oh! He'd unwrapped her like a present.

Shane's breath was coming faster now, but it was more measured than Río's, who heard herself say, in a very ragged voice,

'Yearning – for what, Shane?'

'"For her mouth",' he replied. Oh, God! Río felt herself dissolve as his sleight of hand worked its magic. She clung to him as he drew her down upon the bed and covered her body with his.

'"Her mouth . . ." *Your* mouth . . .' Shane smiled down at her, and she saw that the pupils of his eyes were very, very black. 'That on *your* beauty I might slake my drouth.'

As he lowered his face to hers, Río pulled at the fabric of his shirt and slid her hands beneath, revelling in the sensation of skin on skin. And when he'd finally stopped kissing her mouth and had moved on to many, many other parts of her, playing the instrument of her body *adagio*, *ad libitum*, *appassionata* and *glissando*, she stretched languorously, to allow him full access. 'What's "slake my drouth" mean, Shane?' she asked drowsily, tangling her fingers in his hair.

'It means,' he said, 'to "quench my thirst". I've been parched for you for an awful long time, Río. You are that river you know. The one in the song.'

'Oh!' Río remembered the song they'd listened to in her car earlier, as they drove through the magical landscape of Coolnamara, to their sojourn in this fairytale castle. 'The one twisting through dusty land?'

'The very one.'

Río smiled, and wrapped her limbs around him. 'Drink all you want of me,' she said.

Chapter Twenty-three

Dervla never went to bed with someone on a first date, and she had no intention of doing so this evening, so why had she gone shopping for brand-new lingerie at lunchtime?

Because a girl needs a treat, she persuaded herself, as she stood before the mirror in the ladies' room of the Hamilton Hotel, checking out her look. Having opted for elegance with a dash of sex appeal, she was wearing her 'Chanel' suit. It was actually a very good bespoke copy by her dressmaker comprising a skirt that streamlined her derrière and skimmed her knees, teamed with a beautifully cut jacket, in red and ecru tweed. Her black patent sling-backed stilettos – shiny as her newly styled hair – clicked satisfyingly on the tiled floor as she angled herself this way and that. Did she look the business? Yes, she most certainly did.

Hm. Looking the business was all very well, but it was so long since Dervla had been on a date that she'd forgotten how to behave. Did one flirt? Or was flirting unseemly in a woman hitting forty? Did one talk shop? No, no – please, no – she was fed up talking shop, especially now that house prices were the new weather when it came to small talk. She could small talk about wine. She had consulted her *Bluffer's Guide* in order to bone up on Christian's specialised subject, so hopefully she wouldn't appear too ignorant when the sommelier poured Burgundy or Bordeaux into her glass. She could allow herself wine tonight, since she wasn't driving.

She checked the time on her phone. It was just after seven thirty. If she sprayed herself with scent now and retouched her lipstick she'd be a very acceptable five minutes late, and she could make a poised entrance into the restaurant upstairs.

Unclasping her bag, she took out her atomiser, and as she did, the door to the ladies opened and a young woman with a buggy came through. She was laden with carrier bags, she had a baby strapped to her front, and she was trying to soothe a screaming child, who was struggling against his harness like a miniature King Kong.

She shot Dervla an apologetic look. 'Excuse me,' she said. 'My little boy has been caught short, and he's too young to go into the men's toilet by himself. I hope you don't mind. I know this hotel is dead posh, but there was nowhere else I could go.'

'I don't mind at all,' said Dervla, with a smile, spritzing herself with eau de parfum and reaching for her lipstick. In the mirror, she could see the woman fumbling with the straps on the buggy as the small boy threshed around. 'Stop it, Rocco,' she said. 'Ssh, now. Hush, hush – will you ever give over that racket? Stop – *please* stop. Now lookit! You've gone and made your sister cry!'

Rocco was puce in the face, roaring and shaking his fists like a bad actor playing King Lear, and to add to the drama, the poor baby had started to whimper and squirm in her sling, crushed as she was between Rocco's flailing limbs and her mother's bosom. Free at last, Rocco made a bid for escape, but the minute he propelled himself out of the buggy, the weight of the carrier bags hitched to its handles threatened to topple it over. His mother lunged for the bags and dumped them randomly on the floor where they lay, spilling their contents. Then, grabbing Rocco by the hand, she started pulling him in the direction of one of the cubicles. It was, however, patently clear that all three members of the family were not going to fit in, and it was then that Dervla saw that the woman was pregnant.

She set down her lipstick. 'Please let me help you,' she said.

'Oh!' The woman looked at Dervla as if she were an angel descended from heaven. 'Would you mind? Thank you *so* much – that'd be brilliant. If you could just take Angelina for me while I help Rocco . . . ?' And the woman started unstrapping the bundle attached to her chest.

Dervla hesitated, wishing there was some other way she could help. She wasn't very good with babies. She tended to avoid those of her friends who had become mothers because they talked about nothing else but nappies and formula, and croup, whatever that was. And most babies she thought hideously ugly. But the baby that was handed to her had the face of a Raphael cherub framed by golden curls. Angelina blinked up at Dervla with forget-me-not-blue eyes, and her rosebud mouth rounded in a kissable 'O' of surprise.

'I don't think Angie's ever seen anyone with such red lipstick before,' said her mother. 'Maybe she thinks you're a clown. Um, no offence.'

'None taken,' said Dervla, with a laugh, taking the child into her arms. 'Angie! Hello, Angie! How lovely to meet you! What a pretty girl! What age is she?'

'Four months. She's been growing like the clappers since I put her on solids. I don't know what I'm going to do when she gets too big for the sling. I'll have to get myself a double buggy. More feckin' expense.' Angelina's mum finally succeeded in manoeuvring Rocco into the loo. 'Now. In we go. Good boy. Here, let me help you with that . . .' and as the door shut behind them, Dervla heard Rocco being asked if it was number one or number twos. Her heart sank a little when she heard it was to be number twos. She supposed this could take some time.

There was a gilt boudoir chair on the other side of the ladies. Moseying over to it, Dervla shifted Angelina onto her hip, the way she'd seen mothers of young babies do. It felt right, somehow. It felt – well – *comfortable*, as if her hip had been specifically designed to be a perch for babies. Settling herself down to wait until Rocco had delivered his number two, she transferred Angie from her hip to her lap and checked out her reflection again. Hm. The 'baby as fashion accessory look' suited her rather well, she decided. Particularly one as cute as this Angie was. The child was still gazing up at her mouth with a kind of awe.

'Well, my little Angel!' said Dervla, automatically seguing into the voice used by women all over the world when addressing infants. 'You like my lipstick, do you? You don't need lipstick, Angel! Your mouth is perfect as it is – as pretty as a peony!'

Dervla started to jiggle her knees, and as she did, something miraculous happened. Angelina smiled. It was like watching speeded-up footage of a flower blooming on the National Geographic Channel, and it made Dervla's heart blossom in equal measure.

Uh-oh. It was the first time she had ever, ever felt like this, and Dervla was quite unprepared for it. Was the overwhelming, biological urge to procreate finally kicking in before it was too late? She had read somewhere that the pupils of women's eyes dilate when they look at babies. It could have been her imagination, but her eyes in the mirror really *did* seem darker.

The mirror reflected not just Dervla in her exquisitely tailored suit and bonny little Angelina in her ruffly stuff; it also reflected the detritus scattered on the floor of the ladies' room. The buggy with its stained upholstery and grubby changing bag, the carrier bags disgorging products such as rusks and creams and wipes onto the floor: items as arcane to Dervla as the props of a magician.

Another bag spilled articles of chainstore underwear: a six-pack of plain cotton knickers, a nursing bra, a pair of pyjamas. These were not the shopping bags of a yummy mummy with money to spend. Dervla experienced a stab of guilt when she realised that the combined cost of knickers, bra and pyjamas was probably less than the sum she had splurged on a single pair of Agent Provocateur briefs earlier today.

But looking down at Angelina's little face, Dervla had no doubt that this child was more precious to her mother than the Krupp Diamond. That yearning rose in her again.

'Angelina, Angelina,' she murmured. 'What have you done to me? You are a little minx – that's what you are – to make me feel this way.'

The sound of the minx's mother's voice came from behind the door of the cubicle. 'Good boy!' she said. 'All done!' The door opened, and the pair emerged looking many times less frazzled than when they'd gone in. 'Now, we'll wash our handies, will we? Thank you so much,' she added, turning to Dervla. 'The name's Paula, by the way.'

'I'm Dervla,' said Dervla, turning Angelina round so that she could see her mama. 'Look, look! There's Mummy now! Wave your little handie!' She took Angelina's tiny starfish hand in hers and wiggled it, and Paula waved back, and said, 'Good baba!'

'I have to tell you,' continued Dervla, 'that I have absolutely fallen in love with your baby. She is the cutest thing I've ever seen. I'm very tempted to tuck her under my arm and kidnap her, and— Oh!'

Dervla felt a sudden wash of warmth on her lap. Looking down, she saw that the cutest thing she'd ever seen had been sick all over the skirt of her faux Chanel suit.

'Oh!' she said again, and, 'Oh my God, I am so *sorry*!' said Paula. The two women looked at each other, and it would have been impossible to tell who was the more horrified.

After a second or two of frozen non-action, Paula made the first move. She grabbed Angelina and set her on the floor, where she remained looking serenely up at her mother and gurgling. Then Paula pounced upon the pile of paper towels that lay folded by the wash-hand basin, and fell to her knees in front of Dervla, mopping ineffectually at the pool of sick that was spreading over the front of her skirt.

'No, no!' cried Dervla, leaping up and unzipping herself. 'That's going to make it worse – you're just rubbing it into the fabric.'

She wriggled out of the skirt and teetered in her heels over to the basin, where she saturated a handful of towels and started trying to swipe the sick off under the taps, but even as she did so, she knew it was futile. There was no way she could wear this skirt tonight: even if she got rid of the stain, it would take ages to dry and it would be impossible to get rid of the smell. Could she race home and change? No. By the time she got there and into a new outfit and back to the hotel in a cab it would be at least half-past eight. She'd just have to phone Christian and make some excuse; she couldn't tell him that she wasn't able to have dinner with him because she was covered in puke. But then what? This might be the only evening he had free in Galway. He might decide it wasn't worth asking her out again. He might even decide against doing business with her. She might never see him again. And he was the only man she had met in an awfully long time who had made her feel like a cat that wanted to be stroked. She felt like crying.

'I – I can't tell you how sorry I am,' stammered Paula, and when Dervla turned to the woman, she saw that she *was* crying. 'I've had the worst day, and now this happens. You're probably going to want to sue me. I'd say that suit's worth a fortune.' Paula's face had gone bright red, and she was abject as a beaten dog.

'Of course I'm not going to sue you,' said Dervla.

'Why not?' Paula looked incredulous. 'Doesn't everyone sue everyone these days?'

'No, no. Rest assured that suing you is the last thing on my mind. I'm actually more concerned about how I'm going to get myself out of the bloody hotel. I don't particularly want to have to get back into my skirt and walk through the foyer covered in vomit, and I can hardly walk out in what I'm wearing.'

'No. You'd get arrested,' said Paula, helpfully. 'It looks like you've missed out on a really hot date, and it's all my fault. Oh, Rocco, stop that! I've had to put up with enough from you today.'

Rocco was sitting on the floor beside his baby sister, trying to put a pair of knickers on her. He'd ransacked the carrier bag containing his mother's underwear, and was sporting another pair of knicks on his head. Paula crouched down and started putting things back into the bag, and as she reached for the pyjamas that were still attached to their chainstore plastic hanger, she paused.

'I know!' she said. 'The red on these pyjamas is practically identical to the red of your suit. You could wear them out of the hotel, and nobody would bat an eyelid.' Standing up, she held the pyjama bottoms against Dervla. The colours were a perfect match. 'It's just as well Angel didn't get sick on your jacket, though. You mightn't have gotten away with wearing the top.' Paula's pyjama top, Dervla saw, was emblazoned with the legend 'Porn Star'.

Dervla looked at the pyjama bottoms and shook her head. 'I don't think so.'

'Ah, go on, try them,' urged Paula. 'I bought them for my sister – she's around the same size as you.'

'I – I can't.'

'Why not? Go for it! Nothing ventured . . .'

Paula thrust the pyjamas at her, and, feeling a tad ridiculous, Dervla tentatively slid in first one black nylon-stockinged leg, then the other.

'Yeah!' said Paula. 'That works!'

Dervla surveyed herself in the mirror. Funnily enough, it did work. The pyjama bottoms could have been taken for palazzo pants. They were cut a little on the wide side, but being mid-calf, they displayed to advantage her shapely ankles and her elegant heels. Teamed with the jacket with its nipped-in waist and little peplum, the effect was curiously elegant.

'Could I really get away with it?' she speculated out loud.

'Deffo. Sure loads of people go around in pyjamas all the time. It's the latest thing.'

Possibly not when you're dining in a five-star hotel, thought Dervla. She reassessed her reflection, then nodded. 'Hell. Nothing ventured! I'm gonna go for it,' she said.

'Thank God!' Paula's face was still red, but now she was beaming with pleasure, not crying. 'I'm glad I could help in some way. Listen, give me over that skirt and I'll get my mam to give it a going-over. She swears by bicarbonate of soda to get the smell of sick off clothes. I'll have it right again by the morning, and I'll leave it for you at hotel reception. Unless you'd want me to put it in the post?'

'No, no, hotel reception's grand.'

Dervla handed over her skirt, and Paula rolled it gingerly into one of her bags. 'I'm sorry,' she said again. 'And I'm really grateful to you for not suing me. As for *you*, you bold, bold baba,' she said, stooping down to pick Angelina up from the floor, 'you should thank your lucky stars that you chose a nice lady to get sick on, and not an auld harridan.'

Dervla smiled. 'She's beautiful,' she said. 'She'll be a heart-breaker when she grows up.'

'And if she does that,' said Paula ruefully, 'she'll take after her daddy. Thanks again, Dervla. You need have no worries that that skirt won't be waiting for you tomorrow.'

'I know it will, Paula. Good luck.' Dervla picked up her bag. 'Oh – I'll leave your pyjama bottoms at reception for you too, shall I?'

Paula shook her head. 'Nah. Hang on to them. They look fantastic on you. Honestly. And they only cost six euros.'

As Dervla high-heeled her way back to the foyer, a gaggle of women were emerging from the bar. She braced herself for

318

sniggers as she strode past them in her pyjama bottoms, then realised she didn't care. She just set her shoulders a little further back, and raised her chin an extra half-inch. Halfway across the floor she heard a voice say, 'That's Dervla Kinsella. Doesn't she look fantastic? I wonder what label she's wearing?'

'It's Chanel,' came the categorical response. 'And if it's not, it's a bloody good copy.'

And as Dervla made her presence known to the maître d' standing sentinel at the door to the restaurant, she saw, on the other side of the room, Christian Vaughan rise to greet her, admiration in his eyes.

On Tuesday morning, Dervla was woken by Christian Vaughan kissing her shoulder. 'Oh,' she said, rubbing sleep from her eyes. 'It's you. How strange. I never go to bed with someone on a first date.'

'You just did,' he told her. 'And that has made me a very happy man.'

And half an hour later, when Dervla had made Christian an even happier man, he reached for the room service menu and said, 'Shall we order breakfast?'

'Mm. That would be good.'

'Juice?'

'Orange, please.'

'Let's add a little champagne, and make it a Buck's Fizz. Porridge or cereal?'

'Um . . . Porridge. With cream please.'

'A cooked breakfast?'

'Definitely. Scrambled eggs, tomatoes, mushrooms, bacon and hash browns.'

'Toast or croissant?'

'Croissant.'

'They do *pain au chocolat*.'

'Go for it!'

Christian smiled at her, and she saw that admiration in his eyes again. 'I love a woman with a hearty appetite,' he said. 'It indicates a lust for life.'

'Maybe I'm just hungry after all that exercise,' replied Dervla.

While Christian spoke to room service, she went to the bathroom. From the bedroom, she could hear him talking on the phone with admirable patience: it must have taken nearly five minutes for him to make his order understood.

Dervla took advantage of the extended conversation to improvise a toilette, thanking the good lord that she always carried cosmetic ammo. She splashed her face with water; slapped on some tinted moisturiser; rubbed away last night's mascara from under her eyes and applied a little fresh MAC Coal Black; combed her sleek bob and then changed her mind and messed it up a bit.

And all the time she was thinking about Christian. Christian Vaughan was charming, full of character and extremely well presented. He was finished with a superb eye to detail, and in turn-key condition. An exclusive and elegant jewel of gracious proportions and in excellent decorative order with superb fixtures and fittings, Christian presented a unique opportunity for the discerning individual. He had the wow factor, he had the potential to be a forever investment. And as for the all-important location factor? If Christian Vaughan moved to Coolnamara, location was as perfect as it could get.

Desirability aside, Christian had made her laugh – and it had been a long time since Dervla had worn anything but a polite smile during intercourse (sexual or social) with the opposite sex. She had enjoyed his company so much last night that she had even forgotten to drop into the conversation those little gems from the *Bluffer's Guides* that she usually relied upon to make an impression: it simply didn't seem necessary to make an effort. Dervla had never felt so at ease – so *right* – with anyone in her life before. She remembered how, when she had shown him round

320

the Old Rectory, he had turned to her and said, 'Isn't it a bitch when you fall in love with a house?'

It *was* a bitch when you fell in love with a house. She knew that. But there were ways and means of securing a house. It was even more of a bitch, Dervla decided, when you fell in love with a man.

Chapter Twenty-four

On Tuesday morning, Río was woken by Shane kissing her shoulder.

'Oh,' she said, rubbing sleep from her eyes. 'It's you. How weird. We shouldn't really have done that, should we?'

'I'm glad we did,' he told her. 'It has made me a very happy man.'

'But it was a drunken and irresponsible thing to do.'

'You might have been drunk. I wasn't.'

'It was still irresponsible.'

'Give me one reason why it was irresponsible.'

'Um. You're right. It wasn't irresponsible at all. Yesterday was fun.'

After Shane had un-giftwrapped her and they'd spent a couple of hours beneath the canopy of the four-poster, they had shared a bath and polished off the bottle of champagne. And then a table by the window had been laid with pristine linen and silverware and dinner had been brought to their room, and they'd sat there in the hotel's fluffy complimentary robes and played the 'Remember when . . . ?' game, which didn't last that long because they didn't have a whole lot of shared memories, so they turned it into the 'What if . . . ?' game instead.

'What if Dervla hadn't had a thing for me? Would we have ended up together?' Shane had asked.

'I doubt it. You were dead set on getting out of Ireland. I couldn't have handled the homesickness.'

'But you didn't even have a home in those days! You were living in a squat!'

'I mean homesick for Coolnamara. I couldn't have reared Finn in LA, Shane.'

'What if I'd stayed? What if we'd got married? What if we'd had more kids?'

'You'd have had to give up acting and got yourself a regular job in order to support us. And then you'd have started to resent me and the kids, and taken up drinking, or gone off with another woman. And then we'd have got divorced, and I'd have sued you for maintenance, and we'd have ended up hating each other. And I'd have denied you access to the kids, and Finn would have gone off the rails and ended up on crack, and I'd have been labelled an unfit mother, and the kids would have been taken into care.'

'It's just as well I buggered off then, isn't it? What if I'd applied for shared custody and you'd have had to bring Finn to LA and then decided you liked it? What if . . . ?'

And when they'd finished playing the 'What if . . . ? game they'd snuck downstairs in their robes to the cloakroom where Wellington boots in all shapes and sizes were available for guests of the hotel, and they'd gone for a skinny-dip in the lake where a sickle moon was reflected upside down like a burnished scimitar, and where an owl was hooting in the woods.

'What are we going to do today?' Shane asked, now that he'd admired Río's nakedness all over again (the morning sun made her a little coyer than she'd been last night). 'Can we go skinny-dipping again? That was a hoot.'

'That was irresponsible too. We shouldn't have gone swimming after eating and drinking so much.'

'That's what I love about being with you, Río: the sense of irresponsibility – like something fun could happen at any time and I wouldn't have to worry about what my agent or manager or PR person might have to say, or what my contract stipulates. Being in LA is like being back at school. Do you know that there's even a clause in my contract that prohibits me from going boar-hunting?'

'Dammit! I was going to suggest we go boar-hunting this afternoon. Maybe we should go bungee-jumping instead.'

'I'm not allowed to do that either,' said Shane, gloomily.

'Well, we can't make too many plans. I'll probably have to work. What time is it?'

'I haven't a clue.'

Río reached for her phone and turned it on. 'I'd better find out. I can't run the risk of missing a fare.'

'How come you weren't working yesterday?' asked Shane.

'I decided to take the day off. I thought it would be nice to spend time with my long-lost son. Except he turned out to be a dirty stop-out. I'd love to know where he went on Sunday night. I wonder if he somehow ended up with that horrible little Izzy thing.'

'She's not horrible.'

'Oh, of course you'd know her a lot better than me,' said Río snittily. 'I'd forgotten you spent half of Sunday night flirting with her.'

'Well, what about you and Baldy?'

She shot him a cross look. 'I wish you'd stop calling him that.'

'Why?'

'It's unkind. And he's actually a really sound bloke. The more I get to know him the more I like him.'

'How well *do* you know him?'

'Sunday night was the third time we've met.'

Shane yawned. 'Wow. You're practically soul mates.'

'Ooh. Are we bickering?'

'The best couples bicker.'

'We're not a couple.'

'I haven't given up on that idea.'

'What do you mean?'

'I have another present for you.'

Something about Shane's demeanour told Río what was coming. She felt her heart go into a kind of skid as he swung his legs out of bed, strolled over to where he'd hung his jacket last night, produced a small box from the pocket, and set it on the quilt.

'You know what that is,' he said.

She nodded.

'What is it?' he asked.

'It's a ring.'

'Aren't you going to open the box?'

Río sent him a pleading look. 'No, Shane. Please don't ask me to.'

'Why not?'

'Because I'm not going to marry you.'

'But we're good together, Río! Last night proved that. And if you marry me I can offer you all the security you need. I owe it to you after all these years. You've worked so hard, and you've brought Finn up practically single-handed, and I adore you for that. You've been so brave and good and—'

'No, I haven't – shuttup!' Río clamped her hands over her ears.

'No, *you* shut up!' Shane leaned towards her and kissed her, and she did shut up. 'Don't say anything just yet,' he said, after he'd kissed her quite forcefully. 'Just think about it.'

She knew she shouldn't have opened the box, but she couldn't resist it, any more than she had resisted the offer of champagne and lingerie and a deluxe suite last night.

It was a diamond. It was the prettiest damn diamond she had ever seen. Set in gleaming platinum, it shimmered as if it was alive – and Río knew by the size that it had cost Shane an absurd amount of money.

She looked at the diamond, and she looked at Shane, and then she looked back at the diamond, and she felt choked with gratitude for the quixotic impulse that had compelled him to do this.

'It cost a fortune, didn't it?'

'Maybe.'

'Do you mind me asking how much?'

'A hundred thousand dollars.'

'Sweet Jesus, Shane! I hope it's insured!'

'Damn right it's insured.'

She looked at him sternly. 'You know I can't accept it.'

'I want you to have it, Río. Even if you're not going to marry me, this is something that proves how much I respect you as our son's mother. Look on it as a friendship ring.'

'But I'll never wear it! And if I do, I'll lose it. I'll leave it in the loo of some pub, or it'll come off when I'm swimming, or when I'm weeding someone's garden, or someone will mug me for it. You've got to take it back.'

'I don't want it back.'

'Then what'll I do with it?'

'Sell it.'

There was a long, long silence while Río looked down at the ring.

'Sell it,' said Shane again.

She gave him a look that combined guilt with relief. 'You'd really allow me to do that?'

'It's yours to do what you like with, Río. I'm sure there's a lot you could do with the money.'

She shook her head. 'No. I told you I'm OK for money.' She looked at the ring thoughtfully, slipping it onto one finger, then another. 'But Finn isn't. He's completely skint after Thailand, and the only way he's going to make a living is by getting the hell out of here and looking for work some place foreign. And if he disappeared from my life so soon again, Shane, I don't think I could bear it.'

'What about the dive outfit on Inishclare? Couldn't he get work there?'

'It's closing down. And I know it's a mad idea, but when I heard that, I thought how fantastic it would be if Finn had some capital, and could look into setting up a dive shop here, in Lissamore.'

'He'd still have to get a loan.'

'I know, but he'd never get any kind of loan if he went to the bank empty-handed. A hundred thousand dollars would make a hell of a difference.'

'What if he decides he wants to set up somewhere else?'

'You mean somewhere foreign?'

'Yeah.'

'Then that's what he'd have to do. I'm not going to stand in the way of Finn following his dream – and I know I'm sounding like something out of *Faraway* but I don't care. Whatever way you look at it, Shane, this ring could help finance Finn's future.'

'What about *your* future, Río?' said Shane.

'I told you yesterday. I'm content to carry on as I am.'

'Even without Finn?'

'If he's following his dream, I'm more than content. I'm happy.'

Shane put his hands on either side of Río's face and looked at her, and she realised that the expression he had on was the one he wore when studying a script. He was reading her. 'You really, really mean that, don't you?' he asked.

Río nodded.

'See? That's why I adore you. You are the best mother in the world.'

'No, I'm not. Every mother is the best in the world. Just ask Hallmark.'

'You silly, lovely woman.'

'You silly, lovely man.'

'This is where we kiss in the script.'

They smiled at each other, and as Shane moved in to kiss her, Río's phone went.

'A pox on your phone! Do you have to take that?' he asked.

'Yes, I do,' said Río, checking out the display. 'It's Finn.'

Before she picked up, Río clambered out of bed and slipped into her hotel robe. She didn't much like the idea of talking to her son on the phone while she was in bed with her lover, even if the lover was her son's father, and even if her son's father wasn't going to be her lover any more after today.

'Hello, Finnster!'

'Hey, Ma. Where have you and Dad got to? I came home last night and you were both gone, and your phones were switched off.'

'We're in Coolnamara Castle. Dad decided to take me out for dinner, and we stayed over because we were too over the limit to drive back to Lissamore. Sorry. We should have left a message.'

'You . . . stayed over?'

'In separate rooms, of course!'

'Oh, OK.'

Río moseyed over to the window to get a load of the view while she talked. The sun was admiring its reflection in the lake, but there were big rain clouds on the horizon where a cold front was approaching from the west. 'Where did you get to on Sunday night?' she asked.

'I – er – stayed over at the Bolger house.'

'The *Bolger* house? The Villa Felicity?'

'Yes. Izzy and I have a lot in common. She's cool.'

'Yeah?' said Río. *No!* she thought. The first time Finn had seen the girl, he'd described her as a hottie. The fact that she was cool as well made her even more dangerous.

'Yeah,' continued Finn. 'She's a diver. In fact, turns out we were in Tao at the same time.'

Río felt like coming out with the same quip that Shane had used earlier about Izzy's father – 'So you're practically soul mates' – but she refrained. Instead she said, in what she hoped was a conversational tone: 'They're off today, the Bolgers, aren't they?'

'Well, they were meant to be. But Izzy's persuaded her dad to stay on for a while. I'm meeting her for lunch later.'

'Nice. Well, enjoy!' The exclamation mark cost Río some effort. 'Will we see you later for supper?'

'Probably not. I'm not sure what time I'll be home.'

'OK. Bye-bye, love.'

'What's wrong?' asked Shane, as Río dropped the phone onto the bed.

'Nothing.'

'You were *so* right, Río Kinsella.'

'Right about what?'

'You are a crap liar.'

'Oh, it's stupid.' Río flung herself down beside him. 'It's just that it looks as if Finn might have hooked up with that little Izzy Bolger.'

'And why would that not be a good thing?'

'I don't like her and she can't stand me.'

'How do you know she can't stand you?'

'Women's intuition.'

Shane shrugged. 'Women never like the girls their sons hook up with, do they?'

'I liked loads of his other girlfriends. His last one, Maggie, was the best. She used to bring me breakfast in bed.'

'Why did you tell him we stayed in separate rooms?'

'Why do you think? He'd be mortified to know that we'd slept together.'

'Río, we *conceived* him together! Why would he be mortified?'

'Because nobody likes to imagine their parents having sex.'

'Ah. I guess you have a point. I wonder how he'd have handled it if you'd arrived home wearing a rock?'

'You mustn't tell him about that, Shane. Never, ever tell him that you offered me that ring. He'd be appalled if he thought I'd sold it to give him a step up on the career ladder.'

'What'll I tell him, then?'

'Just say you're prepared to finance him to the tune of €100,000.'

Shane lay back against the pillows and gave her that look again. 'Is there nothing else I can give you, Río, that would make you happy?'

'I just told you that I'm perfectly happy,' she returned, trying to rearrange her features into an unreadable expression. The truth was that she wasn't happy at all with the news of Finn's liaison with Isabella Bolger.

'How about a new car?'

'No.'

'New clothes?'

'No.'

'A dream holiday?'

'No.'

'Because I can afford all that shit now, Río. My agent's signed a really good deal for the next series. I could give you practically anything you want.'

'You are sweet, Shane. But the only thing I want is something you can't give me because it doesn't exist any more.'

'What's that?'

'Coral Cottage.'

'Hm. Maybe I could buy Coral Mansion now that it's up for sale?'

'I don't think even you could afford the asking price.'

'What's Dervla asking?'

'Five and a half million.'

'Fuck me sideways! You could buy the Taj Mahal for that.'

'That's what Dervla has as her screen saver.'

'The Taj Mahal?'

'Yeah. What's your screen saver, by the way?'

'Why do you want to know?'

'You told me when we did that stupid quiz that the photograph on your screen saver was your most treasured possession.'

'My screen saver,' said Shane, reaching out and toying with a strand of Río's hair, 'is the photograph of you and Dervla that I took just before your mother died.'

'Two girls in silk kimonos?'

'Yep.'

Both beautiful, one I adore . . . He adored her, she knew that. He'd offered her love, marriage, a new life in LA. He'd offered her a future beyond the wildest dreams of most women in the world. But he'd offered her the impossible. She could no more leave Coolnamara now than she could have twenty years ago. The reason was implicit in the motto embroidered on the sampler Dervla had given her. *Home is where the Heart is.* And Río's heart belonged, always had and always would belong, in Coolnamara.

She suddenly thought she might cry, but she really, really didn't want to. She, Río, was a strong, independent woman whose name meant 'queenly', and queens never cried. She needed something to distract her. Reaching for the volume of erotic verse, she thrust it at Shane and said, 'Read me something.'

'What?'

'I dunno. Just open it at random.'

'OK.' Shane opened the book, cleared his throat, and in his lovely, sonorous voice read the following:

'In the Garden of Eden lay Adam
Complacently stroking his madam,
And loud was his mirth
For he knew that on earth
There were only two balls – and he had 'em.'

331

'You eejit, Shane Byrne!' laughed Río. 'You deserve a kiss for that!'

'I deserve a kiss for reading a rude limerick? Jeez, Río, I didn't get a kiss when I gave you that stonking great rock!'

'Oh, you deserve more than a kiss for that,' she said, leaning into him with a smile.

But just as the kiss was getting interesting, her phone went again.

'Shit, shit, *shit*!' Shane said, with feeling. 'Do you have to take that?'

'I'd better. It's Dervla.'

'Your phone has the worst timing in the world,' he grumbled, pulling the quilt over his head.

'It actually might have the best. You know what they say about delayed gratification. Hi, Dervla. What's up?' Río slid out of bed and padded back towards the window. The clouds had encroached further into the view, and raindrops had started to dent the pewter surface of the lake.

'Hello, my little sibling!' purred Dervla. 'How are you?'

Río nearly dropped the phone. She wasn't sure she'd ever heard her sister purr before. If she hadn't called her 'little sibling', she'd have thought that Dervla might have dialled a wrong number.

'I've just had the most glorious breakfast!' came Dervla's velvety voice again.

That was weird. To Río's reasonably certain knowledge, Dervla seldom bothered with breakfast.

'Isn't it a bit late for breakfast? You've usually got an entire morning's work behind you at this hour of the day.'

'There's more to life than work, Río. Isn't it a glorious morning?'

'Not where I am.'

'Poor thing!'

Taken aback by this expression of sympathy, Río decided it

was about time they got down to whatever business Dervla was calling about. 'What can I do for you, Dervla?'

'I hope you might do me a favour. I know this is very sudden, but can I ask you to stand in for me on any viewings that may come up in the Lissamore area this week? The team can cover the Galway region, but I hate asking them to travel further afield.'

'Um. Sure. Are you all right, Dervla? You're not sick or anything?' Dervla certainly didn't *sound* sick. She sounded like the cat who'd got the cream.

'No. I'm not sick. Actually, I'm going on holiday.'

'Holy moly.' Río nearly dropped the phone again. 'It's not like you to take off on the spur of the moment.'

'No, it's not, is it? But I've decided I need more spontaneity in my life. I've been too bloody *comme il faut* up till now.'

'Com il fo? What's that?'

'It means, "doing the right thing". I've decided a little more anarchy is called for.'

'Where are you going? Somalia?'

Dervla laughed. Because it was probably the first time ever that she'd laughed at one of Río's juvenile jokes, Río nearly dropped the phone a third time.

'No. I'm not going to Somalia. I'm going to Las Vegas.'

'Las *Vegas*? But that's *so* not you, Dervla!'

'I know. But it's the only place that can organise what I want in a hurry.'

What was *with* her sister? Did she have some secret addiction? Río's grip on the handset tightened. She'd never have dreamed that Dervla might have a gambling problem.

'Are you . . . is it some kind of *gambling* holiday, Dervla?'

Dervla laughed. 'No, Río. If there's one thing I've learned from the business I'm in, it's that gambling never pays.'

'So what *are* you going to do in Vegas?'

'I'm getting married,' said Dervla.

Río's phone clattered to the floor.

Chapter Twenty-five

Río needed to swim. So much had happened in the past few days that she craved time to herself.

After the phone call from Dervla, another had come asking her to pick up a fare from Ardmore. She had said a hasty goodbye to Shane (no time for anything more intimate than a quick kiss) and sped away like Cinderella, stopping off at her apartment on the way to change out of her fairy-tale threads.

Having dropped off her passenger, Río hit the beach. There, she stripped off again, glad to be rid of the obnoxious feeling of the man-made fabric of her suit against her skin. Maybe she should have taken Shane up on his offer of new clothes after all? But the suit was functional and creaseproof, and that was what mattered in her line of work. She had taken the precaution of putting her bathing togs on underneath – she hadn't skinny-dipped on this beach since the Villa Felicity had been built. Yet another reason for her to have taken umbrage against the Bolgers.

The sea was uninviting – a stone grey slab under a leaden sky. The only thing to do was to dive straight in. But Río knew that once the initial shock wore off, the temperature of the water was immaterial. For her, swimming was more about the mind than the body.

She struck out towards the buoy that marked the mooring

for Adair's boat, which she always used to gauge distance. Between that and the slipway was roughly fifty metres, and Río usually managed a swim of at least five laps, which she calculated to be around a quarter of a mile. She couldn't understand why people forked out a fortune to go training in a gym when you could get fresh air and exercise for free.

Once she reached the buoy, she turned over on her back and floated for a few moments. The sun was chiselling its way through the cloud: it looked as though it was going to turn into one of those days the west of Ireland is famous for, when you can experience all four seasons in the course of a single twenty-four-hour period. Launching herself against the tide, Río established a rhythm, arms slicing through the water, feet kicking vigorously, mind rerunning recent headlines in her life. If she were a news reader, they would go like this:

'Film Star on Nostalgic Visit to the Emerald Isle.'

'Dive God Returns Home.'

'Millionaire's Daughter Seduces Dive God.'

'Film Star Proposes to Former Girlfriend.'

'Top Business Woman Elopes with Strange Man.'

This final headline was the one that was of most concern to her right now. Had Dervla lost her mind? In the course of the phone call earlier that morning Río had learned that her big sister had decided to make major changes in her life after a baby had vomited on her and she'd been forced to wear a pair of pyjama bottoms to a hot date. It had been her Eureka moment, Dervla had told her, her Feel the Fear and Do It Anyway Opportunity of a Lifetime. And when the Vaughan bloke (for it had been he who had been the hot date) confessed that he'd invented a wine importers' conference in Galway as an excuse to see her again, Dervla had swooned and – as far as Río could see – lost all reason. They had booked a honeymoon suite in a fabulous resort in some place in Mexico called Careyes – stopping off in Vegas to make it official at the Little White Chapel first – and when they came back, they were going to move into the Old Rectory together and Dervla was going to wind up the business and write a book.

'A Mills & Boon romance?' Río had asked, and Dervla had tinkled with laughter.

Río wasn't so sure that Dervla had anything to laugh about. Mills & Boon romances had happy endings and didn't usually feature an elderly mother and a teenage daughter in their cast of characters, and as she recalled from an earlier conversation with her sister, this Christian Vaughan came with both responsibilities. Río feared that Dervla might have landed herself a man with a lot of baggage. But, hey, she thought – the gal was a grown-up, after all. What she did with her life was her business.

Her quarter-mile dispatched, Río swam ashore and clambered onto the slipway where she'd left her clothes. Her phone was ringing.

'Río Kinsella,' she answered.

'Hello, Río. That was some swim.'

'Who is this?'

'Don't worry. It's not a stalker. It's Adair Bolger. If you look up to your right you'll see me in the yoga pavilion.'

Río turned and looked up at the Villa Felicity. There, sure enough, was Adair standing on the yoga pavilion.

'What do you think you're doing, spying on me swimming?'

'A cat may look at a queen.'

'Not if you put its eyes out,' she retorted. 'What can I do for you, Adair?'

'I thought you might like to join me for refreshments?'

'Thanks, mister. I could do with something warm after that swim.'

'Hot chocolate?'

'Perfect. I'm on my way.'

Río wrapped herself in her beach towel and strolled over to the gate. Someone had been this way recently, she saw. The brambles had been beaten back and there was a shoe lying on the grass amongst the fallen apples under the trees. Izzy's, to judge by the size and style. She picked it up, and carried it along with her clothes across the overgrown lawn and onto the deck. Round the corner, the side door into the sitting room was open.

'Hi, there!' called Río.

'I'm in the kitchen,' came Adair's voice, bouncing off the walls of the cavernous house.

'I'd better stay on the deck. I'm still dripping wet.'

'Would you like a robe?'

'A robe would be great.'

Río set her clothing down, and balanced Izzy's shoe on the railing. She was towelling her hair vigorously when Adair emerged onto the deck carrying a robe that was even fluffier than the one she'd worn earlier that day in Coolnamara Castle.

'Thanks.' Taking it from him, she shrugged into it, noticing as she did so that the logo embroidered on the breast of the garment was that of the überposh Merrion Hotel in Dublin. 'I wouldn't have thought you were the kind of person to steal bathrobes from hotels,' she remarked.

'I didn't steal it. Izzy did.'

'Izzy did?' That the impeccably mannered daughter of the house was capable of stealing came as a surprise to Río.

'She was at some twenty-first shindig where you had to fetch stuff from all over Dublin, as a kind of competition.'

'You mean a party game?'

'Yeah. You know, like a pair of chopsticks from Wagamama or a cocktail glass from the Four Seasons. The one who pilfered the most items won. Izzy beat them to it by a mile.'

Río was curious. 'How did she get the robe?'

'She bribed some hapless hotel porter to let her have it. She can be a minx, sometimes, my Izzy.'

A minx? thought Río. Hm. Sounds more like spoiled brat behaviour to me. She had an image of a load of Hooray Henrys and Henriettas swanning around Dublin, snatching stuff from beleaguered serve persons.

'Let me fetch your chocolate,' said Adair. 'You must be freezing after that swim.'

'Nah, I'm used to it. I'm like a hardy perennial. And it's suddenly turned into a beautiful afternoon.'

It was true. All the weather forecasters were predicting an Indian summer. It would be a real treat to have a couple of weeks of good weather before winter came to claim Coolnamara.

Río watched Adair go back into the house. Then she perched on the rail and scanned the view, swinging her legs. She wondered, if the Bolgers had got planning permission for the helicopter pad that was to facilitate the coming and going of all their D4 pals, would he and Felicity still be married? If he applied for PP for his helipad now, would it be granted? It wouldn't surprise her. Planning permission was being granted for all kinds of projects now that the building market had slumped; projects that wouldn't have got the go-ahead a decade ago were being greenlighted left, right and centre in an effort to keep the economy buoyant.

'Hot chocolate, madam.'

Río turned to see Adair setting a mug down on the table.

'Thanks,' she said, moving across to join him.

'Is that Izzy's shoe?' he asked, nodding at the trainer on the rail.

'Yes. I found it in the garden.'

'She was fretting that it had gone missing. It's some limited edition must-have thing.'

Río sat down and wrapped her hands around her mug. 'I've never understood the appeal of "must-have" stuff.'

'It's a thing of the past now, anyway, isn't it?' Adair said. 'Now that the new austerity's hit.'

'Recession chic suits me. I've been recycling my clothes for years.' She took a sip of hot chocolate. 'Mm. This is delicious.'

'I don't make it as well as Izzy does, unfortunately.'

'I believe she persuaded you to stay on for a few days?'

'Who told you that?'

'Finn.'

They looked at each other guardedly.

'They've – um . . .' said Adair.

'Looks like it,' said Río.

'He – yes – he stayed over the other night. I – er – understand.'

'Yes.'

Río took another sip of her chocolate to cover the awkward silence. The suspicion that his daughter may have been sexually active under his own roof must be difficult for Adair to handle.

'Izzy's at college, is she?' she asked.

'Yes. Doing Business Studies.'

'Finn tells me she dives?'

'Yeah. It's her passion.'

'Finn's too.'

'They're good kids on the whole, scuba-divers, I find. There's a kind of philosophy attached to diving that you don't find in many other sports. A kind of Zen thing.'

'You looked very Zen on the yoga pavilion. What were you contemplating?'

'I was thinking about how hard it will be to let go of this place.'

'You haven't used it much.'

'No. I just never seemed to have the time. It's ironic that we're splitting just as Broadband's finally available.'

'You're hooked up?'

'Only just. Because we're in a dip, the signal couldn't reach us here. If it had happened sooner, I could have spent a great deal more time in Lissamore. I was able to get work done online this morning that I wouldn't have been able to do a year ago.'

'What kind of work?' Río asked, just to be polite.

'I won't bore you with the details.'

'Is your job really boring?'

'It can be stultifyingly boring. Sometimes, during meetings, I look around at all those faces drooping over the boardroom table and I want to stand up and let rip a fart.'

'Do you really?' said Río admiringly.

'Yes. Maybe one day I will. And then I'll retire to Coolnamara and live off the fat of the land. I've always fancied myself as a fisherman.'

Río laughed.

'What's so funny? I'm serious.'

'I'm laughing at the idea of you as a fisherman. It's a bit like Marie Antoinette masquerading as a shepherdess.'

Adair raised an eyebrow at her. 'You don't have a very high opinion of me, Río, do you?'

'On the contrary. I think you're very nice, for a millionaire.'

'How many other millionaires do you know?'

'None. Oh – actually, I think Shane might be one. Or he will be, once *Faraway* goes into a second series.'

'But it's your contention that millionaires are not especially nice people?'

Río shrugged. 'I don't think that many people get rich by being nice.'

'So maybe I'm the exception that proves the rule.'

'Maybe. I've never really understood what that means.' She took another sip of her chocolate, then looked at him speculatively. 'I hope you don't mind me asking, Adair, but how *did* you get rich?'

'I worked hard.'

'It was that easy?'

'Don't be facile, Río. You know as well as I do that getting rich through hard work is no easy thing. Lots of people work hard – you do, Dervla does – but not everybody gets rewarded as a result.' He looked away from her and focused on the shoreline, and she saw a muscle clench in his jaw. 'To answer your question, I started as a bricklayer at the age of fifteen. I suppose you could say that I got lucky, with the property explosion happening when it did, but if I hadn't had an ingrained work ethic, I would never have benefited from the boom.'

'Where did the work ethic come from?' asked Río.

'Generation after generation of my family were forced to emigrate to find work – including my father. My mother scraped by on what my pa sent home from London. That's why I left school so young. I was determined that I would work my arse off to make a better life for her. Sadly, she died before she saw me become a success.'

'Oh. That *is* sad. What about your dad?'

'He died when he got too old to be climbing scaffolding and shovelling concrete. When the work ran out for him, he ran out of hope as well as money.'

'Did he come back to Ireland?'

'No. He died in a doss house in London, clutching a bottle of cheap whiskey for solace.'

'I'm sorry,' said Río. She knew from experience that more words were unnecessary.

'Let's change the subject,' said Adair, turning back to her. 'How exactly are you going to help your sister sell my house? The way things are at the moment, the pair of you might have a tough job on your hands.'

Río looked around at the empty planters and urns and troughs. 'I'll enjoy doing the garden for you.'

'What about the interior? I thought you did – um – how did you describe your job again?'

'Home staging.' Río drained her mug of chocolate. 'I won't have to do anything to this interior. It already looks as if it's been styled.'

'It does?'

'Well, yes, it does. I'll get some flower arrangements in,

341

maybe – a few of those less-is-more Japanese-inspired displays they have in boutique hotel foyers – but otherwise I'll leave it as it is.'

'That suggests you think this house is more like a hotel than a home.'

'Well, it is, isn't it? Didn't your wife use some Philippe Starck-inspired hotel as a template?'

'Yes. She wanted – how did the architect describe it again? Um . . .'

'A home with a kick,' said Río.

'Funny – those were his exact words!'

Río cast her mind back to the afternoon all those summers ago when she had eavesdropped on Adair and his architect. She wondered,would her opinion of him have altered if she'd known then that Felicity, not Adair, had been responsible for the appearance of the barnacle on the beach?

'Did you want a home with a kick, Adair?'

'No. If I'd known my marriage wasn't going to last, I'd have been happy with a fishing lodge – as long as it had a window big enough to frame my view.'

'So you're a man of simple tastes?'

'I like to think so.' Adair regarded her speculatively. 'If you owned this house, Río, and you wanted to give it a more homely vibe, how would you do it?'

'I'd give it a sense of humour.'

'What do you mean?'

'Well, don't you think this house takes itself too seriously? That po-faced goddess on the yoga pavilion, for instance. She could do with a touch of rouge, a little polish on her nails, some fire-engine red lipstick.'

'Are you serious?'

'Yes, I am.'

'What else?'

Río thought hard. 'I'd grow creeper all over the exterior walls,

342

to soften the angles. Creeper hugging a house makes it look as if it's loved. I'd paint the interiors in soft, warm shades of saffron and poppy, and I'd get rid of all that cutting-edge furniture and replace it with floppier stuff. I'd fill the house with plants, and install aquariums in every room and fill them with angel fish and zebra fish and Siamese fighters. And there would have to be a cat. There's nothing like a cat to stop you getting too big for your boots. Cats rule.'

'And on a viewing day? How would you stage it to persuade someone that they'd want to live here?'

'I'd get a long trestle table,' said Río, rising to her feet. 'And I'd put it slap-bang here in the middle of the deck, and cover it in a big white linen cloth. And then I'd set it for dinner, with at least a dozen places.'

'So it would look as if the owner was about to entertain guests?'

'No. So that it would look as if the owner *had* entertained guests.'

'What do you mean?'

'I'd stage it to look as if the guests had enjoyed the grandest dinner imaginable, sitting over great wine and good food in front of one of the most fabulous views in Ireland, laughing and shooting the breeze until the small hours.'

'How on earth would you manage that?'

'Well, think of the dinner we had in O'Toole's the other night. We all had a good time, didn't we?'

'Yes.'

'And how did the table look afterwards?'

'Messy.'

'Go to the top of the class. That's what happens when people have a good time.'

'So you'd set the table as if a load of people had messed it up?'

'Yes. But it would have to be very *carefully* messed up. There'd be no red wine stains on the tablecloth, or rinds of cheese left on plates, or scraps of wilted salad leaves. I'd leave napkins

343

casually draped on table mats, and some of the glasses would have a little wine left in them. Guests would have been at the coffee stage, so there'd be a couple of cafetières with coffee grinds in, and lots of silver teaspoons.' Río furrowed her brow, thinking. 'What else? Wine coolers, of course, and loads of bottles, some half full.'

'Not half empty?' Adair smiled at her, and she smiled back.

'*Never* half empty,' she said. 'There'd be flowers, of course, and I'd scatter the table with petals. A big bowl of oranges, with maybe a little orange peel by some of the side plates. And candles – lots and lots of half-burnt candles all over the deck, and a fiddle propped up by the rail, to show that there'd been music.' Río was really warming to her subject now. 'And by the pool, there'd be a pile of inflatables, to show that kids had been there, and that they'd had a great time too. Staging a house is like telling a story, you see, Adair.'

'I'm impressed,' he said. 'You're good at this, Ms Kinsella.'

'I know. But there's more. Let me think . . . Champagne, of course. A pashmina left hanging on the back of a chair. A discarded bracelet. Maybe a trace of red lipstick on a napkin.'

'A cigar?'

Río shook her head. 'No. These people don't smoke.'

'What were our people celebrating?'

'Um. An anniversary? A birthday?'

'So there'd be presents.'

'Yes. Let's make it a lady's birthday. What does she like?'

'Jo Malone?'

'But of course! Jo Malone candles and body lotion.'

'Lingerie?'

Río considered. 'Maybe not. Too intimate.'

'Books?'

'Yes. Lovely big glossy coffee-table books on gardening and cooking and wildlife.'

'CDs?'

'Definitely. She'd be into trad – that's why the fiddle is there, and maybe a bodhrán too – so you'd have Donal Lunny and Sharon Shannon.'

'And Zoë Conway.'

'Of course! And there'd be wrapping paper and ribbon festooned around the place, and birthday cards with "Happy Birthday" written all over them in different handwriting – and maybe there'd have been dancing, maybe someone had left their shoes on the deck – red shoes with heels – and oh! it would all be so much fun!'

Adair gave her a look of admiration. 'You have some imagination, Río Kinsella. I just wish I had a birthday coming up so that we could do it for real. But then, I have no friends here to invite.'

'My birthday's coming up, weekend after next. Maybe you should throw a party for me.'

'Now, there's a thought. Maybe we should. *I* may have no friends in Lissamore, but you must have loads.'

'Adair. That was a joke.'

'About your birthday?'

'No. About throwing a party for me,' she said, sitting back down beside him. 'Now. Back to business. You see now how important it is, when you're staging a property, to get the ambience just right. Your main aim is to get your viewer to think – Wow! This is a house where fun can be had, where music and laughter and love are on the agenda. You want them to think that when they buy your house, they're buying all these things too.'

'They say that money can't buy you love.'

'But – as Marilyn Monroe claims in *Gentlemen Prefer Blondes* – it certainly can help.'

'*Gentlemen Prefer Blondes*.'

A girl's voice came from the other side of the deck. 'Isn't that the movie where she played the ultimate gold-digger?'

Río turned to see Izzy leaning against the railing, watching them, her gaze bluer and more inscrutable than a Siamese cat's.

'Izzy-Bizz!' said Adair. 'Where did you come from?'

She was clever. Oh, this woman was clever! Clever, devious and dangerous.

From the road above, Izzy had watched Río swimming ostentatiously to and fro between mooring and slipway, before emerging like Halle Berry (she *wished*!) in *Die Another Day*, or Aphrodite in the Botticelli painting, then looking up at the Villa Felicity to see if the lord of the manor had been gazing upon her wondrousness.

He evidently had, because as Izzy rounded the corner of the house several minutes later, the pair of them were having a cosy tête-à-tête on the deck, Río all snuggled up in a towelling robe – *her* towelling robe from the Merrion Hotel, Izzy noticed with some indignation.

She decided that it might be a good idea to stay shtoom for a while before making her presence felt. She listened as Río mouthed on about some fake birthday party she was planning to throw – some kind of a staging ploy to help sell the Villa Felicity, with prop candles and champagne and flowers and a feckin' violin. 'Oh!' she heard the woman say in a breathy, little-girl voice. 'It would all be so much fun!'

The *pièce de résistance* had been when she'd mentioned – oh so casually – that it happened to be *her* birthday, weekend after next. Well, just think! What an astonishing coincidence! Izzy almost had to admire her. The dame had masterminded the scenario so adroitly that she'd even managed to drop in her wish-list of presents. Jo Malone and pashminas didn't come cheap – and as for the 'discarded bracelet'! Izzy was surprised that she hadn't specified the number of diamonds she wanted on said bracelet, or the carat size, or whether it should come from Tiffany or Cartier.

How subtle she'd been! How Machiavellian! But Izzy could be Machiavellian, too, and was not to be underestimated. Sauntering across the deck, she hummed a couple of bars of 'Diamonds Are a Girl's Best Friend' before depositing a kiss on her father's forehead and dropping into the chair beside him.

'Hello, Daddy dearest,' she said. 'I came by to pick up my togs. I'm going snorkelling.'

Río felt uncomfortable beyond belief. With her clothes in a pile on the deck and herself wrapped in a bathrobe, she knew it must look as if she and Adair had had sex. She'd have to disillusion the girl.

'Your father very kindly lent me this,' she stammered, sitting up straighter and pulling the lapels of the robe up to her chin. 'I – I'm wearing it because I was swimming.'

'But of course! Why else would you be wearing it?' asked Izzy ingenuously, widening her eyes. Río felt more uncomfortable than ever now. Oh why did she allow this girl to have such a debilitating effect on her? She felt as if she were back at school, guilty of some misdemeanour.

'I don't know,' she said stupidly.

Izzy gave her a pleasant smile. 'That Marilyn Monroe quote was from the end of the film, wasn't it? When she admits she's marrying for money?'

'Yes.'

'That's what I love about that movie,' said Izzy. 'She's so upfront about the fact that she's venal. It's her candour that makes us root for her.'

Adair looked at his daughter proudly. 'Izzy was originally going to take Film Studies as her degree course,' he told Río, 'until she decided that Business Studies would be more useful.'

'Er, what kind of business are you thinking of going into?' asked Río.

'Funny you should ask that. Finn – your son – and I had lunch

347

earlier, and we were talking about how brilliant it would be to set up a dive centre in Lissamore, now that the one on Inishclare's gone.'

'He was?' Río was taken aback. This was all happening much faster than she planned, nor was it necessarily going in the direction she'd intended. Izzy Bolger and Finn as business partners was a scenario from hell, as far as she was concerned.

'Shane – his dad – has offered to back him,' said Izzy.

'I *know* Shane is his dad!' Río wanted to snap at her. What was all this 'Finn – your son' and 'Shane – his dad' shit? Did the girl think she was such a total imbecile that she had to detail Río's own family tree?

But instead she said, 'Yes. Shane mentioned something about helping him out.'

'It would be an expensive business, setting up a dive outfit,' observed Adair.

'I'll do the maths when I get back to Dublin. The captain of the subaqua club in college is clued in about that stuff. He has contacts in the trade.' Izzy's phone alerted her to a text message. She smiled when she accessed it, and jumped up from her seat. 'I'd better get cracking. Finn's waiting for me up on the road. Apparently the viz off the island is cracking today.'

'You're snorkelling off Inishclare?' asked Adair.

'Yeah. Finn's mate Carl's lent him his boat. I'll see you later, Daddy. Bye!'

Izzy danced away, looking pleased with herself. An awkward silence descended for the second time that afternoon, but Izzy was back before either Río or Adair had a chance to remark upon the burgeoning relationship between their offspring. 'Dad! Could you let me have some money? I'd like to buy a round later, and I'm out of cash.'

'Sure.' Adair got to his feet. 'Just let me find my wallet. Where did I put it?'

'It's on the table in the atrium.'

'Excuse me for a moment, Río,' Adair said. And as he followed his princess inside, Río heard a phone tone and the tinkling sound of Izzy's laughter from the 'atrium'.

Well! It looked as though minxy little Isabella Bolger had well and truly annexed her son. How and why had she done that? Río would have thought that the girl's preference would be for a metrosexual, or a man with 'prospects' in law or accountancy, but she supposed Finn was pretty damn irresistible. He had said something on the phone today about Izzy having visited Koh Tao while he was there. Had they planned to meet? Had they spent much time together? Had they maybe slept together then?

Río remembered how well matched they'd looked all those months ago on the day of Frank's funeral, sitting together on the sea wall across from Harbour View. Perhaps they'd shared contact details that day. That was how young people got to know each other now, carrying on and flirting on Facebook and Bebo and My Space. For all she knew, Finn and Izzy could have been an item for some time. For all she knew, they could be making plans for a future together. She wondered how much information Finn would volunteer about the affair. Very little, knowing him. Not even Dr Phil could have got her son to open up about that kind of stuff.

'Well!' said Adair, with mock heartiness, as he returned to the deck. 'It's nice to see our two young people having fun!'

'Yes.' Río managed an unconvincing smile. 'All that fresh air and messing about in boats is far better for them than playing mindless computer games.' Oh God. She sounded like a bad infomercial for the Scouting movement.

'Would you like something else to drink?' asked Adair. 'A glass of wine?'

'No, thanks. I'd better go.'

Río rose, feeling awkward again. She didn't much fancy the idea of changing back into her clothes on Adair Bolger's deck.

But he must have sensed her discomfort, because: 'Feel free to use the downstairs shower room to change,' he said.

'Thank you.'

She made her way through the massive sitting room and into the 'atrium', where the shower room was located. It could have accommodated three of her puny bathroom, Río thought, as she disrobed and got back into the suit she so hated.

As she went to hang her borrowed bathrobe on the back of the door, she dislodged another from its peg. Stooping to retrieve it from the floor, a citrusy scent hit her. It was a scent that she recognised at once as Acqua di Parma, the aftershave Adair used.

Deep inside her, Río felt something like a flower unfurling.

'You're some waterbaby,' Finn told Izzy.

Having just completed a series of tumbles, Izzy was floating on her back, watching a vapour trail trace its way across the sky.

'You remind me of my mum,' he added.

'What?' Izzy stopped floating, and started vigorously treading water.

'She adores the sea. She does all her soul-searching in the water.'

Izzy did not welcome the news that she reminded Finn of his mother. Pah! Why did boys say the stupidest things? She performed one last tumble, then shook her wet hair back from her face and swam back to the boat, where Finn was leaning back against the stern, looking at her admiringly. Oh! How good it felt to be gazed at admiringly by a beautiful boy!

'Help me out, will you, punk?' she said.

Reaching down, he helped her haul herself out of the water. It felt good to be pulled on board a boat by a beautiful boy too, and to be wrapped in a towel by him, and it felt even better when he took her in his arms her and kissed her.

'You're very beautiful,' he said.

'That's funny,' she said, tracing the line of his mouth with a finger. 'I was just thinking the same thing about you.'

'You're beautiful and you're funny and you're ballsy.'

'Not a spoiled, stuck-up brat?'

'You're one of the least stuck-up girls I've ever met,' said Finn. 'And I've met a few. Some of the divas I've had to train would make Paris Hilton look like a cherub.'

'Tell me!'

'Oh, girls refusing to carry their gear in case they broke a nail. Girls complaining about seats on the boat being wet . . .'

'He*llo*? It's a boat.'

Finn spread his palms. 'Doh, yeah. Girls not wanting to get into hire neoprene suits because they might look fat. Girls moaning about masks ruining their hair and make-up.'

'Girly girls. Barbies. We call them "plastics" in college.'

'"Plastics" is good. That's what's so great about you, Izzy. Sometimes you behave more like a boy than a girl.'

'Hey! Thanks.'

'No, I don't mean it that way.' He pulled her tighter, and smiled down at her. 'Obviously I don't. In fact, when I first met you as a grown-up, on the day of my grandfather's funeral, I thought you looked edibly girly.'

'Don't I look edible today?'

'Oh, yes.' He licked her neck. 'You taste of the sea, and you're making me hungry. Let's go get chowder in O'Toole's.'

'How romantic, to tell a girl that she tastes of fish.'

'You taste delicious, but you need something to warm you up. You're cold.'

'How can you tell?' she asked, disingenuously.

'How do you think?' he asked, running a hand over her nipples. 'God, you're a sexy piece of work, Isabella Bolger.'

The way he was looking at her made her feel sexy too. Winding her arms around his neck, she tangled her fingers in his hair. 'Maybe we should just go home,' she suggested.

'Home?'

'To the Villa Felicity. I have a suspicion that you're horny as hell, Finn Byrne, and there's not a lot you can do about that when you're on a boat in the middle of the bay. There are probably binoculars trained on us as we speak.'

'Won't your dad be at home?'

'He's cool. He didn't bat an eyelid when I told him you'd stayed over on Sunday night.' It was true. But Izzy suspected that it had cost her father an effort not to bat an eyelid.

'I felt kinda bad about that.'

Izzy shrugged. 'Honestly, you needn't worry about him. The house is so big that he probably won't even know you're there. My mother's the one I'd have a problem with. She's not half as easy-going as him.'

'Your mum's Felicity, yeah?'

'Yeah.'

'The Villa Felicity. Imagine if I called a house after myself. The Villa Finn doesn't have the same ring to it, somehow. The Villa Isabella sounds good, though.' Finn moved midstern, and took hold of the oars.

'What if your name was Bob?' mused Izzy. 'The Villa Bob. That's a good one.'

'How about Phyllis? The Villa Phyllis sounds like some kind of a disease.'

'What'll we call our dive shop? Finn Fun?'

'Fizzy Izzy's?'

'*Frizzy* Izzy's if I got dodgy hair extensions again. How about Fish Finn-gers?'

'Crab Catchers?'

'Rude boy! If it was a bicycle shop, you could call it Finn de Siècle.'

'Or if we lived in France we could call it Finny's Terre.'

And as the oars dipped rhythmically in and out of the water and the sun started to sink down below the horizon, Izzy and

Finn giggled like schoolkids as they made their way back to the safe harbour at Lissamore.

From her balcony overlooking the harbour, Río and Shane regarded their son as he made a boat fast to a bollard.

'I'd better go and say goodbye to him,' said Shane.

Shane's bag was packed and waiting for him downstairs. Earlier that day he had received a call from his manager, requesting that he make an appearance on a mid-week television chat show. Well, it was more of a command than a request. Shane couldn't say no. An S-class Merc was on its way to convey him to Dublin, and a suite had been booked for him in the Four Seasons.

'Are you sure you won't come up for the craic?' Shane asked Río. 'I bet there's loads of stuff you could nick from the Four Seasons.'

Río shook her head. 'No. Coolnamara Castle is as fancy as it gets for me. I'd be a fish out of water in the Four Seasons.'

'There's a pool.'

'I hate swimming in pools. Anyway, you'll have no time for craic, Shane. You'll be too busy being a media whore.'

Shane gave a pained expression just as his phone rang. 'Yeah,' he said into the mouthpiece. 'Just opposite the harbour – the house with the balcony and the blue door. Thanks. See you in a minute.' Stuffing the phone back in his pocket, he turned back to Río. 'The car's arrived. Hell, you know I'd much rather have you drive me up to Dublin, Río.'

'No, Seth. It cannot be. Beyond the realm of Coolnamara, I transform into a wraith. You must go alone. And beware the warlord Xerxes.'

'Akasha, it pains me to leave you.'

They stood smiling at each other for a moment or two, and then Río said: 'Send me a message, will you, when you're on telly? For fun. A private one, just for me.'

'A message? Like something encrypted that only you will understand?'

'Yes.'

'OK. Watch out for it.'

Below them, the Merc pulled up by the kerb, and a chauffeur emerged.

'Bummer,' said Shane. 'A man. No one to flirt with. I guess I'll just have to talk about sport. Byebye, love.'

Río raised her face to his and closed her eyes. Shane kissed her lightly on the lips, and then she heard his feet on the stairs, and the door to the street opening.

'Byebye, love,' she echoed. And tried not to think of the next line of the song.

There was a lot of talk about sport on the chat-show the next evening. Snuggled up in front of the fire, Río dozed off until she heard the presenter say: 'He's taken the US by storm in the surprise hit of the season, *Faraway*; he's set a whole new trend in leatherwear, and he's back in his native Ireland for the first time in five years. Ladies and gentlemen, will you welcome please – Mr Shane Byrne!'

Shane loped onto the set and shook hands with the presenter, and then they settled down for their chat. The usual introductory suspects were gone over, and then, some minutes into the interview, Shane was asked how he was dealing with his new-found fame, and how it had changed him.

Shane paused for thought, and then he looked directly into the camera and said, in that voice that made Río melt like chocolate: 'Fame? It's not something I ever had a drouth for.'

'A drouth?' queried the interviewer uncertainly.

'Yes. My drouth is slaked by simpler things. Such as . . . Beauty. Passion. Love wakened from despair. That kind of thing.' And then Shane smiled straight into Rio's eyes.

'I'm sorry?' said the chat show host, looking a bit confused. 'You're maybe being a little too – um – metaphysical for me here.'

'Forgive me,' said Shane, turning back to him. 'I guess I'm just waxing nostalgic. Re-visiting Coolnamara made me prioritise some things in my life. Fame means nothing to me. Love and friendship is all that slakes my drouth. Or – if you prefer – floats my boat.'

And then Shane resumed his affable expression and settled down to be grilled about life in La La Land.

Río laughed out loud and clapped her hands. He'd done it! He'd sent her a message in the form of a quote from the poem he'd read to her as he'd made love to her that night in Coolnamara Castle. She recalled fragments of it now...

I have craved . . . with passion burning
And with my whole heart yearning . . .

And looking at Shane on her plasma screen, she wondered now: did her heart yearn for him? No. She loved him – she loved him with her whole heart – but she didn't yearn for him. Shane had been a revenant – a visitor from another era when Río had been young and irresponsible and – yes – passionate. And now she had put childish things behind her and grown up and moved on, and the men that mattered in her life were moving on, too. And as for passion? Passion was for poems and pop songs and paperback fiction. Passion was for members of that exclusive club known as *jeunesse dorée*. Passion would not be allowed a look-in in Río's life.

Chapter Twenty-six

Dervla was in love. She was in love with a man who looked like Pierce Brosnan and who owned a Dalmatian and who was buying the house she yearned to live in.

For the past week she had felt as if she were floating around in a dream world, like a woman in a Chagall painting. The Vegas wedding had been the most gloriously tacky thing she had ever done, the honeymoon had been the most gloriously romantic thing she had ever done, and the lovemaking had been the most gloriously fulfilling of her life.

Christian Vaughan was the kind of man women dreamed about, the kind of man who populated the Mills & Boon novels she had read so avidly as a teenager. He was tall, dark and handsome, he was authoritative without being domineering, he was polite without being obsequious, and he loved to laugh.

But today – an unseasonably sultry Monday in Galway – the dream had to end. Instead of lounging around in bed or sharing a bath or quaffing champagne, she would have to make phone calls to her accountant and her solicitor and her bank manager.

The decision to fold the business had been a surprisingly easy one. In the current economic meltdown, lots of people were doing the same thing – selling up their businesses, renouncing their lifestyles and making a bid for happiness before it was too late. Dervla was one of the lucky ones. The passion she had once felt for her business had been transmuted to passion for her new husband, and she had never been happier. She pictured a life of serenity, living in the Old Rectory with Christian (*Christian!* Even the name made her swoon!) and Kitty the Dalmatian.

In the Old Rectory she would write every day in the little turret room at the top of the house that she had earmarked as a study. With her mind free from stress, the words would come flowing, and she'd have a manuscript finished in no time! She would walk with Kitty down by the river and through the woods that adjoined the house. She would sit with Christian on the wrought-iron bench by the front door of a summer's evening, sipping chilled Sancerre and reading books. She would make soup in the kitchen – real soup with home-made stock and fresh vegetables. She even entertained the idea of keeping chickens; she'd read somewhere that keeping chickens was a fascinating pastime. Bees? Could she learn about bee-keeping? She rather fancied the idea of herself drifting round the garden of the Old Rectory in wifty-wafty frocks – as per her childhood daydream – and sporting a big hat with a veil. Bees, chickens, vegetables, fruit trees – hey! they could be virtually self-sufficient. Life would be simple and good; life really, really would be worth living.

The phone went. Dervla picked it up with a languid hand, and smiled when she saw the name in the display. 'Hello, Christian,' she purred.

'Hello, beautiful wifelet,' he said. 'What's the weather like on your side of the country?'

'Cloudy, but warm.'

'It's cloudy here too. Depressing. God, I miss you already. I can't wait to get out of Dublin and back to my gorgeous Galway girl.'

'And I can't wait to have you back. I was awfully lonely in my bed last night.'

'Me too. It's funny how easily you get used to falling asleep with your arms wrapped round a heavenly body.'

Dervla felt like purring again. 'You charmer. How's your first day back in the real world?'

'Stressful. How's yours?'

'I haven't got round to it yet. But guilt will get the better of me. When I got in last night the light on the answering machine was fluttering like someone with a nervous tic, and I'm dreading opening my inbox.'

'That's what a week in paradise does to you.'

'It wasn't even a whole week. I could have stayed there for ever, no problem.'

The resort in Careyes had been idyllic. The honeymooners had lived without computers, cars, newspapers, telephones or television. There had been the usual top-class resort facilities – fine dining, spa treatments, leisure activities – but Christian and Dervla had spent most of their time simply enjoying each other's company. Dervla hadn't laughed so much since she was a child, and she realised it was true that laughter was the best medicine. She felt the tension leave her shoulders and her jaw muscles, she stopped worrying her cuticles, and the word 'stress' no longer featured in her vocabulary. Any time she caught a glimpse of herself in the mirror she had a smile on her face, and she suspected that she might look – that word so beloved of pharmaceutical advertising – radiant. Christian Vaughan was better for her than any spa treatment.

'I've good news for you, wifelet,' said Christian. 'I spoke with your putative publisher. He's very keen indeed on the idea of a book on *How to Sell Your Home*, and he'd be delighted to get some sample chapters from you.'

'Heavens!' said Dervla. 'How will I find the time? I'll be bogged down with real-life stuff until we move into the Rectory.'

'Write a couple of hundred words in bed at night, while I'm not there to distract you.'

'There's an idea. The danger of that is it might turn into a steamy novel instead of *How to Sell Your Home*. When are you coming back to me?'

'This weekend's looking good. Megan managed to get an exeat from school.'

Megan was, of course, Christian's seventeen-year-old daughter, who, he'd told her, was keen to meet her new stepmother.

Stepmother! She, Dervla Kinsella, was a stepmother! She was a little apprehensive about it – of course she was – but the internet was there to help her. There were loads of sites with advice for step-parents, and she would work her ass off at being the best damn stepmother a girl could have. She'd find out what Megan's interests were and bone up on them, and she wouldn't nag her if she didn't tidy her room, and they could watch rom-com DVDs together and paint each other's toenails and read *heat* magazine and do girly stuff.

Dervla gave herself a mental slap on the wrist. 'Sorry, Christian, I got a bit distracted there. What did you say the story was on Megan's flight?'

'She's flying out of Gatwick with Mum on Friday afternoon. I've booked Coolnamara Castle for four nights, and I'll drive down and meet them at Galway airport. Mum will be tired after travelling on Friday, so I thought Sunday rather than Saturday would be a good day to view the Rectory.'

'That can be arranged,' Dervla told him. 'I'll get someone down there this week to put the "Sale Agreed" sign up, and I'll have a think about how the outhouses might be converted into a granny flat. I'd better get in touch with my architect as well. You're quite sure you're happy to use him?'

'Why not? He's been highly recommended by the brightest gal in the business, who just happens to be my wife.'

'Except I won't *be* in the business for very much longer,' she reminded him.

'No. You'll be a bestselling author instead.'

'Bestselling?' she scoffed.

'It's bound to be a bestseller, sweetheart. Think of all those endless television programmes advising people on how to make their properties more desirable. Hell!'

On the other end of the line, Dervla had just heard the ping! of mail arriving in Christian's inbox.

'Hell,' he said again. 'I'm going to have to go, darling.'

'What is it?'

'My mother's carer has a problem. Her passport's out of date. That means she won't be able to come over at the weekend.'

'Your mother has a carer?'

'Yes. Nemia's a real treasure – we were incredibly lucky to find her. She and Mum get on like a house on fire. Shit. This is a bummer. Excuse my language.'

'No worries, Christian.'

'Sorry, love. Talk to you soon.'

'Yes. Bye.'

Dervla put the phone down, feeling numb. She knew nothing about this Nemia. Christian hadn't mentioned that his mother had a carer. A carer! What did a carer do exactly, and how much caring did the old lady need? Was this Nemia a full-time or a part-time carer? And how incapacitated was Mrs Vaughan that she required help?

She hadn't a clue what age Christian's mother was. She knew she wore a hearing aid because she was partially deaf, but she'd assumed that the old damê was still reasonably active. Dervla realised now with a chill of apprehension that she had scarcely given her new mother-in-law a thought. She'd pictured, in her rosy-tinted 'Life in the Old Rectory' scenario, an apple-cheeked little old dear who would spend most of her time pottering around in her granny flat, knitting tea cosies and comforters (whatever they were) and dropping in for dinner in the main house occasionally. But now she had an uncomfortable feeling that there might be more to living next door to Mrs Vaughan senior than she'd bargained for.

What could she do? She could hardly phone Christian back and demand to know what condition his mother was in. It was fair enough when you were examining an old property to ask for a surveyor's report or a schedule of derelictions, but it was hardly appropriate to conduct something similar on an old person. Even Trinny and Susannah might draw the line at that.

Of course, Dervla hadn't demurred when Christian had stuck to his idea of converting the Rectory outbuildings into accommodation for Mrs Vaughan. She could hardly marry the man and then insist that there was no room in her life for his mother – or his daughter, come to that. But Megan was at boarding school and spent most weekends and holidays with her mother in London, so she wouldn't impact too much on their lives. Anyway, she looked like a lovely girl – Christian had shown her pictures of a pretty dark-haired teenager with a winning smile. But, she realised now with a sense of awful foreboding, he hadn't shown her any pictures of his mother.

Her phone rang. Dervla's instinct was to ignore it and let the answering facility kick in, but then she changed her mind. She wanted something to distract her from the fluttering she felt in the pit of her stomach at the idea of a mother-in-law in her life.

It was Adair Bolger on the line.

'Hello, Adair,' she said, seguing automatically into unflappable mode. 'How are you?'

'I'm very well, thank you, Dervla – and I believe congratulations are in order. I understand you've just come back from honeymoon.'

'That's right. Careyes, in Mexico.'

'Really? I know it. Any *tortugas* around?'

'No. Wrong time of the year, possibly . . .'

And Dervla and Adair small-talked for a few minutes more before he got round to the point of his phone call, which was to invite her to a party on Saturday night.

'A party at the Villa Felicity?' she asked.

'Yes.'

'What fun! A big party or a small one?'

'A smallish one, followed by a biggish one.'

'What do you mean?'

'Well, I thought I'd do dinner for around a dozen people, and then put word out for anyone who's interested to join us for drinks and dancing afterwards. I'll ask Michael in O'Toole's to spread the word, and I'm going to hire a trad band.'

'What a lovely idea, Adair! May I bring my new husband?'

'Of course you may. Anyone else you'd like to invite?'

'Yes, actually. I'd love to be able to bring my new stepdaughter and my new mother-in-law. They're coming to Coolnamara for the weekend.'

'A whole new family for you and Río!'

'Indeed. I presume Río will be coming to the party?'

'I hope so, but please don't say anything to her about it.'

'Why not?'

'I want to surprise her. It's her birthday.'

'You're throwing a birthday party for Ríonach?' Dervla was astonished.

'Well, not really. I thought that it would be a nice thing to do, to throw a party before I leave Lissamore, and when Río mentioned it was her birthday on Saturday I decided to have it then.'

'How generous of you! You *are* a nice man, Adair Bolger. Lissamore will miss you.'

'No it won't,' Adair said blithely. 'The people in Lissamore hardly know me. That's why I asked you to invite more guests. I only really know you and Río.'

'You could invite Finn.'

'Izzy's already invited him.'

Oh? thought Dervla. The plot thickens.

'And Shane,' she suggested.

'Shane's gone back to LA, unfortunately.'

Dervla wondered how sincere Adair's 'unfortunately' was. He actually sounded rather pleased that Shane had gone back to LA. And then she remembered how Río and Adair had flirted over dinner that evening in O'Toole's, and how Shane had looked a bit cross about it, and she began to wonder if Adair had an ulterior motive for throwing this farewell bash. Was it really more to do with impressing her sister than with bidding farewell to Lissamore?

'What about Fleur?'

'From Fleurissima?'

'Yes.'

'Now that *is* a good idea! She'll be clued in on the kind of stuff Río likes.'

'What do you mean?'

'Well, there will need to be presents for the birthday girl, won't there? Fleur can handpick a few items for me.'

'Fleur's shop is awfully expensive, Adair.' And it's only Río, she wanted to add, but didn't. Fleur's stuff would be wasted on Río; even Dervla balked at the prices on Fleurissima's exclusive stock.

'I can afford to throw my money around, Dervla,' said Adair matter-of-factly, 'and I don't do it often enough. Izzy's the only person I spend my dosh on. Splashing out on a little fun for a few folks this weekend isn't going to break the bank.'

Dervla made a noncommittal sound.

'See you Saturday, eight o'clock-ish?' said Adair.

'Perfect. I look forward to it.'

'Bye, then!'

'Bye, Adair.'

Dervla put the phone down feeling pensive. 'Splashing out on a little fun' was all very well, but there was something else on the agenda here, Dervla was sure of it, and she was pretty sure that it had to do with Río. Was Adair falling for her sister, the way so many men seemed to? If so, Dervla felt sorry for him.

She remembered the way Río had once shimmied around the Villa Felicity, being rude about it and poking fun at the master of the house, and she knew that Adair had a better chance of snaring a selkie than of snaring Río.

She wandered over to where her laptop awaited her and booted it up. Money might buy you fun, Adair Bolger, she thought, as she waited for the Taj Mahal to shimmer onto her screen, and it might buy you a kick-ass lifestyle, but Dervla knew it sure as hell couldn't buy you love.

Chapter Twenty-seven

Izzy really resented the idea of her father throwing a party for Río Kinsella. Even though he denied that he was throwing it specially for her, Izzy suspected otherwise. She had heard him talking on the phone to caterers and florists, and he'd booked a bunch of local Lissamore musicians. She knew that Adair was going to stage this event exactly as Río had suggested, right down to the presents. He had ordered coffee-table books from Amazon – Monty Don's on gardens, and one on wilderness places, and Nigella's latest – and he'd asked Izzy where was the best place to buy a pashmina. She'd even seen his laptop open at Fleurissima's website.

'Why are you going to so much trouble?' she asked him on the evening before they were due to travel back to Coolnamara. They'd been in Dublin for just over a week, during which her father had spoken of little else but the party he was planning. Izzy had swung by Wagamama to bring him home a treat tonight – gyozo and seafood ramen, with chocolate wasabi fudge cake for pudding. Setting her chopsticks down, she gave him a look of enquiry. 'It would make a lot more sense to throw a party here, when you think of it. You could invite all your business contacts.'

'This isn't about business,' Adair told her. 'This is about leaving an impression on Lissamore. I want the locals to look at that house and remember the fantastic shindig they once had there. They've only ever associated the Villa Felicity with nobby parties attended by socialite types from the days when your mother used to entertain. I want people to remember Adair Bolger as someone who could have a good time with the locals too. I want to feel that I might be accepted by them, that I might belong.'

'It's a bit late for that, now that you're selling up,' Izzy pointed out.

Adair shrugged. 'Maybe. But I may never have another opportunity to throw a party in that house, and I want to pull out all the stops.'

'Don't you think that showering Río Kinsella with gifts is overdoing it a bit?'

'No, I don't. She's had a tough life and she works damn hard. She deserves a treat.'

There was no answer to that that wouldn't sound spiteful. Izzy would just have to resign herself to the fact that her father was going to look like a prize loser (if that wasn't a contradiction in terms), fawning over the local sexpot. And if that wasn't bad enough, the local sexpot (for Izzy had seen the way men eyed Río) was the mother of the hottest guy she had ever met.

Finn Byrne was not only beautiful to behold and built like a god, he was also an expert lovemaker. Izzy had only slept with one guy before – more out of curiosity than anything else – and the sex had been less than mind-blowing. But Finn had made her feel like a goddess – Aphrodite rising from the waves – and he, a worshipper at her shrine. Sex with Finn was buoyant and sleek and streamlined and fluid and fun. With Finn, Izzy was in heaven, soaring weightless, an angel without wings, an *Übermensch*, a mermaid, a selkie.

She had a horrible feeling that she was falling in love with him.

The feeling was horrible for three reasons. Reason one: Finn lived on the other side of the country, and long-distance love

366

affairs were notoriously difficult to manage. (However, Izzy thought that there might be a way around this, *if* they were going to take things a stage further.) Reason two: Izzy despised Finn's mother, which did not augur well for any future relationship. Reason three: it looked as if her father, on the other hand, was completely infatuated with the ghastly mother.

Since Adair's divorce from Felicity had finally come through, he was now officially eligible to remarry. There had even been a piece about it in one of the Sunday papers, with a photograph of him leaving a restaurant with a woman on his arm (it had been his PA). People were avid for news of an engagement or an affair or an elopement, and – oh! Izzy thought with a jolt – what if he did the rebound thing? What if he was blithely unaware of the cunning snare that Río Kinsella had set for him? What if he proposed to *her*?

Ew! Imagine – if Izzy and Finn *did* become an item – just *imagine* what it would be like to be involved with a guy whose mother was married to your father? Ew, *ew*! There was something so icky and distasteful about it – something almost incestuous. It made Izzy shudder to think that they might have to end up doing family stuff together. Would they have to go on holiday together? Would they have to have Sunday dinners, or celebrate Christmas at each other's houses? What if there were offspring? Not just her offspring, but the offspring of her father and Río? *Ew!* And what would be the status of said offspring? Would a baby be her sister or brother as well as being Finn's? Or would she be its second something something removed? No, *no*! It was impossible, completely out of the question, and it wasn't going to happen. Her lovely, lovely dad didn't deserve to end up with a blood-sucking gold-digger like Río Kinsella, and Izzy was damn well going to make sure that the bloodsucker backed off.

She got up from the table and picked up their bowls, preparing to scrape the remains of their noodles into the bin.

'I'll do that, Izzy,' said Adair. 'You take it easy. You sorted the food.'

'No worries, Daddy. I'm glad to do it.'

'You're a good girl, you know that? To look after your old dad the way you do.'

'My old dad,' said Izzy, 'is not so old. And he deserves to be looked after.'

'I'm lucky to have you.' Adair leaned back in his chair and smiled at her.

She gave him her best smile back. 'Dad,' she said, 'can I run something by you?'

'Sure.'

'How would you feel if I left college?'

'What?' Adair looked startled. 'Why would you want to do that?'

'Well . . . you know Finn and I were talking about how cool it would be to set up a dive outfit?'

'In Lissamore? I thought that was some kind of daydream.'

'No, not at all. We did some serious talking about it last week, and I've been doing research since I got back to Dublin.'

'Hang on. You're telling me that you're really thinking of going into business with Finn Byrne?'

'Yes.'

Adair furrowed his brow. 'Jeez, Izzy, I don't know. It'd be a pretty risky undertaking.'

'But it's an ideal time, Dad, since the joint on Inishclare's folded.'

'There must be a good reason why it folded,' said Adair. 'Presumably they weren't doing business.'

'That's because the place was ancient. They really needed to upgrade. Equipment, premises – everything needed an overhaul.' Dishes scraped and stacked in the machine, Izzy sat back down beside her father.

'So you wouldn't be able to buy stuff from the Inishclare place secondhand?'

'No.' Izzy shook her head emphatically. 'The whole point of this would be to create a state-of-the art outfit, with brand-new equipment. A rebreather, and camera equipment, and a couple of DPVs.'

'DPVs?'

'Diver propulsion vehicles. You whizz around underwater on them, James Bond-style.'

'Pricey.' Adair looked thoughtful. 'You'd need a dive boat too.'

'Just an RIB, to start with. There's good shore diving to be had in Lissamore.'

'What else might you need?'

'Well, premises-wise, we'd need a shop and reception area. Um.' Izzy started counting on her fingers. 'We'd also need an air room, and a kit room, and a classroom for academic work. A yard for hosing down the gear and a pool for confined water training.'

'Hell, Izzy, this is very ambitious.'

'I know! But you've always encouraged me to be ambitious, Daddy.' She gave him a look of entreaty. 'And there's more . . .'

'Bring it on,' said Adair, weakly.

'We thought we could offer accommodation for people on dedicated Dive Safaris, so we'd need bedrooms and bathrooms and a restaurant and a bar. Of course, we'd have to look into licensing for that. But some outfits operate an honesty bar, and that seems to work. Most divers are people of integrity, Dad. You know that. Look at me!'

'You're some piece of work, all right. You've clearly thought this through.'

'Yes, we have. And just think how convenient it would be to offer a package! Weekends, or weeks – or even fortnights – with bed and board and dives included. And hill-walking and stuff, and Guinness and oysters, and trad sessions in O'Toole's – all that Coolnamara shit.'

'Sweetheart. I'd need to talk to some people about this.

This isn't a venture you can rush into, you know. And giving up college is a big decision to make.'

'I know that, Dad. But Business Studies is boring the arse off me. I'm a bright girl. I already know half the stuff they're teaching me. And I can learn the rest from you. You're the savviest business person I know.'

Adair shifted a little in his seat. 'You and Finn are – um – involved – er – romantically, aren't you?'

'Yes.' It was best to be upfront about this. 'It's not official, but I really like him.'

'And you think it's a good idea to go into business with someone you're romantically involved with?'

'Why not?'

'There's no answer to that, I guess,' Adair said with a sigh. 'Look. This has all happened very suddenly, darling. We're going to have to do a lot of hard thinking.'

'Finn and I have already done loads of hard thinking, Dad. We're really determined to make this work.'

'There's a lot to take on board. You'd have to find the right location, for starters, and look for planning permission.'

Izzy picked up the wine bottle and refilled her father's glass. 'We've thought of that too.'

'So where would you think of setting up this dive centre?'

'In the Villa Felicity,' said Izzy.

Chapter Twenty-eight

Río reread the letter that had arrived in the post that morning. It still didn't make sense, partly because it was written in legalese (Río was dyslexic when it came to legalese), and partly because it was quite simply ludicrous. It was from a Royston Brewer, Attorney-at-Law, and it was to do with a bequest from a Patrick Flaherty (deceased) of Big Piney in Wyoming.

Patrick Flaherty. This could only be the Patrick who had adored her mother, the Patrick with whom Rosaleen had had the passionate affair, the Patrick of the letters. This man Patrick Flaherty had to be her father. Río felt aflutter with apprehension. Her father had left her a parcel of land belonging to him in the Lissamore area. Well hallelujah! She had something to call her own at last, something maybe even to build a little house on! She, Río Kinsella, was a landowner at last!

A landowner like her heroine, Scarlett O'Hara in *Gone With the Wind*, a novel she had loved so much as a child that she had read and reread it until the spine had cracked and the pages had started to fall out. Scarlett's passion for land echoed Río's own. In these recessionary times people were selling cars and jewellery and yachts, but anyone in possession of land knew how very, very important it was to hang on to it until the recession was over. Just looking at the map that had been enclosed with the attorney's letter made Río dizzy with a kind of proprietorial fervour.

There was, however, something odd about the map. The designated parcel of land was very clearly part of the garden of the Villa Felicity. The orchard, to be precise. There was no mistaking it. Río had looked at the map right-ways, sideways, and upside down. According to this map, she owned the best part of the land surrounding Adair Bolger's house.

She'd always known that there had been a right of way through the orchard, but she – and hundreds of other local people – had presumed that the land belonged to what had once been Coral Cottage. She even remembered how her mother had always asked permission to use the short cut any time they went to fetch eggs from the old lady who lived there, even though it was a public right of way.

She needed clarification. Who was the best person to talk to? Dervla clearly didn't have a clue, since she had handled the sale of Coral Cottage in the first place. But it wasn't like Dervla to be remiss. Hadn't she done a search? Or had she connived with Adair Bolger about the orchard? She'd certainly have known about the right of way, because the Bolgers had been careful to keep it open. They'd caused enough controversy when they'd extended their lawn out onto the foreshore.

But it happened a lot with rights of way, didn't it? That they became incorporated somehow into other people's properties? She knew someone in Dublin whose garden had once been part of an unused back laneway, but which had been annexed by a kind of osmosis. And, hey, if it could happen in a capital city, how much easier for it to happen in the country? Especially around the time of the Irish diaspora, when people had been forced to emigrate to obscure and farflung places like – well, like Big Piney.

What had her father done in Wyoming, she wondered. Would this Royston Brewer, Attorney-at-Law, be able to fill her in on him? Had she perhaps, siblings? Half-sisters or -brothers, aunts, uncles, cousins, that she'd never known anything about? She felt like someone in a Frances Hodgson Burnett novel – except she was too old, of course. What an adventure!

She could start by Googling him. But as she scrolled through all the entries that came up when she typed in 'Patrick Flaherty Wyoming', she felt an increasing sense of unease. Did she really want to find out who her father was? Frank, the man she'd assumed to be her father all her life, had been a sad case, but what if her biological father was worse? What if he'd been a murderer, like the Michael Patrick Flaherty she'd just clicked on, who had shot a man in the back of the head after sharing a beer with him? There was something spooky about this, something not quite right.

The letters he'd written to her mother were in a drawer in her bureau. She took them out and regarded the handwriting. Her father's hand gave nothing away. It wasn't jagged or dramatic or scrawly. It wasn't the kind of handwriting that you'd expect from a man besotted. The form belied the content.

And suddenly Río felt shameful. These letters had been written for her mother's eyes alone; the words they contained were not addressed to her. Looking at them made her feel grubby, as if she were reading someone's private journal. She didn't want to go digging around in the past. She didn't want to unearth secrets that should maybe remain just that – secret. *It's a wise child that knows its own father.* Who had said that? Shakespeare? What did it matter who her father was? Río was her own woman. She didn't need to dive into some murky gene pool to find out who she was.

She took the bundle of letters from their hiding place and carried them over to the stove. After burning them, she would visit the headland where the contents of her mother's urn had been scattered, and cast the ashes of the letters too, out over the ocean. It was, she felt, a way of reuniting the lovers at last.

As Río reached for the matches, the final words she read, in her mother's distinctive, swirly script, were: 'I know what it is to be adored . . .'

And so, she thought with a smile, remembering Shane, did Río.

Dervla had just had a call from Río to do with the orchard adjoining the Villa Felicity. Did she know its provenance? Well, yes, Dervla did, and she knew full well that Adair Bolger had helped himself to it. She had warned him years ago that if it ever came to a dispute he would have to relinquish any claim to the pocket of land, and now it looked as if that was exactly what was going to happen. Imagine Río inheriting a prime piece of real estate! Even though it was unlikely that she could ever afford to build there, Dervla was glad for her sister. However, she hadn't been able to proffer much advice right now because she was driving in a hurry to Coolnamara Castle where she was going to meet Christian's family for the first time.

Dervla parked on the avenue that led to the hotel, and checked her appearance in the rear-view mirror. Hair? Check. Make-up? Check. Breath? Check. Oh! There was a tiny mark on her handbag. Wiping it off with a tissue, she unfurled herself from the driver's seat. Christian's Saab was parked further along the driveway, and she felt a sudden flash of anxiety as she high-heeled her way across the gravel and through the front door. *Please God, let me make the right impression. Please God, make them like me.*

The three of them were in the conservatory, as had been arranged.

'Darling!' said Christian, rising to meet her, and kissing her on the cheek. 'You look wonderful.'

'Thank you,' said Dervla, looking not at him, but at the pretty, dark-haired girl and the elderly lady sitting on a rattan sofa next to the French windows.

Christian's mother was immaculately groomed. She was dressed in plain black cashmere and she had a string of pearls around her neck that Dervla suspected were the real thing. Her hair had been styled in an elegant bouffant, and her mouth was lipsticked. There was an autocratic set to her head, and she sat very upright on the sofa. She was, Dervla thought, quite formidable-looking. Her granddaughter too was dressed in black, and Dervla had the sudden uncomfortable feeling that she'd been invited to a funeral. The table in front of the pair had been set for tea, with scones and jam and cream.

'This is Megan, Dervla.' Christian indicated his daughter, who gave a faux smile.

'Pleased to meet you, Megan,' said Dervla.

'Yeah?' said Megan.

'And this is my mother, Daphne.'

'How do you do?' Dervla crossed the room and extended a hand, which Daphne took with a pleasant smile.

'Who are you?' she asked.

'I'm Dervla, who's just been lucky enough to marry Christian,' said Dervla, taking a seat across the table from them.

'Yes. You certainly are lucky to have bagged a dish like him. He's my son, you know.'

'Yes.'

'Will you have some tea, Dervla?' said Christian.

'Yes. I'd love some tea, thank you. And my goodness, those scones look scrumptious.'

'They're from Tesco's,' said Daphne.

'Oh.' Dervla looked at her uncertainly. She knew that the scones were baked here in the hotel, but she could hardly contradict her new mother-in-law so soon after meeting her for the first time. 'Tesco's do excellent baked goods,' she said diplomatically.

'Every little helps.'

'Yes. It does indeed.'

'Excuse me, sir?' A man whom Dervla recognised as the hotel

porter had approached Christian. 'Do you mind if I ask you to move your car? It's blocking the delivery entrance.'

'Certainly.' Christian rose to his feet. 'Excuse me for a moment, ladies.'

Megan sneered at her father as he left the room, and then came the sound of 'My Chemical Romance' from her bag. The girl fished out her phone and, jumping up from the sofa, lurched through the French windows onto the terrace beyond. Here she proceeded to pace up and down, muttering into the handset. Dervla heard snatches of the conversation, which was peppered with such phrases as 'fucking nightmare', 'fucking old bat', and 'fucking fruitcake'.

Dervla turned back to Daphne, who had helped herself to a scone.

'What's that you've got wrapped around your neck?' the old lady asked.

'It's a scarf, Daphne. I got it in Liberty.'

'Aha! Fancy yourself, do you?'

'N-no.'

'You do fancy yourself. I can tell by the way you sit. Have a scone.'

'Thank you.'

'They're Tesco's Finest.'

Dervla reached for a scone and bit into it. It felt like dust in her mouth. From beyond the French windows, Dervla could hear Megan growling, 'I had to change her fucking dress and do her fucking hair. It's like looking after a fucking baby.'

'Who did you say you are again?' enquired Daphne.

'My name's Dervla, Mrs Vaughan.'

'Dervla? *Dervla?* I've heard that name before. Did you marry someone I know?'

'Yes, Daphne. I married Christian.'

'You married Christian? My son, Christian?'

'Yes.'

376

'You don't mean to tell me that you two are married?'

'We are.'

'Why did nobody tell me? That's great news! Well, welcome to our family, my dear.'

Oh God, thought Dervla. What response could she give to that? 'The weather's lovely, isn't it?' she hazarded. 'Although it has got a little cooler.'

'Cooler, cooler, West Coast Cooler,' said Daphne, struggling to get to her feet. 'I need to spend a penny. Where's the bathroom?'

'I – I'll take you,' said Dervla, moving swiftly round the table to give her mother-in-law a hand. She clearly had difficulty keeping her balance, and Dervla could scarcely allow her to go careening off to the loo on her own, in case she did herself an injury. As she linked Daphne's arm, she saw that the old lady had a dollop of cream on her chin.

They made their way out of the conservatory and through the lobby of the hotel to the corridor that led to the ladies' room, Daphne singing, 'When the Red, Red Robin Goes Bob-Bob-Bobbin' Along'. Dervla could tell that people in the lobby were pretending not to look.

Once in the ladies' room, Daphne entered a cubicle, and shut the door behind her without bothering to bolt it. Dervla heard fumbling noises coming from behind the door and then came the sound of a fart, followed by a loud sneeze. Daphne finally emerged looking rather less elegant than she'd done before she'd 'spent her penny'. The cream on her chin had transferred itself to the sleeve of her black cashmere dress, which was rumpled around her hips, revealing a black nylon slip.

'Allow me to straighten your dress for you, Daphne,' said Dervla, stooping to tug at the hem. As she did so, she noticed that Daphne's tights were at half-mast. There was only one thing for it: she'd have to pull them up for her.

'Oh! Your hands are like stones!' cried Daphne, as Dervla's hands made contact with her thighs.

'Yes. I have rather poor circulation, I'm afraid.'

'What?'

'I said I have poor circulation.'

'You're an awful mumbler, you know.'

'Yes! I am!' shouted Dervla.

'There's no need to shout.'

Task completed, Dervla straightened up.

'Who did you say you are again?' asked Daphne, peering into her face.

'My name's Dervla.'

'Dervla? *Dervla?* I've heard that name before. Did you marry someone I know?'

'Yes, Daphne. I married Christian.'

'You married Christian? My son, Christian?'

'Yes.'

'You don't mean to tell me that you two are married?'

'We are.'

'Why did nobody tell me? That's great news! Well, welcome to our family, my dear.'

Oh. My. *God*, thought Dervla.

It got worse. On their return to the conservatory, she could hear that Christian and Megan were having a row on the terrace.

'How could you have allowed them to go off together?' Christian was saying.

'I wasn't going to stop them,' came the retort. 'Anyway, I'm fucking fed up of taking the old bat to the bog. She's disgusting. She never washes her hands, and she sneezed all over my scone. I need a fucking drink. I deserve one after that fucking fiasco at the airport. Stupid fucking Nemia, forgetting to renew her passport.'

'Deal with it, Megan. And stop saying "fucking". It doesn't suit you.'

Megan heaved a sigh.

'I had no idea she'd got this bad,' continued Christian. 'If I'd known, I wouldn't have dreamed of flying her over. Nemia should have warned me.'

'Nemia thinks she's had a stroke. The old bat's, like, totally bananas. She hasn't a clue who I am. When I told her I was Megan, she said, "But Megan's only little! You can't be Megan!"'

Feeling panic rise, Dervla helped Daphne back into her chair. The old lady dropped onto the cushion with an 'Ooof!' Then, 'Who's that talking out there?' she demanded, as Christian came in through the French windows, looking sheepish.

'Hi there, Mum,' he said. 'It's just me and Megan.'

'Come back in and finish your tea,' commanded Daphne.

'No way,' Dervla heard from the terrace. 'I'm going for a fucking walk.' And Megan stormed off down the terrace steps like a thundercloud descending on the lake.

'Where are we?' enquired Daphne.

'We're in the conservatory of Coolnamara Castle Hotel, Mum,' said Christian, sitting down next to her.

'What for?'

'For a nice stay. We've booked you into a lovely room.'

'Did you tell them the name?'

'Yes.'

'Because they'll know us, you know. They'll know the Vaughan name. We're a very well-known family.'

'Yes, Mum.' Christian sent Dervla a look of entreaty.

'Stop giving each other private looks,' said Daphne. 'It's rude.'

'But we're married,' said Christian. 'We're allowed to smile at each other.' He lowered his voice. 'And do rude things.'

'What do you mean you're married?

'Dervla and I got married last week.'

'Why did nobody *tell* me? I don't *believe* that the pair of you are married!' Daphne started to sing 'Congratulations'. 'That's by Cliff Richard, you know.'

'Yes,' said Christian, wearily.

'I love Cliff Richard.'

'Mum?' Christian laid a hand on her arm. 'Do you mind if Dervla and I go for a stroll?'

'Mind? Why should I mind? You can go wherever you like.'

Feeling like an ice sculpture, Dervla rose to her feet and walked onto the terrace. Behind her she could hear Christian saying, 'Are you sure you'll be all right here on your own?' and Daphne's imperious voice telling him that of course she'd be all right on her own and that he was to stop being such a fusspot.

Her new husband followed her onto the terrace, and Dervla turned to face him. He looked utterly stricken.

'I'm sorry,' he said. 'I can't tell you how sorry I am, Dervla. I had no idea she'd got this bad, I really didn't. I'm guessing that Nemia didn't tell me because she wanted to hang on to her job until Mum made the move back to Ireland.'

'You really hadn't a clue?'

Christian shook his head. 'I should have known that something was up when Nemia started making excuses not to put Mum on the phone to me. Any time I've rung of late I've barely had a chance to talk to her because her favourite programme's just come on, or they're about to sit down to dinner, or some such excuse.'

'When was the last time you saw your mother?'

'About a year ago. She was a little forgetful then – leaving pots on the stove and suchlike. That's why we hired Nemia. But Nemia was really just a companion for her, you know – someone to cook and clean and keep her amused.' Christian raked his fingers through his hair. 'It's been a shocking decline.'

'Is it Alzheimer's?' asked Dervla.

'It's more likely dementia. She may have had a stroke. That can bring on dementia.'

'She's pretty far gone, Christian.'

'I know.'

He looked so helpless that Dervla felt a great rush of sympathy for him.

'I hope,' he said, 'I hope to God that you don't think I asked you to marry me to act as a carer for my mother, Dervla. Nothing could be further from the truth, I promise.'

'No,' she said, moving towards him and taking him in her arms. 'I don't think that at all. I just feel so, so sorry for you.'

If she were honest with herself, Dervla would have to admit that she felt pretty damn sorry for herself too. She may have married her dream man, but no dream man came accompanied by a demented mother and a teenage daughter with attitude. Still, she could hardly blame Megan for her strop. If she'd had to ferry Mrs Vaughan over from London, and change her clothes and do her hair, she'd be feeling frazzled too. It had been a Herculean enough task escorting the old lady to the loo.

A kind of tuneless medley came from the conservatory. 'When the red, red robin goes congratulations and celebrations!' they heard. It was followed by a loud crash.

Dervla and Christian looked at each other, then legged it back into the room. The tea tray had crashed to the floor, and Mrs Vaughan was sniggering.

'What a fucking mess,' she said in cut-glass tones, looking directly at Dervla. 'Come here at once, you, and clear it up before my husband gets home.'

Chapter Twenty-nine

Río was cycling along the coast road, singing. She was on her way to inspect her new orchard. She felt like Eve, being invited back into the Garden of Eden. What would she plant there? What plants did well by the seaside? Sea kale and sea pinks, obviously. Cupid's dart flowers, butterfly bush, pineapple guava. Shrubby Mediterranean herbs and New Zealand flax. Flaming montbretia, candy-coloured hydrangea, baby-pink weigela. Buddleia to lure butterflies. Angel's fishing rod and sea holly. She would plant only the leanest and meanest – the survivors.

Like her, she told herself as she rounded the corner that would take her to the Villa Felicity. She was a survivor. What were the odds of survival for a fatherless single parent who had lost her mother at a tender age, been estranged from her sister, and raised by a raging alcoholic? She reckoned she had enough credentials to write a misery memoir. Maybe she should ask Dervla for her putative publisher's contact details.

Her phone tone sounded from her bag. Río dismounted to find Dervla's name displayed.

'Hi, sis!' Río sang into the mouthpiece.

'Río. Where are you?'

'I'm on my way to the Villa Felicity. To re-explore my orchard!'

'You can't go there.'

382

'Why not?'

'Because Adair Bolger's throwing a birthday party for you there tomorrow evening, and he's getting the place ready.'

'*What?*'

'Oh, shit! I've just blown the surprise element. Look, I don't have time to explain now. Just pretend you didn't hear that. Can we meet at your gaff? I'm there now.'

'Sure. What's wrong, Dervla?'

'I need a shoulder to cry on.'

'Then you're talking to the right gal. I'm on my way.'

Río turned her bike around, and cycled back the way she'd come, pondering on the conversation she'd just had. Why was Adair Bolger throwing a surprise birthday party for her? How bizarre! And what was up with Dervla? Surely she couldn't be regretting her marriage to Christian Vaughan already, after her über-romantic honeymoon? She barely knew the man, after all. Even their own mother – poor impulsive Rosaleen – had held off for two months and two days before marrying Frank. Maybe Dervla's new husband had turned out to be an alcoholic? An alcoholic or a gambler or a wife beater, or all three? Río suddenly felt fearful for her sister.

She pulled up outside Harbour View, and dumped her bike against the wall. Dervla was sitting on the sea wall, worrying a cuticle. She jumped up when she saw Río and said, 'Can I get drunk and stay over with you tonight?'

Oh God, thought Río. Things must be really bad. 'Of course you can. Come on in.'

Río led the way upstairs, and into her apartment. Taking a bottle from an off-licence carrier bag, Dervla made straight for the drawer where Río kept her corkscrew, uncorked the wine and sloshed copious amounts into two glasses.

'What's happened?' asked Río.

Dervla told her. She told her about her new mother-in-law and her new stepdaughter and about the myriad unforeseen problems she'd invited into her life.

'Oh God,' said Río, when she'd finished. 'Where's Christian now?'

'He's staying over at the hotel with Megan and his mother. We're going to the Old Rectory on Sunday to check out the feasibility of a granny flat with accommodation for a carer, and he's going to drive them to the airport on Monday.'

'Hell's teeth, Dervla. It'll be some responsibility, living next door to a – what's the politically correct term for someone with dementia?'

'To hell with political correctness,' said Dervla, taking a swig of wine. 'This dame is a cross between a wicked pixie and a dragon.'

'Couldn't she go into a home?'

'I suggested that to Christian, and he literally turned white with horror. We're just going to have to find an excellent support team for her, once we've moved in. I don't know how this Nemia person's been managing all on her own. She must be some kind of Mother Theresa to put up with that kind of abuse.'

'Well,' said Río, activating her laptop. 'Thank God for the internet. The first thing you're going to have to do is bone up on the disease. Let's have a trawl through cyberspace.'

First up was Wikipedia. It made for gloomy reading. So did FamilyDoctor.org, and MedicineNet.com and the self-explanatory Dementia.com. There were pages and pages and pages of articles proffering scholarly words of wisdom and advice, and by the time they'd got to a 'Hobbies, Pastimes and Everyday Activities' page, Río and Dervla were quite drunk.

'"Create a reliable daily routine,"' Río read out loud, '"from washing hands, saying prayers, preparing food, cleaning and singing, to a little dancing before bedtime."'

'Dancing before bedtime?' scoffed Dervla. 'Mrs Vaughan can barely *walk*, let alone dance. And just what kind of dancing do these internet do-gooders have in mind? Old-time waltzes? The hokey cokey? A samba round the garden? Maybe she'll get up and stepdance like Jean Butler at Adair Bolger's party tomorrow night. Ha! What a *danse macabre* that would be.'

It was time to change the subject. It was clear that Dervla was completely wound up about her new situation, and Río really didn't want to hear any more depressing stuff about dementia. She suspected that she might be showing signs of early onset herself – she'd left the apartment in her shower cap yesterday.

'What *is* all this about a party?' she asked.

'Don't let on I told you,' Dervla begged her. 'It's the sweetest thing. Adair decided to throw a farewell bash before the house goes on the market, and when he heard it was your birthday, he hit on the idea of making it a combination farewell-birthday party.'

'Oh' said Río, turning pink. 'That *is* sweet.'

Dervla gave her a knowing look. 'He fancies you, doesn't he?' she asked.

'How should I know?' Río covered her confusion by emptying the wine bottle into their glasses.

'You do so know. You're blushing. And it's mutual. You fancy him too.'

'I do *not* fancy him,' protested Río, knowing even as she said the words that she was lying, and that she had in fact been in denial for some time about the fact that she really, really did fancy Adair Bolger.

'He's a good-looking man,' observed Dervla. 'At least I've always thought so.'

Río made a noncommittal sound.

'He makes you laugh,' continued Dervla. 'And he listens to you.'

'How do you know?'

'I watched the pair of you together in O'Toole's that night. At first I thought that you were flirting with him just to make Shane jealous, but I could tell Adair was really into you. You can't fake body language like that. And he has manners – proper, good, old-fashioned manners. There's nothing sexier than a man with manners.'

Río shrugged, and continued to avoid her sister's eye. She was loath to admit that Dervla had nailed her so adroitly, because in the careless days of her youth, Río had scorned men with manners. She and her pals had flouted convention and subverted regulations and laughed in the face of authority, and as far as she'd been concerned back then, manners were for wimps. The kind of men she'd dated had been musicians and artists and actors, brigands and libertines, all of them, and most of them had been reckless with her heart.

But now she saw that Dervla was right. There *was* nothing sexier than a man with manners. Río was impressed by the way that Adair would hold a door open for her, or rise to his feet when she sat down at a table and – sexiest touch of all – the way he would guide her into or from a room with a decorous hand hovering over the small of her back. Every time he did that, it was an indication of the respect in which he held her. And now he was going further still, by holding a party for her!

'He's a nice man, Río,' said Dervla, whose BlackBerry was bleating at her.

Río demurred. 'Don't you think he might just be on a kind of rebound thing, after Felicity?'

Dervla shook her head. 'No. You don't see the way he looks at you when your back is turned. I think he cares for you. I rather think he might adore you.'

Adore! That word again!

'That's what Mum wrote on the last of those letters that my – that Patrick Flaherty wrote to her. She said that she knew what it was to be adored.'

'It's a good feeling,' said Dervla, with a smile.

'Yes,' admitted Río. 'It is.'

Dervla returned her attention to her BlackBerry. 'Well! This is interesting!' she remarked, as her fingers started buzzing over the keypad.

'What is?'

'I'll tell you in a minute.'

'D'you know something?' resumed Río, reaching for her wineglass again. 'I know I'm flying in the face of my post-feminist convictions here, but I'd really, really like someone to care for me. I'm sick and tired of being all on my own, and fighting every inch of the way.'

'I know exactly how you feel. Beleaguered. That's what made me decide to sell the business.'

Río slumped. 'Pah. I can't afford to give up work.'

'You could if you hooked up with Adair Bolger.'

'*Don't*, Dervla! That's just stupid. We're polar opposites, Adair and me.'

'He's mellowed through the years. And so have you. Hey! Let's play the "What if . . . ?" game.'

'What if? You mean, as in "what if" anything happened between us?' Río looked dubious. 'It's an "if" of gargantuan proportions.'

'Let's play it anyway. Come on! It's fun. Remember the old days when we used to play it all the time?'

In fact Río remembered that she'd played it rather more recently, with Shane in their suite in Coolnamara Castle. She tucked her feet up under her, and started toying with a strand of her hair. 'Well . . .' she began, reluctantly. '*If* Adair and I got together, there's no way I could live in Dublin, for starters.'

'What if you stayed here?'

'There's no room for two people here!'

'No, I don't mean here, in this flat.'

'But you made the stipulation that I wasn't to sell this place, Dervla!'

'What if I changed that stipulation? What if you were to move into the Villa Felicity?'

'Get real! The Villa Felicity's up for sale!'

'What if it weren't?'

'Can you really see *me* living in the Villa Felicity?' Río scoffed.

'You visualised yourself living there once. You pictured yourself being Queen of all you surveyed.'

'I did not!'

'You did, Ríonach. I clearly remember you speculating about what it would be like to wander out on the balcony and go for a skinny-dip before breakfast. And then you slid down the banister and Adair caught you at the bottom of the staircase. You were both laughing like drains.'

'Oh, yeah.' Río squinted at a split end and broke it off. 'I remember now.'

'They say that if you visualise yourself living in a place, you subconsciously want to *actually* live in it,' observed Dervla. 'You've always wanted to live there, Río.'

'I wanted to live in Coral Cottage, not in that house!'

'That's because it's not a home. You could make it one, Río. You know you could. What if—'

'Oh! This is bonkers!' Río swung her legs off the sofa and marched towards the kitchen to get another bottle of wine. 'I don't want to play the "What if . . . ?" game any more, Dervla. We're grown-ups now.'

'But what if it *weren't* a game?' asked Dervla.

'What do you mean?'

'What if it *were* for real?'

'Dervla? Have you been spending too much time with your new mother-in-law? Is dementia catching?'

'I think not.' Dervla smiled her best Sphinx-like smile. 'I've just had an email from Adair.'

'So that's what that was. What did he have to say?'

'He's taking the Villa Felicity off the market,' said Dervla.

Chapter Thirty

Izzy was in a tizzy of excitement. She was wandering through the Villa Felicity, ignoring the caterers and florists who were setting up for tonight's party, visualising how the place would look as a state-of-the-art dive centre. The guest suite had six bedrooms with interconnecting bathrooms en suite, so a dozen or so guests could be accommodated there. She could sleep in her own bedroom, and there were two extra bedrooms for . . . for whatever. She didn't want to pre-empt anything. While she and Finn were clearly compatible, she wasn't going to hex herself by making any assumptions about their sleeping arrangements.

Downstairs, her father's study could be converted into an office. The library could serve as a classroom, and the atrium was easily big enough to accommodate a reception area. The dining room would remain just that, and the catering kitchen – with its Poggenpohl appliances – would be a fantastic workspace for a chef. The sitting room would become a bar and lounge, and the ever-changing view from the massive window would provide an added attraction for Coolnamara-philes.

As Izzy crossed the deck on her way to the pool, she saw that the massive dining table had been carted out and covered with a pristine white cloth. A stage had been set up for the musicians, and a sound engineer was going, 'One two, one two,' into the mic.

A man in overalls was stringing bunting along the railings, and a banner bearing the legend 'Happy Birthday Río' had been strung up above the picture window. There were flowers and candles everywhere.

Izzy's lip curled. Her father was making a monumental fool of himself, but that was his look-out. Izzy had warned him that, instead of presenting the munificent mine host image he was so determined to forge, he might end up looking like the village idiot. But he had simply said that he didn't care what people thought of him. He was clearly going through a midlife crisis, and Izzy hoped to God that he wasn't going to get a tattoo or piercings, or take up Formula One racing. But if she was going to get her mitts on the Villa Felicity, she was going to have to humour him and do as she was told. She was also going to have to work very, very hard indeed at turning her business idea into a success. But hadn't she inherited her father's work ethic as well as his business acumen? The word 'difficult' didn't exist in Adair's vocabulary: he used the word 'challenge' instead. *Challenge. Adrenalin. Danger.* The same words Izzy loved, the words that had spurred her on to become a master scuba-diver. *Experience intense adventure. Take it to the edge . . .*

Strolling past the hot tub to the pool area she saw that the cover of the pool had been rolled back, and flower petals had been scattered on it. It really was ridiculous to get the pool heated for just one weekend, Izzy thought. And as for all those gas-guzzling patio heaters! The more eco-conscious of the guests would have things to say about Adair's carbon footprint.

The pool was easily deep enough for novice divers, Izzy knew. They could do all their confined-water training there. And maybe the changing area could be extended? The garage could house RIB and DPVs, and they could build a kit room and an air room in the old orchard. They'd have to cut down trees to make space for them, but loads of the trees were practically falling down anyway.

It was all so ideal! It was all so utterly perfect that it should have been staring her in the face – when Adair had first announced his intention to sell – that the Villa Felicity would make a fantastic scuba-dive centre. When she and Finn had been dreaming up silly names for their dive outfit that day on his mate Carl's boat, they had suddenly looked at each other in awe and said simultaneously, 'The Villa Felicity!'

Except Izzy didn't want her mother's name appearing on the letterhead of her brand-new business. She knew it was pettish of her, but her mother had become even more of a pain in the arse since Izzy had told her she'd decided to give up college and move to Lissamore. Felicity's plans for her daughter did not include her knocking around with boggers and culchies: she wanted her to make a good marriage with some well-to-do barrister type and settle down in leafy Dublin 4, where Felicity would be able to visit her 2.4 grandchildren whenever it suited her.

No. The Villa Felicity was *so* not a good name for Izzy's business venture. She'd dream up a lovely name – something in Irish, maybe. *Gorm Mhór* had a nice ring to it. The Big Blue.

Rounding the boiler house, beyond which a barbecue area had been set up for the post-dinner party-goers, Izzy saw her father's car roll up under the *porte-cochère*. How lucky that the joint even had a *porte-cochère*, to keep guests dry while they unloaded their scuba gear! Or would she need a porter for unloading? Hm. There were several matters niggling at her that needed her attention. They were, of course, the practicalities that obscured the grand vision of her dream. She was going to need staff: there was only so much she and Finn could do themselves. And once the business was up and running they'd need one or two more qualified instructors – not just transient dive masters who would work in exchange for free diving.

Izzy meandered down the path that led past the orchard. Yes, there was plenty of space for kit room and air room. She knew there was an ancient right of way across this tranch of land, but hardly anyone knew about it, and more sheep than people used it. She was bound to get permission, wasn't she? If her clever daddy had swung it for the Villa Felicity, he could do it again for her.

'Hey, Dad!' she said, turning back to the house, where Adair was unloading the boot of his car. 'Let me give you a hand.'

On joining him, she saw that the boot was full of presents. Lots and lots of gift-wrapped presents. Some of them were wrapped in paper with the discreet Fleurissima logo embossed on it, some of them were encased in expensive gift-wrap, and yet others were shrouded in HMV and Hughes & Hughes bags.

'These aren't all for Río Kinsella?' Izzy asked, incredulity scrawled large on her face.

'No. There's something there for Dervla too, to say thank you for her time.' Adair smiled happily, and hefted the carrier bags out of the boot. 'I can manage these on my own, princess. You probably want to go and get ready, don't you? People will be arriving in an hour.'

'How many are coming for dinner?'

'Me, you, Río, Dervla – and Dervla's new husband, mother-in-law and stepdaughter. She's around the same age as you, I think. Who else? Fleur and her latest man. And Finn, of course.'

'But, Dad, we've way too many women.'

Adair swung through the atrium into his study, and Izzy followed him.

'What about that nice chap I met with you and Finn? With the crutches. What was his name?'

'Carl. I could ask Finn to bring him along, I guess. I'll text him.' Izzy grimaced. Oh God. How humiliating to be asking last-minute guests to her father's dinner party. He was going to look like a complete Norman-No-Friends. 'Um. Don't you think it's scraping the bottom of the barrel a bit, Dad, to be inviting people we hardly know?'

'I told you I owed Dervla for her time, and she specifically requested that she be allowed to bring her new in-laws. And it'll be nice for you to have young people at the table to talk to. Though there will be lots more young people coming to the afters.'

'Any idea how many?'

'The word in O'Toole's is that there'll be around a hundred.'

'Fun,' said Izzy, trying not to sound unenthusiastic. She didn't want to talk to 'young people'. The only young person she wanted to talk to was Finn.

And yet, and yet . . . that wasn't quite true. She so wanted this evening to work for her dad! He'd put so much effort into the event – it would be tragic if no one turned up. She determined to light a candle in her room and pray to Aphrodite, who was her favourite goddess.

'Are you sure there's nothing else I can do, Dad?'

'Not a thing, Izzy-Bizz. You run along and have your shower. Wow! What's that smell? It's amazing!'

There was a fabulous smell coming from the kitchen, of garlic and basil and something Izzy couldn't identify. And she thought again as she climbed the cantilevered staircase, of how she was going to need someone to cook as well as everything else if she was going to do this big thing, and suddenly she wondered if turning the Villa Felicity into a dedicated scuba-dive outfit wasn't way too ambitious a project after all.

In her room, she lit a plain white candle and prayed for several minutes. She so wanted her daddy to be happy! But how could he be happy with that grim gold-digger, Río Kinsella? She wanted him to find love with someone who would make him laugh. *Please, Aphrodite, make it happen for him. Make my lovely, generous dad a happy man. He deserves it. He has too many worry lines around his eyes these days, and he's starting to look gaunt. Please, Aphrodite, make it happen . . .*

When she'd finished praying, Izzy went to her closet and took out the frock she had chosen to wear tonight. Finn had told her that she sometimes behaved more like a boy than a girl. Huh! Well, tonight she wasn't going to *look* anything like a boy. No Comme des Garçons quirky stuff for her! Tonight she was going to look as deliciously, quintessentially girly as she had that time he'd rescued her from the potty-mouthed lager louts.

And as she moved to the bed and laid the confection of white chiffon on her counterpane, she remembered the last time she'd lain there, with Finn's arms around her, and she felt a little rosebud of anticipation in her tummy. No matter how tempting the aromas wafting up from downstairs, Izzy knew that she would not be able to eat anything tonight until she had kissed her beautiful boy.

Dervla was on her way to Adair's party in Christian's car. She had relinquished her claim to the front seat. Daphne was ensconced there now, and Dervla was travelling in the back with Megan, who was plugged into her iPod, and scowling out of the window.

In the front of the car her mother-in-law had forgotten about her fellow passengers, so Dervla didn't have to partake in any riveting conversation.

'Where are we going now?' demanded Daphne.

'We're going to a place called the Villa Felicity for dinner, Mum.'

Daphne started to sing ''S Wonderful. 'S Marvellous'. Christian joined in for a few bars, even though it was clear that he didn't have a clue about the words other than ''S wonderful' and ''S marvellous'. Then: 'Where are we going now?' asked Daphne again.

'We're going to a place called the Villa Felicity.'

'What for?'

'For dinner.'

'Oh. Do you like my trousers?'

Daphne had been dressed in trousers in case it got too cold for her out on Adair's deck this evening. The Indian summer they'd enjoyed was well and truly over.

'Your trousers are very nice, Mum. They're herringbone, are they?'

'What?'

'I said, "Are they herringbone?"'

'I don't know what sort of bone they are. Dum de dum de dum de dum . . .' she went, to the tune of How Much Is That Doggie in the Window?'

'Wuff wuff,' said Christian, obligingly.

'I think I'll get a dog. I'm going to get a dog.' A pause, then: 'Where are we actually heading for?' asked Daphne.

'The Villa Felicity, Mum. In Lissamore.'

'Are you going to stay there?'

'No. We're going for dinner. Yum yum. Yummy dinner. Shall we listen to the radio?' Christian flicked a switch, and some muthafucka came on, rapping about slapping his bitches and hos, so Christian switched it off immediately before his mother could pick up the chorus and start singing along.

'Where did you say we were going?' asked Daphne.

'The Villa Felicity.'

'Will we be able to get anything to eat there?'

'Yes. We're going for dinner.'

Where are we going now? Dervla decided it was like that refrain so beloved of small children. *Are we there yet? Are we there yet?* Except in Daphne's case it was *Where are we going now?* You could record this pointless conversation, she thought, and play it on a loop. You could cut and paste it, cut and paste it, cut and paste it, over and over again.

Daphne's final pearls of wisdom before they pulled up under Adair Bolger's *porte-cochère* consisted of: 'I love not knowing where I am,' and 'If *I'd* been the one who was driving we would have been there by now.' And then, 'This is a lovely place!' she announced, as Christian pulled on the handbrake and killed the ignition. 'I'm going to buy this place.'

A silence fell. And suddenly Dervla knew that they'd been wrong to come this evening. They should have stayed in the hotel, where at least the staff had been savvy enough to make allowances for her mother-in-law's outré behaviour.

'Will we get out now?' Daphne asked.

'No. Let's stay in the car and chat,' said Christian sarcastically, and Dervla could tell by his tone that he was tired.

'I love this car,' said Daphne. 'I love being here with you.'

'Oh God, Mum. I love you too,' said Christian. And then he slumped and rested his head against the steering wheel in an attitude of utter despair.

Río had splashed out on a dress from Fleur's shop for her surprise party this evening. She had decided, since she had inherited a prime piece of real estate, that she should celebrate, and she knew that Fleur would give her the dress at a discount rate. The dress was of slippery red bias-cut silk and felt as fluid as if she were wearing water. The way it moved against her bare legs made her feel like dancing. Río hadn't felt like dancing in years.

When she'd announced that it was her intention to buy a gúna for tonight's party, Fleur had raised one of her perfectly waxed eyebrows and looked at Río askance. 'You do know that this party's supposed to be a surprise for you?' she asked.

'Yes,' Río had answered. 'And I just hate, hate, hate surprise parties. But I'll do my best to look – er – suitably surprised.'

'Why is he doing this for you, Río?' Fleur enquired of her friend as she left the shop, swinging her glossy Fleurissima bag.

'I honestly have no idea,' Río had replied.

And then, as she headed home to shower and wash her hair, Río had had an idea so shocking she almost reeled. Was Adair Bolger doing this out of the goodness of his heart, or was he doing it because he had found out somehow that Río was the rightful owner of the orchard he had pilfered by osmosis? Was he being Machiavellian? Word got round fast in rural communities, she knew – especially when it came to land deals – and Adair had powerful contacts. Dervla had mentioned something about Izzy taking over the Villa Felicity and turning it into some kind of hostel, but Río hadn't really been paying attention. Now she wished she had. Was Adair wooing her because of her newly acquired status as a landowner? Did he hope to persuade her to sell?

No! This lady was not for turning.

The tranch of land by the Villa Felicity was Río's and no one else's. It was hers to cherish and to nurture and adore. It was hers to laze in on a summer's day and pick apples in autumn and plant seedlings in spring. Mr Bigshot Developer would not get his hands on that orchard, no matter how persuasive he was.

And as Río hooked on her earrings and slipped her feet into her red shoes, she found herself hoping that actually, it wasn't the land he was interested in. For some reason she rather hoped that – as Dervla had intimated – Adair Bolger might possibly be interested in her.

That evening, Río and Finn walked to the party. She didn't want to drive, and she suspected that her son might be invited to stay over by pretty little Izzy.

She hadn't told Finn about her inheritance yet. She still hadn't come to terms with it herself. 'When are you moving in with Carl?' she asked as they walked along the road out of town. Nature had painted the landscape in hues of copper and bronze, with here and there a splash of scarlet, and leaves had started to float down from the trees. 'You know if you stay in the duplex downstairs for much longer, Finn, Dervla will have to start charging you rent.'

'I'll move next week,' Finn told her. 'But, Ma, I don't think I'll be living with Carl for very long.'

'What? Why not? He's your best mate.'

'Yeah, but something's come up. Something that could be quite big.'

'What's that?'

'Izzy and I are thinking about starting up a dive outfit together.'

'You said something about that last week. I assumed it was one of those "What if . . . ?" games that never get off the ground.'

'It's real, Ma. We really want to go for it.'

Uh-oh. Río had a dilemma here. On the one hand she didn't want to dissuade Finn; on the other, the notion that Isabella was part of the equation filled her with fear and loathing. When she had told Shane that she'd love Finn to set up a dive outfit in Lissamore, she'd pictured him and Carl messing about in boats, not Finn and the Bolger girl.

'Well, good for you! I mean, I think it's a great idea, Finn. But don't you think that if you're serious about this, it would be better to go into business with Carl? Carl's rock solid, and you know him a lot better than Izzy.'

'Carl has no money.'

'You have money,' Río pointed out. 'Your father's offer was very generous.'

'I know, Ma. But it's not enough.'

'Even if you go to the bank?'

'You know how cagey they are about giving out loans these days. And the brilliant thing is that Izzy has asked her dad if he'd back us. He's said yes.'

'Are you serious?'

'Yeah. With Carl I can only go so far. With Izzy, we can operate a five-star PADI outfit with totally up-to-date equipment.'

'You're . . . involved with each other, aren't you?' Río focused on the evening star, Venus, who was just twinkling her way up above the horizon to the east.

'Um. Yeah. Kind of.'

'It's never a good idea to go into a business partnership with someone you're involved with romantically, Finn.'

'So what am I supposed to do? Turn round to Izzy and say, "Doh, I don't think we can swing this because I like you"? I'd have thought that was a plus, to get on as well with your business partner as I get on with Izzy. She's dead smart, Ma, and she can get us a backer. She's even got premises in mind. Let me give you a clue. Two letters. V.F.'

'Not the Villa Felicity?'

'Got it in one! Wouldn't it be brilliant! You've always said that it looks more like a club house than a place where people live.'

There was no stopping Finn now.

'I was talking to Iz earlier, and she's got it all figured out. The Villa Felicity's got just about everything we need – it's a dead cert! There's even a pool for confined water work. And we can custom-build a kit room to our own spec.'

'In the garden?'

'No. We'll need an air room as well, and it would be a shame to build in the garden.'

'So where are you thinking of building?'

'In the old orchard.'

Inside Río's gut, an icicle started to form. 'You know there's a right of way down to the beach through there,' she said.

'Yeah. But that shouldn't be a problem. We'll just have to get good security. Who'd want to steal a load of scuba gear, anyway?'

Quite a lot of people, thought Río. There'd been a spate of thefts of outboard motors in Coolnamara recently, but that problem wasn't high on her list of concerns right now. 'What about the orchard?' she asked.

'What about it?'

'You'd have to pull down trees.'

'Ma, I know you have a sentimental attachment to that place, but this is my future we're talking about.'

They had reached the main gate to the Villa Felicity. It stood open in welcome.

'We'll talk about this another time, Finn,' Río told him. 'It's not appropriate to discuss it now.'

'Oh, yeah. I forgot. You're supposed to be surprised by this party. Why do you think Izzy's dad is doing this for you, Ma?'

'I honestly have no idea.' Río realised that it was the second time that day she'd uttered those words with regard to Adair Bolger. And as she walked down the path that ran parallel to the orchard she heard the wind soughing in the branches of the trees that had grown there for decades, and she steeled herself for confrontation – pleasant or otherwise – and pulled the lapels of her black cashmere cardigan as close as she could for comfort.

'What a lovely surprise!' Río said, a handful of minutes later, as she stood on Adair's deck listening to people singing 'Happy Birthday, Dear Río'. 'Oh, Adair, you really, really shouldn't have gone to so much trouble!'

The place looked amazing. Adair had followed her suggestions to the letter, and staged this party just as she had described it to him the day she'd come up with her inspired idea of how to transform the Villa Felicity into the kind of house that people would yearn to live in. The only discrepancy was that the white-clothed table in the middle of the deck was set for dinner for ten, as opposed to a dozen.

Upon it gleamed the same crystal and silverware that Izzy had laid out the day she'd entertained Río and Dervla to lunch, but the table this evening had been scattered with flower petals and littered with presents, all of which, she saw now, bore her name. There were countless wine bottles lined up on a trestle table on the other side of the deck, and the hot tub had been drained and filled with ice and beer and bottles of champagne. There were candles everywhere, and flowers, and a stage had been rigged for musicians.

Adair handed her a glass of fizz. 'Sit down and open your presents,' he said.

Part of Río wanted to throw her arms around the man and thank him for this absurdly generous gesture, and part of her wanted to send a stinging slap across his face and denounce him as a devious, land-grabbing louse. She was too confused to do either. Instead, she sat down at the table and did as he'd instructed.

First out of its wrapping was a pashmina, in a shade of poppy red that almost exactly matched her dress. She smiled her thanks, and draped it round her shoulders.

Next was a gift pack containing a Jo Malone candle and body lotion in her favourite fragrance, grapefruit. Had he asked Fleur to advise him? If so, it was very astute of him. Very astute, or wonderfully thoughtful . . .

Jo Malone was followed by Monty Don and David Attenborough and Nigella – all ready to take pride of place on her coffee table. Then came the CDs. Donal Lunny and Sharon Shannon and Zoë Conway. And there were cards, lots and lots of them, all with 'Happy Birthday' written in different hand-writing, and all wishing her well, and by the time Río had finished unwrapping her presents, giftwrap and ribbon were festooned all over Adair Bolger's deck, and the champagne had gone straight to her head.

She couldn't have staged it better herself.

Chapter Thirty-one

Izzy had been careful to stand very close to Finn when he was introduced to foxy little Megan Vaughan. 'Paws off,' said her body language. There was something about the girl that was aloof yet alarmingly predatory at the same time, and Izzy determined not to let her guard slip for a minute.

She had managed to inveigle Finn into the downstairs shower room before dinner, where they had shared such an intense kiss that Izzy's appetite had come bouncing right back. Her place was at the right-hand side of her father, who was seated at the top of the table. Río was at the other end, directly opposite, looking flagrant in scarlet silk.

The food served up by the caterers was so mouthwateringly good that Izzy decided she might try and head-hunt the chef once she'd got her business up and running. They had steamed mussels with watercress sauce to start, followed by parsnip and honey soup. The main course was saffron risotto with grilled sardines and a green salad, and pudding was bitter chocolate sorbet with raspberries. Blue Mountain coffee was served afterwards, and cognac for those who wanted it, and then the table was cleared as guests started to arrive for the main event, which was, of course, music and dancing.

As hostess, Izzy was kept busy. Her *savoir-faire* – courtesy of her mother – was the one thing for which Izzy was grateful to Felicity. Izzy knew she had considerable charm, and she used it to great effect.

She spoke to Devla Kinsella about property, and expressed an interest in the logistics of conversion work. Could she introduce Izzy to a bespoke carpenter? Which design consultant would she recommend? When Dervla put forward her sister, Río, as a potential design guru, Izzy feigned enthusiasm.

She spoke to Christian about his wine importing business, and suggested that he supply the restaurant of her scuba-dive centre. He knew a château in the Loire that could provide an exceptional house white, he told her, and he'd be delighted to draw up a sample wine list for her.

She spoke to Fleur about Fleurissima, and told her it was her favourite shop in the whole world – better than anything Dublin had to offer. She had admired Fleur's dress (Bill Blass) and her shoes (Freelance) and her bag (vintage) and her scent (Chanel No. 5). Of course! How classic! Incidentally, would Fleur be able to recommend someone who could design staff T-shirts for her? Why, yes, indeed. Fleur could recommend her partner, Conrad.

Having pocketed Conrad's card, and crooked a finger under Babette's chin (Babette was dressed for the occasion this evening in a diamanté collar), Izzy noticed that Mrs Vaughan senior was sitting on her own on a seat in the garden, under a patio heater. The old lady had clearly elected to distance herself from the hurly-burly of the party, so Izzy decided that it would be a charitable thing to keep her company for a while. She sought Finn out to tell him that she was going to spend some quality time with Mrs V.

'Aren't you sweet!' said Finn. 'To spend time with a little old lady when you could be dancing with me!'

'I'd rather slow dance with you later,' Izzy replied, with a minxy smile.

She fluttered across the deck like a white butterfly, gracing guests with compliments and smiles (an especially saccharine smile was bestowed upon Megan), and lit next to Mrs Vaughan on her bench under the patio heater.

'Good evening! We didn't get a chance to talk earlier. I'm Izzy.'

'Izzy! What sort of a name is that?' said Mrs Vaughan.

'It's short for Isabella.'

'Is a bell necessary on a bicycle?' said Mrs Vaughan, and Izzy gave a tinkling laugh.

'That's a good one all right!' she said.

'Do you like my trousers?' asked Mrs Vaughan.

Izzy nodded a polite assent. 'Yes,' she said. 'They're lovely!'

'I got them in Ireland, I think. You should get yourself a pair.'

'I – well – I could have a look for them,' said Izzy, uncertainly. 'I could ask Fleur, who has a boutique in the village. She might be able to help.'

'What village?'

'Lissamore.'

'Where's that?'

'Well, it's – kind of where we are now. Just down the road.'

'I see.'

'It's a lovely party, isn't it?' said Izzy, manfully.

'Yes. What are we celebrating?'

'It's a birthday party.'

'Congratulations,' carrolled Mrs V. 'That's Cliff Richard, you know. I love Cliff Richard.'

'Yes. His music is very . . . accessible.'

'What are those people doing?'

From beyond the sea wall, came the sound of a couple making out *con brio*. Izzy ignored the question, and tried to think of another topic of conversation. The weather! Of course. 'The weather's—'

'Are they having sex?' demanded Mrs Vaughan. 'It's very over-rated, you know, sex.'

'The weather's changed a bit for the worse, hasn't it?' said Izzy hurriedly. 'Such a shame, after our glorious Indian summer. It's definitely got a lot cooler.'

'Cooler, cooler . . .'

Some time later, Izzy staggered back onto the deck, feeling as though she'd been over an assault course. She very much wanted to find Finn and fling herself into his arms, but there were two more people she needed to talk to before she could relax and enjoy the party.

The first person she wanted to sweet-talk was her father. The second was Río Kinsella.

She found the former in the kitchen, settling up with the caterers. 'Hello, Daddy, darling!' she sang, linking his arm as the caterers backed off, practically salaaming after clocking the tip they'd received. 'Let's take a stroll.'

'I couldn't think of anything nicer,' said Adair, dropping a kiss on her forehead, 'than an evening stroll through the garden with my gorgeous girl on my arm.'

They walked through the atrium and headed for the orchard.

'I'm sorry Lucy couldn't come,' remarked Adair.

Izzy hadn't actually invited Lucy to the party, but she wasn't going to tell her dad that.

'Yeah. It's an awful shame,' she said. 'But she felt she had to stay in Dublin to be agony aunt to a friend who's going through a really rough time.'

'Oh? What's happened?'

Izzy paused for dramatic effect before launching into a pre-prepared spiel. 'Well, this friend – her name's Sarah – met a boy that she really really liked. And Sarah's dad's divorced, and so is this boy's mum. And when she introduced her dad to the mum, they fell madly in love.'

'The parents did? That's lovely!' said Adair.

'No, it's not,' said Izzy, in the manner of an infant school teacher. 'You see, Sarah and Paul – Sarah's boyfriend's called Paul

– were so mortified by the whole thing that they had to break up. Sarah's inconsolable.'

'Why?'

'She just couldn't hack the idea of her father and Paul's mother being a couple.'

'Why – why not?'

'Oh, come on, Dad! Just *think* what it would be like for a girl to be involved with a guy whose mother was having a thing with her own father? Ew, *ew*! It's so icky it's almost incestuous. What if there were babies? I mean, imagine if Paul's mother got pregnant? Would the baby be her sister or brother as well as being Paul's sister or brother? It's just really, really hard for poor Sarah to even contemplate the idea of her father having sex with her boyfriend's mother. I mean – *ew*! It gives me the shivers to even think what it must be like to be in her situation.' Izzy shook her head mournfully. 'Poor, poor Sarah. Lucy's doing her best, but she thinks she might need medical help.'

'You mean, the girl might have to go on anti-depressants?'

'Yes. And get counselling too, probably. The whole thing's messed her up, bigtime. Without Paul, her life's a meaningless void.'

'That's – that's a dreadful story.'

'Yes. Isn't it?'

Izzy's ringtone went. 'Oh! Sorry, Dad. I'm going to have to take this. It's Lucy. She's probably looking for some advice.'

'Yes, you go ahead and take that call, darling. Dear God – that's a dreadful story!'

And Adair turned and walked back into the house, looking bewildered.

Izzy hung up on her caller (it was a private number; she never picked up on private numbers, but she thanked the anonymous caller for his excellent timing), and went off on the next stage of her mission, which was to find Río.

The scarlet woman had discarded her shoes and was sitting

by the pool. Her feet were dangling in the petal-strewn water and she was sipping champagne, doubtless waiting for her host to come along so that she could flirt with him again.

'Hi, Río!' said Izzy, sitting down beside her. Río choked a little on her champagne, and Izzy banged her on the back. 'Oops! Careful. That happened to my friend Paul recently, and he choked so hard that champagne came out of his nose. He thought he was going to die, but then that wouldn't have been so bad because he actually really *did* want to die.'

'Oh?' said Río, recovering. 'Was he suffering from depression?'

'Yeah. He was going through a really rough time.'

'What happened?'

'Well, Paul had met a girl, Sarah, who he really really liked. And Paul's mum's divorced, and so is Sarah's dad. And when he introduced his mum to the dad, they fell madly in love. Madly being the operative word, at their age.'

'I think that's rather lovely,' said Río, cautiously.

'No, it's *not*,' said Izzy categorically. 'You see, Paul was so mortified by the whole thing that he and Sarah had to break up. He was inconsolable. Neither of them could hack the idea of their parents being a couple.'

'Why – why not?'

'Oh, Río! Just *think* what it would be like for a guy to be involved with a girl whose mother was having a thing with his own father? Ew, *ew*! It's so icky it's almost incestuous. Anyway, Paul knew that his mother didn't even like Sarah very much. Can you imagine what it would be like for them to have to do family stuff together – you know, holidays and Sunday dinners and Christmas and all that jazz? And the other thing is that it's just really, really hard for poor Paul to even contemplate the idea of his mother having sex with Sarah's father. I mean – *ew*! It gives me the shivers to even think what it must be like to be in his situation.' Izzy shook her head mournfully. 'Poor, poor Paul. He's on anti-depressants, and he's probably going to have to get counselling too. The whole thing's messed him up, bigtime. Without Sarah, his life's a meaningless void.'

Izzy was just about to congratulate herself on her performance, when she clocked the expression on Río's face. The woman was looking back at her with a kind of understanding that made Izzy feel . . . petty. Worse than that, she felt ashamed. She felt as ashamed and worthless as she had when her mother had told her 'Don't!' *Don't make a mess! Don't fiddle with your hair! Don't get your dress dirty!* But her mother had never said the word 'Don't' gently, the way Río was saying it now, with her eyes.

'That's a dreadful story,' murmured Río.

'Yes. Isn't it?' Izzy hardened her heart. If she started backtracking now it would be like unravelling a tapestry.

'D'you know something, Izzy?' said Río. 'There's a lot that I'd love to be able to—'

But just then Adair came round the corner, swinging a bottle of champagne. 'Oh, hi, Dad!' said Izzy brightly. 'I was just telling Río that awful story about Sarah and Paul.' There was a pause, as the three of them looked at each other. Then Izzy jumped to her feet. 'Well, I'll leave you two to enjoy your champers. I'd better go and find Finn. We're going to wander round the house and dream-build. Gorm Mhór is going to be sooooo beautiful!'

'Gorm Mhór?' echoed Adair, uncertainly.

'Our dive centre, of course! The Big Blue!'

And, mission accomplished, Izzy danced off in the direction of the deck.

Río was in the downstairs bathroom, trying to resist the temptation to bury her face in Adair's robe so that she could breathe in Acqua di Parma. She was feeling very confused, and it wasn't just from a surfeit of champagne. She was confused about her feelings for Adair, and she was confused about the whole thing with Finn and Izzy, and she was confused about the land issue and how she was going to resolve it.

Oh, how she wanted her orchard! But if Finn was dead set on going ahead with this Gorm Mhór idea, she wanted to be able to help him out too. If he and Izzy needed to build on part of the land in order to realise their dream, she couldn't be the one responsible for thwarting them. However, on anticipating the expression on Izzy's face when she found out that Río had the power to veto any building on the orchard of which she did not approve, she couldn't help but break into a smile. It was petty of her, she knew, to think about scoring points, but after the treatment meted out to her by Adair's daughter, it felt good to have the upper hand for a change. Arra, what the hell – she'd think about all that tomorrow. After all, as her heroine Scarlett O'Hara had said, tomorrow was another day. She was sure they could come to some compromise.

And yet, and yet . . . her smile faltered when she recalled Izzy's story about the guy whose dad had fallen for his girlfriend's mother. If she and Adair did hook up – and the idea had become more and more attractive to her – she'd not just be opening a can of worms, she'd be disturbing a whole nest of vipers. Izzy had started making hissy noises, although, to Río's ear, the hiss was more like a kitten's than a snake's.

She suspected that the girl's story was just a cautionary tale concocted as a warning to Río to back off. She had a point. The thought of padding down to breakfast someplace and bumping into Finn and Izzy after having just left Adair's bed was wildly inappropriate. She couldn't – *wouldn't* – subject Finn to such mortification. It was the kind of scenario you'd find in a Feydeau farce or a Greek tragedy – and look what happened to all those old Greeks: murdered in their baths and killed by their own hands and sacrificed to indifferent gods.

Río moved to the mirror to check out her reflection. She'd made an effort to look good tonight, and she knew she'd made that effort for Adair. But any possibility of a relationship was out of the question now. Things had become far, far too complicated.

She'd have to go to find him and say thank you for the party, and then she'd have to excise him from her life. Excise was the right word, she decided, as she unlocked the door and went out into the atrium. 'Excise' meant to cut away with a knife, and doing what she was going to have to do was going to cause Río some pain.

She moved through the party on bare feet, looking this way and that for Adair. The band was playing something languorous now, and couples were slow-dancing, wrapped in each other's arms and looking at each other with amorous eyes.

Finn was dancing with Izzy. The couple looked so beautiful together that they almost took Río's breath away. He – so like his father, dark and piratical; she – so like something out of a fairy tale, elfin, a golden sylph. Río couldn't do to them what the couple in Izzy's story had done to their children. She couldn't break their hearts.

Christian and Dervla – the new Mrs Vaughan – were waltzing, clearly delighting in their new-found synchronicity. Río was so very happy that Dervla had found love at last, at this (fairly) advanced stage in her life. But love came at a price – Río knew that – and Dervla would have to learn some new life skills to negotiate the web of problems in which her in-laws would be bound to snag her.

Would her sister want to have children of her own? Río wondered. That too, could bring complications. It was strange to contemplate the idea of Dervla with a baby: she still thought of her older sister as formidable, a consummate businesswoman, a princessa.

But then, people changed, circumstances changed, and the world moved on. Río remembered how, in his cups, her father had used to recite the poetic works of William Butler Yeats, and she heard his voice in her head now, uttering the passionate words of 'Easter 1916'. *All changed, changed utterly: A terrible beauty is born.*

410

And then she heard Shane's voice in her head, and the words of the Yeats poem he had adapted to suit her and Dervla:

> The light of morning, Lissamore,
> Sash windows, open to the south,
> Two girls in silk kimonos, both
> Beautiful, one I adore.

Both beautiful, one I adore. She, Río, had ended up being the adored one. Like her mother before her.

Adair was in the orchard. She could see him standing under a tree, gazing at his view. The sea had grown rougher now, with white horses curveting on a horizon where the silver light of a full moon frosted the edge of the world.

Río made her way towards the steps that would take her down to the garden, reaching for the pashmina draped over the back of her chair, the exquisitely embroidered swirl of silk and cashmere that Adair had given her.

Out in the garden, her bare feet made no sound on the newly-mown lawn. Once under the trees, though, the lawn gave way to more luxuriant growth, and grass and fallen leaves rustled underfoot.

Alerted to her presence, Adair turned to her. Río was taken aback to see that there were tears on his face. Raising a hand, he dashed them away.

'I – I'm sorry,' she said, making to move away. 'I'm intruding.'

'You're not intruding, Río. Please don't go. Unless you're embarrassed by seeing a man cry.'

'I'm not easily embarrassed by anything,' she said. 'Is there anything I can do to help?'

'You've already helped.'

'What do you mean?'

'You were responsible for this. All this festivity.' He gestured towards the house, where the shadows of partygoers danced on

411

the candle-lit deck, and the sound of laughter competed with the fiddle-players and bodhrán for supremacy, and the aroma of barbecue rose into the sea air.

'*I* was responsible?'

'Yes. This party wouldn't have happened without you.'

'But that's crap, Adair! This is *your* party.'

He shook his head. 'If I'd announced I was throwing a birthday party for me, people would have made excuses to stay away. Nobody gives a shit about me. But they care for you. That's why all these people are here tonight – they're here for you, Ríonach Kinsella. They adore you. The house is full of your friends, not mine. You've breathed life into the place.'

'Don't be daft!'

'It's true. I'm under no illusions that I haven't made enemies in Lissamore. Well, maybe not enemies, exactly, but I know that people had no very high opinion of the Bolgers. You didn't.'

'I . . .'

'It's all right, Río. You don't have to deny that you thought I was a right plonker. I probably still am. Look at me, blubbing because I'm Norman No-Friends.'

'You're allowed to blub. It's your party, you can cry if you want to.'

'Don't worry. I've finished blubbing. Let's change the subject.'

'We could talk about the weather.'

'We could. Or we could talk about our hopes for the future.'

'No, no. I made the decision earlier today that I was putting off thinking about the future until tomorrow. Let's just try and enjoy the present.'

'Live for the moment?'

'I guess.'

They remained silent for some time. Across the bay, clouds were slinking along the mountain range, draping themselves over the dark peaks like an eiderdown settling over a recumbent figure.

Then Adair said, 'I have something for you.'

Reaching into his pocket, he produced a leather box and held it out to her. Río recognised the logo of an über-exclusive jeweller's, and her hands flew to her face in shock.

'Don't worry,' said Adair hastily. 'It's not a ring. I wouldn't be so presumptuous as to offer you a ring at this stage in our relationship.'

'Our – relationship?'

'I – well – oh God. I've just dug myself into a hole. It is, of course, presumptuous of me to – er – presume that we enjoy such a thing as a relationship. But I have to tell you, Río, that I'd love to think we might. Enjoy one, I mean. I . . . you see, I adore you—'

'Adair! Stop it.'

'But it's true! I *adore* you! I adore everything about you! I adore your feistiness and your lust for life and your laugh. I adore the way you swim in the freezing cold Atlantic to warm it up, and I adore the way you walk barefoot, and I adore the way you swig wine and slide down banisters. I adore your name, Río – Ríonach! I adore the way it feels on my tongue. Look at you! You're beautiful, Río. A goddess. A selkie.'

'Adair—'

But he wouldn't stop.

'I've never met a woman like you before. All the women I know are harpies, and they're all made of plastic. They wouldn't dream of walking barefoot into an orchard. They wouldn't be caught dead bowling along on a bicycle. Can't you see how I adore all those things about you? Don't you know that that's why I want to shower you with gifts?'

'You've showered me with too many gifts already, Adair. I can't possibly accept any more.'

'But you must, Río.' He undid the clasp on the small leather box. 'It's part of the birthday celebration you dreamed up. Please take it.' He proffered the box, looking at her with entreaty. Then he opened it, and revealed the contents.

Inside was a bracelet of beads looped together by a network

of silver filigree. The beads were exquisite, handmade and decorated with tiny whorled pink rosebuds against a blue and silver background – like miniature Fabergé eggs. It was clearly antique, and it had clearly cost him a lot of money.

'It's the last gift on your wish list,' said Adair, lifting it from its bed of creamy satin. 'It's the bracelet your imaginary birthday girl left lying on the table.'

Río looked at the bracelet, and then she looked at Adair and shook her head. 'I won't take jewellery from you, Adair. No, indeed I won't.'

'Take it. Please take it, Río.'

He thrust the box at her, and she put her hands behind her back. But Adair was insistent. Putting his arms around her, he tried to prise her fingers apart so that he could slide the bracelet onto her wrist. And as he did so, her pashmina fell to the ground and Río felt the hardness of him against the slippery silk of her dress. And then she felt a wave of lust so powerful that nothing in the world could have stopped her pulling his face down to hers and kissing him. Adair made a kind of growl deep in his throat, and suddenly they were embracing. The embrace for Río was like tasting water for the first time after travelling through a desert. She had, she realised now, been parched for him, and he likewise for her. She *was* his selkie: she would sacrifice her ocean home for him.

She felt his palms travel down her back, and she felt the hard grip of his hands on her ass as he pulled her closer into him, and then there came a muffled squeal from the garden beyond the orchard, and Río and Adair sprang apart abruptly. There, like a little lost ghost standing in the middle of the lawn, was Izzy. Her hands were covering her mouth, and her eyes were wide in her pale, pale face.

'Daddy!' she cried, and Adair said, 'Darling, it's not what you think!' – the classic line so abused by truly guilty people.

But Izzy just shook her head wildly before turning and fleeing

414

back in the direction of the house, her sobs receding as she left the arena.

Río and Adair regarded each other for a long moment before Río said, 'It's impossible, Adair. You know it is.'

Adair stooped and picked up the pashmina and the bracelet, which had also fallen to the orchard floor.

'Yes,' he said, straightening up wearily. 'I guess it is.'

'It would have been lovely in another place and under different circumstances. Wouldn't it?'

He nodded. Then he held the bracelet out to her. 'Are you sure you won't accept this?' he said.

'I'm sure. You'll find someone else to adore, who would love to wear it. I'm certain of that.' Río smiled at him. 'I'll keep the pashmina, though, if you don't mind. It's starting to get really cold.'

'Of course.' Adair wrapped her in the swathe of crimson cashmere, and then he stuck his hands in his pockets. 'I'd better get back to Izzy,' he said.

'You better had,' said Río. 'Goodbye, Adair. Thank you for the party. It was lovely.'

'You're welcome, Ríonach,' said Adair. He turned with an awkward dip of his head, and retraced his daughter's steps back to the Villa Felicity.

Río watched him go, then pulled the pashmina tighter round her, and wandered further down the orchard. She wouldn't cry, she told herself, as she slid the bolt on the five-bar gate and stepped off her land onto the beach. She had no reason to cry.

Back at the house, Izzy sped upstairs to her room to compose herself before rejoining the party. But someone had got there before her. It was Babette. The little dog was lying in the middle of Izzy's bed, looking like a furry odalisque.

'What are you doing here, sweetie pie?' Izzy asked; then figured that the pooch had been airlifted away by her mistress to prevent her from being trampled to death by the dancers on the deck.

Babette wagged her tail in greeting, then gave Izzy a sympathetic look as she clocked the tears on her cheeks.

'I know – I've been crying. Sorry. They're stupid tears, really.' Izzy helped herself to a Kleenex from the box on her bedside table, then sat down beside Babette, and curled her feet up underneath her. 'It's just that my dad's made a real eejit of himself over that appalling Río woman, Babette. He fancies her, but I so want him to find someone who will love him for himself and make him happy, not a gold-digger like her who'll probably get pregnant and force him into marrying her. And then I'd have to share Dad with a half-sister or -brother, and I couldn't bear that. If that happened I'd be practically an orphan, because I don't have a mother, Babette – at least not a mother in the real sense, who makes comfort food like cottage pie, and does your laundry, and tucks you into bed with a hot-water bottle when you're sick. And I'm horribly, horribly lonely because I've no one to talk to apart from Lucy and she's going to study abroad next year.'

'You have Finn.'

'What?' Izzy looked at the dog in astonishment, before realising that the voice had come from the direction of her en suite bathroom. She turned to see Fleur leaning against the doorjamb, looking at her with concern.

'I'm sorry,' said Fleur. 'Your father told me I could leave Babette here in your room. I came up to check on her and go to the loo, and of course I couldn't help overhearing you. You clearly need someone to talk to, Isabella, and wise as Babette is, she's not the most articulate of agony aunts. Can I help?'

Izzy felt her face flare up, and then, to her mortification, the tears started again. Except this time, they were tears of despair, not tears of anger.

Fleur moved across to the bed, and took Izzy in her arms. And when she'd soothed her and told her 'There, there' over and over again, she pushed Izzy's damp hair back from her face and smiled.

'You're confused about a lot of things, Isabella, and I'd like to put some of your misconceptions right, if I may. The most important thing you need to know is what a remarkable woman Río Kinsella is. Allow me to tell you all about her.'

On the beach, Río walked towards the edge of the water and stood looking out to sea for some time, while wavelets lapped at her feet. Then she reached down and picked up a stick of driftwood that had been washed up onto the shore. Taking a few steps backward, she hunkered down and wrote some words in the sand with her driftwood pen, in great big letters. Then she looked up. Above her a gull screamed, and she wondered idly, if the bird could read, what it would make of the legend looped in Río's swirly capitals on Lissamore strand.

The climb up the cliff path was a stiff one, and by the time she got to the top Río was breathless with exertion and emotion. Looking down, she saw that the words she'd inscribed on the beach were visible, just, by the light of the full moon. There had been a full moon too, on the night Finn had been conceived. '*I know what it is,*' she murmured, '*to be adored.*' She repeated the words, like a mantra, for reassurance. She, Ríonach Kinsella, knew what it was to be adored, and really, that was all that anyone should want from life, because it meant that you were a good person.

She watched, dry-eyed, as waves swept over the words on the sand, erasing them. Erasing them for ever? Maybe. Maybe not. She could write those words again and again, on sand or on paper or in bold graffiti on a wall. She could embroider them in silk or daub them on canvas or carve them upon a tablet of marble. She could blazon them on a banner, or across the sky in fireworks if she damn well pleased.

Río looked to the east upon the gleaming, floodlit Villa Felicity with its glimmering pool and its shadowy orchard, and smiled.

Epilogue

The next morning, very early, Izzy woke. Finn lay beside her, looking like the sleeping prince in some fairy tale. She longed to reach out and trace the curve of his mouth, the contour of his cheekbone, the line of his jaw – but she resisted. She needed time to herself, time to think. Izzy needed to swim.

Downstairs, there was evidence everywhere of last night's party. The deck was littered with a kind of picturesque debris – glasses and bottles glinting in the early morning sun, bunting fluttering overhead, fairy lights gleaming still. There were flowers and half-burned candles and birthday cards and confetti curls and streamers all over the place, and by the steps that led down to the garden was a pair of shoes. Red shoes, with heels.

Looking around, Izzy saw for the first time that this was a house where fun could be had; where music and laughter and love was possible. The house had never looked like this after Felicity's parties. When the sun rose on the morning after one of Felicity's parties, the detritus had all been cleared away – disappeared by an army of house elves while the guests slumbered under goose-down quilts. After Felicity's parties it looked as if no fun or music or laughter had been on the agenda; no dancing, or shenanigans, or shooting the breeze until the small hours. And the house had appeared as unloved as ever.

On the big trestle table – like an island surrounded by a reef of discarded gift wrap – was the stack of presents Adair had given Río: the books, the CDs, the distinctive black-edged Jo Malone boxes. The bracelet. The bracelet that she had seen Río Kinsella decline so categorically last night. *I won't take jewellery from you, Adair,* she had said. *No – indeed I won't . . .*

The whirring sound of powerful wings overhead made Izzy look up. Above the bay to the east, two swans were soaring towards the open Atlantic on snow-white pinions. They said that swans mated for life. Unlike humans. Izzy did not know one single couple of her parents' age who was not already on their second or third marriage. What made them turn their backs on their spouse and children and embark in hot pursuit of a specious happiness elsewhere? Her mother hadn't been made happy by the man who'd presented her with the diamond she coveted and had just split from her third 'boyfriend' since she and Adair had parted company. Izzy didn't want a reconciliation between her parents – she knew that they had never been right for each other. But who *was* right for her father?

There came the sound of a splash from the sea below. Moving to the rail, Izzy saw that someone was swimming in the bay. Río Kinsella. Fleur had told her last night that Río had an affinity with the ocean that was almost spiritual. Just as she, Izzy, had. Fleur had told her that Río was the most loving and generous of souls. Fleur had told her lots of things about Río, and the person that Fleur described bore no resemblance to the floozie who had flounced in front of Felicity's cheval glass all those months ago, badmouthing Adair. Who was the real Río? Was she the ultimate gold-digger? Or was she the woman who said 'Don't' with gentle eyes? Maybe it was time for Izzy to find out.

Moving across the deck, she picked up the red shoes and descended the steps to the garden. She passed under the apple trees and through the gate that led onto the shore, and when she reached the edge of the slipway, she set Río's shoes down and raised a hand to shield her eyes from the sun.

'Hi,' she said, when Río had finished her second lap. 'May I join you?'

Río shook her wet hair back, sending droplets of water spraying. Treading water, she regarded Izzy speculatively for a moment or two. Then she smiled the smile that her son had inherited – the smile that said, 'All's right with the world and aren't we lucky to be living in it?'

'Be my guest,' she said.

Read on for an exclusive extract from Kate Thompson's new novel, coming in 2010.

Chapter One

Fleur O'Farrell felt foolish. She was standing in front of the wardrobe in her bedroom, regarding her reflection in the mirror. Fleur normally took pride in her appearance – but not this afternoon. This afternoon she was wearing a floral print skirt over flouncy petticoats, a cherry-red cummerbund, and a low-cut blouse. Her feet were bare, a silk shawl was slung around her shoulders, and great gilt hoops dangled from her ears. The crowning glory was the wig – a Rapunzel-style confection of synthetic black curls. She looked like a chorus member from a second-rate production of *Carmen*.

Her friend, Río Kinsella, had talked her into playing the fortune teller at this year's summer festival. Río usually took the role upon herself, but she had come down with a nasty viral infection and was stuck in bed, gulping back herbal tea and Echinacea. So Río had furnished Fleur with the gypsy costume, as well as a crystal ball, a chenille table cloth and a manual called *Six Lessons in Crystal Gazing*. The flyleaf told Fleur that these words of wisdom had been published in 1928.

Turning away from the mirror, she reached for the dog-eared booklet. The cover featured a bug-eyed gal transfixed by a blinging crystal ball, and the blurb went: 'Are you lacking in self confidence, unemployed or discouraged? Are you prepared for the future, or blindly groping in the darkness? Do you wish for health, happiness and success?'

Evidently not a lot had changed in the world since 1928. People were still asking the same questions, and still entertaining the same hopes and ambitions. Nowadays, however, instead of using crystal gazing as a means of self help, people were unrolling yoga mats and sticking Hopi candles in their ears to assist them in their navel gazing. Much the same thing, Fleur supposed.

A blast of hip-hop drew her to the open window. A youth was lazily patrolling the main street of the village, posing behind the steering wheel of his soft-top and checking out the talent. Being high season, there was a lot on display. Girls decked out in Diesel, Miss Sixty, and Converse promenaded the footpaths and lounged against the sea wall, hooked up to their iPods or gossiping on their phones or browsing on their BlackBerrys. Beautiful girls with gym-toned figures and sprayed-on tans and GHD hair, sporting must-have designer eyewear and toting must-have designer bags. High-maintenance girls, whose daddies footed the department store bills and whose mummies stole their style. Girls who did not know what the word 'recession' meant.

Lissamore was not usually host to such quantities of deluxe *jeunesse dorée*. The village was, rather, a playground for their parents, a place where those jaded denizens of Dublin 4 came to unwind for a month in the summer and a week at Christmas. Once the yearned-for eighteenth birthdays arrived, the princelings and princesses tended to migrate to hipper locations in Europe or America.

But this summer, because a major motion picture was being made in the countryside surrounding Lissamore, the village had become a must-visit zone. Wannabe film stars had descended in their droves after an article in a national newspaper had mentioned that extras were being recruited for *The O'Hara Affair* – a movie based on the childhood of Gerard O'Hara, father to Scarlett of *Gone with the Wind* fame. An additional allure was the fact that the movie starred Shane Byrne, an Irish actor with the sex appeal of Johnny Depp.

'Did he text back yet?' It was a girl's voice – a princess – to judge by the accent.

'No,' came the morose reply.

Craning her neck a little, Fleur looked down to see two girls sitting on the window sill of her shop below. The girl with the D4 drawl she recognised – she had been in and out of Fleurissima half a dozen times in the past fortnight, helping herself to pricey little wisps of silk and *devoré* velvet paid for by daddy's gold Amex.

'Did you put a question mark at the end of your last message?'

'Yes.'

'Shit. That means you can't text him again, Emily. Like, the ball's in his court now.'

'I know. I should never have put the stupid question mark. He's ignoring me, the bastard.'

'How many x's did you put?'

'Three. But two of them were low case.'

'Ow. Three's a bit heavy. I'd only put two low case ones next time.'

'If there is a next time. There was a message from that Australian girl on his Facebook this morning.'

'Uh-oh . . .'

Fleur felt like leaning out of the window and calling down: 'Just pick up the phone and *talk* to him!' But she knew that the rules laid down by mobile phone etiquette meant that picking up a phone was not an option. Fleur couldn't understand how kids nowadays stuck the uncertainty, the insecurity, the emotional turbulence generated by the text messaging phenomenon. It must be a kind of enforced purgatory, sending texts to-ing and fro-ing through the either – like playing ping-pong in slow motion.

But Fleur was as in thrall to her phone as the girls on the

street below, she realised, because when her text alert sounded she automatically reached for her nifty little Nokia. Accessing the message, she saw that it was from her niece, Daisy. The text read: 'Hey, Flirty! On my way now with cake & wine ☺ XXX'

Because Fleur's middle initial was 'T' for Theresa, Daisy had come up with the nickname 'Flirty' for her. Fleur loved it: it sounded so much more youthful and fun than 'Auntie Fleur', which was what all her other nieces called her.

'Cake & wine sounds good', she texted back, adding ♥ for good measure.

Cake and wine *did* sound good. Especially wine. It had been busy in the shop today: Fleur's jaw was aching from all the smiling she'd been doing, and her feet were killing her from all the standing. Her boutique, Fleurissima, specialised in non-mainstream labels sourced from all over Europe: from evening chic to skinny jeans, from beachwear to accessories, all Fleur's stock was handpicked and exclusive to her – and none of it was cheap. From the month of October, when the tourist trade dropped off and the summer residences were boarded up, Fleur hibernated, opening the shop only at weekends. After today, when two overdue deliveries had arrived at the same time, Fleur was looking forward to hibernating already. She reached up a hand to pull off her gypsy wig, then decided against it. It would give Daisy something to laugh about, and she loved to hear her niece laugh.

Tossing her shawl on the bed, Fleur negotiated the spiral staircase that led down to her living area. In the kitchen, she set a tray with plates, glasses and a wine cooler, and was just about to carry it through to the deck, when the doorbell rang. 'Come on up, Daisy-Belle,' Fleur said into the intercom. 'I'm on the deck.'

Fleur's deck overlooked the Lissamore marina, and was perfect for spying on the comings and goings of yachts and yachtsmen. Her own lover had a yacht berthed there, but so far this summer he'd had few opportunities to use it. He'd been stuck in Dublin, on business. Damien was the creative director of an advertising agency – a mover, shaker and Sabatier-sharp image maker. When Río had asked Fleur to describe him to her, Fleur had laughingly called him her very own Mr Big: but because Río had never seen a single episode of *Sex and the City*, the reference had meant zilch.

'He*llo*! What in God's name are you wearing?' Fleur turned to see Daisy framed in the French windows, regarding her with a curious expression.

'It's my outfit for the summer festival. Ta ra!' Fleur held her skirts out and attempted a flamenco-style twirl. 'I'm the fortune teller. What do you think? Smokin' or what?'

'Mystic Meg, eat your heart out,' replied Daisy, strolling across to the table and dumping a carrier bag on it. 'Let me take a photograph.' Holding up her iPhone, she adopted the exaggerated stance of a pro photographer, segueing into the usual clichéd directive: *Lovely! Chin a little higher! Drop your shoulder!*

Click, click, click went Daisy's camera, while Fleur twirled some more and hummed a little Bizet, and then Daisy slid her phone back into her bag and kissed her aunt on the cheek. 'How did you get roped into being the fortune teller?' she asked. 'I thought that was normally Río's gig.'

'I'll tell you later. I want to hear all your news first. Sit down and give me the wine and cake.' Daisy took a bottle of wine and a cake-box from the carrier bag, and Fleur reached for a corkscrew. 'Have you seen sense and ditched that prick?' she asked, stripping foil from the neck of the bottle.

'Yes. The prick is ancient history, Flirty. But I've got some even better news.'

'Oh? What's that?'

'Guess.'

'You've landed a new contract?'

'No.'

'You've been asked to be a judge on *Ireland's Next Top Model*?'

427

'Yes, I have actually. But that's not the good news.'

'You've got a photo-shoot with Testino?'

'In my dreams.'

The cork popped. Fleur poured wine into the glasses and handed one to Daisy. 'A *Vogue* cover?'

'Get real!'

'OK. Give up,' said Fleur.

'That's it! That's *exactly* what I've done!'

'What are you talking about?'

'I've given up modelling.'

Fleur set her glass down. 'I'm guessing this isn't a joke.'

'No joke. This is earnest; this is real.'

'But why, sweetheart?'

'I've fallen out of love with it. It's that simple. I'm giving it up, and I'm going to Africa to do voluntary work.'

Fleur took a sip of wine, and gave her niece a look of assessment. It was clear from Daisy's expression that she was resolute. Daisy was a Capricorn, and once a Capricorn decides upon a course of action, Fleur knew, there was no turning back.

'Well. Good for you. Was it a tough decision to make?'

Daisy shook her head. 'No. My agent asked if I needed twenty-four hours to think about it, and I said "Yes . . ." and then "*No!*" practically simultaneously. I really didn't need to think twice. I've been miserable in this job for a long time.'

'You've only been a model for two years,' Fleur pointed out.

'Well, I've been miserable for a whole year of those two, and that's a long time to be miserable. I was never cut out to be a model.'

'You're a brave girl.'

'No, I'm not. I'm just doing what I've always wanted to do, and that's make a difference. You've no idea what it's like to be surrounded by size zero girlies moaning about putting on half a kilo when there are people all over the world starving. It makes me feel sick.'

428

'Won't you miss your celebrity status, sweet pea?'

'Nope. I'd rather be famous for having a real talent like singing or dancing or painting. Being famous for being a model is just embarrassing.' Daisy cut two slabs of chocolate sponge and plonked them on to plates. 'Ha! Bye bye, stupid diet. Bring on the calories.'

'What made you decide on Africa?' asked Fleur.

'A friend who's over there told me I *had* to come out. She recruited a whole bunch of people via Facebook.'

'I thought you were a Bebo gal?'

'Nah. Facebook's way better. I've been in touch with everyone else who's going, and they're all really sound. It's brilliant. I don't know how I managed life before Facebook. Have you joined up yet, Flirty?'

'I keep meaning to, but I've just been so insanely busy lately. Maybe I'll get round to it in the winter, when things have calmed down.'

'Things will be hotting up for me this winter. I'll be working in a township in Kwa Zulu Natal, building a school.'

'Actually hands-on building?'

'Yeah. My mate says that she's completely knackered at the end of every day, but that she's never felt better in her life.'

'Wow. I'm full of admiration – and not a little jealous. I'd love to have had the chance to do something like that when I was your age.' Fleur raised her glass in a toast. 'Here's to you, sweet pea, and here's to Africa!'

'And here's to you, Mystic Meg!' Daisy took a sip of wine, then gave Fleur a look of appraisal. 'One question. How are you going to do it?'

'The fortune telling thing?'

'Yeah.'

'Río lent me a crystal ball.'

'A crystal ball? Does it work?'

'Yeah. I looked into it earlier and it told me that at half past

429

seven this evening I'd be drinking Chilean Sauvignon Blanc and tucking into chocolate sponge with my niece. And hey presto, how uncanny is that?'

'So presumably you're just going to gaze into it and come out with mumbo-jumbo stuff about travelling over water and meeting tall dark strangers?'

'I guess. I haven't really thought about it. Río gave me an instruction manual, but it's worse than useless.'

'How does Río usually do it?'

'She spoofs – she's brilliant at it. She has a kind of intuitive thing going on.'

'I hate to say this, Flirty, but you're not very good at spoofing.'

Fleur shrugged. 'I'm going to have to try. Río says she raised nearly four hundred euro last year, and Damien's agreed to double whatever I take in. And all the money raised is going to the Hospice Foundation.'

'But if word gets out that you're rubbish, no one will want to know.'

Fleur looked put out. 'It's only five euros a go, Daisy. And it's for charity.'

'Flirty – if you're not worth it, people are going to spend their five euro on the tombola instead. If you want to make any money, you're going to have to dream up some way of impressing the punters.'

'But I can't be expected to read people's fortunes, Daisy! That's just bonkers!'

'Of course it's bonkers. But . . .' Daisy narrowed her eyes and gave Fleur the benefit of her best Sphinx-like smile '. . . but I have an idea. Where's your crystal ball?'

'Upstairs.'

'Show me.'

'OK.' Fleur got to her feet and eased into a stretch. 'Ouch. I'll get out of this gear while I'm at it. If I don't take off the cummerbund I'll have no room for cake.'

'Why did you lace it so tight?'

'Vanity.'

Upstairs, Fleur doffed her fancy dress and got into sweat pants and T-shirt. There was a message on her phone: Daisy had forwarded the picture she had taken earlier. Her gypsy skirts were all a-twirl around her thighs, the cinched-in waist enhanced her curves, and she was smiling direct to camera. She'd send it to Damien, for a laugh. She composed the caption: 'Gypsy Rose Lee will tell your fortune for a modest remuneration', then sent the message whirling off into the ether. By the time she'd got back downstairs with the crystal ball and *Six Lessons in Crystal Gazing*, Daisy was checking something out on her iPhone.

'My idea is *inspired*, Flirty. Have a look at this.'

'What is it?'

'It's my Facebook profile.'

'Wow. You've masses of friends,' said Fleur, looking over Daisy's shoulder. 'But what has this to do with your inspired idea?'

'Aha! Behold.'

Aiming the cursor at 'status' on the top of her profile page, Daisy typed in 'Anyone in the Coolnamara region this weekend? Check out the fortune teller at the festival in Lissamore. She rocks!'

Fleur gave her niece an 'as if' look. 'Sweetheart – that's just *asking* for disaster!'

'No, it's not. Because this is what you're going to do. Watch this.'

Daisy clicked on a name, and another profile appeared on the screen. The person in question was a pretty girl called Sofia. As Daisy scrolled down, Fleur learned that Sofia's birthday was on the second of October: she was a Libra. Her relationship status was single, she was interested in men. A click told Fleur that Sofia's favourite movies included *Mamma Mia* and Disney's *Beauty and the Beast*, her favourite book was *The Boy in the Striped Pyjamas*, she had a brown belt in karate, and she made

431

excellent pasta because her mother was Italian. Her photo album included shots of herself standing against a variety of landmarks: the Sydney Opera House, the Eiffel Tower, the Coliseum. Remarks that had been posted on her wall read: 'See you when you get back from Coolnamara – Plu bar Friday week?' 'Hm . . . I hear you met a cutie in Paris!' 'You saw Cheryl Cole in Topshop? Awesome!'

'This is most illuminating, sweetie,' said Fleur. 'But why should you want to share with me the information that one of your friends met a cutie in Paris and has a brown belt in karate?'

'I know for a fact that she's in Lissamore this weekend.'

'So?'

'So, picture this. She's messing about on Facebook. She learns that there's a shit-hot fortune teller at the festival, and decides to investigate. Put yourself in her shoes.'

'What do you mean?'

'Pretend you're Sofia.'

Fleur gave Daisy a bemused look, then shrugged and said: 'OK. I'm Sofia.'

'Welcome, Sofia!' said Daisy, doing a kind of salaam and adopting a mysterious expression. Gazing into the crystal ball that Fleur had set on the table, she added in a dodgy Eastern European accent: 'I think you might be a Libra, Sofia, yes? Hm. What else can I tell you about yourself? I see – I think I see you in a pair of trousers – white trousers, with bare feet. You are dancing – no, no! You are kicking! I guess perhaps you might have a talent for karate, Sofia? And there is more – you have travelled, travelled far and wide. I see many foreign countries in the crystal – Sydney, Paris, Rome . . . And what is this? You are in a club, now, and this time you *are* dancing. But dancing in the future. Next Friday, perhaps? Next Friday I think you are going dancing with a friend, to a place called the – could it be the Blue bar?'

'No,' said Fleur with a smile, as the penny dropped. 'It's the Plu bar.'

'There!' Daisy flopped back in her seat with a triumphant smile. 'You see! It's ingenious! Word spreads like lightning through the Facebook community, and anybody who's spending the bank holiday weekend in Coolnamara will come flocking to see – what's your fortune teller name?'

'Madame Spoofetti?'

'The famous Madame Spoofetti, who knows all!'

'Daisy – how exactly do you propose I do this?'

'Simple! You check out profiles on my iPhone, which will be cunningly concealed under the table.'

'But I don't do Facebook.'

'Simple! You log on as me – popular minor celebrity and model, Daisy Delaney. You saw how many friends I have. And those friends have friends, and I have influence. Sometimes being a C-lister can be useful.'

'You've clearly had too much wine. This can't possibly work.'

'Don't be so negative, Flirty!' Daisy reached for *Six Lessons in Crystal Gazing* and started leafing through it. 'Just think of all the moolah you can raise for the Hospice Foundation.'

'But we've got to anticipate the worst. Loads and loads of things could go wrong. What if Norman No-Friends from Nenagh walks into the booth. What do I say to him?'

'You tell Norman that there is no hope of telling his fortune because . . . because he doesn't have one!'

'I couldn't say that! Poor Norman will think he's going to die.'

'Um. OK. Tell him you can't see his aura. Listen to this: "It is quite possible for the gazer to be able to see things in the crystal at one time and not at another. In fact, many of the best crystal gazers have lost their power for weeks. This being so, you should not be discouraged if such images fail to appear at your command." There's your disclaimer. Print it out and display it by the entrance.' Daisy checked out the cover of the booklet. 'It's by Dr R.A. Mayne. There you go! Your spiritual mentor has impressive credentials.'

'But that book was published in 1928.'

'Your punters don't need to know that. Come on – let's have another go. This time you can tell my fortune. My name is . . . Jana.' Daisy's fingers twinkled over her iPhone, then she handed it to Fleur.

'Jana!' said Fleur, peering at the display. 'Um, welcome.'

'Pretend to be gazing into the ball,' instructed Daisy.

'I can't look at the ball and Jana's profile at the same time!'

'Then we'll get you a veil. Try this.' Daisy unwound the length of chiffon she was wearing round her neck and dropped it over her aunt's head. 'Perfect! Go again.'

'Jana,' repeated Fleur. 'I think you might be a Pisces, yes? I see – um – a book with the title *The Time Traveller's Wife* and I see Meryl Streep wearing dungarees – holy moly, is *Mamma Mia everyone*'s favourite film on Facebook?'

'Tch, tch. You're stepping out of character, Madame Spoofeti. Here, have some more wine.'

'Thank you, Jana. Now – where were we? I see you singing – singing in front of Simon Cowell. Might you have auditioned for the *X Factor*?'

Some forty minutes later, Fleur had told half a dozen more fortunes, and was really beginning to have fun.

'Not bad for a Facebook virgin,' remarked Daisy, upending the wine bottle. 'You'll get hooked, Flirty, mark my words. Now, let's do one more. This time I'm going to be Paris Hilton.'

'Paris Hilton's one of your Facebook friends? Wow!'

'No, she's not. But we all know everything there is to know about Paris. You should have no problem uncovering *her* secrets.'

'Welcome!' enthused Fleur, waving her hands over the crystal ball. But just as she was deliberating over questions for Paris, the phone in the kitchen sounded. Reaching for her wineglass, she excused herself and shimmied inside to pick up. It was Damien.

'Hello, darling!' she purred into the mouthpiece.

'I just got your message,' he told her. 'And I have to say, you look pretty damn hot as Gypsy Rose Lee. But you made a mistake.'

'I did?'

'Yeah, Gypsy Rose Lee was a burlesque artist, not a fortune teller.'

'Oops.'

'And she was a *very* sexy lady. The original Dita von Teese.'

'What are you getting at, Mister O'Hara?' Fleur started toying with a strand of hair. She couldn't help flirting with Damien, even on the telephone.

'You know I said I'd double your take, Fleur? I'm prepared to quadruple it. On one condition.'

'Name it.'

'When I call in to you on Friday evening, I want to see you wearing those gypsy threads.'

Fleur's mouth curved in a provocative smile. 'So that you can take them off?'

'No. So that *you* can take them off. While I watch.'

Fleur's smile grew even more provocative. She pretended to buy time while taking a sip from her wineglass. Then she laughed out loud. 'Done deal,' she said.

WIN A ROMANTIC WEEKEND BREAK AT A GRANGE HOTEL
PLUS A FREE ROOM UPGRADE FOR ALL READERS

We are offering one lucky AVON reader a romantic weekend at a Grange Hotel. The winner will enjoy 2 nights' accommodation (Friday to Sunday) at a Grange Hotel, including a continental breakfast on both mornings.

To enter this free prize draw, simple visit www.avon-books.co.uk and answer the question below or send your postal entry to Kinsella Sisters Competition, HarperCollins Publishers, 77–85 Fulham Palace Road, Hammersmith, London, W6 8JB. The closing date for this competition is July 31st 2009. No entries received after this date will be valid.

Whereabouts in Ireland is Lissamore?
A. The East coast of Ireland.
B. The South coast of Ireland.
C. The West coast of Ireland.

We are also offering all readers the chance to receive a complimentary room upgrade (subject to availability) when making a booking at a Grange hotel. Please quote KINSELLA when making your booking. The free room upgrade offer is only valid on bookings made before 31st August 2009. For more information on Grange Hotels, please visit www.grangehotels.com

Terms and Conditions:
1. This competition is promoted by HarperCollins Publishers Ltd, 77–85 Fulham Palace Road, London, W6 8JB.
2. This promotion is open to all UK residents aged 18 years or over except employees of HarperCollins, TLC Marketing or Grange Hotels (or their parent, subsidiaries or any affiliated companies) and their immediate families, who are precluded from entry.
3. The Competition prize consists of a weekend break for 2 in a superior twin or double room, (2 nights between Friday and Sunday) including continental breakfast on both mornings in a Grange Hotel.
4. Dates for the weekend break are subject to availability, the hotel choice is limited to the UK and the prize must be redeemed by 31st October 2009. It will be the winner's sole responsibility to book the prize.
5. All meals, transport and other costs are excluded.
6. The weekend break competition offer and complimentary upgrade offer can not be combined.
7. Grange Hotels booking terms and conditions apply. Visit www.grangehotels.com for details.
8. No purchase necessary. Only one offer may be used per person, per household and per booking group (group is defined as more than one person accompanying the voucher holder). Responsibility can not be taken for entries which are not received. Proof of sending is not proof of receipt. Any application containing incorrect, misleading or illegible information will be invalid. Third party or bulk entries will

be excluded from the competition. The closing date for competition entries is 31st July 2009.

9. Winner will be drawn at random from all correct competition entries. HarperCollins' decision as to who has won the competition shall be final and HarperCollins will not enter into any correspondence relating to the winning entry, The winner will be notified in writing by 30th August 2009

10. All additional costs incurred during the stay such as meals, telephone calls, television/films and mini bar bills must be paid on departure. On arrival, your card details will be taken by the hotel. All costs incurred during the stay will be charged to this card when you check out at the end of your stay.

11. Prices (if any) and information presented are valid at the time of going to press and could be subject to change.

12. The complimentary room upgrade is subject to availability and is only valid on bookings made by 31st August 2009.

13. The complimentary upgrade offer and weekend break competition offer has no monetary value, is non-transferable, cannot be resold and cannot be used in conjunction with any other promotional offer or redeemed in whole or part for cash.

14. Entry instructions are deemed to form part of the Terms and Conditions into the promotion is deemed to signify acceptance of the Terms and Conditions. Any breach of these Terms and Conditions by an entrant will void their entry. Misrepresentative or fraudulent entries will be declared invalid.

15. By entering, you are agreeing that if you win, your name and image may be used for the purpose of announcing the winner in any related publicity with AVON, without additional payment or permission.

16. The Promoter, TLC and distributors are not responsible for the management of the hotels and will accept neither liability nor claims for disappointments or dispute in relation to management of the hotels. The Promoter makes no guarantee about any aspect of the quality or performance of the hotels.

17. The Promoter, its agents and distributors do not guarantee the quality and/or availability of the services offered by the hotels and cannot be held responsible for any resulting disagreements. Liability is not accepted for any personal loss (including but not limited to wasted expenditure), resulting from you or any other member(s) of your Group attending the hotel, caused by matters beyond the Promoter's reasonable control. Your statutory rights are unaffected.

18. In the event of unforeseen circumstances TLC reserve the right to withdraw or substitute the offer with one of equal or greater value.

19. The terms of this promotion are as stated here and no other representations (written or oral) shall apply.

20. Any persons taking advantage of this promotion do so on complete acceptance of these terms and conditions.

21. TLC reserves the right to vary these terms without notice.

22. HarperCollins shall also be bound by these Terms and Conditions and shall not encourage, persuade, promote, support or in any way assist in their breach.

23. Promoter: HarperCollins Publishers Ltd, 77–85 Fulham Palace Road, Hammersmith, London, W6 8JB.

24. This is administered by TLC Marketing plc, PO Box 468, Swansea, SA1 3WY

25. This competition is governed by the laws of England and Wales and is subject to the exclusive jurisdiction of the English courts

26. HarperCollins Publishers excludes all liability as far as is permitted by law, which may arise in connection with this offer and reserves the right to cancel the offer at any stage.

What's next?

Tell us the name of an author you love

Kate Thompson Go

and we'll find your next great book.